NOURIS...
THE ...
REVENGE GROW.

Sobbing with rage, Krulshards, the Master of Nightmares, spat at the ground.

"Thanehand! Galloper's spawn!" he ground the name of Hand between his teeth, watching the boy reach up towards the owl stooping out of the clear evening sky, stretching his fingers for the long Galloping sword in the owl's talons. Krulshards struck his fist against the rough tunnel wall and began to turn towards the secret roads that led to his high chambers in the center of the city, far away from the light, but Thane cried out to the stooping owl, making Krulshards turn back and listen.

"Eagle Owl! I am Thanehand, Thoronhand's grandson, and I have great need of the blade you carry, for Grandfather is still a prisoner in the City of Night. Lend me the sword, so that I can rescue him. Please help me."

The owl was shunning Thane's hand, taking the sword up away from him, casting fear and doubt through the advancing warriors. Krulshards laughed and, cupping his bone black skinless fingers to his mouth, called back into the darkness, summoning the Nightshards he had bred to defend the high chambers.

"Come to me, blind beasts!" he shouted. "Form a shadowless circle in the dark while I seek the weakness in this warrior and find a way to kill him."

Also by Mike Jefferies

Loremasters of Elundium:

The Road to Underfall
Shadowlight

THE SECOND VOLUME OF
LOREMASTERS OF ELUNDIUM

PALACE OF KINGS

MIKE JEFFERIES

Harper Paperbacks a division of Harper & Row, Publishers, Inc.
10 East 53rd Street, New York, N.Y. 10022

This book was first published in 1987 in Great Britain by
Fontana Paperbacks, a division of William Collins Sons
& Co. Ltd.

First Harper Paperbacks printing: March, 1990

Printed in the United States of America

HARPER PAPERBACKS and colophon are trademarks of
Harper & Row, Publishers, Inc.

10 9 8 7 6 5 4 3 2

To my wife, Sheila,
who heard the Nightbeasts's roar
and lit the first spark
against their darkness.
To you I give all Elundium.

Into the
City of Night

*T*HANEHAND balanced lightly on the balls
of his feet, stretching his hand towards the
hovering owl. Laughing, he closed his fingers around the hilt of his grandfather's sword and
took it easily from Eagle Owl's talons.

"Thoron is somewhere beyond the black gates,"
he whispered to the owl. "But I will find him no
matter how thick the darkness becomes."

Thane turned towards the plateau and lifted his
sword to catch all the evening light, sweeping it in
a glittering arc above his head. The warriors surged
forward, a shout of victory on their lips.

"Who will follow me into the darkness?" he
cried, taking a step towards the black marble gates
that led into the City of Night. Behind him an eerie
battle silence spread across the plateau. Thane hesitated and looked back towards the warriors beneath
the standard of the owl in blue and gold and saw
their fear of the dark pass like a shadow across their
faces.

"Is there none brave enough to hold my spark

while I fight with the Master of Night to free Thoron?" he shouted.

All the Marchers, Gallopers and Archers had shuffled to a halt, unable to face their fears and look Thanehand in the eye. Tombel, the greatest Marcher Captain in all Elundium, shouldered his way through the press of warriors until he stood before Thane. Lifting his broad Marching sword he pointed at the body of Amarch, Thoron's warhorse, where she lay, stabbed to death, before the black gates. He lowered his eyes and wept.

"Dearly would I love to avenge her death and help you to free your grandfather but without a glimmer of starlight, no matter how faint, how can I? I fear the dark and I cannot be at your side, not even to hold the spark."

"I will lead you, Thane," rang a clear voice near the black gates.

Tombel spun around and stared in bewilderment at Willow Leaf, the tunnel slave who had helped to defeat the Nightbeast army at Battle's End from within the City of Night.

"Who in all Elundium . . . ?" gasped Tombel, his look passing from Willow's shell-like ears and huge round eyes to his white, almost transparent, skin.

Thane laughed, for a moment forgetting his haste. "Willow, come and meet the greatest Lord of the Marchers ever to cross Elundium."

"The horse at Willow's side is a greater lord than I could ever be!" said Tombel, admiringly.

"He is the Lord of Horses, Equestrius," Willow

replied, proudly, moving forward to stand before Tombel. "He is the greatest warhorse ever to live. He took me back into the City of Night and helped me to rally my people into a great army. Together we won the black gates and the beautiful sunlight."

Then he remembered the old mare, Evening Star, who had started it all an age ago when the Lord of Horses had served her while the Night-beasts slept; and his large eyes grew soft, filling with a far away look. "Well, almost the greatest horse ever to live."

Equestrius snorted, nudging Willow with his head. Tombel laughed, saying, "You go too fast for an old Marcher, child. Start at the beginning, tell me who you are."

Thane turned impatiently towards the setting sun. "Thoron's life may hang on each word we waste. Let it be enough for now to know that without Willow and the black warhorse you would have found us trampled beneath the Nightbeast army."

"Lord, I will lead you to the very heart of our torment, through black chambers that are choked with the forgotten bones of our people. I will guide you to the chamber where Thoron hangs, but you can only travel that road if you are not afraid of the dark, for within the City of Night there is a blackness so complete that you will be lost, even within yourself, if night holds any fear for you."

Willow turned, grim-faced, towards the warrior army and called in a loud voice, "I will take anyone who is not afraid of the dark."

Thane laughed, moving into the entrance. "I was born to the Candlelighter in Candlebane Hall. I fear nothing in the dark."

"There are no candles in the City of Night," added Willow.

"I will stand by your side," cried out Kyotorm, a little nervously. "The dash to World's End made us brothers. I will go with you."

Tombel moved close to Thane and whispered, "My heart yearns to follow you, but I cannot face the darkness. Forgive me."

Thane took Tombel's hand and gripped it tightly. "Oh, Lord and greatest Marcher Captain, when I came to your house, a low and humble Candleman's son, you made me strong with patient hours of teaching. You readied me for this task and taught me that we must use the strengths we have. Your place is here beneath the stars, marshalling day's end and setting fair the wreck of battle. Wait for us two daylights on the high plateau. If we have not returned by then, go back to Underfall and strengthen it against the Master of Darkness. We are ready to go now."

"There are no candles beneath the mountain to light the way," repeated Willow.

"Nor were there candles on the road," answered Thane. "Mulcade, chief Loftmaster Owl, shall come with us and be my eyes for he can see in the dark."

Esteron, the Warhorse who had carried Thane the length of Elundium, snorted and pawed the ground. "Esteron shall come, for he fears nothing that moves by night."

Kyot hesitated between the great marble portals as a hot wind blew on his face and cries of terror came out of the dark. "I cannot come with you into that blackness!"

"Take my hand, brother," Thane whispered as Rockspray the Battle Owl stooped to Kyot's shoulder and hooted a challenge at the darkness.

Kyot laughed, lifted his hand and caressed the owl's chest feathers. "You will be my eyes, great bird of war. Now I can follow!"

Willow passed into the darkness, his eyes widening as the Nightshapes closed off the last shades of evening light, and followed the main highway into the heart of Mantern's Mountain. "Take care," Willow whispered, "for the Nightbeast armor has poison in the spikes."

They carefully picked their way between the fallen carcasses that littered and in some places almost blocked their road.

"You fought a great battle here in the darkness," Thane called out softly to Willow, lighting his spark to find a way through the heaps of dead.

"Put out the light!" hissed Willow. "I can hear voices far ahead of us retreating into the high chambers."

Seeds
of Revenge

"*C*URSE you, Thanehand!" screamed Krulshards, the Master of Nightbeasts, with-
drawing farther into the safety of the City
of Night, forcing a passage through the piles of
Nightbeast dead.

"Thanehand!" he snarled, halting between the
now lifeless Gatewatchers and turning to stare
hatefully at the figure of the young warrior standing defiantly between the black gates. "I know your
name, foul Galloperspawn," he cried, drawing the
battle-torn black malice he wore tightly around his
shoulders. "And I curse the day you crawled out
of your mother's belly to seek my ruin."

Sobbing with rage Krulshards, the Master of
Nightmares, spat at the ground. He looked past
Thane at the Marchers and Gallopers of Elundium
crowding towards the gates and saw the measure
of his defeat. The last shadowy mass of his Nightbeast army was being trampled and overrun by the
wild Warhorses.

"Thanehand! Galloper's spawn!" He ground the

name of Hand between his teeth, watching the boy
reach up towards the owl stooping out of the clear
evening sky, stretching his fingers for the long Galloping sword in the owl's talons. Krulshards struck
his fist against the rough tunnel wall and began to
turn towards the secret roads that led to his high
chambers in the center of the city, far away from
the light, but Thane cried out to the stooping owl,
making Krulshards turn back and listen.

"Eagle Owl! I am Thanehand, Thoronhand's
grandson, and I have great need of the blade you
carry, for Grandfather is still a prisoner in the City
of Night. Lend me the sword, so that I can rescue
him. Please help me."

"Thoron! Thoron!" Krulshards whispered,
creeping back towards the black gates, searching
his memory, going through each and every black
chamber of his nightmare city, trying to remember
where he had chained this Thoron.

The owl was shunning Thane's hand, taking the
sword up away from him, casting fear and doubt
through the advancing warriors. Krulshards
laughed and cupping his bone black, skinless fingers to his mouth, called back into the darkness,
summoning the Nightshards he had bred to defend
the high chambers.

"Come to me, blind beasts!" he shouted. "Link
your spare blades and defend me here in the entrance of night. Form a shadowless circle in the
dark while I seek the weakness in this warrior and
find a way to kill him."

The Master of Nightmares watched the owl hesitate and hover above the high plateau. "Thoron!" he laughed, roughly pushing aside two of the gathering Nightshards that blocked his view of the black marble entrance. "Now I see his weakness," he hissed, scratching at his raw gray layers of jaw muscle where they fused on to the bone.

"He seeks to free his blood kin. He seeks to free the ancient Galloper!" Krulshards laughed again, remembering the ancient rider he had unhorsed and captured near the black gates an age ago and hung up for torture in the high domed chamber deep in the heart of the city. He had almost forgotten the old Galloper, but now if he was quick he could spoil Thanehand's victory.

"I'll skin him. Peel the strips of skin . . ." Greedy for revenge Krulshards spun around towards the fastest, darkest road but stumbled, catching at the broken arrow shaft embedded in his shoulder.

"Curse all Archers!" he screamed, digging his fingernails between the layers of rotten flesh beneath the black malice, searching for the arrowhead that Kyotorm had true-aimed at him during the height of the battle. Closing his fingers around the broken shaft and screwing his red eyes shut against the pain he wrenched at the blade, gasping as it tore free.

"I will take your eyes for this, Archer, and feed them to my blind beasts," he snarled, lifting what he thought was nothing more than a steel arrowhead to his mouth. Savagely he bit at it, clamping his jaws together.

"No!" he cried, too late as the blade crushed between his teeth and ground to a fine powder. "Curse glass arrowheads of Clatterford!" he choked as the core of the arrowhead snapped, releasing a tiny point of sunlight that had long ago been trapped within the battle-blackened glass. It exploded in a blinding flash of pure white light that burned on his tongue, etching his foul shadow against the tunnel wall.

Krulshards screamed, clutching at his throat as the white light seared across the roof of his mouth. He staggered backwards, trying to spit out the light but he fell against the blind beasts and swallowed the burning flame. Burying his head in the shadowy folds of the malice he wept as his new-made shadow leapt up and plunged amongst the circle of Nightshards.

"Curse all light!" he snarled, struggling to his feet and trying to smother the shadow.

"Master! Master!" a harsh voice called out.

Krulshards shook his head free from the malice and stared, blinking, towards the black gates.

"Who dares to enter the City of Night?" he hissed, drawing the long dagger he had used to kill the Warhorse, Amarch, as he retreated between the gates.

Heavy, dragging footsteps drew closer. Krulshards put the dagger blade against his lips and licked at the Warhorse blood, easing away the bitter taste of the pure sunlight the arrowhead had left on his tongue.

"Master, are you hurt?" the harsh voice cried out. The footfalls slowed to a shuffle, and then stopped a few paces from the Nightshards. Blind heads turned, following the voice.

"Quiet, fool!" hissed Krulshards, seeing the bulky, misshapen form of Kerzolde, his one-eyed, broken-clawed Captain, just beyond the circle.

"What do you bring me, Nightmare, except whispers of defeat? I saw you attack the Galloper-spawn between the gates and yet you failed to kill him!"

Krulshards turned towards the captain, took one giant step and roughly pulled Kerzolde into the circle beside him.

"Master! I bring you news!" cried Kerzolde.

"What news, but the victory of the cursed sunlight, fool? I can see the rout, the destruction, without the help of your eye. But they shall pay. Every one of them will pay; one by one, alone and in the dark. I will take their skin, fresh-stripped, before their bones grow cold, to make new Nightbeast armor. None shall escape!"

"Master!" Kerzolde begged. "Elundium is empty. Every warrior that could lift a sword is beyond the gates. But the great Nightbeast army you sent against the Granite City is safe and still unknown to the warriors that have defeated us here. We must escape and destroy the Granite King while they rejoice in their victory."

"Escape with this shadow!" hissed Krulshards, pointing at the dark shape that followed his every movement. "We must wait until the cursed light of Clatterford pales, then we shall enter Elundium, but first we will torture the Galloper hanging in the high chamber and then throw his corpse out onto the high plateau."

Kerzolde lifted his broken claw to salute the Master of Nightbeasts and caught something hanging in the battle tears of his cloak.

Krulshards pointed at the claw. "What is this?"

Kerzolde laughed, holding up the delicate silver finger bowl he had snatched from Thane's belt as they fought between the black gates.

"It belonged to the foul Thanehand, Master. I took it, his treasure, the moment before he escaped my last hammer blow."

"Treasure indeed!" whispered the Master of Nightmares, stretching out a hand to take the finger bowl. It was smooth and perfectly round in shape, finely blennished from the purest silver, and yet its touch was as ice in Krulshards's hands and he recoiled, letting it slip through his fingers and fall to the ground. It struck the tunnel floor with a clear sweet note that rang out in the darkness, and rolled into the lower folds of the malice where they swept across the ground. Bending quickly, Krulshards chased the silver cup and caught it up in his fingers by the fine, broken, silver chain. Twitching at the burning coldness of the chain against his skinless sinews he lifted it up. He turned it over and over, scratching with his fingernails at the finely engraved legend that ran around the lip of the bowl.

"Elionbel of Woodsedge, my finger bowl," the letters spelled, and woven into the loops and tails of the letters a new word had been etched, sharp to the touch.

"Thaneband," Krulshards spat, following the groove with his fingernails.

"Thaneband," he whispered again, gathering a ball of hot venom in his mouth and spitting it into the cup. The venom hissed and bubbled, burning into the silver, staining it black with hatred.

"Who is Elionbel?" he cried, turning on Kerzolde.

Kerzolde shivered. The Master of Nightmares' hands were on his throat, his new-made shadow towering over him, searching for the truth.

"Master, she was the . . ." Kerzolde hesitated, choking on his own lies, feeling the iron grip begin to tighten.

"The truth, you fool," Krulshards hissed. "I made you in my image to destroy others, not to lie to me."

"I was afraid, Master," Kerzolde gurgled. The hand slackened and allowed him to fall to the ground.

"Who is Elionbel?" Krulshards hissed again, pressing the finger bowl hard against Kerzolde's cheek.

"She is Marcher Tombel's daughter, Master," Kerzolde wept, clutching at the hem of the malice.

"You lied me into ignorance, Captainbeast! You knew of her ties with the Thanehand and kept it a secret."

"No, Master! I knew nothing of the love between them. I had captured her as a delicacy for your table."

"The truth!" Krulshards roared, casting back the malice to expose the raw sinews and rotten flesh of his shadowy body. "Only the truth."

"Master, it was when you sent us after the messenger who rode towards the Granite City. We had chased him far across Elundium and almost overtaken him on the edge of the Black Forest but he escaped the circle of Nightbeasts we set against him and sought refuge in the Wayhouse at Woodsedge. Under cover of darkness, in the eye of a blizzard, we attacked and sacked the Wayhouse, but the messenger had gone, his tracks hidden beneath the snow. We killed all the Marchers we could find and stole Elionbel, Master. I was afraid to return empty-handed. I was going to bring her to you for torture, but the foul Galloperspawn, Thanehand, and Elionbel's father, Tombel, overran us as the sun was rising and took her back. Great Master, I know nothing more."

"You dared to keep this a secret and lie to me about the messenger's death?" Krulshards screamed, tearing his fingernails in deep plow lines across Kerzolde's face. "In better times I would have stripped back your armor and thrown your skinless body onto the high plateau, to die when the sun rose. But I have some need of you now."

"Master," Kerzolde cried, crawling forward, "fear of your rage made me lie to you. The Galloperspawn has plagued me, Lord. I could not kill him. He is a true nightmare that follows me everywhere."

Krulshards turned towards the entrance, licking at his dagger blade, curling his tongue around it as he looked out across the battle-strewn plateau. "You say every warrior in Elundium was gathered here?" he asked. "Even Tombel, the Marcher?"

"Yes, Master," Kerzolde cried, rising to his knees. "Perhaps the messenger died in the snow and never reached the Granite City."

Krulshards turned harshly on his Captainbeast where he knelt, huddled against the tunnel wall, and pressed the dagger blade into the coarse hairy skin below his jaw.

"You fool," he hissed. "The messenger escaped. I know it now, and he warned the Granite King that my Nightbeasts were once more loose in Elundium. Why else would the King have gathered the Marchers, Gallopers and Archers into a great army. He was weak, terrified of the dark, and strangled by indecision; but the messenger must have given him strength and purpose, and the time to march against me. Unless . . ."

Krulshards hesitated, curling his lips back across

his ragged teeth, "Unless Nevian, the Master of Magic, warned him."

"But he did not march, great Lord," Kerzolde whispered. "He is siege-locked in the Granite City, and nowhere to be seen on this battlefield."

Krulshards shrank back into his malice, wrapping himself in dark thoughts.

"There is a new power in Elundium," he whispered, turning his hooded eyes towards the gates. "It is more powerful than the Granite King's. And this power does not fear the dark."

"Thanehand, the Galloperspawn!" cried Kerzolde. "He brought the warriors to our doors, following the bright banner of the sun that he carries."

Krulshards laughed, drawing Kerzolde so close to him that their foul breaths mixed, filling the tunnel with yellow sulphurous fumes.

"Captainbeast," he whispered, "you have stumbled on the truth, blindly. He is the one I must destroy, and you have brought me his weakness. This foul finger bowl will be his undoing, and in time will lure him alone, into the darkness."

"How, Master?" Kerzolde asked in a nervous voice.

"How?" laughed the Master of Nightbeasts. "Why, you shall lead me to the Wayhouse on the edge of Mantern's Forest, and there I will steal the fair Elionbel, and bring her back to the City of Night. She will be my lure. But first we will spoil Thanehand's victory. Come quickly, follow me into the high chambers where I hung that ancient Galloper, for he is another weakness in Thanehand, and I think the most trivial reason for the great army massing at our gates. Magicians and messengers had nothing to do with this battle."

Krulshards spat at the ground and laughed. "Victory will be a skinless corpse to carry home, Thanehand, and ruin and disaster will meet your every footstep. For I shall go before you, burning and destroying all you hold dear."

Breathlessly Krulshards ran along the darkened narrow roads that led into the domed chamber where Thoronhand hung, suspended by two iron chains from a giant stake driven into the rough chamber roof.

"Thoronhand!" he hissed, prodding at the ancient warrior's dangling feet, cutting easily into the ruined leather of his riding boots with a spear blade he had snatched from one of the Nightshards, and sending him spinning giddily in the darkness.

"I bring you news, Thoron," he mocked, holding up the silver finger bowl above his head.

"Battle's end has now come and I have a hard-won trophy to show you, cut from your dead grandson's hand. Look! Look, foul Galloper, for all is lost in the battle before my gates, and all those who gathered to take you back into the light have perished. The sun is setting over the ruin, Thoron, casting long shadows from where they lie, piled high in carrion heaps for an age of Nightbeasts' feasts."

Krulshards laughed cruelly, shaking the dead locks of twisted hair he had plaited across the top of his head.

"Listen, Warrior," he whispered. "Listen to the silence of your defeat. Listen to the darkness, Thoronhand. You are the last warrior in all Elundium, and the sun will never rise for you again."

Krulshards unsheathed his skinning hook, wetting the blade with his tongue.

"What say you now, Warrior?" he hissed, drawing the Nightshards into a circle around the dangling prisoner.

Thoron lifted his ancient head and stared down at the Master of Nightbeasts, catching a glimmer of the faint rays of sunlight that shone out beneath the malice. Throwing his head back he let a shout of laughter fall from his cracked and dirty lips. "Rumor is a poor truth, Nightmare. Look to your cloak, for that tells of real day's end. What is it you hide beneath that foul black rag? Is it arrow-lights from Clatterford, or ruin before the Gates of Night?"

"Truth! This is the truth!" screamed Krulshards, wrapping the weakening sunlight within the folds of the malice and thrusting the finger bowl up into Thoron's face, catching the fine silver chain in the straggly ends of the old man's beard.

"There are few in all Elundium who could remember the Crystal Maker of Clatterford and his foul glass arrowheads," hissed the Nightbeast, "but one lucky strike does not win a battle or speak of victory. Read the names upon the bowl, Thoron-hand, and then see who speaks the truth of battle's end!"

Thoron narrowed his eyes and traced each letter, spelling out the words written on the bowl. "Thane!" he whispered, remembering the young lad, imagining him clearly in the darkness sitting astride the great Warhorse, Amarch, with Battle Owls perching on his shoulders. Thoron let his head fall forward.

"Thane!" he whispered again, only this time fiercely, squeezing back the tears, gathering his failing courage. Proudly he lifted his head and stared into Krulshards's hooded eyes.

"Nightmare!" he whispered. "One look from you, the Master of Nightmares, is rumored to kill a man, and one shout to turn him deaf, but I do not fear you, not even now, at the end. You are nothing but a stench that spoils the air. A creeping darkness that hides from the light."

Thoron sobbed bitterly, shaking the chains that bound his wrists. "I have nothing to fear from you, Nightmare. You have already destroyed everything I love."

"All dead!" laughed Krulshards. "Warhorses, Owls, Border Hounds and all the warriors of Elundium, and between the gates of this beautiful city lies your blood kin. Here, smell his blood on my blade. Taste it before it dries."

Thoron shuddered, turning his head away from the dagger.

"But Elionbel, she lives!" whispered the Master of Nightmares. "And she will be mine, taken in victory as I sweep across Elundium, destroying the light."

"Elionbel?" Thoron cried, turning his face back towards Krulshards, remembering her; fair, gentle Elionbel of Woodsedge. "Take my life, but spare hers!"

Krulshards laughed, reaching up with the curved skinning hook and piercing the leathery wrinkled skin beneath Thoron's chin.

"I already have your life, Thoronhand. You are nothing here in the darkness but a lost moment from the sunlight world of Elundium. You are helpless and alone."

Thoron gurgled, feeling the sharp edge of the hook touch his jawbone, and flinched against the pain. Suddenly he cried out, "Fly, great bird of war. Escape into the dying hours of sunlight. Fly!"

Krulshards hesitated, letting his hand slip from the handle of the hook. Spinning around he snarled, "Who has dared to enter the darkness?"

Thoron laughed, choking against the curve of the hook, and watched the dark shape of Silverwing spread his wings to stoop. Silent and unseen in the darkness above Thoron's head, the owl had waited, turning his aged head from side to side, catching every tiny sound in the chamber. Now he was ready and knew where each beast stood. Blindly he stared down at the Master of Darkness and flexed his talons to strike.

Kerzolde pointed into the domed roof with his broken claw. "There, Master, above Thoron's head. I can see the white eyes. Look!"

Krulshards looked up, unhooding his eyes to stare the owl to death, but Silverwing, blind to the look, stooped at the Nightmare's face, tearing his razor-sharp talons across the raw, unguarded flesh. Krulshards staggered backwards, screaming as the owl's strike cut into his face. Thrusting upwards with both hands he drove the dagger deep into the owl's chest.

Running footsteps echoed in the high domed chamber, drawn on by Kerzolde's warning shout as he leapt to defend the entrance. Blind beasts stumbled into each other in the rising tide of sound. Thoron kicked with both feet at Krulshards, catching his boots in the malice.

"I am not alone, Nightmare," he cried. "Listen! Listen!"

"Run! Run!" hissed Willow, urging Thane to follow him. "The Master of Nightbeasts has your grandfather's life in his hands."

"How many Nightbeasts?" Thane asked, running hard to keep pace with Willow, stumbling against unseen faults in the tunnel floor.

"Many!" Willow replied, suddenly disappearing into a black void on Thane's left. Thane hesitated and Kyot collided into him, dropping his father's bow.

"Curse this darkness," he muttered, feeling gingerly in the gritty marble dust for the weapon.

"Is this what you seek?" Thane asked, holding it up. "You can see in the dark!" exclaimed Kyot, feeling along the length of the bow for any damage to the oiled wood.

"A little," Thane replied, turning into the black entrance Willow had taken. The narrow tunnel spiraled upwards, well marked with Nightbeast claw prints. The air was hot and stifling, filling their noses with the stench of rotten flesh.

"Nightmares," Willow whispered, halting for a moment to sniff the air. "We are close to them now."

"Did you use this tunnel to escape from the darkness?" Thane asked, keeping his voice to a whisper.

"No!" Willow replied, "Our route was by old, long-forgotten roads, dug by my grandelders. Look at this tunnel floor. This was a well-used road before the battle."

"But will it lead us to where Thoron hangs?" Thane asked.

Willow smiled in the darkness, and replied, "Smell the air, Thane."

Thane wrinkled his nose against the stench of rotting flesh. It had grown stronger the higher they had climbed and was now making him feel dizzy.

"This stench is far worse than any Nightbeast I have ever smelled," he choked. "It is even worse than the Nightmare, Kerzolde, and he smelled bad enough."

Willow laughed. "It is the smell of death. It is the smell of Krulshards, the Master of Nightbeasts, and he is the most terrifying and powerful beast that ever walked in Elundium. Do not look into his eyes, or listen to his voice, for he will blind you and send you mad with deafness."

"How can I fight against him?" Thane hissed, gripping Willow's arm.

"First you must tread on his shadow. The Elder told me in his last death rattle that to tread on the Master of Nightbeasts' shadow traps him, frozen, for the killing stroke."

"But he is shadowless in the dark!" Thane cried.

"And all-powerful, beyond man's power to kill," Willow whispered.

Thane ran his finger along the cutting edge of Thoron's sword, feeling helpless at the task ahead. Esteron nickered softly, nudging Thane's shoulder, and Mulcade hooted in the darkness. Thane laughed, "We are more than men, Willow. Lead us to this Nightmare."

Willow moved forward again, crouching against the tunnel wall. The voice ahead of them had grown louder, almost to shouting pitch.

"Quickly," Willow cried, "Krulshards is going to kill your grandfather! Run! Run!"

The tunnel turned a sharp corner and came to an abrupt end in the high-domed chamber. Thoron hung in the center of the chamber, kicking wildly at Krulshards, his feet tangled in the malice. The dark shape of an owl, hooked by its talons onto Krulshards's face, beat its wings, shrieking as the Nightbeast plunged a black-bladed dagger into its chest. Blind beasts in a circle around Thoron thrust their spears at his struggling body.

"Nightshards!" Willow cried, cowering in the entrance of the chamber. "They were in the Elders' stories. Only light can harm them in the darkness, or penetrate their armor!"

The Nightshards had turned as one towards the sound of Willow's voice, and his words were lost beneath their snarling screams. Slowly they advanced, step by step, spears thrusting, on the entrance.

Thane leapt into the chamber, plunging his sword at the closest beast, but the blade turned harmlessly against its armor. Ducking beneath the thrusting spear he struck again, a slashing stroke that sent up a shower of bright sparks in the darkness as the blade bounced off the Nightshard's arm. Thane's hand burned with numbness from the force of a stroke and he quickly stepped back into the entrance.

"Thanehand!" Krulshards screamed, tearing the owl from his face and throwing it to the floor. The Nightshards had broken the circle around Thoron and now filled the entrance of the chamber. Rage dribbled from their mouths and jagged spears were raised to kill Thane. Esteron reared, thrashing with his forelegs at the Nightshards' armor. Thane drew his dagger that Duclos the swordsman had given him, and ducking beneath Esteron's hooves he slashed helplessly at the Nightmare shapes that towered over them. Mulcade stooped at the Nightshards' faces, ripping at their eyes, but his talons only screeched across their smooth, blind faces.

"Grandfather!" Thane cried, as he lost his footing and slipped beneath the leading Nightshard, the beast's spear blade now a handspan from his heart.

Suddenly a rushing wind filled the entrance, passing so close to Thane's shoulder that he felt it touch his face, and something carried by the wind forced the Nightshard back, sending his spear harmlessly into the ground beside Thane's head. A blinding flash of light filled the chamber, then another and another, each one killing a Nightbeast as it exploded, sending them crashing to the floor. Krulshards screamed, covering his face with his malice against the flashes of light and reached up, scrambling wildly with outstretched fingers for the skinning hook.

"They will not find you alive, foul Galloper," he spat at the old man, gripping the handle of his hook and pulling hard at Thoron's throat. Thoron struggled desperately as the blade tore through the muscles below his jaw. Kicking with all his strength at Krulshards's bone black fingers he toppled the Master of Nightmares, sending him stumbling backwards to trip over the body of Silverwing where it lay on the chamber floor. Thoron screamed as the hook tore free, his head slumping forward. Darkness closed about him, shutting out the pain.

"Thane," he gurgled, his mouth falling uselessly open.

Krulshards sprang quickly to his feet, clutched at Thoron's limp and lifeless legs and spun him once.

"He is dead, Master!" Kerzolde cried, jumping between two Nightshards still defending the chamber and swinging his hammer at Thane. Krulshards looked from his weakening shadow to his dying blind beasts and grabbed Kerzolde by his iron collar.

"We must escape," he hissed, "before that Archer of Clatterford strengthens my shadow with his foul blades of glass. Quickly, come! There are secret roads where even the Galloperspawn will not dare to follow us."

"Master, I follow!" Kerzolde cried, disappearing into a low entrance on the far side of the chamber, running at the heels of the Master of Nightbeasts into the bowels of the mountain, where night grew thick enough to touch and tasted bitter on the tongue.

Thane had watched Krulshards attack his grandfather but was powerless to help him. Whatever was killing the Nightshards was traveling in the rushing wind passing just above his head. Carefully he turned, rolling onto his stomach, and saw the great Bow of Orm in Kyot's hand, the string still singing softly from the last arrow shaft to touch it.

Glancing back into the chamber he saw the floor littered with the Nightshards' tangled bodies.

"You overcame the darkness!" Thane whispered, rising to his knees.

"No!" replied Kyot. "Rockspray took each arrow out of the quiver; he guided my hands and became my eyes. He really is a mighty bird of war!"

Thane laughed, rising to his feet. "And the Armorers of Stumble Hill must have great skill with the hammer to forge such arrowheads, for each one brought sunlight into the darkness. I clearly saw Krulshards's shadow."

Kyot frowned, and moving forward, turned over the nearest Nightshard, pulled out the arrow shaft and examined it.

"These arrows are not from Stumble Hill," he exclaimed, passing the charred shaft to Thane. "We have great skill to forge steel arrowheads but these are made of glass!"

Kyot reached into his quiver, withdrew the remaining arrows and passed them to Thane. "These arrows were made at Stumble Hill; look how the Armorer forged the fine steel points, but I do not know who made the glass arrowheads, or why Rockspray chose them out of the quiver. My father gave me the quiver ready-loaded just before I left the tower of Stumble Hill. All he said before we took to the Greenway was "Use each one sparingly, for there are none to match them in all Elundium.'"

Thane frowned, passing the arrows back to Kyot.

"Well, whoever made them, they had a great power in the darkness, but do not forget it is in the arm that pulls the string that the greatness lies."

Willow called out urgently, "Hurry, Thoron is wounded."

Thane, with Mulcade on his shoulder, Kyot with Rockspray on his, and Esteron, followed Willow into the high-domed chamber and stood below Thoron's dangling boots. Slowly he turned in the icy draft of mountain air, warm drops of blood dripping from the gaping wound in his neck.

"Grandfather," Thane whispered, reaching up to touch the old man's boots, but they were beyond his reach.

"Do you think he is still alive?" asked Kyot, feeling the blood splash on his face as he looked up into the darkness.

"It is safe to light your spark now," Willow said, turning to Thane.

Thane lit the spark and handed it to Kyot. Esteron whinnied softly and knelt for Thane to climb onto the saddle. Thane held on with both hands as Esteron rose to his feet, and then balanced on tiptoe and tried to listen for his grandfather's heartbeat. Thoron's beard had grown into a thick and tangled mess, full of half-eaten scraps of food that were stiff and greasy to the touch. Gingerly Thane gathered the beard in his left hand and cut it away just below the chin, and putting his ear to the old man's chest, he listened and heard in the night's silence a faint heartbeat.

"He is still alive," he whispered, feeling tears of joy well up in his eyes.

"Quick, bind the wound in his neck before he bleeds to death," Kyot called. "Use the scarf!"

Thane let the dirty beard fall to the ground and untied the summer scarf from his arm. It had become his banner of light in the shadows of World's End, somehow catching and holding the sunlight, and even here in the darkness the words of love that Elionbel had sewn into the silk shone and sparkled.

"Elionbel," Thane whispered, lifting his grandfather's head and carefully wrapping the scarf across the gaping wound. Thoron's blood quickly soaked into the silk, turning the picture of the sun bright red and it seemed almost as if it were glowing in the dark.

Willow gasped, looking at the bright colors in the scarf, "The sun has come into the City of Night!"

"That scarf has great powers," Kyot muttered, gripping the spark to stop his hand from shaking.

"No!" Thane whispered fiercely. "It is my mother's summer scarf. I took it from her at our parting. If it shines at all it is because it reflects her love of the sunlight, for she wove it in the shadows of the great wall that rings the Granite City." The anger in Thane's voice ebbed away as he whispered, "She did not dabble in magic."

Kyot bit his tongue, wishing he had kept his thoughts to himself. There *was* something about the scarf, something magical, that made it shine. He had seen it during the battle, catching all the glories of the sun, and driving back the Nightbeasts' shadows. Sighing, he quickly changed the subject. He pointed at Thoron's wrists and asked how they were going to cut through the chains to get him down. Thane examined the iron shackles and saw that the lock was a simple iron bolt, rusty with age, that passed through two crudely hammered flanges on either side of the shackles.

"Two hammer blows should break open these chains," he answered, searching the chamber floor for something heavy enough to use.

"Will this do?" Willow called from the far side of the chamber, holding up the mace that Kerzolde had dropped as he fled at Krulshards's heels.

Thane took the long-handled hammer and struck a sharp blow at the shackle on Thoron's left wrist. The force of the blow sent the iron pin flying across the chamber and the shackle broke in two, releasing Thoron's arm and sending him spinning against Thane, knocking him off the saddle onto the chamber floor. Esteron knelt again for Thane to climb back into the saddle.

"Let me help you," Willow called out, springing lightly onto the saddle beside Thane and steadying the old man's legs. Thane swung the hammer again and broke open the second shackle. Thoron slumped into his grandson's arms and Thane gently lowered him into the saddle.

"We must get him to the Healer's," he urged, putting his ear to the old man's chest again. The heartbeat was weaker now, and stumbling erratically.

"What of Krulshards?" Willow asked. "He is escaping through the lower roads. I would lead you down into the heart of the mountain following his voice. But we must go now!"

Thane hesitated, looking from the low entrance where Willow waited on his answer back to the tunnel that led to the black gates and the late evening sunlight.

"I must follow the Nightmare, Grandfather," he whispered, taking the old man's fragile hand into his. "I saw the light beneath the malice and I dare not lose this moment to tread on his shadow and rid all Elundium of his terror."

"The warriors are waiting for us, Thane," whispered Kyot, fearing to follow another darker road. "It would seal a great victory to take your grandfather out of the darkness," he urged.

"But the Nightbeast had a shadow. I saw it!" cried Thane. "It followed him through that black entrance!"

"Hurry," urged Willow. "Their footsteps are growing ever fainter."

Thane twisted around, biting on his knuckles and took half a step.

"Thoron will die without the Healer's hand," hissed Kyot, catching hold of Thane's sleeve. "Is that what you crossed Elundium for, to leave him in the dark?"

"All Elundium will be covered in darkness if the Master of Nightbeasts escapes!" cried Willow.

Thane turned, his mind torn in two. He knelt to

gather up Silverwing's lifeless body into his arms.
"What would you have done, brave Battle Owl?"
he whispered in despair. "Which road would you
have taken?"

"All roads will be dark and dangerous if Krulshards lives," cried out Willow. "Hurry before
your victory on the high plateau turns against you."

"I know I should follow the Nightmare, but I
cannot," cried Thane wretchedly. "I cannot let
Grandfather die!"

"Fools!" cried Willow, thrusting the broken
splinter of steel he used as a dagger back into his
belt. "If I was half the warrior you are, Thanehand,
I would follow Krulshards and rid Elundium of his
foul darkness, but I cannot do it alone."

"Forgive me," cried Thane, wringing his hands.
"But to have found Grandfather alive was beyond
my wildest dreams."

"One life against so many," muttered Willow,
turning his back on Krulshards's fading footsteps.
"He will haunt us all, I know it."

Tombel had paced a thousand steps between the
Gates of Night as the evening light faded. Battle's
end had come quickly and the Nightbeasts' carcasses were piled high in great mounds waiting for
a burning torch to set them alight. Tombel saw
movement inside the gates. Someone was emerging.

First Willow and then Thane walked out of the

darkness. Tombel laughed with relief and gave the signal to light the giant Nightbeast piles.

"Thane!" he shouted, silhouetted against the streams of crackling sparks that floated up into the darkening sky, "You have rescued Thoron! Is he still alive?"

Thane hurried onto the plateau and carefully laid Thoron beside Amarch's cold body.

"Call for the Healer!" he begged, unclasping his cloak and casting it across his grandfather's body to keep out the night chills.

Thoron shivered and slowly opened his eyes. Above him stretched a limitless sky, sewn with a thousand pale stars.

"Thane," he whispered, searching the dark shapes that stood around him.

Thane knelt, taking the old man's hand into his. "Sleep, Grandfather, you are safe now, beyond the Nightmares' reach. I have sent for the Healer."

"Thane," croaked the old man, trying to rise, "has Krulshards . . . ?" The blood gurgled in his throat, making him choke.

Gently Thane eased him back onto the ground. "Amarch came to your rescue, Grandfather, she chased the Master of Nightbeasts to the very Gates of Night. She is here at your side."

Thoron slowly turned his head and looked into her soft eyes. Death had clouded them and age had whitened her muzzle.

"Amarch," he whispered, large tears forming in the corners of his eyes.

"She was the first into battle," Thane whispered. "She led us to victory!"

Slowly Thoron lifted his hand and closed her eyes. Tears were running down his face and his shoulders shook with grief.

"She was the bravest Warhorse in all Elundium," sang out the musical voice of Duclos the Swordsman, and he came forward and knelt beside Thoron, putting his hand on the old man's shoulder.

"A hanging basket of the sweetest lucerne grass will be set in the gardens of Gildersleeves in her memory."

"And Sprint, the Archers' mount, shall run in her memory carrying a quiver of silver-tipped arrows," whispered Kyot, kneeling beside Duclos and blinking back his tears.

"Then in memory of her greatness let us weave tales in the firelight, of all she did," said Tombel, bringing Willow to kneel beside Thane.

"Tombel!" Thoron whispered, hearing his old friend's voice, and looking up from face to face. "If tales of memory are threaded through the firelight then they must also tell of Silverwing who once rode to war on my shoulders, for he cast aside the cloak of a blind beggar and rose up to be the mightiest Lord of Owls in the darkness of the City of Night."

Lowering his voice to little more than a sob he continued, "He found me in the dark following rumors through a wild and dangerous land, long after all the other owls had come to my rescue with dead mice and stalks of grass for me to eat. He came, searching blindly, flapping damaged wings against the tunnel walls, to take up a lonely station in the mountain's heart, and guarded me with his life."

"He is beside you, Grandfather," Thane said. "I brought his body out of that black place and laid him in great honor beside Amarch."

Mulcade stooped to Thane's shoulder, hooting proudly as he looked down with sadness at his father's cold and lifeless body. Equestrius, the Lord of Horses, raised his head, calling out to the stars, the Border Runners howled and all the owls hooted in a chorus, while the warriors of Elundium talked until the gray hours touched the sky. They talked of the braveness and the beauty that they should never see again.

All night long the great mounds of Nightbeasts burned and crackled, sending sparks drifting across the high plateau. Tombel called Willow to sit beside him, and while the Healer tended Thoron's wounds he listened to the boy's story, marveling at the young man's courage and the quiet dignity of a people stolen by the Nightmare, Krulshards, and kept for time beyond counting from the light.

"And you know nothing of where you came from? Whether there were mountains, forests or streams?" asked Tombel, looking across the plateau to where Willow's people had gathered around a Nightbeast pyre. As one they were gazing up at the stars, their eyes shining with delight.

"Nevian, Master of Magic and Lord of the Daylight, he came into the City of Night and found my grandelder, Leaf, and gave him a tiny point of light, and with that light he showed him all the beautiful things above the ground in Elundium. Even our names came from that meeting," Willow replied.

Tombel sighed, vowing in his heart that a place would be found for these strange people with their shell-shaped ears and large round eyes. A safe place, in the sunlight, somewhere in Elundium.

Thane left the fire and the talk of darkness beneath Mantern's Mountain, and walked to the edge of the high plateau. Behind him, around each bonfire, rose the murmur of victory, but in his heart he knew that this was a long way from the truth. Far below in the darkness one lamp shone out brilliant white.

"Underfall!" he whispered, smiling as he remembered how he had first seen the great fortress of World's End rising up out of the morning mist, clinging on to the mountain's bleak shoulders, all those daylights ago.

"What troubles you, Thane?" Tombel quietly asked, moving to stand beside him.

"Krulshards lives," Thane replied. "I had the chance to follow and to kill him, or to choose to rescue my grandfather."

Tombel put his hand on Thane's arm. "Choices are never easy, Thane," he whispered.

Far below a great cry shook the mountainside and the lamp on the highest gallery of Underfall flickered and went out.

"By Nevian! What has happened?" Tombel cried, drawing his Marching sword.

"Underfall is under attack!" Thane shouted. "Krulshards has escaped into Elundium! I know it! I am the fool who chose wrongly!"

"But he will never be able to break into Underfall. It is the Palace of Kings, built against the Master of Nightmares!" cried Tiethorm, the First Archer of Underfall.

Below, a terrible booming sound shook the mountain's roots. Twice it sounded, drawing all the warriors to the plateau's edge.

"Form the Gallopers into a column," Thane shouted, "and follow us with the Marchers as quickly as you can."

Tombel gripped Thane's arm and pointed with his sword down into the darkness. "Look, the great lamp has been relit!"

"But it does not shine as before; it is weak against the darkness," Kyot mused. "Something terrible has happened there."

Tombel raised his hands and shouted for silence. "Warriors," he called against the panic.

Thane looked down at the broken lamps burning feebly below. "Nowhere is safe now!"

"Warriors!" Tombel shouted again, demanding order across the high plateau. Thane turned towards him and thought of Tombel's house, the Wayhouse at Woodsedge, and Elionbel, the beautiful Elionbel. His hand moved to his belt to touch her gift, the silver finger bowl, but his hand found only the broken silver chain.

"Elionbel!" he cried, spinning around and feeling in all of his pockets, but the chain was broken, the last link on his belt twisted out of shape by the wrench of Kerzolde's claw.

"Kerzolde!" he whispered, remembering how the Nightmare had leapt on him in the dark entrance, wrestling him to the ground. Thane felt Tombel's iron grip shake him and heard his voice shouting him back out of his memories.

"Thane! Thane! What is it? Why do you stare at the black gates?"

Thane shook his head. "They have her bowl," he cried. "They have her finger bowl. She sent it to me as a love gift with the messenger, Errant."

Tombel leapt back a pace, his knuckles whitening on the hilt of his Marching sword as he turned the blade point-first into the soft skin just below the angle of Thane's jaw. "There were moments in the battle before the Gates of Night as we fought side by side when I thought that you had grown beyond your base beginnings, Candleman, and my heart was warming towards you. But now I should kill you for taking my daughter's love token into battle."

Tombel slowly leveled the sword and blinked away the tears that blurred his eyes. "I forbade it!" he cried, turning to where Thoron lay. "I pledged her to turn away from Thane, and I was right, for he is not bloodworthy of her. Yet she broke her honor pledge and disobeyed me and now the Master of Night knows her name, he will take her, Thoron, he will take her in revenge. What do you say to that?"

Thoron weakly lifted his hand and pointed a shaking finger at Thane: "You took comfort from the cold in the Wayhouse at Woodsedge; you took everything that was offered, and it was gladly given, and yet you, my grandson, the treasure of our house, you took Elionbel's heart out into the darkness. Why, oh why?"

Thane took a step towards Thoron, spreading his empty hands. "She did not break her honor pledge, Grandfather," he replied bitterly, seeing clearly now the coldness of his last few days at Woodsedge, understanding Tombel's haste for him to continue his journey to World's End and the great fortress at Underfall. Lifting his head, he met Tombel's gaze and held it.

"I stole nothing, Grandfather, for nothing seemed to be withheld from me. I did not know that Tombel was against my love for Elionbel or that I should leave the finger bowl within the safety of Underfall."

"Ignorance is no excuse, Thane," answered Thoron in an angry voice.

"Behind my back like whispering thieves in the night," hissed Tombel, pushing Thane aside.

"No, no!" cried Thane. "She never spoke one word of her love for me and each time I would have talked of it she pressed a finger to my lips. She kept her pledge, but with her crippled hands, in silent needlepoint, she embroidered her passion onto my summer scarf. Look!"

Thane ducked quickly beneath Tombel's angry hand and knelt beside his grandfather. He lifted up the summer scarf from where the Healer had laid it on the grass and it shone and sparkled, reflecting the starlight from the fine gold and silver threads that Elionbel had woven.

Tombel took the scarf and slowly read each word, seeing in the careful stitches a story of love that shone brighter than the daylight and it burned his fingers to touch it. Dropping the scarf back into Thane's hands he knelt beside Thoron and took hold of the ancient Galloper's hand.

"I love you, Thoron, as a brother," he whispered. "For we were battle close and once, in better times, used the same shadow, but to tie my blood to yours now that the Nightmare knows of Elionbel's name, that is beyond any love."

Thoron nodded, tears of shame and sorrow wetting his wrinkled cheeks. "You have lost much, perhaps everything, dear friend, to rescue a worthless fool from the darkness."

Tombel lifted his head and stared out past the bright-burning pyres of Nightbeasts into the dark, limitless sky. "I came not to free you, friend—I knew nothing of your plight—but on King Holbian's orders to strengthen Underfall. I was against such a march and would with each step we took have turned back to break the siege lock that the

Nightbeasts have ringed around the Granite City. But I am not a pledge breaker and I followed the path set for me to these very Gates of Night."

"Honor has played you hard and cruel with no reward, but the Nightmare is free to plunder Woodsedge and terrorize all Elundium," whispered Thoron. "Perhaps in some small part I am to blame, perhaps if Thane had kept on the Nightmare's heels . . ."

"Would you rather I had left you to die?" cried Thane in anguish, gathering Esteron's reins ready to mount.

"No! No!" answered Tombel quickly, rising and putting his hand on Esteron's bridle. "Much as I may curse you for the finger bowl, every warrior here on the high plateau would have made your choice in the City of Night and brought Thoron out into the light."

"But I am to blame for the Nightmare knowing Elionbel's name. It was my choice that set him free. Bloodworthy or not I will follow Krulshards and destroy him, and win back what little honor I can in your eyes, for I love your daughter and one day-light would beg you for her hand."

"Ask not for Elionbel's hand, or ever let her name slip past your lips again, for now she will fall beneath the Nightmare's shadow where none can save her."

"I will outrun the Nightmare," shouted Thane, setting his foot into Esteron's stirrup and springing lightly into the saddle. "Give me room to chase Krulshards!"

Tombel laughed bitterly, releasing the bridle. "You cannot catch the Master of Nightbeasts. He can outrun a shadow as it crosses the moon."

"Esteron is a Lord amongst the Warhorses and he can outrun the wind," cried Thane, spurring him forward.

"Halt!" cried Thoron, his fragile voice cutting through the night air. "Beware that your love for Elionbel does not blind your purpose, for there is more at stake than a loving cup. All Elundium totters on the brink of darkness now that Krulshards is loose. Destruction and death will shadow every road he takes."

Thane halted, turned and rode back to where his grandfather lay. "I must hasten to put right all my wrongs and reach Woodsedge before Krulshards and take Elion. . . ."

"Easy, be easy," whispered Thoron, beckoning Thane to dismount. "You must take counsel before choosing such a wild and dangerous road. Even Tombel, I am sure, would agree to that!"

Tombel nodded gravely, pointing his hand towards the warriors spread out across the plateau. "Whatever stands between us, Thane, you are a leader of men. Strikes of Archers and whole squadrons of Gallopers stand poised to follow you. Think carefully which way the wind blows before you move."

Thane looked steadily into Tombel's eyes. "What

of Elionbel? How will that matter stand between us if I stay here on the high plateau and follow counsel to take a different road?"

Tombel bowed his head, remembering Elionbel's soft touch and her gentle voice. Blinking away his tears he looked up and caught sight of the summer scarf, re-tied to Thane's armored arm. It fluttered in the chill night breezes, her stitches sparkling in the darkness. "Although I am against it and it darkens my heart, I see that a great love is between you. Let it be enough that when Krulshards is dead and the siege of the Granite City is over, then we shall talk again."

Thane gripped Tombel's arm and offered up the hilt of his sword. "I will be bloodworthy yet, my Lord, and rid Elundium of Krulshards's foul shadow. That much I promise!"

"First you must bury your warrior dead, or the carrion crows will pick their bones clean before the new sun reaches noon," interrupted Thoron, his hand gently caressing Amarch's cold muzzle.

Thane frowned and looked beyond the Nightbeast pyres and saw for the first time the rows of battle dead: warriors, Warhorses, Border Runners and Battle Owls laid ready for burial.

"So many brave hearts," he whispered, seeing the price of victory.

"Walk with me," he asked, drawing Tombel towards the rows of battle dead, "and tell me each and every warrior's name that marched or galloped beneath the standard of the owl, that I may never forget who came when hope was gone and who brought evening sunshine beneath the Nightbeasts' shadows."

Tombel frowned, gripping the hilt of his sword. "There is tragedy in this victory, Thane, for it will take us two daylights to bury our dead before we can chase Krulshards and by then he will be far ahead of us, destroying and shadowing all that is beautiful in Elundium."

"Let us help you, Lord Tombel," Willow called, leading his people to where Thane and Tombel stood. "My people have great skill with the pick and shovel and it would be an honor to serve you here in the light. Just show us where to dig."

Tombel frowned as he lifted Willow up. "Your people have suffered great hurts and I would not add to them by having you serve me or any Marcher on this battlefield. Today you have won your freedom and all Elundium waits to show you its beauty."

"Freedom!" Willow cried, looking at the Warhorses, the Border Runners and the great army of men gathered around them. "You mean we shall really be free and bound to serve no one?"

Tombel laughed and lifted Willow high enough for all to see and shouted, "Warriors of Elundium, look upon this lad and all his people. Let no man stand in their path, or cross their purpose with his shadow, for by their feats this day they are forever free!"

Before the sun began to burn World's Edge with

the morning light four great mounds had arisen on the plateau. They were laid in a crescent facing the Gates of Night. One for the Warhorses, one for the Battle Owls, one for the Border Runners and one for the warriors of Elundium. In front of them a small mound stood on its own. Amarch and Silverwing were laid together and Thane and Tombel between them placed the last heather turf over their bodies as the new sun rose.

Thane lifted his grandfather's sword above his head, catching all the morning's glory on the bright steel, and shouted their names out loud. Spears clashed on shields, Border Runners barked, the Warhorses stamped their hooves and all the Battle Owls, large and small, rose into the air, casting moving shadows across the black gate.

Thane lowered the sword, calling in a strong voice, "We leave many we have loved to guard this foul place forever. The gate is shut to all Nightbeasts. The way is closed for all time!"

He lifted the sword again, reflecting a sunbeam into the blackness, and the keystones above the gate split, crashing to the ground.

"Mantern's Gate is shut. Now we must return to Underfall and chase the Master of Nightmares into the heart of Elundium," Tombel said, turning towards the plateau's edge.

Thoron rose shakily to his knees, brushing aside helping hands, and crawled to Amarch's burial mound.

"Leave him," whispered Tombel, putting a hand on Thane's arm to restrain him.

"Two Gallopers will wait just below the plateau's rim and bring your grandfather down when he has watched awhile beside Amarch's grave, for he has a lifetime of memories to search amongst and grief blinds him to everything else. Come with me, Thane, to Underfall."

Thane reluctantly followed Tombel, but looking back he saw that Equestrius, the Lord of Horses, had moved to his grandfather's side. Sighing he called to Willow, offering him a place on Esteron's saddle for the long descent to Underfall.

Thoron knelt beside the single grave mound, his hands pressed into the heather. Eagle Owl descended on silent wings to perch on his shoulder and Equestrius moved to his side, snorting and whinnying softly, but the old man was unaware of their presence; he was far away, re-living the memory of riding into morning, the first day he had ever sat upon Amarch's back. A proud voice broke through the memory.

"Thoron, lift up your eyes. Look into the sunlight and put an end to your grief!"

"Equestrius! Why do you stand next to me, a ragged old man who has nothing but grief on his shoulders? Why?"

"Because grief must end. Amarch feared that your heart would break. She knew that her death was woven into your triumph over the darkness."

"And yet she came to free me," Thoron said bitterly.

"Yes," replied Equestrius, looking down at the mound where she lay. "And none could, or wished to stop her coming, for Nevian commanded it many sunlights ago at the Bondbreaking. Love drew her to you and love drew all the others who came to rescue you from the darkness. Even those with you at the Bondbreaking were drawn to Underfall and the battle on this high plateau, for the tattoo that Nevian traced upon their arms, of the owl in blue and gold, binds them."

"All just to set me free! A wanderer of the Greenway turf?"

"You are but a small part in these things, Thoron, but many threads of fate have stretched far across Elundium to set you free."

"How can I ever repay what they have sacrificed?" Thoron cried, looking at the wide crescent of burial mounds.

"You cannot, and must not try. The price of your freedom had no measure set against it. Come now and ride upon my back to Underfall."

Siege-Locked

*K*ING Holbian cantered up through the Granite City, reined Beacon Light to a halt before Candlebane Hall and dismounted. "Another daylight!" he laughed, shivering in the chill dawn wind as he unbuckled his sword and rested the hilt against the broken Candledoors. Breakmaster reined Mulberry, his rough-coated pony, in beside Beacon Light and also dismounted.

"We have won another daylight from the Nightbeasts, my Lord," he sighed, rubbing his hand wearily across his battle-smudged face, and smiled at the edge of sunlight climbing over the horizon. "But how long can we hold out against those foul Nightbeasts that hammer on the gates of the city?"

"Each daylight is a victory in itself, Breakmaster, we can ask no more. The shadow of the Nightbeast army has shrunk a little, I think. Look beyond the outer walls, near the horizon. There is a green strip fresh-painted in dawn colors. Come, we have rested enough, let us make ready for the long night ahead."

"Do you never tire, Lord?" Breakmaster asked, hurrying after the King and catching up with him as he strode through the empty Candle Hall. Early shafts of sunlight streamed through the high vaulted windows, chasing the night shadows into gloomy corners.

King Holbian laughed, drawing his fingers musically across the rows of empty tallow-stained candlesticks that ran in concentric circles up towards the high throne. His armored boots echoed across the polished marble floor as he climbed to the throne. "The wicks of my life are guttering, Breakmaster, and the great Candleman hovers with the snuffer behind my shoulder. Ruin looms tall and bleak enough almost to blot out the sunlight. No! I dare not tire, for I am the last Granite King and I must not fail the people of Elundium. Only kings can walk in the darkness and destroy the terrible Nightmares. I will leave this throne fit for a new king!"

Breakmaster stepped up to the throne and knelt before the King. "Lord," he whispered, "I meant no disrespect. You are always first where the Nightbeasts swarm over the walls, fighting with the strength and energy of ten warriors. Lord, you are the greatest Granite King."

Holbian reached down, putting his hand under Breakmaster's chin, and gently motioned him to rise.

"There are plenty here who would plot and scheme and show disrespect at every footstep, but

I have never doubted you, not since that day when you hid Thanehand from the Chancellors' rage. Now, sit by me and help me marshal the Chancellors, for they are a treacherous lot who would open the gates of the city if they feared the Nightbeasts less and if they could see a little profit in it."

"Shall I summon the Chancellors and the defenders of the outer walls into a full Battle Council, my Lord?" Breakmaster asked, turning towards the throne.

Holbian lifted his hand in silent approval; he was leaning forward, engrossed in watching the morning shafts of sunlight pick their way between the tall candle stems, filling the Candle Hall with beautiful light, and he was unaware of how closely the horse-breaker was studying his ungloved hands and his face.

Breakmaster gasped and swallowed; he had never sat so close to the King before and his hands trembled as he picked up the calling bell.

"Granite Kings," he whispered, stealing another look at the King's face, following with his eyes the tiny hairline fractures in the skin, until they disappeared beneath his flowing locks of pure white hair.

"Surely," he muttered, ringing the calling bell as loudly as he could, "the King is not made of stone? That is a night tale, one whispered by the aging crones and witches in the lower circle of the city."

A movement in the darkness behind the throne caught Breakmaster's eye and he turned quickly to see a dissolving flash of bright colors.

"Nevian! Is that you?" he whispered nervously, searching the shadows for the magician's rainbow cloak.

"Guard him well, Breakmaster," a voice whispered out of the darkness. "For he is the last Granite King." Nevian paused, gathered the rainbow cloak into tight folds to hide its light and peered intently at the maze of age cracks on the King's hands and face. "He grows brittle with age, horseman. I fear that only one winter is left to King Holbian. You must help him reach the Palace of Kings by high summer so that he may be laid to rest in his father's house."

"Palace of Kings?" asked Breakmaster. "I would not know where to look for such a place even if we could escape the siege lock the Nightbeasts have ringed around the Granite City."

Nevian laughed quietly. "Within the shadows of Mantern's Mountain lies the fortress of Underfall. That, horseman, is the Palace of Kings, but if you cannot escape, keep the King warm in the chill winds before the dawn; that will stop him from turning into stone."

Breakmaster rose to his feet and took a step towards the shadows. "Nevian?" he whispered. "How do I keep the King warm? He spurns all cloaks since the Chancellors destroyed the cloak of jewels."

The voice in the darkness chuckled, "You must search, horseman, for something of great value. Something that you would treasure against the

Nightbeasts, and wrap it around the King's shoulders."

"Search? Where?" Breakmaster hissed, stretching out a hand towards the voice.

"Something you would treasure, horseman." The voice chuckled, turned hollow and vanished as the first morning sunbeam reached the last dark space in Candlebane Hall.

Armored footsteps interrupted Breakmaster's whisperings, ringing out through the upper circle of the city. Strong voices laughed and shouted together above the murmur of battle talk as the defenders of the Granite City filed into Candlebane Hall.

"Well met, warriors, to a new daylight!" shouted the King, motioning them with a sweep of his hand to be seated.

"Chancellors!" he called, the smile fading from the corners of his mouth. "Come forward, grief-mongers, you are blotting out the sunlight. Sit by the wax channel and tell us what news the new daylight brings."

Chancellor Proudpurse hunched his shoulders, glanced furtively at the warriors as they moved aside, and led the other Chancellors through into the Candlehall. "Lord," he cried, taking his place on the edge of the cold wax channels. "The lower city larders are near to empty. Soon the people will have nothing to eat but the sewer vermin."

"They will be in darkness, my Lord," cried out Chancellor Overlord, rising to his feet, "for the lower tallow house is drained of wax and only one in twenty men has a spark to light his way."

King Holbian glared darkly at the Chancellors. "Enough of this pantomime," he hissed, pointing an accusing finger. Archer Gray Goose rose quietly to his feet and slipped unnoticed out of the room, gathering a small strike of Archers around him. He entered the Chancellors' houses in the third circle of the city, going from chamber to chamber, searching out the truth.

"I have watched you for many suns and countless daylights," the King roared, standing directly above the Chancellors, "plotting, taking and hoarding, lining your pockets and growing fat on the people of Elundium."

"Great King," Proudpurse soothed, spreading his smile as wide as his outspread hands, "our toil is the life blood of Elundium, and all that is ours we would gladly give to the people of the Granite City, but . . ."

"But . . ." laughed Gray Goose, standing between the Candledoors, a rough hemp sack slung across his shoulder. Proudpurse turned, frowning at the Archer. "You dare to interrupt a Chancellor?"

Gray Goose strode forward and cast the contents of the sack across the polished marble floor at the Chancellors' feet, laughing. He knelt before the King. "I bring gifts for the people, my Lord, from the Chancellors. I bring sparks to light the night, blocks of pure tallow, coils and loops of unused wick, cotton . . ."

"Lord! Lord!" Proudpurse cried, treading on the sharp sparks as he retreated to the edge of the wax channel, "I . . ."

Holbian stared the Chancellor into silence, his face set in lines of anger. "What else do the Chancellors offer to the people of the Granite City to ease their siege plight?" he asked and turned smiling eyes towards his Captain Archer.

"Why, my Lord, they are so generous that whole wagonloads of oatmeal, smoked meats and bagged forest fruits are being sent into the lower circles of the city as we talk. They have emptied their houses in their generosity."

Proudpurse bit his knuckles, shaking with rage.

"What say you now to the Archer's interruption?" King Holbian asked, turning searching eyes to the Chancellors.

Proudpurse opened and shut his mouth, the color draining out of his cheeks, but all he could utter was, "The people, the people will . . ."

"Benefit?" prompted Breakmaster, laughing.

"Benefit, my Lord!" choked Overlord, sitting down heavily beside the wax channel.

King Holbian looked beyond the Chancellors into the throng of warriors. "Who can tell me how the outer wall withstood the night's attacks?"

"The great wall is crumbling, my Lord, under the Nightbeast attacks. My mason gangs cannot keep pace with the damage they do."

"Come forward, Mastermason, and tell us what must be done to strengthen the outer walls."

Arachatt, the Mastermason, squeezed through the press of warriors until he stood shyly before the King. Kneeling, he kissed the King's foot. "We cannot repair the damage, my Lord. The houses built against the inner surface of the wall are no more than piles of broken granite. The Nightbeasts are breaking through."

"How so?" asked the King, leaning forward. "The narrow road along the top of the wall feels firm enough. It trembles and shakes under the Nightbeasts' assaults, but it seems strong and safe."

"Lord, they are battering with whole tree trunks against the lower sections of the wall, shaking the very foundations of the city."

"But the walls are seventeen paces thick, and each great granite block is the height and width of three grown men. Surely trees are no match against granite?"

"They are using ironwood, my Lord," Arachatt replied. "Splinters too heavy for my masons to carry have been hurled into the city."

"Ironwood!" Gray Goose mouthed. Once he had seen an ironwood tree in the heart of the black forest. "You can cast sparks with the blade of your sword, or blunt arrows on that wood. It is match enough for granite."

"They pound the walls all night without rest, my Lord, grinding the granite to a fine powder. I fear they will break through into the lower city tonight," Arachatt insisted. "We have piled the rubble from the houses against the weakest sections of the wall but the first circle of the city is a tangle of wreckage."

King Holbian rose to his feet and paced the high dais, deep in thought. "If we abandon the first circle, Mastermason, how will we defend the city once the Nightbeasts have breached the wall?"

"The second level has a strong granite wall, my Lord, but it has been hidden for many suns beneath new buildings. It is said that the houses on that wall have a view second only to the views from the Granite Towers."

Holbian smiled. "But there are no gates. How will you stop the Nightbeasts from swarming up through every level until they reach Candlebane Hall? We will be overrun before the new sun rises."

"Lord, my masons will demolish every house on the second wall and render it smooth, without a handhold for the Nightbeasts. We will block the gateway with the rubble, building a new strong wall in the gap."

Angry mutterings rose amongst the Marchers near the Candledoors and Marcher Cherink pushed his way through the Battle Council to stand before the King.

"We will be homeless, Lord, if the masons strip the inner wall. We will be left with nothing but the stars over our heads at night."

The King looked steadily into Marcher Cherink's eyes and answered him softly, yet all could hear his words. "What would you have, Marcher? Nightbeasts staring down at us from every window on the wall, filling your homely chambers with their foul stench? What of the people from the lower city? They already have the stars for a roof."

Marcher Cherink hung his head and shuffled his feet in confusion.

"We are siege-locked warriors," the King called out in a strong voice. "And every one of us, even the Chancellors, must give a little and bend beneath the Nightbeasts' foul shadows, but remember this, in the bending we are only crouching, waiting for the moment to spring back and tear their black hearts out!"

"Elundium! Elundium!" shouted the warriors, clashing their spear butts on the marble floor and beating the flat blades of their swords against the fire-fluted candle stems. Holbian lifted his hands and called for silence.

"Saddle the horses, Breakmaster!" he cried, unsheathing his sword. The Battle Council leaned forward, hushed and anxious to catch his every word.

"We will clear the lower circle of the city before night falls, Mastermason. Set your stonechippers to work on the inner wall. Use every Marcher, man or boy, use everyone, but strip it bare. Gallopers, spread out through the shadow of the great wall and bring the low-born people up into the safety of the inner circle. Archer Gray Goose, take your Archers up to the great wall and with your careful sharp eyes watch over us and marshal our retreat."

* * *

"Lord we are ready!" Breakmaster cried, holding Beacon Light by the bridle.

"Ride with me, faithful friend," the King whispered as Breakmaster held the stirrup for him to mount, "for never in all the history of Elundium has the Granite City fallen so far under the Nightmare's shadow and I am afraid."

Breakmaster tightened the horse's girth and handed the reins to the King. "I am your shadow, Lord. Even in the Nightmare's darkness I will be at your side."

"Not as a shadow," resolved the King, "but as a fearless and proud friend whom I trust with my life!" Holbian laughed, stood in the stirrups and beckoned his small squadron of Gallopers to follow, and their hoofbeats sounded as thunder in the narrow cobbled streets that wound their way down into the shadow of the great wall.

Fine stone dust hung in a gritty fog, blurring the lower limits of the city. King Holbian coughed, choking on each breath that he swallowed and his eyes watered in the stinging dust. The lower city lanes and winding alleyways had been reduced to heaps of granite rubble, and rough sacking shelters had sprung up wherever a wall remained standing. Cooking fires lit the gloomy scene, sending up the stench of roasting sewer vermin or worse.

"What chaos!" muttered Breakmaster, wrinkling up his nose and reining his pony to a slow walk as he picked his way amongst the temporary shelters.

"Bring the cryers forward!" shouted the King,

twisting in the saddle and sweeping his eyes across the wreckage of the lower city. Far above him in the upper circle of the city the noon bell tolled out the measure of the daylight.

"Cryers!" he shouted, "the daylight runs away from us. Marshal the people up into the second level."

Holbian spurred Beacon Light forward, riding amongst the shuffling low-born dwellers, urging them to hurry. "The people are slow to move to safety," he called across to Breakmaster as the evening shadows lengthened.

"They have suffered great hardship in the siege, my Lord, and their spirits are near to breaking." Breakmaster hesitated. "And they fear death in the upper circles of the city at the hands of the Chancellors."

A loud clap of thunder drowned out any more of Breakmaster's words and the ground beneath their feet rocked and trembled.

"Death waits for them here if they drag their footsteps," shouted Holbian. "The Nightbeasts are battering on the walls. Drive the stragglers to safety."

Galloper Earit saw the wall begin to bulge above him. He spun his horse away and galloped clear as a shower of sharp granite stone fell all around him. His horse stumbled, floundering in the wreckage as a section of wall collapsed behind him. Blinding clouds of stone dust rose. The Nightbeasts were swarming through the breach, roaring and screaming, reaching out with cruel claws for the last fleeing dwellers of the lower city.

King Holbian wheeled Beacon Light towards the Nightbeasts and spurred her forward.

"The King! The King!" shouted Breakmaster, seeing his Lord's peril as the Nightbeasts surrounded him. Beating the flat of his sword against his pony's side he charged after the King into the terrible shadows, calling to the Gallopers to follow. King Holbian slipped the reins and, double-handed, gripped the hilt of his Galloping sword. Boldly he scythed through the Nightbeasts' mail-clad arms and iron caps, as Beacon Light reared and plunged, thrashing the air with her forelegs, taking the King nearer and nearer to the breach; farther and farther into the Nightbeasts' shadows.

Gray Goose knelt at the edge of the great wall and watched the King's perilous charge.

"Wait for my signal!" he commanded quietly. His strike of Archers were spread out on either side of him. Lifting his right hand, the Archers nocked new-forged arrows onto their bows and drew them tight until the feathered flights lightly touched their cheeks. Beyond the piles of granite rubble the Gallopers had rallied into a fast-moving line. Spears lowered, they closed in on the Nightbeasts to rescue the King.

Gray Goose's hand trembled and fell, the oiled wooden bows cried out as the arrows sang and shrieked their way down into the Nightbeast army below. The wall of Nightbeasts crumbled and Breakmaster galloped over them.

"Abandon the breach, my Lord," he urged, arriving breathlessly at the King's side.

Holbian laughed, sweeping his sword in a glittering arc. "Well met, Captain Archer," he cried, looking up at the strike of Archers on the wall. The Gallopers closed about the King, their spears turned outwards in defense.

"The lower circle of the city is abandoned, Lord, it is time to retreat," urged Breakmaster. More Nightbeasts were already surging through the breach, climbing over the carcasses of those the Archers had felled.

"Abandon the wall!" Holbian shouted up to Gray Goose. "We will wait for you beneath the second wall."

Gray Goose saluted to Holbian, then turned and quickly led the Archers towards the ramp that led down into the shadow of the great wall, but ahead of them siege ladders crashed against its stones.

"Form a moving strike!" Gray Goose shouted as the first Nightbeasts swarmed up onto the narrow road, blocking it with their hideous shapes.

"What keeps them?" fretted the King, pirouetting Beacon Light in the lengthening shadows.

"Lord," a voice shouted from the top of the wall, "we are trapped! The Nightbeasts have the road against us!"

Holbian looked up at the black shapes crowding

towards his Archers, then spurred his horse forward.

"Lord, the narrow road is too dangerous. We must abandon the great wall!" cried out one of the Gallopers.

"And lose my only strike of Archers?" Holbian angrily replied, checking his horse's stride and bending to snatch up a siege hook from where it hung at the bottom of the ramp.

"Follow me if you dare, Gallopers!" he cried, turning the shaft of the siege hook until the smooth curve of shining steel was level with the edge of the wall. Leaning forward he stroked Beacon Light's neck with his rein hand. "Gallop for me, greathearted friend, against the blackest shadows," he whispered, pressing her forward with his spurs.

Breakmaster galloped level with the King, a siege hook in his left hand. "Let me go before you, Lord. Let me go and cut the Nightbeasts down."

"It is the place of Kings," Holbian shouted against the thunder of their hoofbeats, "to be first, and tread where the danger is the greatest. But ride with me, true friend; match me stride for stride and help me tear the Nightbeast ladders down."

Breakmaster laughed, urging his pony forward, and galloped beside the King to the top of the ramp. Low evening sunlight shone on their faces, but before them the edge of the narrow road was a forest of siege ladders. Beacon Light neighed and sprang forward. Holbian swung the siege hook against the first crude wooden ladder and toppled it, sending it crashing backwards into the deep dyke that surrounded the great wall. Breakmaster attacked the second ladder, pushing it out away from the wall until it overbalanced, shedding its Nightbeast load onto the ground far below. Galloping hard, they cleared away the siege ladders one by one between them and their Archers. Gray Goose saw the sunlight blood red on the King's mail-clad arms as he came to their rescue. Their quivers were empty and their bows clasped securely to their belts. The Archers were beating their way towards the ramp. The column of Gallopers rode up onto the narrow road and quickly overtook the King. Lowering their spears they ploughed through the Nightbeasts, clearing a gap for the fleeing Archers.

Bending low and running as fast as they could Gray Goose and the Archers reached the safety of the ramp and descended into the shadows of the great wall. Their footsteps echoed loudly in the eerie silence, and behind them they could hear the roar of hoofbeats as the Gallopers led the King and Breakmaster down off the narrow road. Beyond the great wall they could hear the screams of the Nightbeasts, distantly muffled by the wall's thickness.

"Do not stop until you are within the second circle," shouted the King, swinging the siege hook behind him, knocking the nearest pursuing Nightbeast to his death on the piles of rubbish below.

Arachatt, the Mastermason, had driven his stonechippers without rest from the moment the King rode down into the lower circle of the city, and, as he had promised, the inner wall rose bare and imposing in the evening sunlight. The granite rubble from the demolished houses had been carried down in wicker baskets and piled into the gateway by the Marchers, but Arachatt himself had built the new wall, packing the granite in tight layers and troweling in the mortar against the Nightbeasts. He had left a narrow gap for the retreating warriors and every Marcher, man and boy, waited behind the wall, a block of granite held ready to fill the gap. Two carts of wet mortar were poised upon the top of the wall to seal it once the King was safely inside.

Breathlessly the Archers ran through the gap, with the Gallopers only a length behind. Breakmaster and the King reached the wall together. Briefly they halted and looked back at the ruin below.

"We are siege-locked now, my Lord," Breakmaster muttered, watching the Nightbeasts pouring through new breach-holes all along the length of the great wall.

"Siege-locked and desperate," answered the King in a tired voice, turning Beacon Light into the entrance and riding up into the second level of the city.

Underfall

*T*HE giant doors of Underfall lay shattered and splintered away from their hinges. The inner courtyards were a jumble of wreckage and broken stonework.

"Thunderstone!" Thane shouted, quickly dismounting from Esteron's back and unsheathing his grandfather's sword.

"Who lives in this great fortress?" Willow asked, jumping lightly to the ground.

"The Keeper of World's End. The Lampmaster of Elundium," Tombel replied, grimly striding across the Causeway to join the others standing between the broken doors.

"Who could have wrought such damage?" cried Tiethorm, looking up at the ruined tree-thick doors.

"Krulshards, the Master of Nightbeasts!" cried a voice from the shadows of the first stone stairway that led up to the galleries. Faltering, with his hand upon the rail, Thunderstone descended the last few steps into the main courtyard.

"Thunderstone!" Thane cried, running to the Keeper's side and catching him in his arms as he stumbled forward.

"Give me room!" Thunderstone wept, struggling to raise the horsetail sword, but it slipped from his hand and clattered onto the cobblestones.

"Fetch Merion the Healer!" Tombel ordered, bending to pick up Thunderstone's sword.

"An army of Healers will not stop him now," whispered Thunderstone, climbing dizzily to his feet, and taking back his sword.

"How did the Master of Nightmares break into Underfall?" Thane asked, helping Thunderstone to a stone bench at the edge of the courtyard.

Merion the Healer burst into the courtyard, his bag of oils and herbs bumping heavily against his legs. Thunderstone stared absently at him for a moment, his forehead wrinkled in a frown.

"The lamp gallery. Go quickly. Morolda is tending Errant beside the lamp."

Merion ignored him, dipped into his bag for an oiled cotton and pressed it against the ragged tear in the side of the Keeper's face.

"Go, fool!" Thunderstone roared, angrily pushing Merion away. "Errant needs you more than I. This is nothing but the mark from a broken Nightbeast claw."

"Kerzolde!" Thane exclaimed, grimly.

"You know of this beast?" Thunderstone asked, picking up the oiled cotton that Merion had dropped and pressing it against his wound.

"We have fought many times, even yesterlight in the City of Night, but he escaped. I had the choice between his death and Thoron's life."

"Thoron lives?" Thunderstone cried, jumping to his feet and letting the oiled cotton fall to the ground again.

"He follows us with Equestrius, the Lord of Horses."

"Who?" gasped Thunderstone, looking from face to face and seeing Willow for the first time standing on the edge of the gathering crowd.

"There is much to tell you, Master," Thane laughed, stooping for the oiled cotton and returning it to Thunderstone's head. "It is a long story, and many parts need others to fit the pieces together. But tell us, how did Krulshards break into Underfall?"

Thunderstone turned his head and looked fearfully into the innermost courtyard where it touched the side of Mantern's Mountain. "He did not break in. He came from within, out of the very roots of the mountain. Up through the earth we stand upon."

The listening warriors shuffled uneasily, as if the ground beneath their feet had suddenly grown too hot for them.

"In a great screaming wind he stormed up through the galleries, burning the wooden floors and tearing down the stonework, until he reached the lamp gallery. He charged at the lamp, his black malice billowing out with hatred."

Thunderstone hid his face in his hands and his shoulders shook with terror as he remembered what he had seen. "Out of the earth," he whispered. "A face of raw sinews, more horrible than death itself to look upon."

Thane knelt and took Thunderstone's hands into his own and steadied them before he continued with his story.

"Errant tried to come between Krulshards and the lamp but Krulshards picked him up and tossed him the length of the gallery and then he snapped Errant's sword in two as if it had been a stick of straw. The one-eyed monster attacked me in the instant that Krulshards smashed the crystal in the lamp, but I caught a glimpse of that broken claw as he slashed at my face. Darkness descended across the gallery, even the starlight seemed blacked out. Krulshards destroyed the glass of the lamp and laughed as he crunched the crystal into a fine powder, but with the horsetail sword gripped firmly in both hands I tried to cut into the malice, slashing at the black fabric."

Thunderstone smiled and touched the horsetail sword. "The silver strands of horsehair bound into the hilt of the sword glowed in the darkness, and whenever they touched or wrapped themselves about my hands they seemed to give me strength, the strength of the great warhorse, Equion, who feared nothing in the dark. Twice Krulshards drove me to my knees but each time as he tried to make the killing stroke the horsetail shone so brightly that it gave the Nightmare a shadow, blinding him with a silver light. Cursing and snarling he turned on the shadow, trampling it as he fled from the lamp gallery down towards the great doors."

Thunderstone paused for breath and all eyes turned towards the ruined doors. "I followed the Nightmare sticking as close as I dared and watched the awesome power of Krulshards as he wound the malice tightly around his shoulders and attacked the doors. Twice he hammered on them, once to the left and once to the right, filling the courtyard with blinding sparks. The iron studding melted at his touch. The doors fell, collapsing outwards onto the Causeway and Krulshards was gone, escaping into the night."

"We saw the great lamp falter and feared for you," Tombel said, quietly taking his old friend's hand and leading him into the sunlight.

"Tell me," he whispered when they were beyond the others' hearing, "did the Master of Nightmares, or the other beast, have a small silver finger bowl?"

Thunderstone thought for a moment, and then shrugged his shoulders. "Black-bladed daggers, cruel rusty iron spears and the gruesome trophies from earlier battles hung from the one-eyed beast's belt, but nothing that shone like silver. The malice hid much of Krulshards's Nightmare shape and I could not guess at what he might have carried but he did cry out to the one-eyed beast to hurry for they had easier meat to catch than the Lampmaster of Underfall."

*　　*　　*

Kyot cantered Sprint easily up onto the Causeway, leading the Archers. Laughing, he jumped to the ground. "Thunderstone! We come back to eat the chair you sit upon!"

"And so you shall," boomed Morolda's voice as she entered the courtyard. Softly she smiled at Duclos and took his hand in quiet finger-talk of all that had happened on the high plateau.

"There was no finger bowl to see," Thunderstone concluded, turning back towards the main courtyard and taking Esteron's bridle to lead him towards the stables.

Tombel sighed with relief and fell into step with the Keeper.

"We heard the battle on the high plateau," Thunderstone said quietly, "and we feared for you. The tattoo of the owl on my arm began to fade as the afternoon wore on. Despair darkened our hearts. Then a great shout filled the air and the tattoo burned with new colors. What happened?"

"Defeat towered over your warriors. Thane and Kyot had prepared to make a last stand; we could hear their defiant singing as we breasted the edge of the plateau. That shout you heard was the Archers of Stumble Hill and the Warriors of Underfall finding new heart to see us—late but in the nick of time."

"And the small boy with the strange ears and the bulging eyes?"

"Willow! He led his people out from within the City of Night and won the black gates."

"Master! Master!" a voice cried out, interrupting Tombel's explanation of Willow's part in the battle. "Thoron is on the Causeway!"

With a rush of feet across the cobbles every man and beast ran to the broken doors, and the roar of their welcome echoed across the Causeway Field.

Thunderstone waited until Thoron had been helped to dismount before he offered him the hilt of the horsetail sword saying, "Welcome home, old friend. You have been greatly missed."

Tombel knelt, offering up the hilt of his Marching sword, shouting, "Hail to the greatest rider in all Elundium, who has defeated the darkness and returned!"

Thane pushed his way through the crowding warriors and clasped his grandfather's hands. "Beyond my wildest dreams . . . you have returned from the dead!"

Thoron laughed, his eyes sparkling with joy. "You have grown, child, into a strong young man that your father, Ironhand, would be proud of."

A shadow crossed Thane's face, his eyes growing wet around the edges.

"He is dead, Grandfather."

"Dead?" cried Thoron, the laughter fading from his lips. The warriors fell into a hushed silence. Thane turned his eyes toward the pine-clad slopes of Mantern's Mountain and told Thoron how his father had died.

"He was the King's standard-bearer, Grandfather, running at his stirrup through a long weary day of retreating before the Granite City. At evening time he fell, driven into the shadows by a Nightbeast blade."

"The King rode back for him," Errant called out from where he leaned on the Healer's arm, "and took his body up into Candlebane Hall. The standard he carried to his death was laid across his funeral bier and was taken in great honor to the buriers' yard."

Thoron looked up at the standard of the owl in blue and gold where it fluttered in the sunshine and wept. Willow squeezed through the press of warriors until he stood before Thoron.

"Lord. Equestrius told me that you are a great lord, so great that all the animals came to help you. I am sure that they will grieve at your loss."

Thoron smiled down at Willow, brushing the back of his age-stained hand across his cheeks to wipe away the tears. "You are the boy, Willow. The one who escaped into the daylight before the battle began. There was an old horse with you."

Willow smiled, but a sadness haunted his face. "Her name was Evening Star, but I have lost her, Lord. We were together the night before the battle, when she gave birth to a beautiful foal, but after the battle she vanished. I looked everywhere and I cannot find her."

The warriors smiled at each other and began moving forward toward the row of tables the servers had set upon the Causeway for the victory feast, but Thoron straightened up, his eyebrows drawn fiercely together, and bade them remember who stood before them. Who, when all had seemed lost, had won the black gates and turned defeat into victory.

"We shall ask the Owls and the Warhorses to search for Evening Star and her newborn foal, but if she is not found before tomorrow's sun sets every Galloper here at World's End will ride out and scour the countryside."

"Come warriors, Marchers, Archers and Tunnelers, we are going to eat this victory table bare, and then young Kyot will keep his promise and eat the chair I sit upon!" shouted Thunderstone, leading Thoron to the Honor Chair at the center of the highest table.

"We must call a Battle Council," Tombel demanded, taking the chair on the left of Thoron.

"The Nightmare is loose in Elundium," replied Thunderstone from Thoron's right.

"And the King is siege-locked in the Granite City," Errant called from farther down the table.

Thane watched his grandfather picking at his food, lifting it to his mouth, chewing a little and then returning it to the plate. Quietly he caught a server's eye and beckoned him. "Give me your serving cloth. I will serve my grandfather; he is not yet strong enough for raw meats."

Thoron smiled as Thane came to his aid, and pulling him close he whispered, "I cannot eat. Krulshards fills my mind with dread. We must speak privately of him before the Battle Council is called."

Thane felt a cold shiver at the mention of the Nightmare's name, as if an icy hand had touched his spine. Kyot came laughing to Thoron's chair and linked his arm through Thane's. "We are brothers, Thoron, and closer friends you have never seen. Let me wait with him and serve you all you desire."

Evening had drawn the shadows long before the feast was finished and huge bonfires were lit upon the Causeway Field. The Warhorses, Owls, Border Runners and men of Elundium gathered for the Battle Council. Thunderstone took the center of the field, drove the point of the horsetail sword deep into the turf and waited for silence before he spoke. "When this blade draws a shadow from the new sun then this council will end."

"We should ride with the rising sun and break the siege of the Granite City!" Tombel shouted.

"Follow the Master of Nightbeasts," called another voice.

"Both paths will be along the same road," said another.

"Strengthen Underfall and repair the doors," Tiethorm shouted against the rising clamor of anxious voices.

"Thane," Thoron whispered, an edge of worry in his voice, taking his grandson into the shadows away from the firelight and sitting down by his side. "I urged you to take battle council, for that is

the warrior way, but now that I am sure that Krulshards has escaped into Elundium I know you must
follow him. He has linked your name with fair
Elionbel's; he knows of your love through that
cursed finger bowl and he will take the fastest road
through Notley Marsh to the Wayhouse at Woodsedge to take her in revenge for his defeat before
the Gates of Night. I know it."

"Elionbel," Thane cried, closing his fingers on
the broken chain that hung from his belt.

"No matter what Tombel thinks of you, low
born or base, bloodworthy or not, you must follow
the Nightmare," urged Thoron. "There are leaders
here, my boy, plenty enough to rescue ten Granite
Kings, but you dared to enter the darkness to rescue
me. I know you have the power to follow Krulshards. Go! Take the wild road through Notley
Marsh. Go! Go now, or it will be too late!"

Thane rose to his feet and called softly into the
flickering firelight for Esteron and Mulcade. "Will
you follow me?" he asked, his hand on Thoron's
arm.

"When darkness holds the Greenway's edge and
the gray hours have yet to light the sky, look for
me then, or call my name, and I shall come to you
with the soft jingle of battle harness and the thunder of Warhorse hooves." Esteron nudged Thane's
arm and Mulcade silently stooped onto his shoulder.

Thoron turned his head towards the darker edges
of the Causeway. "Men will council, Thane, strut-

ting and shouting to make themselves strong in the darkness, but listen—out there beyond the fire-light, there is the greatest power in all Elundium!" Thane turned his head and heard beyond the noisy Battle Council the thunder of hoofbeats on the edge of the wind. "I will follow you, Thane, on Equestrius, the Lord of Horses, but first I must honor my pledge to Willow and find Evening Star and her newborn foal."

Thane quickly mounted Esteron and handed the sword he carried to Thoron. "Eagle Owl carried your blade the length of Elundium. I only bor-rowed it to set you free."

"But you will need it against the Nightmare," Thoron insisted, making to give it back.

"I am well armed. I have the dagger Duclos gave to me on the lawns of Gildersleeves. Give my fare-well to Thunderstone, tell him we will meet again before the great lamp of Underfall."

"Beware the Nightbeasts on the road," Thoron called into the darkness, but Thane had gone, gal-loping over the soft turf of the Causeway Field to-wards the ancient road that led to Notley Marsh.

"Men will council," laughed a voice at Thoron's side.

"Nevian!" Thoron cried, spinning round to-wards the shrouded figure. For long moments they stood eye to eye.

"You did not forget me or abandon me in the darkness," Thoron whispered, reaching out a hand to touch the muted colors in the rainbow cloak.

"Many threads were pulled, old friend, to set you free."

"But what is the bidding? What is the pledge-task that you would take in payment?" Thoron asked, sinking to his knees and offering up the hilt of his sword.

Nevian laughed, a sharp glint in his eye. "You see deeper than most men, Thoronhand, and you know that nothing is ever given without a price. The fate of Elundium may yet balance on Thane's shoulders and he may need your sword again. I pledge you to keep it safe for him and in his hour of need offer up the hilt to Eagle Owl, for he will wait, ready perched on your shoulder, to carry the blade to Thane's hand. For when the Nightmare haunts Elundium no more, a new King will stand upon the Causeway Field, his banner shining in the sunlight."

"Nevian!" Thoron cried, feeling the rainbow cloak melt beneath his touch. "Who will be that King?"

Woodsedge

*B*RANCH fingers scratched against the windows of Woodsedge, rattling and tapping in the chill evening breeze. Martbel shivered and drew her shawl more tightly around her shoulders and, for the hundredth time since the noon bell had rung, she looked along the Greenway that ran past the Wayhouse close to the eaves of the black forest. "I was against it," she muttered, fretting with the shawl's edge. "Night is no time to wander out of doors." Behind her a server coughed, hovering in the doorway. "We will wait," Martbel called out, without taking her eyes off the darkening strip of Greenway turf that led towards the Granite City.

"Elion," she whispered, screwing the shawl between her fingers.

Far off, three shadows broke away from the forest gloom, hurrying towards the Wayhouse. Silver laughter rang out clearly in the evening light.

"Elion! Elion!" Martbel shouted, throwing open the Wayhouse door.

Laughing and teasing, Arbel and Rubel raced their sister the last league to Woodsedge and tumbled, fresh-faced and breathless, onto the cool flagstones of the great hall. Martbel stood before them, her face dark with anger.

"You fools!" she scolded, pointing through the open door to the forest eaves. "Listen! Nightbeasts are close at hand. Your father charged you to keep the Wayhouse safe and hold the Greenway open for his return. You spend the days in idle foolishness, risking your sister's life in silly games!"

The laughter died away. Arbel shuffled, blushing, and unbuckled his broad Marching sword. "Mother . . ." he began, but she glared him into silence and turned hard eyes onto Elionbel.

"The Wayhouse should have been locked and bolted long ago. You have risked all our lives with your foolishness."

Elionbel hung her head and offered up a basket of sweet-smelling forest fruits. "Arbel and Rubel were guarding me while I collected these for our table."

Martbel's face softened as she took the basket. "You are a foolish girl, Elion. Light-headed with flights of fancy, always dreaming, you are leagues away from the dangerous world you live in. Beware, child!" Beyond the forest's edge a Nightbeast roared, cutting short Martbel's anger. She dropped the basket and threw her weight against the door, slamming it home.

"Bolt and bar the shutters," she cried, drawing

the short sword she carried from her belt and bracing herself for the Nightbeasts' attack.

Elionbel and her brothers raced from window to window, making the Wayhouse safe, shutting out the last shades of evening light. The Wayhouse Candleman hurried into the Great Hall, a spark blazing in his hand, and went from wick to wick, filling the hall with soft yellow light.

"We will eat as we stand, armed and ready," Martbel ordered, calling all the servers into the safety of the hall and bolting the outer doors. "The Nightbeasts are on the Greenway and it will not take them long to realize we are alone and defenseless."

"Mother!" Rubel cried, striking sparks off the stone chimney breast with his Marching sword. "Arbel and I will defend the Wayhouse. We are Marchers; pledged to it by our father!"

Martbel smiled. "I know you are Marchers, proud and brave, but you are only two against a swarm of shadows that goes beyond my skill to count. Listen! They are gathering all around us."

"If Thane were here with us he would drive the Nightbeasts away," Elionbel said, smiling as she remembered how he fought his way across the hollow to rescue her, but it seemed so long ago now, even the scars from the Nightbeasts' teeth on her hands had paled beneath new skin.

Martbel frowned at Elionbel, shushing her into silence. "Count with me, girl." She ordered Elionbel to put away her memories of Thane and listen to the Nightbeasts roaring on the Greenway's edge. One, two, three, they were getting closer, crowding in with the darkness.

"Light the stairhead fire," Martbel whispered to Elionbel, "and set branding irons to warm in it. Arbel, Rubel, arm the servers."

"There are at least twenty Nightbeasts!" Elionbel called out softly from the stairhead. "I can see them through the casement slits in the bell tower. They are leaving the eaves of the forest to ring the Wayhouse!"

Martbel quickly threw more logs onto the hall fire, making it blaze halfway up the chimney. "We will eat now," she ordered, "before the night attack."

Rubel tried to laugh but failed to mask his nervousness as he carved thick chunks of cold nightboar and filled the waiting plates. Elionbel pushed her plate away but Martbel insisted that she eat. "Strength for the night ahead," she whispered, splitting a hard-skinned yellow apple on the blade of her sword.

"But the noise of them screaming ties my stomach in a knot," Elionbel whispered.

"Eat!" commanded her mother, listening to the Nightbeasts drawing closer. Elionbel closed her eyes and chewed on the coarse dark meat. She swallowed and filled her fork again. The taste and smell of the meat reminded her of the Nightbeasts in that awful hollow, pawing and touching her, breathing their foul odor in her face. Choking, she pushed the plate away, drew the long dagger from her belt and tested the blade by cutting a deep groove in the stairhead banister.

"You will not take me again," she hissed, gripping the hilt of her dagger hard enough to make her knuckles turn white.

"They are upon us," Arbel cried, leaping backwards a pace, away from the Wayhouse door as it shook and rattled, bulging inwards.

Rubel dropped the carving knife and quickly moved across the hall to take his place, a sword's length from his brother. "Ready," he whispered, as they raised their Marching swords, gripping them to strike.

Elionbel stoked the stairhead fire and rearranged the branding irons to glow sparkling white beneath the logs before she ran down the broad stairway and took her place beside her mother. Both held a long Marcher spear, the butt firmly placed against the third stair riser, the sharp pear-shaped blades pointing towards the main doorway. Behind them at each stair tread the servers crouched, swords and spears glittering in the candlelight.

"One stroke only, boys, and then retreat to the stairway," Martbel called anxiously to her sons as the door shook violently, splintering on its hinges.

Nightmare screams rose to a deafening pitch as the Nightbeasts hurled themselves against the Wayhouse. Window glass shattered, the shutters flew splintering across the Great Hall. The iron-studded door shuddered, bulged and burst apart.

"Sing! Sing!" shouted Rubel, feeling the icy strength of hatred flooding through his veins. "Keep these monsters out of Woodsedge!"

Hideous Nightbeast shapes were crowding through the broken doorway and spilling over the window sills.

"*Elundium . . . a place of sunlight hours . . .*" Arbel sang at the top of his voice, lunging forward and slashing his blade at the cruel spears and wicked razor-sharp claws that reached out towards him.

"One stroke only," Martbel shouted above the Nightbeast roar.

Elionbel watched, horror-stricken, as her brothers waded into the writhing mass of Nightbeasts, slashing and cutting to left and right.

"Arbel, Rubel," she cried as the shadows closed around them. "We must save them," she shouted across to her mother.

Elionbel and Martbel sprang forward, their spear shafts gripped firmly in both hands and charged, heads down, across the hall. With reckless speed they crashed into the monsters, driving their spear blades deep into the Nightbeasts' armor, sending up bright showers of burning sparks.

"Arbel, Rubel, back to the stairway," the women shouted as the impaled Nightbeasts crumpled before them, leaving a clear gap for the boys to retreat through.

Turning, they fled in a tight knot to the safety of the stairs and fell exhausted behind the wall of servers' spears.

"Next time I give an order you must obey it!" Martbel snapped breathlessly.

The Nightbeasts renewed their attack, surging in a mass of black shadows against the stairway. Elionbel snatched up two hot firebrands and thrust them down into the Nightbeasts' faces, searing into their coarse hairy flesh with the burning metal. Rubel took up a spear, and Arbel a broad Marching sword, and together they defended the lower stairway.

"Bring every light and spark to the stairway," Martbel cried, thrusting her dagger between the banister rails, and with one sweep of the blade cutting a Nightbeast's throat. "It will weaken them."

Elionbel returned to the stairhead fire and quickly passed out the white-hot firebrands. "We are ready, Mother," she whispered, turning her head and looking back up the stairway to where the servers waited, the glowing firebrands in their hands.

Martbel counted what were left of the Nightbeasts in the Great Hall and sprang forward. "Now," she shouted, leading the defenders of the Wayhouse down onto the broad flagstones and singing in a clear voice of the beautiful sunlight that would fill Elundium with the coming dawn. Screaming and howling, the Nightbeasts retreated, fighting each other to escape the hot irons and bright lights that burned through their scaly armor. The Great Hall quickly became fogged with bitter smoke, heavy with the smell of seared skin. Rubel and Arbel chased the last fleeing Nightbeasts to the doorway and slew them on the threshold stone. "Victory, mother," they laughed, returning into the ruined hall and resting wearily on their swords' hilts.

Martbel surveyed the wreckage and a frown drew her eyebrows together. "Victory is only a short breath away from defeat. We have little time to rest. Quickly, barricade the door and windows before the Nightbeasts return."

Elionbel stepped over the Nightbeasts' carcasses that littered the floor, her face grim with disgust.

"They will come back, mark my words. They will return in black hordes to smother the starlight," Martbel muttered, sheathing her sword, and turning to the servers.

"Clear the hall, pile the Nightbeasts in a heap beside the doorway. We will burn them before the new sun rises."

Turning back to her sons she ordered them to fortify the Great Hall as for a siege. Elionbel she sent to the larders with baskets for all the food she could carry. "Before the new sun sets this Wayhouse must become a fortress. Something terrible is loose in Elundium, I can feel it, a black shadow at my shoulder, a gnawing coldness in my bones."

Elionbel shivered, feeling the coldness of her mother's fear, and looked out at the black forest's edge. "The gray hours have come," she whispered without hope.

The Hut
of Thorns

DARKNESS blurred the Causeway Fields and spread in deep shadows under the eaves of Mantern's Forest as Esteron passed between the trees and took the ancient road that led towards Notley Marsh. Thane crouched low in the saddle, hunched against the rushing wind, his eyes narrowed by streaming tears.

"Forgive me, Elion. Forgive me . . ." he whispered in rhythm with Esteron's pounding hoofbeats. Without a backward glance at the Battle Council or a thought of the danger on the road ahead he pressed Esteron for all the speed he could give, keeping him to the crown of the road, racing between the fleeting moonshadows. Before them, less than half a league distant, stood the tumbledown Wayhouse hut of thorns that Thane remembered from his earlier journey to Underfall. Mulcade suddenly shrieked a warning, digging his talons sharply into Thane's shoulder. All about them Nightbeasts swarmed up onto the Greenway, roaring and screaming.

"The hut! Run for the hut!" Thane shouted, urging Esteron to gallop faster. Mulcade spread his wings and stooped, sinking his talons into the nearest Nightbeast. Thane drew his dagger and slashed at the black Nightbeasts that blocked his path. The door of the hut shimmered in the night air, barbed thorns were shining in the moonlight. Esteron surged forward, taking the last stride to safety, rising from the ground in a graceful arch. He did not see the Nightbeast spring out from the shadows of the hut and thrust the cruel spear at his flank, but the force of the crippling blade sent him crashing to his knees. Thane, unbalanced, fell beside him, rolled once and leapt back to his feet.

"Into the hut! Into the hut!" he cried, as the injured horse staggered through the doorway. The Nightbeast was hanging on to the spear shaft, driving it deeper into Esteron's flank. Thane ducked under the monster's outstretched arms and drove his dagger upwards through the thin strips of foul armor with both hands on the hilt. He pushed his weight against the Nightbeast and sent the screaming animal toppling backwards, releasing his grip on the spear shaft. Thane pulled the blood-sticky dagger out of the Nightbeast's chest and followed Esteron, jumping through the door of thorns.

Snorting and whinnying with pain Esteron half lay, half knelt on the earth floor, beads of sweat forming on his neck as he tried to rise. Thane sheathed the dagger and knelt beside him. Mulcade stooped through the doorway and perched on

Thane's shoulder. The curtain of thorns fell across the opening and rustled and shook as the Night-beasts tried to force their way through, but it remained impenetrable.

Thane shivered in the darkness and felt his way along the spear shaft until his fingers reached the blade. The force of the thrust had driven the barbed blade deep into Esteron's flank and it would clearly need a Healer's skill to cut it out.

"I cannot pull it out!" cried Thane, taking Esteron's head into his arms. "The more I touch it the deeper it sinks."

Esteron snorted through the pain, the whites of his eyes showing in the darkness, and rose to his feet. With each painful movement the spear shaft dipped and swayed wildly, making the pain worse. Thane grasped the shaft as close to the blade as he dared and, raising his knee, he snapped it in two. Esteron shrieked and backed away until he stood against the far wall black with sweat. He was trembling from head to foot. Thane moved quickly to his side, gently unbuckled the girths, removed the saddle and cut the bridle knot, taking the steel bit out of Esteron's mouth.

"Tomorrow," he whispered, untying the summer scarf from his arm and binding it around the spear blade to stem the flow of blood, "tomorrow, when a new sun burns above World's Edge the magic will fade and the Nightbeasts will overrun this Wayhouse. We must escape in the first shafts of sunlight. I will go alone to Woodsedge and you must return to Underfall, for only Merion the Healer has the skill to remove the Nightbeast's spear blade."

Esteron neighed fiercely, arching his sweat-soaked neck, and tried to cross the Wayhouse, forgetting for a moment the crippling spear in his side. Thane watched his slow halting steps and whispered to himself, "They will cut you down long before you reach the Greenway!"

Quickly he unclasped his cloak and pulled off his fine chainmail shirt. With the edge of his dagger he unpicked the rows of fine glittering steel loops and spread the opened shirt across Esteron's back. Taking his cloak he cut the lower half into strips and bound the shirt securely. Stepping back he smiled in the darkness. "Now you have a battle coat that even Equestrius, the Lord of Horses, would be proud to wear. It is not steelsilver, but it will turn the Nightbeasts' blades."

Esteron snorted, rubbing his head wearily against Thane's arm.

"Merion is the only one with the power and the skill to pull that black blade. You must go to him," said Thane as he pulled the shortened cloak about his shoulders. He felt the owl's talons squeeze his shoulder and lifted his hand to caress the soft downy chest feathers. "Mulcade will go with you and defend you on the road. I will clear a path through the Nightbeasts as the new sun rises and win you the best road that I can."

Thane paused, biting his knuckles with despair,

knowing that the road to Woodsedge would be endless without Esteron, yet he had no other choice.
Sighing, he pulled off his boots, and with two swift
cuts of the dagger he cut them down to just above
the ankles so that he could run in them. Esteron
whinnied. He would go as Thane had begged him
and seek the Healer of Underfall, but once the spear
blade had been removed he would use the gift of
speed and raise a Warhorse army greater than the
one that had gathered on the high plateau to free
Thoronhand, and they would follow Thane into
the heart of Elundium to rescue Elionbel; and Mulcade, the Lord of Owls, would call a stoop of Battle
Owls great enough to darken the sun. Thane would
not stand alone against the Master of Nightmares!

Beyond the door of thorns dense black shadows
were crowding in; the gray hours would soon touch
the horizon's edge with pale moving fingers. Thane
shivered in the darkness, drawing his cloak tightly
around his shoulders; night silence prickled at his
scalp, for he knew that beyond the thorn-covered
walls the powers of night crouched encircling the
Wayhouse, waiting for the magic to fade. Thane
rose to his feet and quietly lifted Mulcade up towards the blackened smoke hole.

"Fly high, great bird of war," he whispered.
"Rise above the Nightbeasts' shadows that trap us
here, be our eyes and find the morning. Bring a new
sun to the Greenway's edge to drive our enemies
back."

Mulcade dug his talons into Thane's arm, hooted

softly, and lifted on silent wings, spiraling up through the sooty chimney towards the distant stars. Thane stood for a moment peering upwards, searching the night sky for a hint of the gray hours that would herald the dawn, but only cold faraway stars filled the blackness. He shuddered and turned back to comfort Esteron, weeping as he looked upon the ugly spear blade embedded in his flank. As Thane crossed the Wayhouse floor, moving silently between the upturned furniture, something made him pause and hold his breath. Something of terrible malice had arrived outside and was circling, testing the tumbledown walls for weakness.

"Krulshards!" Thane whispered, drawing his dagger and hurrying to stand between Esteron and the door, following the Nightmare threat with his eyes as it circled their refuge.

"I wish we had Kyot's great bow and those glass arrowheads from Stumble Hill," he hissed, summoning up the courage to shout a challenge at the Master of Nightmares. "None can enter this Wayhouse against the power of Nevian, for he is the Master of Magic who built it!" he cried, drymouthed.

A cry of hatred froze Thane's heart as Krulshards watched the owl escape up into the night sky. Turning back to the hut he called out Thane's name. "Killhand! Killhand!" he hissed, rising in a blanket of shadows to envelop the hut. "Bring his head to the City of Night for torment!"

He laughed bitterly, pushing the ring of Nightbeasts forward against the Wayhouse, and it began to crumble beneath the assault. The walls cried out as black brittle claws tore into them, and the barrier of living thorns that protected the doorway shook and rattled as the Nightbeasts began to tear it down.

"You cannot enter!" Thane cried, advancing a step towards the door.

"Killhand! Killhand!" chanted the Nightbeasts, thrusting their way through the thorn barrier.

"Galloperspawn, you are mine!" dribbled Krulshards, advancing on the door, his bone black fingers between the thorns.

"No!" shouted Thane, slashing with his dagger at the Nightbeast's claws, but instead of Nightbeast his blade touched a soft white wall of tiny flowers.

"It is the magic!" he whispered, gazing in wonder at the night flowers. "Nevian will keep us safe until the new sun rises. It is carved in the legend on the lintel above the door. Esteron, we are safe!"

The heavy, sweet scent from the nightflowers filled the Wayhouse, bringing blissful sleep to Thane and Esteron, shutting out their fear and pain. For it was written by the Lord of Daylight that none who treasure the light need fear the powers of darkness for the space of one night while they rested in the Wayhouse hut of thorns.

"Killhand! Galloperspawn!" screamed Krulshards, retreating from the Wayhouse and spreading his malice to blot out the starlight that reflected from the tiny white flowers. But the more the

Nightbeasts assaulted the walls or tore at the doorway the more petal cases opened until the Wayhouse was buried beneath deep banks of brilliant nightflowers that dazzled and blinded, and where the Nightbeasts touched the white petals they burned their claws, giving off a bitter smell that drove them back. Krulshards spat at the hut and looked at the graying sky. He drew his Nightbeasts around him into a circle of blackest shadows.

"Tomorrow," he dribbled, touching the raw sinews that Silverwing had torn open, "when the sun touches the World's Edge as these foul flowers close, put on your wolfskin eye shields and destroy the Wayhouse. Tear it stone from stone and bring Hand's head to the City of Night. In the darkness I shall pluck out his eyes and feed them to my blind beasts."

"Killhand! Killhand!" the Nightbeasts chanted, moving in a slow circle, spears interlocked, waiting for the magic to fade.

Krulshards gathered the malice into heavy black folds of hatred about his shoulders and summoned Kerzolde to his side.

"We are too few to risk battle here. If that owl brings warriors or Warhorses to Thanehand's aid we are doomed. Come, there is an old enemy in Elundium, with a tattoo in blue and gold upon his arm, we shall destroy him before the new sun rises."

"Who, Master?" Kerzolde asked, running to keep

pace with Krulshards's giant strides as he took the ancient road into the heart of Elundium.

"Archerorm, the begetter of the foul Archer who did this!" snarled Krulshards, throwing back the malice to reveal the ragged hole Kyot's arrow had made in his shoulder.

A noise in the blackened smoke hole brought Thane to his feet, dagger ready, but he eased his grip on the hilt and laughed with joy as the shadow of Mulcade crossed the Wayhouse floor. "You have brought the morning," he cried, feeling the owl's dew-wet talons on his arm. Mulcade hooted softly, bobbing his head backward and forward.

"Esteron," Thane whispered as the Warhorse struggled to his feet, "Mulcade has seen the new sun. Here, touch the jewels of daybreak before they vanish."

Esteron stretched his neck and brushed his muzzle across Mulcade's talons, feeling the beginnings of a new day.

"Soon we must part," whispered Thane, collecting his courage and turning towards the door, remembering now in their last brief moments together all the little things that had bound them, that had made their love so strong. That first moment in the sand school, far away in the Granite City, when Esteron had been wild and set on killing him, but the owl had made him spare his life. He smiled, remembering how he had named him Esteron. Mulcade tightened his talons on Thane's arm, making him look into his own eyes.

"How could I forget," he laughed, "how you stooped to my shoulder and we started our journey to World's End so long ago? I love you both more than life itself. Hurry to Underfall and seek out the Healer."

Esteron snorted fiercely, nudging Thane's shoulder. The flowers were fading and the new morning's light was streaming into the hut through the ruined walls. Mulcade shrieked a warning, for beyond the closing petal cases he saw the Nightbeasts' shadow circle rising up to hide the sunlight. Thane ran to the doorway and looked out into the sun. The Nightbeasts were advancing on the hut.

"Give me a moment to clear the way," he called and jumping through the thorn barrier he plunged the dagger into the nearest beast. It screamed, stumbling blindly against him, slashing with a rusty jagged blade above Thane's head. Thane jerked the dagger free and attacked the next, felling it with one upward thrust. He hesitated before tackling the third and circled it on tiptoe, carefully studying its face. It was blind; it had a layer of skin over its eyes to protect them from the daylight. Thane laughed; the beast spun around, following his voice. Roaring, it called the other beasts to where Thane stood. He stayed perfectly still with bated breath, poised on the balls of his feet, until the Nightbeasts' spear blades were a handspan from his chest.

"Nightbeasts!" he shouted, ducking and scooping up a handful of stones before he slipped sideways as the Nightbeasts lunged forward, impaling each other, screaming as the spear blades tore through their scaly armor. "Now go!" Thane shouted, scattering the stones amongst the Nightbeasts as he urged Esteron over the threshold stone. The Nightbeasts stumbled into one another, following the noise of the stones while, far away, beyond the Nightbeasts' screams, the first blackbird burst into song and the new sun spread its warmth across the ancient road, drying out the jewels of the morning.

"Go quickly," Thane urged, helping the crippled horse onto the empty Greenway. Esteron snorted through the pain and tried to trot; Mulcade hovered above him, talons spread ready to stoop to his defense.

"I love you both," Thane called out, running back through the Nightbeasts, taunting them with his voice and throwing handfuls of sharp stones to distract them from the fleeing horse, drawing them after him towards Notley Marsh.

"Killhand! Killhand!" the Nightbeasts chanted, following his voice in a ragged line. Thane ran on ahead of them as fast as he could, keeping to the center of the road. When he reached the rim of the steep valley that led down into Notley Marsh he looked back and saw them spread out across the road, close to his heels.

Krulshards at Stumble Hill

SOMETHING more terrible than death had come with the gray hours, that much old Archerorm could feel in his bones and smell on the dry nightwind. It made him shiver and the fear of it gnawed at his stomach as he paced the empty Wayhouse Tower on Stumble Hill. It had come in the dead of night, encircling the Wayhouse, looking for weakness and a way to enter, but finding none it had settled before the great wooden doors, pressing against the iron studding and fiercely rattling the locks. Archer dared not guess at what, or who, had come to the tower, and he feared each shadow that filled the dark courtyard. The tattoo of the owl carrying the sword itched upon his arm and, pulling his sleeve away, he gazed at the mark Nevian had traced all those suns ago beneath the walls of Underfall and gasped, for the colors burned with a fierce light, driving the shadows out of the courtyard.

"Nevian," he cried, lifting his bow arm above his head. "You have lit my darkest hour. Now I have the power to see who haunts the road before my door!"

Archer hurried into the armory and selected the best, strongest bow and the heaviest quiver of new-forged arrows. He climbed to the top of the tower and looked through the Glass of Orm at the road below.

"Krulshards!" he cried, stepping quickly back from the glass, not daring to raise his eyes to look at the Nightmare that had covered the Causeway and pressed his black hatred against the door.

"Trueflightorm," a voice hissed, splitting the night air as it rose up out of the malice. "I have not forgotten your name, foul Archer, nor have I forgotten how you once stood between me and victory over the daylight, destroying my shadow circle with the Bow of Orm."

Archer took shallow breaths; the palms of his hands were growing wet with fear as he gripped the oiled wooden bow tightly.

"I have come to claim you, Trueflightorm, and keep you in the darkness, forever sightless from the sun," sneered the voice of hatred.

"Nightmare!" cried Archer, nocking an arrow onto the string and aiming into the shadowy folds of the malice. "You could not kill me on the Causeway Road before the gates of Underfall. You shall not, by the might of my arm, take me now!"

Cruel laughter filled the night air as a gnarled bone black hand reached up out of the malice, snatched the arrow as it flew and snapped it in two.

"Your son, foul Archer, has the Bow of Orm," mocked Krulshards, "and he lies dead in the City of Night. You cannot harm me, Archerorm, nor can these doors keep me out."

Krulshards snarled, curling his lips back across his ragged teeth, and threw the weight of his malice against the doors. Twice the tree-thick timbers rocked backward and forward before the locks smashed into a thousand pieces. "You are mine!" he hissed, entering the courtyard.

"NO!" shouted Archer, leaping down the tower steps four at a time. Tears of rage filled his eyes and anger boiled in his heart. "I shall avenge Kyot's death even without the Bow of Orm, and I will bring his body out of the depths of night to see the sunlight once more. Do you hear me, foulest Nightmare, dirtier of daylight? I shall drive you out of my house before the new sun rises!"

"Run!" mocked Krulshards, moving forward. "Hide, puller of toy bows, but I will find you and keep you beyond the candlelight forever."

"Run!" replied Archer, coldly, stepping into the courtyard and nocking another arrow onto the string. "You have dared to enter my house without my leave, bringing black news of despair."

"I bring more than black news!" spat the Master of Nightmares, "I bring defeat and darkness to all Elundium!"

Archer drew the bow taut and released the arrow at the center of the malice, putting all his strength behind the shot, but Krulshards laughed, opened the malice and again caught the arrow in mid-flight, throwing it harmlessly across the cobbles.

"You cannot hurt me, foolish Archer. You gave away the only bow in all Elundium with that power and it now lies broken in the City of Night beneath your son's body!"

The anger in Archer's heart turned icy cold as he remembered Nevian's words, *"Keep safe the Bow of Orm, and let no other hand but yours upon the string until the Nightmare is dead. Use none but the fine-forged glass arrowheads of Clatterford if you wish to pierce the center of the darkness."*

"I have been a blind fool, over-anxious to let Kyot do my work. I should never have let him lead the Archers of Stumble Hill into battle before the Gates of Night. It was my place with the Bow of Orm to stand against this Nightmare."

Rubbing away a tear upon his sleeve Archer reached back into the quiver and took the third arrow, cursing its blunt steel edge and wishing his hand was closing upon the cold crystal blades of Clatterford. Wetting the dull steel point with his tongue he nocked the arrow onto his bow and faced the dark shape that stood between the ruined doors.

"Krulshards!" he cried, moving quickly across the courtyard until his back was firmly braced against the solid oak shooting butt. "I remember your name, Nightmare, and the curse you laid on Elundium. I am the Wayhouse Keeper of Stumble Hill, set upon the Greenway's edge to defeat your foul kind. Even without the Bow of Orm I have the power to send an arrow strike into your black heart. Look to the tattoo upon my arm!"

Krulshards hesitated, wrapping the malice tightly about his shoulders. Perhaps this Archer had more strength. Perhaps he did have the power to stand against the darkness. "Kerzolde!" he rasped, pushing his Captain before him. "Take the Archer's bow and break it across your knee."

Kerzolde rushed at the Archer, a broad-bladed spear in his good claw, only to be knocked off his feet, screaming, as Archer's arrow pierced his armor and sank deep into his chest. Kerzolde crawled back to his Master, clutching at the embedded shaft with his broken claw.

"Guard the door!" Krulshards hissed, wrenching the blade of the arrow free and pushing Kerzolde roughly out of his path.

Archer acted quickly in the few moments it took Krulshards to pull the arrow. He dug deeply into his jerkin pocket to find the spare bowstring and with it he bound himself against the oak shooting butt. "None will pass this spot," he whispered through trembling lips, pulling the string so tight that it cut painfully into his sides. Now his mind would be free to face the Master of Nightmares. No matter how much he wanted to run there was no escape. Grimly he nocked another arrow onto the string and sang Kyot's name aloud as he brought his eyes level with the Master of Nightmares.

"Now, Nightmare, you shall know who is the Keeper of Stumble Hill. By the light that burns on my arm you shall not enter this Wayhouse. It is closed to all your foul kind."

Krulshards threw the malice back across his shoulder and charged at Archer, a black-bladed spear in his hands. Archer bent the bow until it cried out, and loosed the arrow at the Nightmare's heart. He laughed to see a ragged tear in Krulshards's shoulder and knew that Kyot had used well the great Bow of Orm before his death. Archer's laughter turned into a scream as Krulshards's spear blade struck his chest, shattering his rib cage, tearing through his chest to pin him onto the shooting butt.

"Kyot, I love you!" he cried, grinding his teeth against the pain, but lifting his eyes he saw Krulshards on his knees, both hands clutching on the arrow shaft in his chest.

Krulshards rose to his feet, the malice boiling with hatred, and snapped the arrow shaft in two, closing his fingers around the steel arrowhead. He advanced across the cobbles, molten steel from the arrowhead dripping between his fingers. Slowly, painfully, and without hope, the old Archer reached back into his quiver, knowing the steel was no match for the Nightmare, wishing with all his heart that his fingers could touch an arrow from Clatterford, with sunlight trapped in the cool glass blade. That would have found a way through the malice and it would have avenged Kyot's death.

"Death! Darkness!" spat Krulshards, throwing his weight against the spear shaft, forcing the blade deeper into the oak post. Archer screamed as the steel bit into him, his hand gripping the smooth polished shaft of the arrow. With the last of his strength he took the arrow and nocked it onto the bow. Screwing his eyes tightly shut he cursed all Nightmare shapes, drew the string tight and let the arrow go, aiming it deep into the black shadows of the malice. Bright blazed the tattooed owl upon his arm, lighting a path through the shadowy folds that threatened to engulf him. "With this arrow I have fulfilled my pledges to the Granite King, and kept this Wayhouse safe through the darkest reaches of the night."

"You shall not see the new sun rise!" Krulshards screamed at him as the arrow knocked him backwards, forcing him across the cobbles, slicing through his rotten flesh and cutting him to the bone. "You will die slowly for this," he hissed, rage dribbling through his quivering lips as he advanced on Archer, his hands outstretched to tear at his face. Archer looked up through his tears at the paling dawn sky, knowing that he lacked the strength to take another arrow from the quiver.

"I have won the morning," he whispered, hearing far away the first blackbird break the dawn silence, filling the Greenway with sweet music. Krulshards's shadow blocked out the dawn light as he spread the malice in terrible hatred above Archer's head.

"Trueflightorm," Krulshards whispered in a

voice heavy with the gloat of victory, "you will pay dearly for your skill with the bow."

He reached back into the shadows of the malice, unhooked a long curved knife and tested the cutting edge against Archer's throat, drawing a fine trickle of blood across the black metal blade. "I could kill you now, Archer, with one stroke of this blade, but that is far too humble a death for one who dares to stand against me, the Master of Nightbeasts. No, oh no!" he hissed, putting his face so close to Archer's that the old man could almost taste the foul odor of death.

"I shall leave you alive, Trueflight, the greatest Archer in all Elundium. You will be blind to your quarry and unable to reach into the quiver or take up the bow."

Laughing, Krulshards gripped both of Archer's hands, raised the curved blade to flash in the dawn sunlight and brought it slicing down across the bowman's wrists. Archer screamed, straining against the binding bowstring, but there was no escape. The tattoo of the owl in blue and gold burst into blinding light above his bleeding stump.

"Curse you, Nevian," Krulshards hissed, burying his head from the light in the malice and reaching for Archer's eyes with his bone black fingers. Archer sobbed through the pain, gasping in shallow breaths as he twisted his head from left to right trying to avoid the Nightmare fingernails that tore at his face.

"I can see you without eyes," he cried, as the

Nightmare's nails hooked and gouged into his face, "and I will avenge the death of my son, Kyot, without my hands upon the bow. Mark well my words, Nightmare, for I shall follow you beyond death. The Great Bow of Orm will haunt you and bring light into the City of Night."

Slowly Archer lifted his bleeding tattooed arm and thrust it through the folds of the malice into Krulshards's face, and the tattoo burned the Nightmare's raw muscles with the colors of a new morning, driving the Master of Nightbeasts out beyond the Wayhouse doors onto the Greenway.

"I shall follow you," Archer wept through bloody tears, tensing himself for the next attack, but the Wayhouse was empty. Krulshards had fled, taking his Captainbeast, Kerzolde, with him. Early sunlight filled the courtyard, falling gently in a golden halo around Archer's bowed head, and he wept, mumbling over and over as his lifeblood soaked into the cobbles. He did not feel the sun move through the stations of the day, nor see the shadows draw long in the evening, nor hear nor sense the lone figure enter through the broken doorway.

"Archer, oh Archer," a soft voice called out, "what has the Nightmare done to you?"

The Passing of Archerorm

*T*HANE moved quickly down the steep slope into the marshes. Behind him he could hear the pursuing Nightbeasts chanting his name, "Killhand, Galloperspawn!" He knew they were almost blind in the daylight but all hope of slipping past them vanished for they had spread out in a grim arc of hate. They were beating every tree and bush with their cruel-bladed spears and long curved scythes.

"Nightbeasts!" he whispered, catching his breath and plunging into the undergrowth beside the road for a moment's rest. "I will have to run faster than the east wind to reach Woodsedge before these Nightbeasts catch me."

Rising shakily to his feet he took off his heavy metal helm and threw it aside. He missed the protection of the metal shirt outside the hut of thorns as he dodged amongst the Nightbeasts' spear blades but now he was truly glad he had spread it across Esteron's back; the cut-down half-cloak was easier to wear and did not snag his every stride. Bending low, he ran forward, drawing in deep breaths with every loping stride. Gradually as the day wore on he drew ahead of the Nightbeasts and the sounds of pursuit fell away to a distant murmur. Now he was in the center of the marsh and all around him the air grew heavy with the smell of stagnant water as it hissed and bubbled in black pools beside the road. Giant dragonflies hovered, beating the still air with their wings; marsh spiders scuttled away from beneath his hurrying feet. There was no rest as he forced his feet on.

Ahead of him he saw the ring of ash from his earlier battle with the Nightbeasts on his way to Underfall. He laughed and paused for breath, crouching to suck in great lungfuls of air. "If the Battle Owls or the Border Runners were with me I would turn and fight," he muttered, rising to his feet. Holding his breath he listened to the marsh silence, straining his ears for sounds of pursuit. Far away he could hear that they were still following him, closing the gap with each moment he rested. He leapt forward in the stagnant silence. "I must run until my bones crack and my muscles knot with cramp," he hissed in the silence. "I must run to Elionbel."

With each footfall the ground grew firmer beneath his feet. He was climbing out of Notley Marsh towards the great Greenway crossroads that led to Stumble Hill. "I must not stop again," he said to himself, "until I reach the Wayhouse Tower.

There I will take breath and fight these Nightbeasts with a strike of Archers at my side."

Bending low he pushed on, kicking against the steepness of the valley, following the winding road up until it breasted the valley's rim. Here he paused to look back and he saw the Nightbeasts spread out across the fire-burned road. They were fewer now, running in close order and gaining on him with every stride.

"The darkness!" he gasped, in a tired voice, looking at the lengthening shadows on the valley floor. "It must give the Nightbeasts new strength. Oh Esteron, if only I had your gift of speed to outrun these beasts, or Mulcade's power to rise up into the soft evening air and escape!"

"Killhand! Killhand!" rose the distant chant from the black bubbling marshes below. Thane could just hear the dry rattle of their armor; they were on the first steps of the steep ascent. Turning, he fled, running as fast as his tired legs would take him. "Run or die," he repeated in rhythm with his pounding heart, "run or die," until he could run no farther. He stopped, bent double, shaking and choking for breath. Slowly he straightened, blinking against the stinging sweat that was trickling into his eyes and looked at the silhouette of the Wayhouse Tower, etched in dark colors against the evening sky.

"Stumble Hill," he gasped, looking back across his shoulder towards the marshes. The road was straight and empty; he had outrun the Nightbeasts and safety waited a hundred paces before him. Clenching his fist he hurried forward, eager to take a strike of Archer's best bowmen back towards Notley Marsh and destroy the Nightbeasts.

Looking up at the Wayhouse he hesitated; a frown creased his dirty, sweat-stained forehead. Something was wrong. He took deep breaths to steady his racing heart and listened to the early night sounds. He strained his ears for the slightest clue. The hairs at the base of his neck began to prickle. Far away on the edge of the wind he could hear the sounds of pursuit, but here on Stumble Hill the evening held its breath, there were no night sounds. He searched the dark bulk of the Wayhouse but nothing moved, the tower stood wrapped in silence. Fearfully he drew his dagger and began cautiously to climb the hill, looking into each shadow and testing each dark shape with the point of his blade until he stood upon the Causeway, between the broken doors.

"Krulshards!" he hissed, moving noiselessly into the center of the courtyard, balancing lightly on his toes as he swept his gaze from left to right.

"Archer?" he whispered, seeing the shape of the figure in the gloomy darkness beneath the center archway that led into the Wayhouse.

"Who dares enter?" a weak voice cried out. A blinding light suddenly burned upon the figure's arm, casting a giant shadow across the cobbles from the cruel spear shaft that pinned it onto the oaken shooting butt.

"Archer," Thane called softly, crossing the courtyard and kneeling beside the old man. "Who has done this to you?" he wept, gently taking the bleeding stumps into his hands.

"Thane, Thane is that you?" Archer cried, searching in the direction of Thane's voice. "The Nightmare said that Kyot is dead, lost forever in the City of Night. He said that the Bow of Orm lay broken beneath him." Archer coughed, choking over the words, crying bloody tears. "Oh, Thane, I know it was the truth for I saw with my own eyes the mark of the arrow strike in the Nightmare's shoulder. I know that Kyot used the bow well before he died."

Thane lifted Archer's ruined arm and kissed the tattoo mark, then taking the scarred and bloody head into his arms, he whispered gently, "Kyot is alive and well; he sits at the Battle Council before the doors of Underfall. Together we won a great victory before the Gates of Night. In the new daylight he will lead your strikes of Archers back home. Have courage, my Lord, he will be with you soon."

"There is no time to waste," Archer whispered urgently. "Listen to me, child, while there is still breath in my body. Kyot must be well armed to face the Nightmare, Krulshards. He must follow him and stand in my place."

Thane leaned closer to catch every word, putting his ear to Archer's blood-encrusted lips.

"Before you were born, long before the great battle to win World's End had even begun, Nevian, the Master of Magic, took me into the heart of Mantern's Forest into a secret grove of black yew trees and showed me the tree, the perfect yew tree, and ordered me to cut only enough wood for two great bows." Archer paused, drawing in shallow breaths. "If ever the Bow of Orm is broken seek out that other bow. Remember it has my mark upon it."

"Who has the other bow?" Thane asked. "Where is it hidden?"

Archer coughed, new blood gurgled in his throat. "The arrows," he mumbled, deaf to the question, "must be hot-forged and drawn sharp at Clatterford by the Arrowmaster who knows of the light!"

"What is his name?" Thane urged gently, feeling Archer begin to slump against him.

"Fairday of Clatterford," Archer cried, straining against the spear blade. "Tell him that you need new arrows shaped in glass. Tell him that Krulshards, the Nightmare of Darkness, has come forth into Elundium. Tell him, child, that I have sent you."

Archer slumped forward and then feebly tried to lift his head. "Free me, Thane," he whispered, turning his bloody head towards where Thane knelt. "Free me, Thane, from the binding cord of my fate. Cut me loose." Thane gripped the spear shaft with both hands and, using all his strength, wrenched it free. Archer slumped forward against the bloody bowstring. Thane cut the string with one sweep of his dagger and carefully laid the old man on the cobbles. Suddenly, roaring screams broke the night silence just beyond the broken entrance. Thane's pursuers had reached the Wayhouse. Turning, he crouched ready.

"I will avenge you, Archer!" he cried, reaching for the fallen bow at Archer's side, but he hesitated. He was a swordsman trained with the skills of Gildersleeves. Quickly he threw the bow aside and drew the dagger that Duclos had given him.

"Killhand, the Galloperspawn!" rose the Nightbeast chant. Five shapes, perhaps ten, their numbers were difficult to count as they swayed forward in an ever-changing pattern, swallowing the courtyard beneath their foul shadows.

Archer lifted his head, a frown cracking the dried blood on his forehead. As he listened, a large tear, blood-streaked, escaped down his cheek. "Thane!" he whispered, "I can hear the Nightbeast chant, but I cannot see them. I am powerless in this darkness, alone and helpless!"

"No, no," whispered Thane, cradling Archer's head. "I will keep you safe until Kyot comes. You need fear nothing that moves in the night." Archer wept, lifting his mutilated arm with the tattoo mark towards the Nightbeasts. "There is no time left for me, Thane. Fate's hand is upon my shoulder. Tell Kyot of Clatterford."

Archer's head slipped sideways and his last breath misted the steel arrowhead that lay unused in the quiver. Thane rose to his feet and leapt forward. Through blurring, angry tears Thane slashed with the dagger, cutting into the nearest Nightbeast, and as the first drop of its blood splashed onto the cobbles the tattoo on Archer's arm burned with a white fire, blinding the Nightbeasts, sending them stumbling into one another. Thane strode forward amongst them, slashing and stabbing, driven on by the terrible sight of Kyot's father.

"I will build a wall of Nightmare dead! Carrion heaps to shadow the sun!" he cried, letting the rage and anger guide his dagger arm. Silence once again filled the courtyard, and the light from the tattoo began to fade. The shadows softened and grew deeper. Thane lowered the dagger and let the anger melt away. Before him, in a wide crescent, the Nightbeasts lay piled to the height of his shoulders, and none had come within a dagger's length of where Archer lay. The anger had now gone; he felt alone, empty and drained of strength. He shivered, drawing the ragged half-cloak tightly about his shoulders, and knelt beside Archer.

"I have killed the Nightbeasts. You can rest the watches of the night in peace," he whispered, unclasping the old man's cloak and laying it across his body. Already the cold air had taken the warmth out of Archer's flesh and the tattoo had faded to a soft phosphorescent glow.

A noise from the stable yard made Thane freeze. Silently he rose, his hand on his dagger, and made to step across the courtyard, but as he left Archer's side the tattoo flared brightly through the weave of the cloak and then faded back into a soft glow.

"Beyond death, this Wayhouse will be safe. None will dare enter while the tattoo glows!" he thought in wonder.

Widening his eyes against the darkness Thane entered the stable yard and slipped the iron latch upon the long barn where the relay horses were stabled. Hooves clattered on the cobbles and somewhere in the shadows a horse snorted. There was fear in the horse, Thane could sense it, the silent fear of the hunted who, with bated breath and pounding heart, crouch waiting for the hunter to pass. Quietly Thane sought the spark he carried in his pocket, closed his fingers around it and lifted it high above his head, squeezing it into life. White eyes flashed in the darkness. Hoofbeats crashed on the cobbles. Stumble, the last relay horse of the Wayhouse Tower, lowered his head to charge. Bright spark light reflected from the finely woven battle coat that lay across his back and long shadows leapt up from the bow and the quiver of new-forged arrows fixed onto the pommel of the saddle. Proudly he sprang forward.

"Stumble!" Thane cried, jumping out of the horse's path. "It is Thane!"

Stumble stopped and turned, casting sparks with his near fore as he pawed the cobbles. "Have you forgotten me? I am Thane, Esteron's rider, Kyot's friend."

The horse hesitated, snorting, uncertain, the

whites of his eyes still showing fear. Thane sheathed the dagger and walked forward, his empty hands outstretched, remembering the story Kyot had told him of how Archer had found Stumble wandering on the Greenway, an orphan foal, how he had taken him in and how every warrior loved him for his quiet courage.

"Your master is dead," he whispered, stroking the frightened horse. "He gave his life defending this house against the most terrible Nightmare that has ever walked Elundium."

Stumble whinnied, bowing his head, a great sadness filling his soft gentle eyes. "Will you help me?" Thane asked. "Will you carry me and follow the Master of Nightmares to seek revenge?"

Stumble arched his neck, stretching the battle plaits woven through his flowing mane and rubbed his muzzle against Thane's arm, smelling the fabric of his ragged cloak and remembering who stood before him.

"Come," whispered Thane, taking the reins in his hand, "come and see the greatness of your master. See how in death he still protects his house!"

They stood together, side by side, in the main courtyard, and watched the tattoo's warm colors glow blue and gold beneath Archer's cloak. Stumble stretched his neck and brushed his lips on the old man's cold cheek. Anger flashed in his eyes and his ears flattened against the side of his head.

"Take me to Woodsedge!" Thane urged, springing up into the saddle. "I know the Nightmare seeks to destroy that Wayhouse and steal Elionbel, the Keeper's daughter!"

Thane ran his hand across Stumble's shoulder until he reached the heavy steel-ringed battle coat. "We need speed to catch Krulshards and this battle coat will slow us down. Better to leave it here defending your master," he said, dismounting and loosening the girths. Gently Thane removed the heavy chainmail coat and spread it over Archer's body. Before rising from his knees he took the arm with the tattoo and laid it on top of the battle coat across the old man's chest.

Stumble whinnied and stood quietly while Thane refitted the saddle and remounted. "Let us gallop to the Nightmare's death," he shouted, wheeling Stumble towards the ruined doors and urging him into a canter.

"Wait!" he cried, reining the horse to a halt. "I must leave word for Kyot, his father pledged me to it."

Dismounting, he ran back into the courtyard. "How do I leave a message?" he asked the empty shadows, "how?"

The Battle Council Breaks Up

"*CANDLEFOOL!* Base meddler!" Tombel shouted, red-faced, his hand upon the hilt of his Marching sword. Thoron stood before him, waiting for the rage to subside, waiting for Tombel to draw breath.

"I sent him to protect your daughter, Elionbel. It is his duty to repair the damage he did by taking her love token into the City of Night," Thoron answered, in a firm quiet voice.

"Love token!" Tombel hissed, stepping a pace nearer to Thoron. "Not only is he not bloodworthy to carry Elionbel's token but now he has gone galloping off at the Nightmare's heels and I ordered him to the Battle Council!"

Thunderstone stepped quickly between them, pushing both fighting blades down into the ground. "Warriors, warriors," he soothed, "this is not the place to settle differences of blood. All Elundium totters on the brink of ruin. We must act quickly, with bold purpose, to save the daylight."

"He is not blood-worthy," Tombel muttered, darkly, sheathing his Marching sword.

Thunderstone frowned, caught Tombel by the arm and turned him sharply towards the assembled warriors, whispering, "You are the greatest Marcher Captain that Elundium has ever known and yet you cannot see past the end of your nose. Thane is more than just the son of a Candleman, he is a leader of men, a force in the darkness stronger than any man at this Battle Council. He brings life to old legends and prophecies. Beware how you treat him!"

Tombel shrugged and begrudgingly extended his hand towards Thoron. "We will settle this squabble in the privacy of the trophy room at Woodsedge when the siege lock on the Granite City has been broken and Krulshards is no more."

Thoron reached out and took Tombel's hand. "So be it!" he replied, adding, "If any Wayhouse stands for us to meet within!"

"Lord! Lord!" Kyot cried, turning all eyes towards the ancient road that led down from the hut of thorns. "Esteron is on the road, and my eyes tell me that he is gravely injured."

Four Warhorses led by Equestrius broke away from the crescent and galloped out across the Causeway to escort Esteron to the Battle Council. Slowly he passed through the ranks of silent warriors who watched the morning sunlight shining on the steel links of Thane's torn mail shirt where it protected his back and reflected the bright colors of the summer scarf that he had wound about the cruel spear blade in his flank.

"Esteron!" Thoron cried, unbinding the scarf to reveal the terrible spear wound.

"Call for the Healer!" Thunderstone shouted, cutting away the strips of cloak that held the metal shirt across the horse's back.

Merion broke through the press of warriors and, without a word, led Esteron away into the fortress of Underfall. "It will take all my skill," he whispered to Esteron, as he set out a tray of curved silver knives and needles threaded with twists of gold, "but I will make you whole again to run the Greenways."

Mulcade hooted and settled on a low beam to watch the Healer perform his magic.

"Thane must lie injured somewhere out there!" Kyot cried, throwing his saddle across Sprint's back.

"More likely he is dead," Tombel answered crossly. "I feared to let him go alone. The Greenways are a dangerous place now that Krulshards is loose in Elundium. Nevian only knows how many Nightbeasts are ahead on the Greenways."

"I will find him!" Kyot shouted, leaping into the saddle and spurring Sprint up through the bordering dyke on to the Causeway.

"Wait! Wait!" shouted Tombel, striding after Kyot, but his voice was lost in the thunder of Sprint's hooves.

"It is madness of youth to tread beyond our counseling," Thunderstone muttered, taking the summer scarf from Thoron's hands and carefully folding it away beneath his cloak.

The Battle Council was dissolving into a rout. Men and horses swept this way and that, leaderless, across the Causeway Field. The Archer strikes that Kyot had led to the battle on the high plateau were readying themselves to follow him. The Gallopers of World's End milled in disorder, calling Thoron to lead them. Duclos, the Swordsman, looked at the rising tide of chaos and ran into the fortress of Underfall. He climbed up through the galleries until he stood before the daylight bell. Unsheathing his best blade he struck the bell. Full seven strokes it took to bring order to the Causeway Field below.

Thunderstone raised his horsetail sword in salute to Duclos and without delay or further council he marshalled the warriors into long lines of Marching men, squadrons of Gallopers and tightly formed strikes of Archers.

"Warriors!" he shouted in a grim voice, "you march without delay on the Granite City to break the siege lock and rescue the King. Tombel will lead the Marchers and the Archers, Thoron will lead the horsemen and scout the road ahead. Prepare the baggage trains!"

The traveling gear was packed away. The horses were saddled, and the crowded courtyards were a bustle of activity as the warriors assembled in two long widening columns that led down to the Causeway. Thunderstone's eyes were full of tears as he stood between the ruined doors awaiting the final farewells. Equestrius had gathered all the War-horses until they stood, rank upon rank, on either side of the warriors, and the Border Runners had assembled in a great pack that stretched across the Causeway Fields. Eagle Owl rose up from Thoron's shoulder and drew the Battle Birds into a mighty stoop whose shadow darkened the sky as they wheeled and swooped across the roofs of Underfall.

"It is time!" Tombel said, moving forward and taking Thunderstone's hand, "for old friends to say goodbye, and follow their fate at the Nightmare's heels."

"So be it!" Thunderstone cried, lifting the horse-tail sword to flash in the noonday sunlight. "We shall meet again beneath these very walls!"

"You have no saddle or bridle!" Thunderstone called out to Thoron as he climbed onto Equestri-us's back.

Thoron laughed, and bent low over the horse's back. "My saddle and bridle lie somewhere on the road to Woodsedge, wherever Esteron ran onto that foul spear blade. I will find them, and in his honor will put them on Equestrius. Meanwhile keep Esteron safe for Thane and heal him quickly, for I know he frets for the road."

"Kingspeed!" shouted Thunderstone, as the two columns began to move slowly forward.

"Wait!" called Thoron, halting the procession, as Willow rushed to stand before him. "What is it, child?" he asked, bending forward.

"Forgive me," Willow whispered timidly, "but I still cannot find Evening Star and we are about to start on the journey."

Thoron frowned, saying, "She must be found. I will help you, Willow, but first a question, little warrior. Does freedom from the City of Night belong to both of you?"

"Yes, of course, but we must be together; she is all I have."

"Willow," Thoron said sadly, "you have everything. The sun, the stars, the wind upon your face. Evening Star has her freedom, which may lead her on a different path from yours. Would you begrudge her the wild forest or the empty grasslands, to follow you and your people to the Granite City? Remember she is an Errant horse and all Elundium is her home. You have yet to seek a place to call your own."

Willow looked down at the cobbles and felt the noonday breezes ruffle his hair. "No," he whispered. "No. I would rather have died in the City of Night than hold her for one moment against her wishes."

"Then look up, champion of the heather meadows, and warrior of the high plateau, look up and rejoice!" laughed Thoron, pointing past Willow towards the Causeway Road.

"Star! Star!" shouted Willow, seeing the old mare for the first time, and he turned and rushed down onto the Causeway to the place where she stood surrounded by a small crescent of Warhorses. The shouts of his battle honors before the Gates of Night were but whispers in his ears as he threw his arms around Evening Star's neck. With a great effort he blinked back his tears as the old mare rubbed her head against his chest.

"Run wild and free," he whispered, then Star's gentle voice filled his mind.

"Our escape from the darkness made a bond that nothing can break."

Willow moved back a pace and looked at the beautiful foal nudging at Star's flank and smiled.

"You will be safer with the Warhorses. They will be able to guard you far better than I!"

Star whinnied, brushing her soft muzzle against his cheek. "We shall meet again, Willow, I promise. When my foal is full grown and powerful we shall see each other, for fate has bound us together."

"Star, one thing before we part."

"Ask, Willow. If it is within my power you shall have it."

"A lock of mane to hold when I am all alone, to touch and remember how we won the light."

"Use the blade that freed us and gladly take it," the old mare replied.

With a careful hand Willow cut a lock of mane and held it tightly, swallowing back the tears.

"If danger threatens you, wherever you are in this beautiful land, call out my name and I shall come, no matter how great the distance that lies between us."

Willow quickly turned his head, bowed with

grief, and retraced his footsteps to Equestrius's side. A strong familiar voice floated through his head as Equestrius spoke. "Willow Leaf. Fate has driven you hard for others' benefit, leaving you with a great sorrow in your heart. Yet you shall leave this place with a gift too great to give to Kings. Evening Star must travel with the Warhorses for the foal's protection, but when he comes of age he shall be yours to ride, and as a mark of the giving you shall name him the first time you sit upon his back."

"Then I really will see Evening Star again?"

"Yes, many times."

Willow turned, shading his eyes, and saw Star trotting away towards the eaves of Mantern's Forest, surrounded by a great company of Warhorses.

"Many times!" he laughed, running to lead his people onto the Causeway. "We will clear the Greenways and garden the roads as we travel!" he shouted. "We will repay these people for our freedom. Come, Tunnelers!"

"Forward, warriors!" shouted Tombel.

"Forward!" hooted Eagle Owl, hovering impatiently, far above World's End, watching the ruin and chaos spreading as a black shadow across Elundium.

Finding the Secret Road

*F*INE stone chips crunched beneath King Holbian's iron-shod boots as he paced along the top of the innermost wall of the Granite City.

"We are near defeat, Breakmaster," he muttered, without turning his head towards the horseman or checking the measure of his stride. Breakmaster hunched his shoulders and looked out despairingly across the ruins of the city.

"Where are all those foul Nightbeasts hatched?" he asked, watching the shadows begin to move, with the weakening of the sunlight. "They have us siege-trapped, caught tighter than rats in a barrel of wax."

Holbian turned, grim-faced, to Breakmaster. "Would you still, if you had the choice, ride with me now that defeat washes in a black tide against our last defense? We have nowhere left to run, brave warrior."

Breakmaster quickly knelt. "Lord, greatest of Granite Kings," he said, and drawing the hilt of his sword he offered it up to the King.

"Rise, true friend," whispered Holbian, stretching a hand to Breakmaster, "for we shall face death together as the new sun rises whether we wish it or not."

"Take the Marchers and the Gallopers, Lord. Marshal them into a hollow column and force a passage through the lower circles of the city. Lead us out onto the Greenway."

King Holbian slowly shook his head and pointed down into the innermost circle. "I could not abandon them, Breakmaster, they are my people. I could not save myself and leave them here. The Nightbeasts would be amongst them before we had ridden two leagues."

Breakmaster looked down, blinking his eyes against the haze of blue smoke that rose up from the cluster of cooking fires in the shadow of the inner wall. The crowds of city folk moved slowly, almost aimlessly, around and around the sheer walls of Candlebane Hall. Clearly there was nowhere to escape these Nightbeasts.

King Holbian sighed and turned to the narrow steps that led down into the inner circle. "We have come to it, friend, the last night of the Granite Kings. I will fall with my city. Set my standard before the doors of Candlebane Hall that I may die defending my people with the rays of a new sun shining on my face."

"Lord, Lord!" implored Breakmaster. "Arm the people. Let them make the Nightbeasts pay dearly for the doors of Candlebane Hall."

Holbian smiled softly at Breakmaster. "These people are not warriors, my friend, but simple craftsmen, cryers, servers and candlemen, they are the lifeblood of the city. You and I and those few Marchers and Gallopers with us must carry the burden of defending what is left of the city, but arm them if you wish. Break open the armory, let every man, woman and child be armed if they wish it."

"Who has the key?" Breakmaster asked, his foot upon the first step.

"Chancellor Proudpurse," called the King, turning for a last look at the setting sun.

Breakmaster searched through the crowds in the Inner Circle but Proudpurse was nowhere to be found. Gray Goose fell into step with the hurrying horseman, asking whom he sought, and laughed at the reply, pointing with the tip of a steel arrowhead towards the towers of Granite.

"I saw him and his son, Silverpurse, making for the armory just as the masons were sealing the inner circle of the city."

Breakmaster muttered under his breath and turned towards the Granite towers, his lips pressed into a thin grim line. "Come with me, Archer," he hissed, his knuckles white with anger upon the hilt of his sword.

The doors of the armory were slightly ajar. Breakmaster put his foot against them and roughly kicked them open. Evening light flooded into the dark granite halls, reflecting back in a thousand points of light from armored battle plates, chainmail shirts and battle helms. Whole forests of spears marched back into the darkness beside rows of polished sword blades, waiting for eager hands to snatch them up.

"Proudpurse!" Breakmaster shouted, striding forward, scooping up the nearest sword in his free hand. "Where are you, rat shadow?"

"There is treachery afoot in this place," muttered Gray Goose, searching along a broad avenue of horse armor. As he strode forward a figure broke away from the shadows directly in front of him and raced towards the far end of the armory.

"Stop! Stop!" Gray Goose cried, nocking an arrow onto the bow and loosing it after the fleeing body.

"Chancellor Proudpurse?" he shouted again, trying to cross the armory by forcing a passage through a tall stand of spears, sending them crashing and spilling onto the broad aisles. Gray Goose's arrow struck a steel breastplate and, glancing off, sent a shower of sparks into the darkness.

"There! By the far wall!" Gray Goose called, nocking another arrow onto his bow.

"Where?" cried Breakmaster, fumbling in his pocket for a spark. The spark hissed, spluttering into life, driving the shadows back between the rows of battle armor. Both warriors strode forward through the armory, eyes sharp for Proudpurse and his son.

"They must be somewhere in here. Nobody, not

even a Chancellor, could have slipped past us," whispered Gray Goose as they reached the far wall.

"Look!" he hissed, stretching out his hand to direct the horseman's spark towards a well-hidden corner where a stand of horse armor had been disturbed. Something glittered with the colors of watered silk.

"Steelsilver!" Breakmaster cried, kneeling and touching the ancient battle coat with his finger tips.

"No, beyond that. Look, three steps lead down to a heavily studded door."

Gray Goose moved past the kneeling horseman to the stairhead and descended the three steps to the door. He tested it, pressing with the palm of his bow hand. It creaked a handspan ajar. Cold musty air flowed out touching his face and far away he heard the echo of running footsteps.

"Chancellors!" he hissed, running back up the steps and almost stumbling over Breakmaster's kneeling figure as he made for the main door to the inner circle of the city.

"Find the King!" he shouted, "and bring him to the Armory!"

"Steelsilver!" Breakmaster whispered to himself, putting his spark back into his pocket and letting the fine battle coat slip through his fingers. It sang as it moved, in whispering tones, with the sound of horse bells in a gentle breeze. "Steelsilver," he sighed, gathering the coat to his chest, feeling its warmth through his rough leather jerkin and steel-ringed shirt. Running footsteps made him start and quickly hide the steelsilver coat, pushing it hastily beneath a pile of fallen shields.

"My Lord," he cried, rising to his feet and stepping forward to meet the King. "It smells of treachery, my Lord. A dark hole beneath the city that echoes to the sound of Chancellors' feet."

King Holbian put his hand on Gray Goose's arm, motioning him into silence. He bent his head in thought and paced up and down the long aisle. "Light two candles!" he commanded, turning at length to Breakmaster. "And then tell me, who was fleeing?" he asked, peering beyond the heavily studded door and looking down into the black winding passage.

"It is darker than the City of Night!" he whispered fearfully before hastily moving back from the darkness.

"It is a black hole, without a glint of starlight to show the way, my Lord," replied Breakmaster, lighting his spark and stepping bravely between the door and the King.

"Who has fled?" he asked again, looking away along the rows of armor.

"I think Proudpurse and his son, my Lord," answered Breakmaster.

"Lord!" Gray Goose shouted, running back into the armory. "The tallow house has been sacked. The grain stores have been plundered. There are no more than ten candles in the entire inner circle."

"Chancellors!" shouted Breakmaster, flinging

shut the studded door. "They have all fled and gone, no doubt, to sell us to the Nightbeasts!"

"Everyone? Even Overlord?" asked the King, gathering his courage to inspect the rough granite wall on either side of the door.

"The city is without a Chancellor, and all the better for it. It is without their treacherous ways at last," replied Gray Goose, standing at the King's elbow.

"Who would have known of this black hole?" asked the King. "Who would have told the Chancellors? They had no dealings with weapons or cause to visit this armory. It was only after the siege lock was put on the city that Proudpurse came to me and asked for the key."

Taking both Gray Goose and Breakmaster by the arm Holbian led them out beyond the armory doors. "Find me the Mastermason, he might know . . ."

Suddenly shouting broke out near the Candledoors.

"Lord," called Adarius, the Archer, breaking away from the frightened, milling crowd and sprinting towards the armory. "All the Marchers have gone, all the Gallopers and the Archers; they have abandoned the top of the wall and vanished. We are defenseless, without food or light."

"Steady, steady," soothed the King, his forehead creasing into a hundred folds of worry as he checked Adarius with a strong hand. "Now tell me slowly, who has gone?"

"Lord, we three are your army. We three are the only defenders of Granite City!"

"The horses!" cried Breakmaster. "Have they taken the horses?"

"Only Beacon Light and your pony, Mulberry, are still here," Adarius replied, turning anxious eyes on the advancing city dwellers.

King Holbian turned to face the frightened city folk and with one raised hand he brought them to a halt. "Be easy, my people," he soothed, "Chancellors are but chaff before the rising wind, who scatter easily at the first sign of danger. Wait with me a while and find and bring me the Loremaster of this once great city, for he may be able to tell us much of the treachery that shadows our last daylights."

Gray Goose moved quickly through the crowd, ducking into the shadows near the armory doors. "Here, Lord," he shouted, "I have the Loremaster. I saw him creeping through the shadows towards the armory with a heavy bag over his shoulder."

Holbian gripped the Loremaster's arm and fiercely shook him.

"Tell the people—tell them how you betrayed them and sold your knowledge of the winding path that leads through the darkness. Tell them!"

"Greatest Lord. Mightiest of Kings . . ." Pinchface the Loremaster pleaded. "The Chancellors forced me to tell my secrets."

"And did they also force you to take what belonged to others?" Gray Goose asked, tipping the contents of the Loremaster's bag across the cobbles.

"Lord," Pinchface wept as new tallow candles and satchels of grain spilled out at his feet.

"You sold them your knowledge of the secret way and bargained with it for a place with them in the escape to safety far from this city."

"Yes, Lord," Pinchface whispered, hanging his head.

Holbian laughed grimly, pushing the Loremaster onto his knees. "You did not have the power to deal in treachery with the treacherous, you simple-minded fool. The Chancellors have long gone, they have no place for Loremasters. You have served your purpose; they have abandoned you!"

"Lord, forgive me," pleaded Pinchface, stretching his hands towards the King's armored boots.

"Bind him between the Candledoors as an offering to the Nightbeasts. Perhaps they will take his treacherous tongue!" shouted Breakmaster.

"No! I will leave nothing for those Nightbeasts, not even my enemies. Bind him, we will sit in his judgment in better times."

"How did you guess that the Loremaster knew of the secret way in the armory, my Lord?" asked Gray Goose as he bound Pinchface's wrists.

Holbian smiled. "It was written clearly above the door in King Mantern's own hand, *'The wise shall know the way. They shall have the knowledge to reveal the winding path through the darkness. For it shall be written for all to share in the Books of Lore.'*"

"Lord, the Nightbeasts are assaulting the walls. How shall we defend the city?" shouted Breakmaster above their roaring screams and the renewed thunder of their battering rams.

King Holbian looked into the darkening sky. "Light every candle and spark we have left. Take the people into the armory and as they pass through, arm them and lead them down through the secret way. I will wait here until the last person is beyond the door and then I will follow. Mastermason! Where is Mastermason?"

"Lord, I am here!" cried Arachatt, brushing the stone dust out of his eyes.

"Look at the secret path and find a way to seal it after we have retreated. Breakmaster!" cried the King, turning quickly to the horseman.

"Lord?" Breakmaster answered, leading Beacon Light and Mulberry, ready-saddled, across the cobbles.

"You are a great Captain," laughed the King, running his hands through Beacon Light's silky coat, "to know my commands before I utter them!"

Breakmaster smiled, unclipping the siege hooks from both saddles. "Are we to ride once more to the top of the wall and battle with the Nightbeasts beneath the shining stars?"

"No, my friend, we will marshal the people into the armory and follow them wherever the secret way leads."

Long after darkness had descended across the empty Candle Hall and swallowed all the shadows in the inner city the King and Breakmaster waited, holding the horses, while Arachatt sealed and bolted the great outer armory doors. Holbian shivered in the feeble sparks of light and looked fearfully beyond the doorway that led down into the bowels of the earth.

Hesitantly he tried to follow the muffled noise of the descending city folk as they trod the secret road but he could not move, his iron-shod boots seemed frozen to the granite floor. "All I strove to overcome has shriveled to nothing," he whispered, tears of helpless despair wetting his eyes.

"Once in all my power I chased the Master of Nightmares to the very Gates of Night but I could not follow him into the darkness and destroy him, and now a lifetime later that same weakness leaves my people abandoned in their moment of greatest need, for I cannot lead them through that same darkness."

Slowly the King turned away from the black entrance and called Breakmaster to come forward. "You have been a strength at my right hand in these last grim daylights but I would ask one more thing, perhaps the most difficult any man could undertake." King Holbian paused, looking for long moments into the horseman's eyes before he slowly lifted his hands towards the crown upon his head. "I pledge you to take this crown of Elundium and keep it safe until the new King is found. There is none save you, dear friend, that I could trust with such a task, for you are true-hearted beyond fault."

"No, Lord!" cried Breakmaster, fearing that the King would stay alone in the armory to defend the entrance to the secret road, buying them time to escape. "Follow the city folk, my Lord, and let me be the one to defend the door. Let my sword arm grow weary that you might lead the people back into the sunlight."

King Holbian smiled and then fiercely gripped the horseman's arm. "Your love for me blinds you, fool. I have no choice. I, the last Granite King, cannot walk in the darkness because, because . . ." King Holbian looked away, blinking at his tears, "because I am afraid of the dark. Now you know my weakness. Go and do my bidding and let me hide my shame beneath a wall of Nightbeasts. Go, I command it."

"Keep him warm," whispered a voice in Breakmaster's head. "Cloak him with something you value above everything else, something that will give him courage in the dark, for he is old and brittle with age and afraid of the weakness that other men will see."

Breakmaster struck his fist against the wall, ashamed at how close he had come to deceiving the King, seeing clearly his own weakness, knowing that he would have kept the steelsilver coat to himself. Nevian's words shouted at him as he bent and searched amongst the fallen shields until his hands closed on the silken warmth of the battle coat.

"Lord," he called, barely able to meet the King's eyes as he held up the battle coat. "This will give you courage to walk in the dark, for it is steelsilver of the finest weave. Listen to the soft sounds of morning as it moves, feel the touch of sunlight it still holds. Come, my Lord, and let me wrap it around your shoulders."

"Steelsilver!" whispered the King. "I thought Errant took the last steelsilver battlecoat for Dawnrise to wear on their dash to World's End!"

"This is the only one in the armory, my Lord, perhaps the only one in all Elundium, and of a much finer quality than the one Errant took. It is . . ." Breakmaster fell silent as he draped the coat around the King's shoulders, his hands trembling with relief as he threaded the fine silver buckle at the King's throat.

"Pure steelsilver," whispered the King, running his brittle fingers across the fine metal weave, reflecting the joy of a summer's day in his eyes as he looked down into its soft shimmering colors. Tilting his head he could, for a moment, hear the whispers of a meadow lark and the first blackbird of the morning. "Breakmaster," he smiled, taking the horseman's hand, "I know the measure of this giving, I can feel it through your fingertips and hear it in your silence. I promise you, my dearest friend, when we reach the light this coat will be yours, and I will find a Lord of Horses to wear it."

Breakmaster looked up into the King's eyes and saw how the hairline fractures on his face had crazed in fine starshaped patterns and he felt glad to have given away the beautiful coat. "Lord, I shall follow the soft sound of bells, for the coat makes a gentle music. It will guide me in the dark."

Beyond the bolted doors the faint thunder of iron trees battering against the inner walls shook the armory floor. "It is time to abandon the city, Arachatt. Seal the secret way behind us. The daylights of the Granite City are now at an end."

King Holbian passed sadly through the doorway, with one hand holding tightly to Beacon Light's bridle and Breakmaster following with Mulberry. Arachatt waited until the King was safe, then pulled the studded door shut, and with his iron spike of the steel hammer he quietly loosened the middle granite blocks around the door until he could ease the spike into the narrow crack.

"Now!" he whispered, swinging the hammer and jumping quickly back. The heavy granite block fell. For a second nothing happened, fine granite dust settled on the mason's hands as he fled down the secret way, and then slowly the wall began to bulge and sway. Then the sheer tower that rose above the armory began to subside. Roaring and rumbling it collapsed, burying the armory and the beginnings of the secret road forever.

"It is done, my Lord," panted Arachatt, catching up with the King.

"It is done!" whispered Holbian, blinking the tears from his eyes as he moved forward.

Lures For Thanehand

"**G**ILDERSLEEVES!**" snarled Krulshards, uprooting the neat, well-clipped hedge figures of fencing men as he strode in black hatred towards the swordsman's house.

"Gildersleeves!" he dribbled, reading the name carved above the doorway and lifting hate-filled eyes towards the strengthening sun that had risen above the tree tops of the black forest. Turning away, he buried his head in the malice and gingerly touched the raw wound Archer had inflicted on him with the last arrow strike. "Foul tattoo that burned white with a light that could enter the malice!" he muttered, searching the early morning tree line for Kerzolde, his Captainbeast.

"We will rest here, Captain," he shouted impatiently as Kerzolde broke through the trees and staggered across the dew-wet lawns.

"Master," he gasped, crawling into the long shadows of a flower-filled gallery, "the Archer's arrow has weakened me. I cannot keep to your pace."

Krulshards snarled, snapping at his Captain,

"Keep pace, or we lose the advantage. We must reach Woodsedge before the Galloperspawn."

"But the Nightbeasts that ring the hut of thorns will have captured and killed him, Master!"

Krulshards curled his lips back across his teeth. "He has a rare gift for life, but he will die, when I have the Elionbel."

Krulshards reached up and tore a handful of newly opened flowers from a hanging basket and squeezed them between his fingers, drawing out all the sweet nectars. Laughing, he dropped the flowers, now gray-pressed, dry crumbs, onto the gallery floor.

"I owe this swordsman much for the skill of his arms before my black gates. Repay him now by destroying this house of Gildersleeves and leave it night-black and burned before the sun sets."

Kerzolde rose wearily to his feet and swung his broken claw through the stem-woven chains of the flower baskets, tearing them from their hooks and treading them into a black tangle along the galleries and walkways. Krulshards laughed with spite as he spread the malice through the lower chambers, wilting the hanging vines, burning and withering the living garden that Morolda had grown with care.

"Night treads in my footprints," he whispered, gathering the malice into folds of contentment and waited with hooded eyes for the sun to set.

"Master!" hissed Kerzolde, slipping through the

doorway. "Two young Marchers are at the edge of the lawn."

Krulshards moved noiselessly to the nearest window and watched the advancing warriors, closing his eyes to mere slits against the noonday glare. "Take them. Net them in darkness as they enter the doorway!" whispered the Master of Night, taking a shadowy nightmesh from within the malice and spreading it above the doorway.

"There is danger here," whispered Rubel, pointing with his sword at the uprooted hedges and blackened footprints that crisscrossed the lawn.

"Nightbeasts have been here," answered Arbel, boldly stepping into the first gallery and stopping a pace from the main doorway.

"Wait!" called Rubel, wrinkling his nose. "Whatever has done this damage is still here, I can smell it. Do not enter!"

Arbel froze. The acrid fumes were spilling through the open doorway, making him choke with each breath. "Rubel, help me!" he cried, trying to turn and run.

Rubel leapt forward, gripped Arbel's hand in his and pulled him backwards out of the gallery. Krulshards screamed with rage and pushed Kerzolde through the doorway after them.

"Kill them! Kill!" he snarled, spinning the nightmesh above his head and hurling it at Arbel, catching the young warrior's feet in the slippery black threads and bringing him crashing to the ground. Rubel slashed at the black threads, Arbel kicked his legs, but the more he struggled the tighter the nightmesh wound around his ankles.

"I cannot move!" he cried, swinging his sword with all his strength at Kerzolde, splitting the Nightmare's spear shaft just above the cruel barbed blade. Rubel sheathed his sword. He bent low and lifted his brother over his shoulder and ran as fast as he could for the safety of the tree line at the lawn's edge. Kerzolde followed them, swinging a long-handled scythe at Arbel's heels, trying to catch the hooked blade in the flowing threads of the nightmesh, but the noon sunlight blinded him and he cursed, stumbling over the uprooted box hedges, and crashed to his knees.

"Marchers!" he cursed as the two warriors reached the clearing's edge. Rubel had run himself to a standstill; he could go no farther with Arbel's weight on his shoulder so he lowered his brother to the ground and hid behind a tree.

"Cut yourself free with your dagger," he whispered, turning back towards the lawns. "I will keep watch for the Nightbeasts."

Arbel sighed and closed his eyes against the darkness that was sweeping over him. It was warm and crowded with visions of the great Marcher he would one day be, clothed in black armor, the most powerful warrior in . . ."

"Hurry, night will be with us soon!" hissed his brother, shaking his arm.

Arbel jolted awake, shivering at what he had seen and hid the black visions deep in his heart as he began cutting at the nightmesh. "I am going as fast as I can, only the cut threads keep trying to catch hold of me again. It is as if it has a life of its own, it is so horrible and clinging."

Rubel watched the shadows lengthen across the lawn of Gildersleeves. "Hush!" he warned, putting his middle finger to his lips. "The Nightbeast has come with the most terrible beast I have ever seen, they are leaving the house, I . . ." Rubel sank to his knees, his mouth silently opening and closing, his eyes wide with terror.

The Master of Nightbeasts stood in the center of the lawn, enfolded in his malice, and stared at the forest edge, searching for the warriors' fear, sniffing the cool evening breeze for the scent of his enemies. Slowly his raw, skinless head turned towards Rubel, dead locks of lank hair falling across the folds of his malice. Rubel shrank into a tight ball, his knuckles white. Arbel felt the Nightmare stare and hacked quickly through the last of the writhing threads. He wanted to see more of the dark dreams and touch the Nightmare's promises.

"Rubel," he whispered, jumping free and turning to his brother. "Rubel . . ." he swallowed the word, falling onto his knees beside his brother as he saw the face of Krulshards for the first time through the leafy undergrowth. It was so different from the dreams, more awesome and powerful, cruel and without mercy. His tongue felt rough and swollen and all he could do was press the palms of his hands over his eyes to blot out the Nightmare's stare.

"Marchers!" Krulshards sneered, drawing a black blade from the folds of his malice; he could see them at the forest edge, covered by the undergrowth. Putting the blade to his tongue he licked the cutting edge, leaving a thin line of bubbling spittle on the bare metal.

A fast-moving shadow spread across the lawns, blocking out the sunlight.

"Owls' breath!" hissed Krulshards, raising his arm to protect his face as he fled from the owls, his blade upturned towards the sky.

Arbel felt the Nightmare's eyes turn away, releasing him. He raised his head and stole a glance at the empty lawn, knowing that one daylight he would touch that power and take some of it for his own. He shivered and pulled at Rubel's sleeve, urging him to follow. "Rubel, come on, run!"

Together they fled deep into the forest, following a little-used path that led towards the flat grasslands and the Tower of Stumble Hill. The stoop of Battle Owls flew low over the swordsman's house, calling in shrill hoots at the Master of Nightmares as he disappeared beneath the eaves of the forest, running in the direction of Woodsedge.

"Krulshards, the Master of Darkness!" they hooted as the Wayhouse of Woodsedge passed beneath their wingtips. "Beware, the Nightmare is near!"

Martbel looked up into the evening sky at the

darkening stoop of owls, her forehead drawn in a frown. "They have bad omens in their call," she said to Elionbel. "Listen girl, bad omens!"

"The boys are late," Elionbel worried, looking up at the owls and biting her lips before she turned her eyes back to the road that led towards Gildersleeves.

"Bad omens from Underfall. Defeat at World's End. I'm sure that was in their voices," mused Martbel, shivering as she thought of Tombel and drawing her shawl more tightly around her shoulders.

"They were fools to go," Elionbel muttered.

"The King ordered it. It was beyond their choice!" snapped Martbel, her face blood red with anger.

"No, no! I mean the boys! Gildersleeves is empty. I am sure Father said Duclos and Morolda would follow the Marchers and the Gallopers to Underfall. There was no need for them to check that the swordsman's house was safe."

"They are Marchers, set to follow in their father's footprints. It was hard enough keeping them here, away from the glories of battle, to guard us. Be not over-hard on them, Elion. If your father, Tombel, is dead they will take the Keepership."

Elionbel smiled, remembering how they had boldly driven the Nightbeasts out of the Wayhouse. "Brave warriors or not, Mother, they are late, and I hope they will have the sense to shelter the dark hours at Gildersleeves."

"Come, daughter, worrying will not shorten their road. Come, bolt the doors. There is something in the air that bodes great evil, something on the Greenway. I can feel it gnawing and nagging at me. Come, stoke up the stairhead fire and prepare for the dark night ahead."

Elionbel shivered, taking a last quick look towards Gildersleeves and paused, frowning. For a moment she thought she saw two figures in the half-light. "Nightbeasts on the road," she cried, as the two figures came closer, emerging from beneath the eaves of the forest. She could see them clearly now, one a humped grotesque Nightbeast with a broken claw, the other a taller, more hideous figure, wrapped in a dark cloak that billowed out, spreading in ragged, tangled shadows about his feet. Elionbel turned and fled into the Wayhouse, slamming the door and shooting home the bolts as fast as she could. Without pausing for breath she raced to the stairhead and stoked the fire into a roaring blaze, thrusting as many fire-irons into the fire as she could.

"Nightbeasts! Nightbeasts!" she shouted, stumbling over the words. "On the road from Gildersleeves!"

"Nightbeasts? Before the sun sets?" Martbel cried.

"Come up here, Mother, to the safety of the fire. They were more terrible than anything I have ever seen before. Please come!" Elionbel's voice faded away; she could hear their footsteps on the gravel outside, and smelled an odor of death.

"Mother," she wept, backing into a corner of the hearth and sinking to her knees. The footsteps had stopped and in the darkening silence that followed a faint whisper began.

"Elionbel. Elionbel," it whispered as softly as a gentle breeze in the treetops. Louder now it called her name, forcefully laughing from the darkness, "Elionbel. I have come to take you!"

Elionbel shrank into a tight ball, the palms of her hands trying to press the sound of the Nightbeast voice out of her ears. Martbel took a defiant step towards the door, her sword arm raised, but the voice turned to shrieking laughter that froze her to the flagstones. The door frame shook, the door bulged and rattled.

"Elionbel! I have come for you with a gift from Thanehand, the Galloperspawn!" screamed the voice. "Come, stand before me, the Master of Darkness, and take the gift!"

The great door shook again, the wood tearing away from the iron studding, splitting across the main beam brace. Krulshards drew back his arm and punched at the door, shattering the timbers apart. His bone black hand appeared through the jagged hole, delicately holding the silver finger bowl by its broken chain. The hand flexed and threw the silver cup across the great hall, bouncing it on the flagstones.

"Thane!" Elionbel cried, watching the cup come

to rest. For a long moment she stared in silence at her love token, seeking in it Thane's pale blue eyes and laughing lips. "Thane," she whispered again as the picture faded and she shuddered to think of his death at the Nightbeast's hand.

"I promised him that I would come for you!" sneered the Nightmare voice of Krulshards. Elionbel looked up across the hall at the skinless, beckoning hand that had blackened and despoiled her love token, and felt anger swell up, pushing back the despair, and giving her strength. For a moment she had more strength than ten Granite Kings. "I love you, Thane," she whispered, pulling a white-hot fire-iron out of the flames, "and I will avenge your death!"

Springing forward, both hands holding the hot iron in front of her, she rushed headlong down the stairway, glittering tears of rage and hate streaming down her face. She charged blindly across the hall, plunging the fire-iron deep into the center of the Nightmare hand. Black, acrid smoke billowed up from the rotten flesh as the fire-white metal seared through to the bone. Krulshards screamed with pain, shutting his fingers on the dull red-hot iron shaft, cooling it in his grasp before snatching it back through the hole in the door.

"Elionbel!" he thundered, swelling the malice with rage and throwing it against the entrance to the Wayhouse. With one devastating blow it destroyed the door and wall in a shower of crumbling masonry. "Elionbel!" he hissed, dribbling her name across the flagstones as he entered, "you shall pay dearly for this, just as Thanehand paid for daring to enter the City of Night."

"You can take nothing more than my life!" answered Elionbel coldly, the strength fading as she retreated to the foot of the stairs and took a Marcher long spear from the server who was crouched, defending the first stair riser.

"Living death in the darkness. Life without light," laughed Krulshards, advancing towards her. "I bring darkness to all Elundium, but to you, Elionbel, I bring the key to the City of Night."

Elionbel tightened her grip on the smooth polished spear shaft and hurled it at the center of the Nightmare, shouting as it left her hand, "Die, foul Nightdemon. Die!" But Krulshards laughed, stretched out his smoldering hand and caught the spear long before it reached the malice. He turned the blade and drove it through the first server kneeling beside Elionbel.

Elionbel stared, open-mouthed, at the quivering spear shaft and retreated as Krulshards stepped forward, his shadowy foot on the first step. "I want you, Elionbel, it is payment for the love token I took from Thanehand. You have hurt me with a power that I do not understand, but only a king can kill me and he is far away in Granite City. Come to me!"

"No!" Elionbel hissed, proudly lifting her head, "My power comes through love, and with that love I shall defend this house against you." Bending, she took the second server's spear and turned it towards Krulshards.

"You are as weak as Thanehand," cackled Kerzolde, creeping forward in the shadow of the malice. Elionbel spun around angrily and flung the spear at Kerzolde, catching him a glancing blow on the shoulder. He snarled and leapt at the stairway, hooking his broken claw in the second server's cloak and pulling her through the splintered banisters. One sweeping stroke from his cruel curved scythe cut short her screams. Elionbel hesitated, poised to take a spear from the third server. Krulshards now had his foot upon the second step.

"Thane is dead, Elionbel," whispered the Nightmare, casting back the malice, "and to prove it I have a second gift for you. Here, hold his hand once more."

Laughing, Krulshards unhooked from his belt one of the Archer's hands, severed in the Tower at Stumble Hill and threw it at Elionbel. She screamed, stumbling backwards, as the hand fell onto the flagstones below, rolled once and touched the hem of Martbel's skirt. Martbel spun around, the spell from Krulshards's shout broken, and looked carefully at the severed hand.

"Nightmare!" she cried, sweeping her sword at the bulk of the malice. Krulshards snarled, snatched Sethot from beside Elionbel, turned and used her as a shield against the sword stroke. Elionbel cried out as Martbel's thrust cut into the server.

"Enough!" she shouted. "What do you want of me if not my death?"

Krulshards grinned, a trickle of saliva wetting his chin and let Sethot's lifeless body fall and tumble its way down to the great hall. "You!" he hissed, reaching out. "I want your life in payment. Your death would be nothing but a moment's pleasure!"

"You choose wrongly!" cried out Martbel, slipping between them. "I am Elionbel. It was my love token you brought here!"

Krulshards looked from mother to daughter; the gray strips of flesh bound across his forehead drew into a frown. "Elionbel?" he whispered, holding them both at arm's length in a viselike grip. Undecided, he turned to Kerzolde.

"Which one is Elionbel?"

"Master, Master!" Kerzolde cried, cleaning the Server's blood from his chin. "The younger one is the one we took from this Wayhouse, but we did not ask her name."

"I am Elionbel!" Martbel shouted, struggling to bite Krulshards's hand. Elionbel slipped her hand inside her cloak and unsheathed a small narrow-bladed dagger. "Nightmare!" she hissed as she thrust the blade upwards into the folds of the malice.

Krulshards felt the point of the blade tear through the malice and shrank away from it. Lifting his foot he kicked Elionbel's wrist, numbing her hand into dropping the knife. Frowning he pushed both women towards Kerzolde. There was a strange power in the Wayhouse, clearly these women were not kings and yet twice they had hurt him. "I have two queen-like creatures who have dared to hurt me, the Master of Darkness. I shall take you both!" he hissed. "Both of you shall come into the darkness of the City of Night."

Kerzolde snarled and held them tightly, pinching the skin of their arms in his one good claw. Krulshards reached into the malice, digging with his long sharp fingernails into the layers of rotten flesh that covered his black heart, and carefully pulled out his life thread. Thin and spider-fine, it glistened in his hands. Carefully he looped it around both Elionbel and Martbel's necks and tied the end in a bloody knot. Stepping back he laughed and turned his head toward the remaining servers crouching in the stairhead hearth.

"Darkness is spreading across all Elundium," he sneered. Elionbel bent, scooped up the dagger and made to plunge it into Krulshards's back, but as the blade touched the malice the life thread looped around her neck began to tighten, choking her to her knees. Krulshards turned his head back towards her, a sneer of delight wetting his lips.

"You are mine now, you are a part of me, joined by my life thread. If danger threatens me the thread will shrink. Sleeping or waking you are bound to me!" Gripping Elionbel by the folds of her cloak he pulled her close, lifting her off the ground, and spat the words into her face. "If the foul Marchers or Gallopers attack me it will be you that suffers my pain. If an Archer's strike of arrows breaks through this malice, it will be your lives they threaten. You are nothing now, nothing!"

Krulshards dropped Elionbel onto the hard stone floor and turned away. The thread slackened around her neck but she could feel it pulsating with every beat of the Nightbeast's heart.

"You have us in your power. Please let the servers go," pleaded Martbel.

"My Captain is hungry, he needs food for the long road ahead of us," mocked Krulshards, letting Kerzolde climb onto the first step.

"Please," begged Elionbel.

"Wait!" ordered the Master of Nightbeasts, halting his Captain on the second stair. "We must leave our mark in this Wayhouse for all Nightbeasts to see."

Picking up the finger bowl he placed it at the center of the hall, and in a pattern around it he stamped his name into the flagstones, shattering them with large black letters, *"KRULSHARDS THE MASTER OF NIGHT."*

"Meet me beneath the walls of Granite City," he shouted to Kerzolde. "I shall be with your brother Kerhunge who is leading my Nightbeast army. Together we will finish the siege and destroy the last Granite King!"

Krulshards turned away from the stairway and strode out onto the dark Greenway, dragging Elionbel and Martbel behind him.

"The servers, please, spare them," Martbel cried. Krulshards only laughed and quickened his pace.

"My Captain is hungry, but he is kind, he will save some for you!"

"We are better off dead!" gasped Elionbel as she tried to keep pace with the Nightmare. "Father is dead! Thane is dead!"

"No!" whispered Martbel. "That hand he threw at you. It was not Thane's!"

Dawn streaked the sky and the Nightbeast had slowed down. Elionbel and Martbel moved closer. "Whom did it belong to? Do you know?"

"Do not ask, child. Names are dangerous things to utter when Nightbeasts are near."

News of Krulshards

DAWNLIGHT had spread the jewels of morning all along the Greenway's edge. Skylarks climbed into the early sky and sang of the new daylight. Thane slid quietly to the ground, easing his weight out of Stumble's saddle and thanked him for a great run against the darkness.

"You are as bold as a Warhorse, and as tireless as a greyhound," he laughed, running his hand down the horse's sweat-soaked shoulder and he fell silent for a moment, remembering that the little relay horse had none of Esteron's fine breeding. "Forgive me, I have ridden you too hard in my haste to reach Woodsedge before the Nightmare, Krulshards."

Stumble snorted, his eyes full of fire, and arching his aching neck he lengthened his stride to keep pace with Thane.

"You have a great heart," he laughed, "just like your brother, Sprint. He knew nothing of defeat and ran tirelessly for Kyot."

Thane was quiet again, hoping against hope that

Kyot would find and understand the message he had left at Stumble Hill. He sighed gently, pulling at Stumble's ears as he took the reins over his head and led him forward through the grasslands. Stumble's coarse coat dried quickly in the fresh morning breeze and shimmered, reflecting the sun from the fine layer of salt he had sweated on their night gallop. The quiver of steel-tipped arrows, clipped onto the pommel of the saddle, rattled with each measured stride he took and the oiled wooden bow hanging next to it sang out a haunting music as the wind tugged at the fibers of the bowstring. Thane listened to the bow.

"Follow me, Kyot, with new-forged arrowheads from Clatterford," he whispered, wondering what and where was Clatterford; he certainly had not passed it on his way to Underfall.

Looking ahead he could see a faint smudge on the horizon's edge; a dark line that marked the eaves of the black forest. "Elundium is a limitless place," he muttered between panting breaths as the sun climbed across the sky, shrinking his hurrying shadow. Thane slowed to a walk and chose a solitary clump of trees for a short noonday rest. The Nightbeasts' tracks would still be there to follow, blackened footprints burned into the Greenway, no matter how long he rested. Even the heat of the sun had not dispelled the foul odor of death that Krulshards had spilled onto the grass as he passed through Elundium. And Tombel had been right in his counsel; he could not match the Nightbeast's pace no matter how hard he tried.

But Thane could not rest while Elionbel's life was at risk and he fidgeted in the shade of the trees, waiting while Stumble took a long drink from a shallow pool. "I will run until the sun sets," he said, brushing the salt out of Stumble's coat with the flat of his hand, "and I shall only mount you for our ride through the night. Come, we must take the road again, or arrive late."

Evening time had drawn Thane's shadow out far behind him before they reached the eaves of the black forest and passed beneath the trees. Thane climbed wearily up into the saddle and Stumble forged bravely ahead, cantering hard over a muffling carpet of leaf mold. Twilight had darkened the forest floor and Thane slumped forward in the saddle, his head nodding in half sleep to the rhythm of the horse's stride. Suddenly Stumble halted, whinnying fiercely, jolting Thane awake. He reached for the dagger and searched the shadows. Two figures crouched at the edge of the Greenway. Clearly he could see their Marching swords glittering in the darkness.

"Who, in all Elundium, hides in the darkness?" he challenged, squeezing Stumble forward.

"Thane?" a voice called as the figures rose.

"Arbel! Rubel!" Thane cried, recognizing Tombel's sons. He jumped quickly to the ground. "What brings you this far from Woodsedge? Is the Wayhouse safe?"

"The Nightmare! The most fearsome, terrible . . ." Arbel began.

"Woodsedge! Has he overrun the Wayhouse? Is Elionbel safe?" Thane interrupted, but he could not finish; his voice shook with fear and he gripped Rubel's arm painfully.

"No! We saw it at Gildersleeves. It has destroyed the gardens and the baskets. Only the stoop of owls that flew overhead saved us."

"Where did the Nightmare go?" Thane asked, re-mounting Stumble.

"It was on the lawns when we fled, less than two hours ago."

"Run! Gallop as fast as you can. Krulshards, the Master of all Nightbeasts, is on his way to destroy Woodsedge. Run!"

Thane spun Stumble back onto the crown of the road and urged him forward. Arbel and Rubel followed, running as if all the Nightbeasts ever dreamed of were at their heels. Thane hardly drew rein as they entered the lawns of Gildersleeves, and even in the night darkness before the moon rose above the trees he could see the destruction in the gardens and the galleries. The sack of the fencing master's home seemed complete. He looked in anger at the empty windows, circled the house once before returning to the Greenway. Bending low in the saddle he searched the road, sniffing at the night air. Behind him Tombel's sons entered the lawns.

"They are before us on the road!" Thane shouted, pointing to the burnt footprints and asking Stumble to gallop as he had never done before. "Do not draw breath until you reach the Wayhouse!" he shouted to Arbel and Rubel as Stumble carried him forward under the eaves of the black forest.

A New Keeper at Stumble Hill

KYOT reined Sprint to a halt before the ruined hut of thorns and dismounted, covering his nose and mouth with his sleeve, and picked a way through the carcasses of the slaughtered Nightbeasts. A quick glance showed him Esteron's saddle and bridle with the broken spear shaft lying beside them. "Thane must be on the road through Notley Marsh," Kyot muttered, stroking Rockspray's chest feathers as he left the hut and remounted Sprint. For a moment he sat, undecided. He knew the quicker, straighter road through Mantern's and Meremire Forest but if he rode that way he would miss Thane who could be lying wounded, less than half a league into the marsh. He shivered, nocked an arrow onto his bow and spurred Sprint onto the ancient road that led through the marshes.

"Father would counsel against this road, but need pushes us to it," he thought as they descended, leaving behind the clean afternoon air and the bright sunlight on the valley top. Lifting his arm he sent Rockspray up into the sky, bidding him to search the road ahead.

"Run, Sprint, run! And keep us to the center of the road through this foul place," he shouted as the little horse lengthened his stride.

By late afternoon they had passed the bubbling pools and ascended the steep slope on the far side of the marshes. Reaching the great divide Kyot pulled Sprint to a halt and dismounted.

"Thane can run as fast as I can ride," he exclaimed, examining the footprints that led towards Stumble Hill. Kyot pointed with an arrow at the Nightbeasts' prints that spread across the road. Moving on with care and with a sharp eye on the lengthening shadows Kyot covered the last league to the Tower and stood before the ruined doors.

"Nightbeasts!" he hissed, tying Sprint's reins in a knot on the saddle, leaving him free to fight in true Warhorse fashion. Crouching, he drew the bowstring and, with his careful Archer's eyes, he searched every shadow, tree and stone before he darted forward into the darkened courtyard. A blinding white light stopped and dazed him, making him loose the arrow, sending it shrieking across the courtyard to strike sparks off the tower wall.

"Father!" he cried, seeing Archer in the center of the white light that glittered beneath the horse's battle coat. "Father," he whispered, running forward and falling onto his knees at his side. Gently he touched the cold mutilated arms, pressing his fingers into the tattoo mark that burned with white fire.

"Who has done this?" he wept, looking up at the towering crescent of dead Nightbeasts a dagger's length away. "Who has done this thing?" he shouted in rage, leaping to his feet, nocking every arrow in the quiver onto his bow and loosing them into the pile of Nightbeast dead until he fell back in despair onto his knees whispering over and over, "I love you. I love you." Bending down he gathered his father up into his arms and rocked him, crying out against the night for revenge.

Gradually his weeping stopped and he laid his father gently back onto the cobbles, drawing the coarse steel-ringed battle coat up over his head. Sitting quietly the emptiness of the moment overtook him.

"Who did this?" he questioned, looking at the wall of the Nightbeast dead. "You could not have taken his hands. None of you trod close enough to do that. But who stood here with you, Father?" Kyot frowned, looking around the courtyard, and his eyes rested on the barbed spear blade lying beside the oaken shooting butt with the neatly cut bowstring. "Thane! He must have brought the Nightbeasts close on his heels through Notley Marsh and found Father tied to the shooting butt."

Kyot examined the lifeless Nightbeasts and nodded to himself. The only arrows used against them were his own, loosed in anger, long after they were dead. Each one had a dagger wound. Thane had obviously fought them alone.

"I will avenge your death, Father!" he cried, kneeling and gripping the hem of the battle coat so hard that the steel rings bit into the palms of his hands.

"Only one foul Nightmare could have done this . . ." Kyot shook with a new rage and rose to his feet. "Sprint!" he called, summoning the relay horse to his side. "Krulshards, the Master of Nightmares, has destroyed my father. I shall hunt him throughout Elundium, no matter where he hides. Will you take me and carry me into such danger?"

Sprint arched his neck and sniffed the battle coat, his eyes glittering with anger. Lifting his head he neighed at the darkness and struck sparks from the cobbles as he pawed the ground. Kyot leapt into the saddle and turned Sprint swiftly towards the broken doors and cantered him hard out into the dark night.

"Which way?" he cried, pulling Sprint to a halt ten paces beyond the doors and reaching into the quiver for an arrow. "Fool!" he muttered to himself, his hand closing on emptiness, remembering that every spine had been loosed into the Night-beast dead. Turning, he rode back into the courtyard, shielding his eyes against the tattoo's blinding light that shone even through the steel rings of the battle coat.

"Father, you still guard this place, but I will ring

your body with new-forged arrows. They will protect you until the Archer strikes return."

Dismounting, Kyot entered the armory and lit his spark. "By Nevian!" he hissed, dropping the Bow of Orm and jumping backwards. The spark fizzled and died in his hand. Quickly he took a tardipped torch from the wall beside the door, lit it and held it aloft to face the far wall.

"*KRULSHARDS!*" He read in large-scrawled, bloody letters painted across the wall, "*Go to Clatterford, seek out Fairday, he knews the measure of your revenge. He will arm you against the Nightmare.*"

Kyot ran to the armory wall and touched the blood-sticky letters.

"Thane wrote this," he cried, "but where is Clatterford? And how will I be armed, why must I go there? Surely I should hunt down the Master of Nightmares; he cannot be more than one daylight ahead."

Kyot sank down, his back resting against the wall, and absentmindedly kicked over the armorer's iron pot that Thane had filled with Nightbeast blood to paint the letters. He sat and thought hard as the night hours passed away, trying to riddle out the meaning of the words. "Clatterford! Clatterford! What or where can it be?" he sighed, twisting his head and looking up at the other name written on the wall. Rockspray flew into the armory and stooped back to his shoulder, hooted and spread his wings before lifting from his shoulder and hovering by each blood-painted word. Stooping to the arrow stands he hooked an empty quiver up in his talons and brought it to Kyot, dropping it at his feet.

"Yes we will take new arrows with us. If only I could know who Fairday is or where Clatterford lies," sighed Kyot again. Pushing aside the quiver he began to rise. The tar-dipped torch spluttered, guttering on its wick, and went out, plunging the armory back into darkness. Kyot searched in his pocket for another spark, muttering to himself. "The gray hours are upon us and I am still none the wiser which path to take. The Nightbeast tracks will be cold and more difficult to follow if I hesitate here any longer."

"Keeper of the Tower," whispered a voice in the darkness. Archer's tattoo blazed for a moment in the courtyard, casting long shadows in the armory. Kyot drew his knife and crouched, his eyes wide and steady, watching the doorway. "Keeper of the Wayhouse on Stumble Hill—come forward and be named!"

The hair on the back of Kyot's neck prickled and he shivered. A single tiny point of light had begun to glow in the doorway. Now it was moving, growing stronger as it traveled between the rows of hanging, oiled wooden bows. Past the arrow stands it came, filling the armory with a beautiful soft light. "Come forward, Keeper, be not afraid," soothed an ancient voice. The light had changed and taken the shape of a rainbow cloak.

"Nevian!" Kyot cried, dropping the knife and

falling onto his knees. "Father has been mutilated by the Nightmare, Krulshards, and tied onto the shooting butt. Thane has been here, I think he defended Father, look, he has left me a message I cannot understand."

"Peace," whispered the Master of Magic, stepping forward and spreading the rainbow cloak over Kyot's shoulders. "Know the measure of your father's battle with the Master of Darkness and understand the words that Thane wrote upon the wall, for I have come to give you the Keepership of this Wayhouse and release your father from the pledges."

Kyot looked up into Nevian's caring face and asked, "Hasn't death given him rest?"

Nevian smiled and covered Kyot's head with the cloak, taking him back in time to the dark empty tower before the Nightmare arrived. "Father," he whispered, tears in his eyes as the battle unfolded before him and he watched the courage in his father's death. "Fairday of Clatterford—the Crystal Maker!" he cried, listening to his father's faltering words as Thane held him in his arms. Now he understood the power of the glass arrowheads and where they had come from. The rainbow cloak had dimmed, the armory was full of gray dawn light.

"You, Kyotorm, are the Keeper now, and I bind you by words alone to guard this place and keep it safe against the powers of the night, for you are a part of the new Elundium that has a strength that stretches far beyond a binding mark upon your arm."

"But how can I seek out Clatterford if I must guard the Tower?" Kyot cried.

Nevian smiled and handed Kyot the great Bow of Orm. "Revenge will dim the power of this bow and it will blur your vision and blunt the arrow's edge. Seek more than revenge and when Elundium is safe once more from the Nightmare, Krulshards, then you will keep this Wayhouse. It is as much a gift as a duty. Follow the sun to Clatterford and be at Thane's right hand in the darkness, for he will have great need of your skill with this bow. Hurry, lest the sun sets before you have reached the Crystal Maker's house."

"Nevian!" Kyot cried as the rainbow cloak melted. "Thunderstone said that Thane brought old legends to life, that he might one day be King, or carry a King's standard—is this true?"

Nevian laughed and melted into the first ray of sunlight that entered the armory, leaving Kyot alone with the great Bow of Orm in his hand, and Rockspray battle-perched on his shoulder. Beyond the tower Kyot could hear the swift running feet of his Archer strikes and hurried out to meet them.

Despair at Woodsedge

WOODSEDGE loomed up, a black shape on the Greenway's edge. "Elionbel," Thane called out quietly, slipping to the ground, dagger drawn. He moved forward cautiously, watching the spiral of smoke that rose from the main chimney stack. Nothing else moved in the darkened Wayhouse. Arbel and Rubel ran silently to his side and together they entered the great hall, picking their way between the broken blocks of masonry and shattered beams.

"Curse this darkness!" Rubel whispered, tripping over something soft on the stone floor. Thane lit his spark and gasped with horror. Before him, his face gorged with blood, crouched Kerzolde, the torn remains of a server held in his one good claw.

"Galloperspawn!" the Nightbeast screamed, hurling the half-eaten girl at Thane's face, knocking him over backwards and making him drop the spark.

"Kerzolde!" Thane shouted, stabbing at the fleeing shape as it escaped into the night. Rubel turned and chased it to the Greenway's edge, but he was near to nightblind and soon lost trace of the fading footsteps.

"Elionbel!" Thane called, lighting every candle he could find in the hall.

"Mother!" Arbel cried, searching among the fallen servers.

Thane suddenly stopped in the center of the hall and fell to his knees. "Elionbel!" he cried, closing his fingers on the silver finger bowl and lifting it up. "Oh, Elionbel!"

"What is it?" Arbel asked, looking at Thane's clenched fist.

"The Nightmare has her. Look!" Arbel followed Thane's shaking finger to the cruel name shattered into the flagstone floor and gasped, catching his breath. "Krulshards, the Master of Nightbeasts, he has her. He has taken her in revenge," cried Thane, pressing the silver cup to his forehead.

"Revenge? Why revenge, how did he know my sister?" asked Rubel, standing before Thane.

"That evil beast we found here stole Elionbel's love token from my belt as we fought between the Gates of Night."

"You took her token into battle!" screamed Rubel. "You—you stupid fool! I will kill you for that!" Arbel moved quickly, he could smell the Nightmare's darkness and the taste of it made him dizzy with desire. Shaking his head he turned his brother's sword stroke wide, sending a shower of sparks up into the air as both Marching swords clashed.

"Enough of this madness. To lose Elionbel and our mother is enough to break my heart, but to kill Thane would only add to the Nightbeast's deed. We must follow him and rescue them, quickly, without delay!"

Rubel turned away, hurling his blade across the great hall and stood shaking with rage. Turning back to Thane he gripped him by the cloak clasp. "Find her, Candleman, and return her safe home, or I will take your life in payment."

"No!" cried Arbel, prying his brother's fingers from Thane's throat. "I am the eldest and I say there will be no bad blood between us."

"Father called him a base Candleman; he was against him ever looking at our sister. I heard him tell her that Thane was not bloodworthy of this house."

Arbel turned savagely on his brother. "Bloodworthy or not, Elionbel loved him and gave the token of her own free will." Lowering his voice he turned to Thane. "She loved you, Thane, and whispered your name each evening time. Will you come with me on the Nightmare's heels and try to bring her back?"

Thane took Arbel's hand and gripped it firmly. "I have run and ridden on the heels of this Nightmare across Elundium only to arrive too late. But we will follow Krulshards together, no matter how bleak the path, for I love your sister more than life itself and to be without her would be to live in the shadows."

Arbel looked past Thane into the darkness beyond the door and heard a black voice in his head, "Hurry, Marcher, on your dark and dangerous road for one day we will be brothers, brothers in the darkness, I know it!" Arbel shivered at Krulshards's whispers and tried to shut them out. "We must hurry," he said, "or the trail will grow cold."

"Go quickly then," Rubel shouted, angry at seeing Arbel standing so closely with Thane, "and do not cross the threshold of this Wayhouse again if Elionbel is not by your side. For if you do I will kill you!"

Thane turned and gripped Arbel's hand. "I will gallop ahead; follow as quickly as you can." Without another word he left the Wayhouse, running the short distance to where Stumble waited. "The Nightmare has taken Elionbel," he whispered, quickly mounting the horse and searching for the black footprints. "He has taken her to the Granite City!"

"Wait!" shouted Arbel, running out onto the Greenway. "I think the Nightmare took our mother as well. She is nowhere to be found!"

"We will find them both," Thane shouted, holding Stumble by the bridle. Turning in the saddle he called out as the horse surged forward, "We will not rest until they are safe and the Nightmare is dead. You have my word on it!"

Arbel turned back into the Wayhouse and for a

moment watched his brother searching amongst the dead servers. A darkness was filling his body, spreading upwards in itching lines from where the Nightmesh had entangled his legs, it was making him move forward across the Wayhouse floor, forcing him to loose the dagger at his belt.

"Rubel," he whispered, drawing the blade, "you must not follow the Master of Darkness. You must stay here."

Rubel spun around and cried out as the dagger cut into his outflung arm, sending him crashing heavily against the first stair riser, knocking him unconscious. "No! No!" Arbel cried, as the darkness dissolved and he saw what he had done. Bending, he gathered up his brother's body and laid him carefully across a broken chair. "I could not help it!" he cried. "That foul mesh that entangled me at Gildersleeves, sometimes it seems that it is still there, filling me with darkness, making me do things."

Mumbling and crying Arbel bound his brother's wound and then ran to the doorway and looked out at the lightening sky. "The darkness draws me, beckons me to follow, but somehow I must overcome it and rescue Elionbel and Mother."

In the Ruins
of the
Granite City

*E*LIONBEL ran wearily at Krulshards's heels, pulled along by the life thread looped around her throat. Behind her Martbel stumbled to keep the Nightmare's hurrying pace. Dawn brought little but chill winds to comfort them as the early light changed from dismal gray to soft green as the sun climbed above World's Edge. Before them on the rising ground black shadows surrounded a huge mound of granite gray blocks, piled, it seemed, in tumbling disorder. Each slab was thrown upon the other as if the bones of Elundium had erupted from the ground; only on the summit of the mound above the edges of the shadows did the chaos end in a smooth wall that rose sheer against the morning light. Just above the ruin of the wall Elionbel could see the steep gables of weathered slate that covered an ancient hall.

"Mother," she whispered between running steps, "what place is this?"

Martbel peered around the billowing folds of the malice that Krulshards had spread across his eyes against the light and her face drained of color. "It was once the Granite City," she replied, falling back behind Elionbel.

Krulshards turned his hideous head, dead locks of tangled hair streamed in the wind, and he laughed, cruelly and without pity. Spreading his arms he shouted, "Behold the last of the Granite Kings. You see the beginning of a long night of darkness where only I, Krulshards, the Master of Darkness, rule! Nightbeasts—your Master!"

The dense black shadows began to sway and in answer to the Nightmare's cry they chanted, heralding his victory, "Krulshards, Master of Darkness. Krulshards, the King of all Elundium!"

Elionbel shrank in horror and hung back against the pull of the life thread. "The shadows are Nightbeasts! The city is surrounded by the Nightmare's army!"

Krulshards laughed and tugged both women along on their knees through the ranks of his beasts. Cruel claws pinched and slapped their arms and legs. Nightbeast faces leered and laughed at them and everywhere hung the stench of rotting flesh and the dry rattle of Nightbeast armor. Only when they stood in the shadows of the highest innermost wall did Krulshards halt. Reaching out he pressed his bone black fingers against the smooth granite, scratching his sharp nails across the fine grooves left by the masons.

"Kerhunge!" he boomed, "come to your master!"

Kerhunge, Kerzolde's brother, heard the summons, quickly clambered out of a dark hole between the granite blocks and hurried forward to kneel at Krulshards's feet, offering up the handle of his twelve-tailed whip. "Master, the Granite City is yours!"

"You lie! This city will not be mine while the Granite King lives," Krulshards shouted, hooking his fingers into Kerhunge's iron collar and pulling him to his feet. "Where is the Granite King's head? Bring it to me now!"

Elionbel listened in horror as Kerhunge stammered out the last moments of the Granite King, pointing to the top of the wall, and telling the Master of Night how King Holbian had retreated into one of the Granite Towers seconds before it collapsed, burying him forever beneath a thousand granite blocks. "The inner circle of the city is empty, Master. There is only the strange light in the Candlehall and a stoop of owls guarding the ancient roof. Nothing more."

Krulshards seethed with new anger. Picking Kerhunge up by his collar he tossed him down towards the lower ruins of the city. "I want the King's head!" he roared. "Destroy the inner circle and find me the King. Tear out every brick and stone, dig down into the bones of Elundium and find the King. Elundium cannot be mine until I have his head!"

"Master, it will be done!" cried Kerhunge, crawling back to lie at the Nightbeast's feet.

"Now!" screamed Krulshards, cracking the twelve-tailed whip in Kerhunge's face. Kerhunge fled towards the siege ladders that lay propped against the inner wall ready for the final assault. Shouting and screaming he drove the waiting Nightbeasts forward in a black mass and they scaled the ladders and breasted the top of the wall, spears and scythes casting a forest of shadows across the empty cobbles below.

Krulshards stretched out a long impatient hand, caught Kerhunge by the collar and pulled him close. "Why do you hesitate?" he hissed, watching the Nightbeasts pause on the top of the wall.

"Master it is the light!"

"Light?" snarled Krulshards, climbing onto the first rung of the ladder.

"There is a strange light that shines blue and gold in the Candle Hall. It burns into our eyes even through the wolfskin shields."

"Light!" sneered the Master of Darkness, reaching the top of the wall and roughly pulling Elionbel and Martbel up with him. "I will destroy this hall and all the light that ever shone in this foul city!"

"It was beautiful once," Martbel whispered to her daughter, stealing a furtive glance back across the ruined lower circles of the city. "The sheer strong walls once cast deep velvet shadows over the maze of narrow streets that wound their way up towards Candlebane Hall."

Krulshards hissed and tugged sharply at his life thread, silencing Martbel's whisperings. "It is more beautiful now that my army has rebuilt it!"

Elionbel laughed bitterly, pointing at the broken doors of the Candle Hall, "That is a hallowed place that you cannot destroy, look!"

Krulshards turned back towards the Candle Hall, his face blood red with anger and screamed out with rage and pain, throwing the malice over his head against the light.

"It is a hallowed place!" laughed Elionbel, her hair blowing in the clear morning breeze, her face reflecting all the brilliant light that flooded out of Candlebane Hall. Krulshards lashed out at Elionbel, catching her behind the knees with his black knuckles, almost sending her toppling over the inner edge of the wall to plunge to her death on the cobbles below. Martbel sprang forward and wrapped the life thread around her hands. "Elionbel! I will save you," she shouted as the thread went taut, cutting into the palms of her hands.

"Elionbel!" Krulshards hissed, knowing now which one of the Marcherwomen he sought. He reached down into the blinding light and hooked his fingers into the fabric of Elionbel's cloak, pulling her back to the safety of the top of the wall. "Now I know!" he sneered through the folds of his malice. Sitting back on his haunches he laughed and grabbed Martbel by his other hand. Holding both women before him he stared at them through a crack in his malice, looking from one to the other.

"You are payment against Thanehand," he hissed at Elionbel. "For his crimes you shall hang in torment in the City of Night. But you, Marcher-woman," he sneered, dribbling the word across his malice, "you shall serve me a purpose." Half turning his head, he looked down at the Candle Hall shielding his eyes against the light. "I cannot enter the Candle Hall, or destroy the inner circle of the city, the light is against me, but you, Marcher-woman, I can take, and enter, and spoil. You shall be my last act of destruction in the Granite City."

"No! No!" Martbel screamed, struggling against Krulshards's strong grip as he dragged her into the malice. "NO!" Elionbel bit at the Nightmare's hand and wriggled free. Turning she kicked and beat on the outer folds of the malice but it was closed against her. Muffled and far away she could hear her mother's screams as Krulshards took her, raping her without mercy. "She is mine!" gloated the Master of Nightmares, his eyes blood red and swollen with victory.

"I will kill you for this, you foul Nightmare!" Elionbel cried, falling to her knees. "I will tear out your black heart for what you have done this day-light, by Nevian I will!"

Krulshards laughed at her, pushing her aside as he opened up the malice. "Magicians cannot help you, Thanehand cannot help. I take what I please!

I am the Master of Elundium!" With a sneer of satisfaction he thrust Martbel back into the daylight. Stumbling forward, the bloody torn hems of her skirts wetting the granite dust, she fell into Elionbel's arms. Her mouth was trembling, her eyes were wide with terror.

Krulshards reached out for Elionbel, a cruel snarl on his lips, but before his fingers could touch her the ground shook and a piercing cry tore the shadows apart. Pure blinding light spilled out of Candlebane Hall across the cobbles. Krulshards screamed as the light entered his malice, burning into his face. Turning, he fled scrambling down the nearest siege ladder.

Elionbel stood her ground, the light edging her cloak in blue and gold. "Even the bones of Elundium cry out against what you have done!" she shouted as the Nightmare dragged her after him. "Elundium will have its revenge, and I shall be its sword maiden, I swear it!" she cried, tumbling down the ladder, bruising her shins on the rough granite rubble as she landed on the ground.

"I may not have taken the inner circle of this city but I have planted something more powerful and awesome here in its ruins. Come," commanded Krulshards, pulling at the life thread. "We travel a secret wild road back to the City of Night. A road that is safe from roving bands of Marchers or columns of Gallopers seeking revenge for all that I have destroyed."

"Master!" Kerzolde gasped, climbing breathlessly over the rubble and falling at the Nightmare's feet, "Thanehand has reached Woodsedge. He is on my heels and behind him on the road is the Marcher we trapped with the nightmesh."

"Thanehand?" the Nightmare snarled, staring back across the ruins at what was once the beginnings of the green winding road to Underfall. For a moment fear crossed his cruel face and the life thread tightened on Elionbel and Martbel's throats then he laughed, spitting out fine trails of saliva onto the front of his malice. "He will never find us, Captainbeast. Look, the ground is spoiled and trodden black for leagues around the city. There is nothing here to tell the Galloperspawn of our passing. We leave no waymark save the destruction of the city!"

"Thane is alive and he will find us, Nightmare!" Elionbel shouted defiantly.

Krulshards turned fiercely on Elionbel. "You are lost forever, Marcherwoman, lost in my darkness. There is no one left to search for you. Thanehand is dead!"

"He is alive. I heard that foul, broken-clawed beast speak his name. He will never stop searching for us, no matter how dark the road."

"Quiet, Marcherwoman," Krulshards hissed, shrugging his shoulders against Elionbel's whisperings as he summoned his Nightbeast army into a great shadow that covered the lower ruins of the city. Lifting his arms he spread the malice and waited for silence. "Nightbeasts!" he cried, thrusting a bone black finger towards the trampled Greenway. "You have taken the Granite City and made it yours, go now into all Elundium and spread my darkness. Render everything that loves the daylight into ruins, but while you travel, sweeping as a black tide, search carefully for one called Thanehand, and if you find him bring him to the City of Night, for he is mine, mine alone to destroy!"

Amidst the roar and rattle of Nightbeast armor the black shadowy army spread out beyond the city. Kerzolde and his brother jostled Elionbel and Martbel to follow the Master of Nightbeasts into the wild lands beyond the outer edges of the Granite City and they vanished without a trace on the heels of the billowing malice, for Kerzolde and Kerhunge were careful that nothing was dropped as a waymark for Thanehand.

The Battle Crescent is Formed

*T*OMBEL raised his hand and with a single twist of his armored gloves he halted the swift column of marching men. Without further command, the warriors unsheathed their broad, double-edged swords and drove them point first into the soft edges of the Greenway. Removing their metal helms they laid them, emblems facing inwards, on the short cropped grass and knelt in respect as the slow-moving Archer funeral passed between them. Tombel saw Kyot leading the strike of Archers that followed the funeral litter, each bowman with an arrow nocked lightly onto the string.

"Whom do you bury?" Tombel asked in a whisper, falling in step with the young Archer.

"My father lies on the litter of oiled bows," he answered gray-faced with grief. "He defended this Wayhouse alone against Krulshards, the Master of Nightbeasts, and paid cruelly with his life!"

"Then the Nightmare is before us on the road!" Tombel gasped, looking up at the sinking sun.

"He is at least one daylight ahead of you, my Lord," answered Kyot. "My father's body was cold long before I dismounted."

"Where do you bury your father?" Tombel asked, looking past the litter along the broad and empty Greenway.

"My father was the Keeper of this tower. It was his wish to walk the Buryman's path as far as a true-aimed arrow will fly from the platform in the top of the tower. Once around the arrow we carry him, then back to the grave niche beside the great wooden door. This was carved out by the armorers long ago. Father will watch over us even in death. It is the custom."

"He was the greatest Archer in all Elundium," Tombel whispered as they walked around the spent arrow.

"And his grave niche will be set with one hundred silver arrows. He will not want for a bow-string nor oil to wet and supple the bow, it will be placed before him each daylight as the sun rises," whispered Kyot, blinking back the tears in his eyes. They had passed into the shadow cast by the tower and stood, heads bowed, before the grave niche. Carefully Kyot pulled back the blue and gold cloak that covered his father's body, lifted him off the litter and set him into the niche. The armorers moved forward and with swift strokes they hammered the silver arrows into the stone wall of the tower. Kyot knelt and kissed the tattoo mark on his father's arm.

"I will avenge your death, even though Nevian was against it," he whispered, pouring cedar oil onto the bow resting against Archer's shoulder.

"Will you take the Keepership if the King deems you fit to take such a post?" Tombel asked as Kyot rose and turned away from the grave.

"Nevian has already pledged me to it," Kyot answered as Sprint trotted forward neighing a greeting, "but first I will seek revenge on the Master of Nightbeasts, for he tortured my father to death."

"You would take the Keepership without the blessing of the King?" Tombel cried as Kyot sprang lightly into the saddle.

"No," answered the young Archer, his eyes hard with anger. "First I will seek out the Crystal Maker, Fairday of Clatterford, for he alone can forge glass arrowheads to pierce the Nightbeast's heart, and then, well-armed, I shall stand at Thane's right hand and rid this land of Krulshards. Only then, when the great Bow of Orm is silent, will I take the Keepership, King willing."

"Will you ride alone?" asked Tombel, searching the courtyard for signs of other Archers preparing for the road.

But Kyot only laughed and pointed out along the dusty Greenway towards Notley Marsh. "I have other friends, my Lord, who have helped me through great danger. Loyal friends who sleep lighter than a downy feather and are fearless in the dark. Look, here come the Border Runners who defended me against the Nightbeasts on the road to Underfall, they will help me to find Clatterford."

Tombel stepped hastily backwards as two huge savage dogs bounded into the courtyard and ran to Kyot's side. Turning towards Tombel, their hackles rose razor sharp along their backs and their lips curled in long-toothed snarls. Crouching, step by step, they advanced, hard amber eyes fixed on Tombel. "Be easy, Tombel is a friend," laughed Kyot, calling the dogs back to sit by his stirrups. "You see, my Lord," he smiled, reaching down to rub his hand through their thick sable coats, "I am better armed than I look!"

"Go, then, with my blessing, and follow the sun to Clatterford," shouted Tombel with an edge of relief in his voice after Sprint's receding hoofbeats.

The Marchers crowded into the courtyards of Stumble Hill, filling them to overflowing. "Rest until eventime. Eat and be ready for the road before the sun sets," called out Tombel.

"It is all so wonderful. The colors, the touch and feel, the smells, so wonderful; so much better than the Elder's stories!" Tombel turned and smiled, seeing Willow standing between the broken doors looking out across the flat grasslands that led towards the Granite City.

"Perhaps the stories would have held more color

if your Elder had seen the daylight!" laughed Tombel, moving to Willow's side and putting his hand upon the young Tunneler's shoulder.

"It is so much larger. So much . . . different!" Willow fell silent, remembering the Elder's stories; remembering how the old man would take the tiny point of light and carefully build the picture of a tree, branch by branch, leaf by leaf. His large, round eyes blinking, he gazed across the forest of trees that grew along the Greenway's edge and sighed; each one was so different in all its tiny details, and yet they were so much the same. He frowned, looking up at Tombel. "How many trees are there in Elundium?"

Tombel laughed, "They are all individual, Willow, because each one grows alone and wind and weather touch them differently. They are beyond counting."

Willow frowned, shading his eyes and pointing out beyond the trees. "There is a column of dust, my Lord, rising out of that dark valley beyond the road that we used. What can that be?"

"That is the direction of Notley Marsh," Tombel muttered darkly, drawing out his sword and calling the Marchers into battle order.

"Gallopers are on the road from the Marshes!" cried out a watchman from the tower platform. Tombel relaxed and waited easily between the doors as long columns of Gallopers rode into view.

"Nightbeasts have used the Marsh Road," Thoron cried, dismounting stiffly from Equestrius's saddle and grasping Tombel's arm in greeting.

"Equestrius!" Willow shouted, running forward and throwing his arms around the great Warhorse's neck.

Thoron laughed, "Guard him well, young warrior, for we ride a hard and dangerous road on the Nightbeast's heels."

Willow looked up at the proud lines of Warhorses that had halted behind Equestrius before turning back towards Thoron. "You have bridled him and put a saddle on his back," Willow cried. "I thought the Lord of Horses ran free with no man as his master!"

Thoron smiled, stretching stiffly. "No man will ever be master of Equestrius, his freedom is beyond question. We hunt the Nightbeasts together as friends; he wears Esteron's saddle and bridle to help an old man on a hard road. We found the tack in the hut of thorns beside a broken spear shaft. Thane must have fought a great battle there and littered the Greenway with many slain Nightbeasts before he escaped. We followed the Nightbeasts' footprints through the marshes; they were close on Thane's heels."

"How can you be sure he did escape them?" Willow asked.

Thoron reached up and unclipped a battered and dirty helm from the pommel of the saddle. "I found this helm beside the road in the marshes."

"Thane reached this Wayhouse!" Tombel interrupted, nodding in the direction of a huge bonfire that crackled in the evening air. "Those are the Nightbeasts that he slaughtered defending Archer in the last moments of the Keeper's life."

"Archer dead?" Thoron cried, seeing for the first time the grave niche beside the broken doors. "How so?"

"Krulshards, the Master of Nightbeasts," Tombel replied, honing the edge of his sword with a sharp stone attached to his belt.

"Which road did he take?"

Tombel silently pointed with the stone across the grasslands towards Woodsedge.

"Horsemen! We ride before the sun sets!" cried Thoron, summoning Errant to his side. He hurried to kneel before the grave niche. "We will make the Nightmare pay dear, friend," he whispered. "All those that love the morning light and soft shadows at noon will gather. You have my word!" Reaching forward he tipped a trickle of oil onto Archer's bow and then stood.

"Errant," he said quietly, taking him amongst the spelled horses, "will you turn north through the far edge of the black forest? I fear we run on too tight a road and may miss the Nightmare in our headlong dash for Granite City."

Errant lifted his head and called for Dawnrise in a loud voice above the clatter of hooves and jingling of harness along the horse lines. The first stallion of Underfall came forward, snorting, his steelsilver battle coat glittering in the evening light. Catching the reins Errant asked, "Will you run for me again on a darker wilder road than the one that leads to the gates of the Granite City? Will you take me out to the wildlands beyond the black forest?" Dawnrise stamped his hoof and snorted and waited for Errant to mount.

"I will take the Nighthorses of Underfall, for they were bred on the dark side of morning and gathered from all the wilder places. Thunderstone has readied them for such a gallop," Errant cried, calling all the Nighthorses and their riders into neat columns. "We ride beyond the Elundium of legends into wild lands where Nightbeasts crouch in every dark shadow!" Quickly he reached down and gripped Thoron's hand. "To a safe King and a land without Nightbeasts!"

Equestrius reared up, neighing fiercely and called forward half of the Warhorses that had traveled with Thoron through Notley Marsh. "The bonds were broken," he snorted to the old warrior, "but the Warhorses will follow Errant to fight for the sunlight."

Eagle Owl flexed his talons and hooted, rising up from Thoron's shoulder into the evening sky. "Battle Owls," he shrieked in piercing notes, calling all the owls that had survived the battle before the Gates of Night into a stoop that darkened the sky. "Fly with the warriors of Underfall and search out the way, be their eyes on the dark road ahead."

Wild barking broke out along the Greenway's edge as huge Border Runners bounded onto the road. Grannog, Lord of Dogs, crossed the Greenway to sit at Thoron's feet, yawned lazily, then licked his ancient hands.

"You will not be alone," cried Thoron, against the thunder of hoofbeats, as Errant led the horses across the Greenway and out into the grasslands beyond. Grannog growled softly and rose, wagging his tail, and led the Border Runners into the grasslands, fanning them out on either side of the columns of horses. Stoop by stoop the owls flew ahead, searching out the way.

"We will meet again in better daylights," cried Thoron, turning back into the Tower of Stumble Hill.

Tombel frowned, doubting Thoron's counsel as he marshalled the Marchers into readiness for the long night's journey ahead. Thoron sighed, taking Tombel's hand. "There was a time long ago when each of us trusted the other's second sight, and knew that wisdom tempered each move."

Tombel looked steadily into Thoron's eyes. "I fear for Elionbel. It weakens me and blinds my purpose."

Thoron drew Tombel close. "I fear for Thane, yet it strengthens my resolve and clears all other things aside. Lean on me now, old friend, put your hand upon my shoulder and let me lead you through the blindness."

"What would you counsel?" Tombel whispered, afraid that his Marchers would see his weakness.

Thoron drew Tombel out onto the Greenway

and pointed along the narrow road that led through
the grasslands. "If we come too late to Woodsedge
or the Granite City, Krulshards has all Elundium
in which to vanish. Spread your Marchers into a
great crescent twenty leagues wide. Take only one
column of your fastest men along the Greenway
and let my horsemen be spread throughout the
crescent in swift-moving squadrons. The Warhorses and the Border Runners that remain with
us are already moving in a wide crescent; follow
their wisdom."

Tombel squeezed Thoron's hand and saw the
wisdom in his counsel. "Thank you, old friend," he
whispered before calling for his captains to come
forward into a marshalling council.

Shortly after darkness had fallen the two old warriors climbed onto the platform in the Wayhouse
Tower and looked out over the wide crescent of advancing lights that now twinkled across the grasslands. "When the farthest lights reach the horizon
we will follow you," Thoron said, smiling at his
friend in the darkness.

"None will escape us!" Tombel whispered, his
foot upon the first step. "But ride hard and fast that
you may be at my side at Woodsedge," he called,
running down the tower's winding steps.

Thoron leaned out of the arched window and
looked down at his waiting column of horsemen beside the tower fretting for the road. "We will not
be far behind you," he cried. "You will see us, a

string of fast-moving lights shining out in the darkness. Look for the lights of our candles!"

"Kingspeed!" shouted Tombel from the Greenway as the tramp of marching feet faded into the night air.

The wound on Thoron's neck ached as he descended the tower stairway, dully throbbing with each footfall. "Kingspeed, Thane," he said, knowing that his grandson was all alone somewhere out there in the darkness.

On the Nightmare's Heels

"*GALLOP*, Stumble, gallop!" urged Thane, driving the little relay horse as hard as he dared, trying to catch up with Kerzolde. The gray hours had come, spreading cold mist between the close, crowding trees on either side of the road. Thane cursed the half-light; ghost tails fogged the Greenway, making him duck beneath low branches or jump fallen trees that suddenly appeared across the path.

"Nightbeasts have used this road," he shouted, looking at the damage all about him. Stumble suddenly lurched forward, crashing to his knees, sending Thane head over heels onto the wet grass. Thane grumbled and climbed to his feet. Taking the reins he put his foot back into the stirrup to remount but Stumble snorted with pain and backed away from him, his head nodding violently with each step. Thane slipped the reins over Stumble's head and bent down to pick up the horse's foreleg. The shoe had been partly torn away from the hoof and a jagged splinter of ironwood was embedded in the sole of the horse's foot. Thane gripped the splinter between his thumb and first two fingers and wrenched it free. Blood oozed from the narrow wound onto Thane's hand as he cleaned out the foot. Taking Stumble's fetlock between his knees he used his dagger to pry off the shoe, unbent the nails and tucked the twisted shoe into his belt.

"We will never catch Kerzolde now!" he muttered angrily, walking a few paces ahead into the mist. "Everything that I touch seems cursed with ill luck." Stumble limped painfully forward and brushed his mist-wet muzzle on Thane's cheek. Thane stroked Stumble's neck and gently pulled his ears. "Forgive me. I pushed you too hard and hurt you with my haste."

Stumble whinnied, pushed past Thane and limped on towards the Granite City. Thane called after him, calling him to stop. "I am pledged to chase the Nightmare. Love of Elionbel drives me forward, but you, great heart, need not follow this road. You are free to return to Stumble Hill or wander where you please in Elundium, but first give me your foreleg and I will plug the wound."

Stumble neighed, lifted his front leg and stood patiently still while Thane cut a strip of leather from the top of his ruined boot and forced it up into the wound. "That will keep the dirt out," he smiled, putting the foreleg back on the ground and running his hand through Stumble's mane. Stumble arched his neck and moved slowly forward, nodding his head each time he put the injured foot onto the ground. Thane quickly overtook him and walked at his shoulder. "You are a great warrior, Stumble, and a better friend than I deserve in these dark times."

Stumble forged ahead, biting on the bit, grinding his teeth against the pain. He fixed his eyes on the horizon's rim, looking for the sunrise. Thane bent low, searching the Greenway. "The Nightmare's prints have vanished amongst all these other foul Nightbeast tracks. All we can do is to follow the Greenway to the Granite City."

Stumble snorted and tried to lengthen his stride. "Easy!" whispered Thane, catching the rein and gently pulling him back to a slower pace. "Haste will cripple you forever, Stumble. I have caused you enough pain in bringing me this far, please walk carefully."

Stumble slowed his pace and the noon hour slipped quickly by before the giant mound of granite blocks that had once been the proud City of Granite Kings came into view. Thane paused, gazing in horror at the ruins. "It was so beautiful," he whispered, his hand tightening on the reins. He narrowed his eyes and stared at the devastation. "But there is a shadow around the base of the city. It is more solid than a dust haze and stiller than smoke." Frowning he muttered, "How can a ring of shadows form in clear sunlight? Look, the shadows are moving, spreading out across the field towards us!"

Turning, Thane searched the Greenway and saw

far behind him a single figure hurrying forward. "That must be Arbel. I wonder if he has seen the shadows yet?"

As the shadows drew closer they took on hideous shapes and Thane saw clearly what they were. "Nightbeasts!" he cried, looking around frantically for a place to hide. "Quickly, we will go to that copse of tangle-trees and brambles beside the road."

Together they disappeared between the close-grown tress, squeezing under their low branches, forcing a passage through the thick clumps of brambles, until, scratched and bleeding, they were completely hidden in the center of the copse. "Hush," whispered Thane, putting a bloody thorn-pricked finger to his lips. Stumble whinnied softly and knelt, his ears twisting in the direction of the coarse Nightbeast voices and the dry rattle of their armor as they passed all around them.

"Master rules now!" laughed a voice, its owner slashing at the tangle-trees with a hooked scythe.

"Everywhere will soon be covered in beautiful darkness," shouted another.

"Find and kill Thanehand!" roared a deeper voice. "He is somewhere on this road. Destroy the tangle-trees, search under every stone."

"Kerhunge has set watchers by the ruined gates. They will kill him if he slips by us!"

"Kill!" sneered another. "Master will hang him up beside the dirty Marcher woman he has captured and peel off his skin, layer by layer."

Laughter amongst the Nightbeasts turned into roars of delight.

"He will pull his nails out one by one!"

"He will nibble on his eyeballs!"

"Find the Galloperspawn!" screamed the deep voice, driving the Nightbeasts forward with a twelve-tailed whip that cracked at their heels. "Spread the darkness throughout Elundium."

The tangle-trees were being torn branch from branch; closer and closer the cruel curved scythes slashed through the undergrowth.

"Look! Look over there," snarled a Nightbeast voice less than two paces from where Thane and Stumble were hiding. "There is the Galloperspawn the Master seeks, running towards us along the Greenway. Quickly, set a trap and catch him alive, bind him tightly for our Master of Darkness."

The search through the copse of tangle-trees abruptly stopped and Thane bit on his knuckles, powerless to go to Arbel's aid as he heard the faint ring of steel and cries for help on the Greenway. He dare not reveal where he was hiding, he had little hope of helping Arbel against so many Nightbeasts. He must wait until the Nightbeast army had passed and then try to follow Krulshards. Yet the screams of Arbel's defeat burned in his ears and echoed long after he had been taken prisoner, and he felt wretched and cowardly hiding beneath a canopy of thorns.

Thane and Stumble crouched in statue stillness, hardly daring to take more than shallow breaths.

Only after late afternoon had pulled the shadows long did the last wave of Nightbeasts pass their hiding place. Gradually the dry rattle of their horrible armor faded and silence settled over the black trampled fields around them. Thane frowned and slowly rose from their hiding place. Why had the Nightbeasts not returned with Arbel towards the city? Where had they taken him? Krulshards had taken Elionbel from Woodsedge and from what the Nightbeasts had said he had her prisoner somewhere in the Granite City. Touching Stumble's mane he whispered, "We must tread carefully, there are watchers set by the gates."

Darkness had fallen and the night sky was sewn with a thousand stars before Thane and Stumble moved cautiously from shadow to shadow, working their way along the last league of the Greenway that led to the ruined gates. Far above them, on the summit of the hill, a sheer wall rose, blocking out the stars and within the wall a fierce light burned with the color of molten gold. "Look at Candlebane Hall!" Thane whispered. "It must still be held against the Nightmare. Look at that light!"

Thane laughed and stared hard at the roof of the Candle Hall; he blinked, shook his head and looked again. "Either the stonemasons have been busy or owls perched on the roof. We may yet have friends in this dark place."

The broken columns of the gate loomed before them. Thane listened to the night wind and caught the faint rattle of Nightbeasts' armor. Drawing the dagger he slipped down into the dyke beside the road. Following the wet bottom of the ditch he entered the shadows of the gate. The first watcher stood above him, silhouetted against the stars. Thane looked to the left and the right, but the second watcher was nowhere to be seen. Hand over hand he scaled the steep slope of the dyke, the long blade of his dagger gripped between his teeth. Near the top his foot slipped, sending broken granite chippings cascading down behind him.

"Who?" snarled the watcher, spinning around, his spear blade held out menacingly against the blackness of the dyke. "Galloperspawn!"

Thane rolled aside as the spear blade sank into the steep gravel slope beside his head. Reaching up he thrust the dagger, following the shape of the watcher's arm, keeping the blade parallel. He felt it slice through the thin armor beneath the armpit and sink deep into the heart.

"Galloperspawn!" the watcher cried again as Thane pulled the blade free. A noise behind Thane made him jump forward, away from a curving scythe that cut through the air just above his head. Turning he saw three watchers, two with spears drawn back ready to throw; the third was turning the scythe ready to strike again. Thane crouched and for the first time wished he had kept his grandfather's sword. Putting his free hand onto the ground he scooped up a fistful of granite chips and flung it at the watchers. Ducking to the left, the dagger held firmly with both hands, he rolled into a ball, expecting the watchers to pounce upon him but instead he heard piercing screams and the clatter of spear shafts falling onto the Greenway. He jumped up and saw the watchers struggling and clawing at three Battle Owls that had stooped out of the darkness to attack their faces. He leapt forward and three times he plunged the dagger.

"Thank you, owls!" he called softly as the Nightbeast watchers fell forward, faces torn and bleeding, onto the Greenway. "Quickly," he whispered, summoning Stumble out of the darkness. "There must be dozens of watchers. Follow me into the first circle of the city. I know all the secret ways."

Without a sound the owls hovered above the ruined gates, looking from left to right before they lifted up and away into the darkness as silently as they had come.

Together Stumble and Thane entered the city, picking their way carefully through the rubble-strewn streets.

" 'Ware the shadows!" Thane whispered, his eyes wide against the dark silence. "The Learning Hall once stood here," he whispered, touching the smooth broken door posts with his free hand. He tried to laugh, but it came out as a dry sound without humor, remembering that this was where it had all begun: the Loremaster and the Chancellors' sons hot on his heels for revenge.

"Oh, Nevian," he whispered, "I have failed the Granite King and brought nothing but ruin to this beautiful city. Help me now, Master of Magic, to find Elionbel, just as you once gave me justice here in this Learning Hall and made the Loremaster tell the truth. Help me now!" Running his hand through Stumble's mane he tried hard to push back the beginnings of despair. "We must search every lane and back alleyway, every dark corner and secret hole and if need drives us we must turn over every fallen block of stone, but we must find Elionbel!"

A long night of searching led them up through the ruined but empty circles of the city. Twice they hid behind huge slabs of stone as Nightbeast watchers passed them by, but they found nothing, not a whisper of Elionbel. Thane stood wearily looking up at the sheer granite wall of the inner circle.

"Too late, always too late!" he shouted, clenching his fist and striking it angrily against the wall. Sinking onto his knees he bowed his head and wept. "Whatever I touch, wherever I go, the Nightmare runs before me, destroying, ruining and taking. I am a curse of all Elundium!"

Thane drew his dagger and stared through his tears at the blade.

"Eversharp," Duclos had said; "when all hope fades then take out this blade." Thane gripped the hilt and waited. "Well," he sobbed at the darkness. "Where is hope? Gone before this Nightmare just like everything else." He laughed bitterly, and then turned the blade inwards towards his heart.

"Elionbel, I have failed. I know not where to look for you. The city is ringed with black, burned footprints, watchers walk in each ruined circle. Elionbel, oh Elionbel! This ruin is all my fault."

Thane pressed the point of the blade against the coarse weave of his undershirt and it cut through, bringing a small trickle of blood onto the blade. Stumble whinnied and lowered his head to push Thane's hand away.

"Tombel was right, I am not bloodworthy, I am not even brave enough to stand beside your brother, Arbel, and die like a man!"

Stumble neighed fiercely, forcing his head between the dagger and Thane's chest, pushing the blade away. Thane suddenly realized the bond which had grown between him and the little relay horse and, ashamed, he resheathed the dagger. He stroked the horse's ears and whispered, "Duclos was right. The dagger does bring hope and together we will hunt this Nightmare and make him pay dearly for what he has done!"

A soft voice laughed in the darkness, "Hope is the power that comes from within. It is the thread that weaves our fate and separates the weak from the strong."

"Nevian!" Thane cried, leaping to his feet and looking from left to right. "Nevian, where are you?"

"Enter the part of the city that the Nightbeasts could not defeat and we shall meet," whispered the voice.

Thane looked quickly about him, scrambling through the rubble. Somehow he had to scale the

wall. Stumble snorted, scraping at a Nightbeast
siege ladder that lay at the foot of the wall. "I'll
never be able to move it," Thane hissed, gripping
the top rung and pulling it away from the wall. It
moved quickly and lightly, bumping over the granite blocks, and tripped Thane over. Laughing, he
leapt to his feet and balanced the ladder, resting the
top rung near the rim of the wall.

"Stay hidden from the watchers and wait for
me," he whispered to Stumble, climbing hand over
hand into the darkness. Chill nightwinds tugged at
his ragged half-cloak making him shiver and he
pulled it tightly around his shoulders. Below him
in deep shadow the Candle Hall stood, the roof
crowded with a stoop of staring Battle Owls, but
the inner circle of the city was empty, nothing
moved. Thane stared along the inner curve of the
wall looking for a way down. Twenty paces farther
along the wall he could see the shadow of the narrow set of winding steps that led down to the cobbles.

"Stay well hidden," he called down to Stumble
before he ran lightly down the steps and crossed the
cobbles to the doors of Candlebane Hall.

"Nevian?" he called, entering the tall echoing
hall. "Where are you, Nevian?"

A soft light glowed on the high dais of the throne,
moving through all the hues and colors of a summer
afternoon.

"I am here, Thanehand, sitting at the feet of
Kings. Come to me." Thane crossed the smooth pol-

ished marble floor, frowning at the emptiness, and hurried between the high fluted columns of broken candle stems to the throne.

"Where are all the candles?" he asked. "This place was once so full of light it hurt your eyes to enter on a dark night."

Nevian laughed, taking Thane's hand and guiding him to sit on the empty throne. "The city has been siege-locked by the Nightbeasts, Thane, and it cost every candle for King Holbian to break the siege and rise triumphant against their shadows."

Thane frowned, "Break the siege? The city is weak and the King is gone, how can that be a triumph?"

Nevian smiled and turned to watch the gray hours flood the sky with cold dawn light. "Long ago, young man, when Elundium was new formed, Krulshards, the Master of Darkness, strove to steal my daylight. We both fought and argued, setting his Nightbeasts and Nightmares against my Warhorses and the Granite Kings until," Nevian paused, drawing the rainbow cloak over Thane's legs against the chill dawn winds, "until in haste I took King Holbian, the last Granite King, from the living rock wall before he was whole, before he was fit to be a King. He had a terrible flaw that I had overlooked. He feared the dark. Krulshards was quick to find his weakness and through it he has brought darkness and despair to all Elundium."

"Where is the triumph then?" demanded Thane.

Nevian laughed, clapping his hands together.

"Where is the King? That should be your question. Where is the last Granite King? Show me which corner he hides in."

Thane stared in bewilderment at the Master of Magic and answered, "Perhaps he lies crushed beneath the fallen tower."

Nevian's laughter faded. "He has gone, Thane. I know not where, but he overcame his fear of the dark and used every candle from this hall to keep back the Nightbeasts. He cheated Krulshards out of his victory and left him only ruin!"

"But the Nightbeasts are bringing darkness and ruin everywhere. Elionbel and her mother are with Krulshards!" Thane cried. "I heard the Nightbeasts talking about their victory while we hid from them in a clump of tanglewood trees. We only escaped capture when the Nightbeasts saw Arbel on the Greenway; they thought it was me."

Nevian sighed, putting his hands on Thane's shoulders. "Krulshards has gone, and the ruins of this city are nothing but a fool's victory. Revenge against you, Thane, ran him clear across Elundium to take Elionbel and fear of you, Thane, drives him onwards."

"Fear of me?" asked Thane. "How could the Nightmare fear me?"

"Because you do not fear his darkness. Thane, Krulshards has a weakness as great as King Holbian's; he has shown how his power is born of fear, of fearing the dark, but you fight amongst his Nightbeasts and brush his Nightmares aside. You enter the City of Night and bring light to all his secret places; you drove him out of the darkness. You are the beginning of a new age and he knows not how to fight you, save through revenge."

"Through Elionbel!"

"Yes, Thane, she has in many ways been your weakness, drawing you, luring you. Krulshards sees this and through her he will try and destroy you. He has Elionbel and her mother, Martbel, tied by his life thread. Harm him and the thread tightens around their throats choking them to death."

"How can I fight against this Nightmare? How can I ever rescue Elionbel?"

"I know not," whispered Nevian, "but you must follow in Krulshards's footsteps and find the way. You must follow your fate wherever it leads for all Elundium waits on your purpose."

Thane rose to his feet and gripped Nevian's hand. "I feel so weak and helpless against Krulshards and so afraid that I will fail."

"Yet you have trodden where only Kings can go and brought defeat to the very doors of night. Look to the morning, Thane, and find hope in the new daylight. Look for the Nightmare's shadow, for that is his greatest weakness."

"Everything I have touched the Nightmare has destroyed," Thane whispered, turning to face the beginnings of a new daylight.

"He is desperate, Thane, and sees his own ruin in you. You are the new Elundium that does not fear the dark. The power that will one day put an end to his Nightmares and his Nightbeasts."

Thane laughed bitterly. "You talk of power and Kings and yet I walk alone in the darkness with only a lame friend at my side. I have nothing with which to fight this Nightmare but the blade Duclos gave me at our parting on the lawns of Gilder-sleeves."

Nevian turned sharply, throwing the rainbow cloak across his shoulder, filling the Candle Hall with the light and beauty of a summer day. "You are a fool if you think that, Thane. Even now the armorers are hammering out hot iron on the anvil and the Warhorses, Border Runners and Battle Owls are fretting to fight the darkness. Come with me to the top of the wall and see if you strive alone."

Catching Thane's hand in his own, Nevian ran out through the Candledoors across the cobbles and up the narrow winding steps. "Look!" he commanded, throwing his arms open. Thane caught his breath and gazed out across the still, dark fields and hedgerows to the black horizon—everywhere there were lights, ribbons of slow-moving lights spread out in a wide crescent as far as he could see. Columns of faster-moving lights pressed through the crescent and raced up over the hillocks or vanished into small valleys only to reappear moments later.

"You are not alone!" Nevian laughed. "That is the vanguard of the army you led on the high plateau. They have marched and galloped without rest on your heels."

"They come too late. Too late to save the Granite City and too late to save Elionbel."

"It is your place to follow the Master of Nightbeasts, Thane. Tombel and your grandfather Thoron will turn the warriors and hunt the Nightbeasts throughout Elundium."

"Which way do I travel?" Thane asked, his foot on the top rung of the siege ladder.

Nevian looked to the horizon edge to where the sun was beginning to burn with a bright red fire. "Look in all the wild places where the sun does not shine. Follow the flight of the gray swans."

"Stumble is lame!" Thane called as he descended the ladder.

Nevian laughed, "I am the Master of Magic and I say he is sound and ready for the road!"

"You are a great power!" Thane answered, calling up into the gray morning light.

Nevian sighed quietly to himself, "I am but a shadow against your power, Thane, for in you there is a power that succeeds without magic." Thane reached the first rung of the ladder and jumped down onto the ground. Stumble whinnied and trotted to meet him.

"Nevian has touched you," Thane cried, seeing the horse moving soundly, "and he has taken the horseshoe from my belt without me seeing or feeling it go. He is truly a great magician."

"Follow the swans!" Nevian cried. "Hurry, hurry!"

"Which way?" Thane shouted, looking up at the rainbow coat flapping in the morning breeze.

Nevian lifted his hand and silently pointed towards the rising sun. Thane shaded his eyes and followed the hand, searching the dark horizon line, looking past the slow-moving crescent of lights.

"There, Stumble, just above the horizon. Look! There are two lines of dark shapes that beat the morning wind into a gale beneath their sweeping wingspans. Look at the gray swans!" Slowly the swans flew over the ruined city, their long slender necks and sharp orange beaks held out before them. Ogion, the leading swan whose feathers were the color of winter shadows, cried out in haunting notes of the Nightbeasts he had seen and the destruction that was spreading as a black tide across Elundium.

"Lead this warrior, Thanehand!" Nevian cried. "Show him the Nightmare's footprints."

Ogion flew low across the roof of Candlebane Hall, circling once around the Master of Magic. "Old legends foretell of this search for the Nightmare, Krulshards, they cry out bad omens that will lead us into silence. It would be our peril to help this warrior, Thanehand."

Nevian laughed, letting the rainbow cloak flow out in the wind the swans had stirred up. "He carries the fate of all Elundium in his sword arm and he cares nothing for ancient tales. He hunts the Nightmare, Krulshards, and greatly needs your sharp eyes to guide him."

Ogion circled again. "There would be nothing but despair in such a search," he hissed, turning towards the wildlands.

"The Battle Owls have perched upon this warrior's shoulders and Equestrius's son has let him ride upon his back; he would protect you and make all Elundium safe for your cygnets once Krulshards is dead."

Ogion hissed and turned back, swooping low across the place where Thane stood. Looking down he searched Thane's heart and found it full of sorrow and pain. "Why does he follow the Nightmare?" he asked, sharply.

"Because," whispered Thane, lifting his head, "because he has stolen everything I love, and destroyed everything I once held dear."

"Lead him to the Nightmare and all Elundium will be safe for you," urged Nevian.

Ogion circled again and flew low over Thane, calling out his name, before he turned away from the city. Thane sprang into the saddle and spurred Stumble to follow the vanishing swans. Ogion cried out Thane's name against the rising wind. Far, far ahead, not yet touched by the rising sun, he saw Krulshards's hurrying figure, the malice streaming out with his haste. Ogion beat his black wings faster, urging the horseman on.

A Council in Candlebane Hall

WEARILY Tombel reached the top of the siege ladder and offered an armor-gloved hand to Thoron as he climbed the last few rungs. Together they turned and looked out into the sunrise to see the jumbled wreck of the Granite City spread out below them.

"We have run hard to this defeat," Tombel muttered bitterly, watching the great crescent of lights stop at the outer edges of the city and let the faster-moving columns of Gallopers pass into the lower rubble-strewn streets.

Thoron turned and stared down into the empty inner circle, searching the shadows. "Something is out of place," he whispered, touching Tombel's arm. "There is no destruction beyond the wall. The Nightbeasts did not take the inner circle!"

"The Candle Hall doors are broken, and one of the Granite Towers has collapsed destroying the armory, but otherwise it is untouched," Tombel observed.

"Come," whispered Thoron, treading carefully

down the narrow steps. "There must be survivors of the siege, perhaps even the King. Perhaps they are hiding in Candlebane Hall."

The silence felt eerie and unnatural as their armored boots echoed on the cobblestones. Tombel unsheathed his broad Marching sword and Thoron drew his long Galloping blade as they came level with the doors of the Candle Hall.

"We came hard-riding to break the siege and free our King!" Tombel shouted.

"Come out into the new daylight!" Thoron cried, striding into the gloomy hall. The emptiness stopped him one pace inside the doors and he stared in disbelief at the broken candlestems and cold wax channels.

"Who in all Elundium," he hissed, "has dared to strip the Candle Hall of all its beauty and let the night overpower the light? Who?"

"Enter, warriors. Come forward, siege-breakers. The Candle Hall is yours!"

"Nevian!" Thoron cried, running forward across the polished marble floor. "We are come too late! The King has gone. Has Krulshards, the Nightmare, taken him?"

"What of Thane? He rode before us, that much we know from Stumble Hill and Tombel's son, Rubel, whom we found badly wounded at Woodsedge."

"Nevian, Nevian," Tombel cried, falling to his knees beside Thoron. "The Nightmare has Martbel and Elion. He took them in revenge from Woodsedge. We fear for them. Arbel is on the road with Thanehand, that much we know."

Nevian reached out his hands and laid them gently on Tombel's shoulders, letting the rainbow cloak fall in soft folds across the Marcher's back.

"Be at peace, my mightiest Captain," he whispered. "Elionbel and Martbel are safe for the moment. Krulshards will not kill them while Thane lives; he took them to lure Thanehand to his death. But of Arbel I know little more than you, only that the Nightbeasts overtook him on the road and took him prisoner."

"All my family are destroyed," cried Tombel, casting himself down onto the cold polished floor.

"Fate has played you hard, and even I, the Master of Magic, cannot change it," Nevian answered, helping Tombel to his feet.

"Come, come, my warriors," Nevian urged before he turned and climbed the high dais to the empty throne and sat down.

"Sit!" he commanded, pointing to the lower step. "Sit and listen and grow wise. I do not make your fates, nor choose which ones should come forward. At the Bondbreaking you both stood before me, raw-boned and young, the survivors of that great battle on the Causeway road and to each of you I gave a task. Thoron, through earlier deeds, was to ride the Warhorse, Amarch, and thus travel into legends as the last Errant rider of the Granite Kings. It cost you much, dear friend: the loss of Amarch and the Lord of Owls, Silverwing, but still you served me well and kept hope in men's hearts during the dark years, riding the lonely Greenways at my bidding."

Turning to Tombel Nevian smiled. "Yours was the more difficult task, the Keepership of Woodsedge, which became with the passing suns a place that the Nightbeasts might attack, but more than that, the keeping and remembering of all the Lore of Elundium; that was a heavy burden for even the bravest Marcher Captain."

"And I did not fail you, my Lord," Tombel cried, his face flushed and angry. "Although I have lost everything, I did not fail you. I remembered every jot of Lore."

"No, you did not fail me," Nevian whispered, "but on that lonely road you lost your way and found more in men's deeds than you did in the men themselves. The glitter of glory blinded you and the shock and crash of battle deafened your ears."

Tombel hung his head and replied, "I strove to serve you, Lord, and keep pure all the Lore you taught me."

Nevian smiled and leaned forward. "If that is so, which is the greater man—he who lights the way in the darkness or he who carries the King's standard into battle?"

Tombel frowned. "Only a king can choose who carries the standard!"

"But the man who pays for the candle chooses the Candleman. King Holbian chose Thane's father to carry the emblem that is now furled at your side.

He carried the standard of the owl in blue and gold and on his death the King laid him across this throne as honor to all he had done lighting the way in a dark world."

"Then I judged Thane wrongly," Tombel whispered.

"No! You only judged him blindly. There was no malice or greed, just blindness."

Tombel turned to Thoron, with tears in his eyes, and took his hand. "My loss will be ten thousand times worse if I lose your friendship for the way I treated Thane and how I spoke to you on the high plateau."

Thoron smiled and gripped his friend's hands. "When the Nightmare is dead and Elionbel and Martbel are safe home then you can welcome Thane into your house, that will be enough."

Nevian smiled and clapped his hands, shaking folds of the rainbow cloak to fill the Candle Hall with a bright light.

"Now to more pressing matters—to King Holbian and the Nightmare, Krulshards. Two nights ago I entered the Granite City, secretly passing through the Nightbeast ranks up towards the sheer granite wall you scaled to reach this hall. I saw the Granite Tower tremble and collapse and in the dense stonelike fog that hung over the city I entered the Candle Hall and defended it against the Nightbeasts, lighting the sky with a blinding light of blue and gold."

"The King," Tombel asked. "Where was the King?"

"In the morning light I searched the summit of the city but the King and all the city folk, high and low born, had vanished. It was empty."

"Perhaps they are beneath the tower," Thoron ventured, looking darkly at the mound of granite blocks heaped up beyond the Candledoors.

"No. I have searched amongst the rubble and the King has gone. All I know is that he overcame his fear of the dark and sent the light of this hall out against the Nightbeasts."

"When did Krulshards reach the city?" Tombel asked. "Were we far behind him?"

"He was one daylight before you, hard-pressed and desperate for victory."

"We will follow the Nightmare now without rest and rescue Martbel and Elionbel," Tombel said, honing his sword on the sharp stone that hung from his belt.

"No!" answered Nevian firmly. "Thane is on the Nightmare's heels, guided by Ogion the gray swan. Your purpose is to turn the warrior army you led to this city and hunt the Nightbeasts through all Elundium."

"But Thane is only one man. How can he destroy Krulshards?"

"Who followed Krulshards into the City of Night to rescue Thoron and bring him out into the light? Who else can face the darkness of Krulshards?"

Tombel stood silently, looking down at the polished marble, seeing clearly his weakness reflecting back.

"Kyot was with Thane, and Willow the Tunneler led them both to the high chamber where I hung," Thoron answered quietly. "Only they have the power to face the darkness."

"But Thane is alone," cried Tombel. "Kyot is riding to Clatterford to seek Fairday the Crystal Maker."

Nevian smiled. "Let them follow their fates, just as you must follow yours. Marshal the warriors and turn the crescent back into Elundium."

A movement between the doors of the Candle Hall turned Tombel's head and he laughed aloud. "Willow, Willow, come forward and meet the Master of Magic. Come and meet Nevian."

Willow shyly crossed Candlebane Hall, his eyes full of the beautiful colors in the rainbow cloak. Kneeling at Nevian's feet he touched the hem of the cloak and said, "It is so much more beautiful than the Elder's stories—the colors! The light!"

Nevian reached down and took Willow's hand. "The Elder only saw the light of the pictures I painted in the darkness of the City of Night, but he had a great power, for he remembered every leaf and branch and subtle shade I showed him, and in his turn he painted the pictures for you."

"He named me after the willow tree, my Lord," Willow answered, looking up into the face of the magician.

Nevian smiled, "And he named you well, for you

will put firm roots into the soil of Elundium and be a blessing to its people."

"Lord," Willow asked, hesitating. "Was this once a beautiful city? Only I felt it in the bones of the land beneath the piles of rubble as I climbed up to this hall."

"It was the jewel of Elundium, Willow, built by King Mantern, the last Mason King before the Granite Kings arose. But why do you ask?"

"We have labored, Lord, for time beyond counting in the darkness. Let us celebrate our freedom by rebuilding this city out of the rubble. Let us use our skills, learned through torture and pain, to raise the fallen Granite Tower sheer and beautiful up into the sunlight!"

Thoron laughed, and Eagle Owl, who had sat silently so far on his shoulder, hooted at the sunlight, and Tombel lifted Willow up onto his shoulders.

"It will be fit for a new King, and more beautiful than before!" Nevian cried, leading the way out into the sunlight and up the winding steps to the top of the wall.

"Each house and hall, each lane and winding alleyway, will grow up out of the ruins, you have our word on it," Willow laughed.

"And you have my word that Elundium will be cleared of Nightbeasts!" Tombel said grimly, turning towards the siege ladder.

Thoron gripped Nevian's hand in parting. "The sword is ready and honed to a razor's edge. Eagle Owl is perched, and eager to carry it!"

"Eagle Owl will hear the call," Nevian whispered, taking the hilt of the sword and drawing it from its sheath. "But age has weakened the blade. Look how it chips and nicks against the granite wall."

Nevian handed back the sword. "Find Durondell, the Armorer, show him the blade and he will reforge it strong enough to shatter stone."

"Durondell is a legend!" Thoron answered. "How can you find such a thing?"

Nevian smiled. "If he has become a legend you must find the truth that the legend grew from and there have the blade reforged. Go now with the new morning and seek the forge of Durondell."

Willow stood beside Nevian and, taking the magician's hand, he watched the crescent of Marchers, Gallopers and Archers slowly turn and spread out across the fields below the city. The Warhorses and the Border Runners fanned out beyond the farthest points of the crescent, running hard on the Nightbeasts' heels, following them into the wildlands where the people of Elundium seldom went.

Nevian sighed as if a great task had been completed and smiled down at Willow.

"The future of Elundium has gone beyond my sight but Fate will weave its webs and show us all its twists and turns in the fullness of time. Evening Star will come to you when the city is nearly rebuilt. She will bring her foal to the gates. Be ready for that day; be ready to ride and take only a stone searcher in your hand."

"Will I ride on Evening Star?" asked Willow, looking up into Nevian's face.

"She will carry you," Nevian cried, the rainbow cloak fading as the sun passed behind towering rain clouds, "and she will take you to the ends of the world!"

Doubts in the Fortress of Underfall

ESTERON fretted and pulled at the hay piled in the manger. Mulcade sat statue-still upon the king post beam and watched. Merion the Healer was fussing at the ugly wound in the horse's side, touching the fine gold threads he had sewn across to draw the edges together after removing the Nightbeast spear blade.

"Many daylights' rest yet," he sang in a high-pitched voice. "But you will be as good as new."

Esteron snorted, his ears flat against the sides of his head, and struck out impatiently at the stable wall.

Merion turned his head, making a disapproving sound with his tongue.

"Patience will heal the wound—bad manners will split it open again!"

Esteron neighed, shaking his head from side to side.

"How long, Healer?" Thunderstone asked, opening the stable door and giving Esteron a sugar slice he had kept. "How long?"

"Many daylights, Lord, perhaps even a season or at most a sun. The spear blade had severed more than just flesh and the long road back to us only worsened the wound."

Thunderstone sighed, taking Esteron's head into his arms; a season had passed already and he feared for Thane's safety as he stood silently in the straw, worrying. His fingers moved beneath the heavy blue cloak he wore and touched the summer scarf, feeling the fine needlepoint Elionbel had sewn with silver and gold threads. The picture of the sun seemed almost to burn the tips of his fingers. "We will keep it safe for his return," he whispered, "for it brings old legends to life."

"Old legends, my Lord?" asked Merion, rummaging in his sack for an oiled cotton to dab at the wound. Thunderstone had forgotten Merion and his voice startled him.

Gruffly he answered, "Don't you remember, old fool? The saying, 'And his standard shall light the Causeway Field and it will be the sign of the new King.'"

Merion smiled blankly at Thunderstone, turned and pressed the oiled cloth to the wound.

"Fool!" muttered Thunderstone, leaving the stable and climbing to the highest gallery to clean the wick in the great lamp. Winter would soon be on them and still there was no word. What was happening beyond the Causeway Field and the dark trees of Mantern's Forest? What had happened to the great army Tombel and Thoron had led towards the Granite City? Closing the lamp he paced the gallery, watching the shadows lengthen as the sun dropped towards World's Edge.

"What news?" he shouted as he passed the watching chair.

"News, Lord?" answered Tiethorm, startled back to wakefulness. "Nothing but the whisper of the wind through the grasses of the Causeway Field and the murmur of doves on the high roof slates. The Greenway is an empty road, my Lord."

Across the Grasslands to Clatterford

*K*YOT followed the sun, but no matter how hard he pressed Sprint the sun overtook him each daylight and sank in a ball of fire beyond World's Edge.

At evening time Sprint slowed at a touch on the rein and began to look for a place to rest. Kyot nocked an arrow onto the string and slipped noiselessly from the saddle, his eyes fixed on a grassland hare. The arrow sang, the hare twitched and cried out just once as the steel blade struck it down.

"Supper!" Kyot shouted, sending the two huge Border Runners out through the long grass to pick up the hare. Darkness had fallen before Kyot had built a ring of dead wood in readiness against the Nightbeasts and lit a fire in the center to cook his supper. Sprint stood close to the fire, his saddle lying on the ground as a pillow for Kyot.

"Elundium has limitless horizons," Kyot said, pointing a nibbled hare bone out past the watchful dogs, back from their own hunting, into the darkness. "No matter how far we travel the sun still seems just as far away. I always thought that World's Edge was just beyond the horizon, and that Clatterford would be less than a day's ride away."

Sprint snorted, pulling at the rough grasses within their ring. Rockspray hooted and lifted off Kyot's shoulder to hunt his supper in the darkness beyond the firelight, while the dogs yawned and settled down on either side of Kyot. He arranged six arrows in a makeshift arrow stand, their points thrust lightly into the ground a hand's reach beyond the saddle, but the seventh arrow he nocked onto the bow, and thus armed he settled back, his head resting against the saddle, and tried to sleep. Beyond the firelight the grasslands rustled in the soft night breezes. Rockspray hooted once and was silent. Sprint snorted and moved a pace in search of better grazing. Kyot opened his eyes and looked up at the stars. He felt so small, so tiny, so alone; a mere speck in the wild dark grasslands that stretched away in every direction towards the flat black horizon. He shivered, pulled his cloak up around his ears and tried again to sleep but sleep would not come.

"We have been traveling for twenty daylights," he sighed, sitting up, "and nobody can tell us where

Clatterford is." Kyot remembered grimly how the villagers from whom he had asked the way had closed their gates against him and how they had thrown sharp stones to drive away the dogs. Only twice had he been coldly welcomed inside the deep-dyked barricades and given bad meat to eat and a rough place to sleep. "Clatterford!" the villagers had sneered, "is a legend from the time of Kings that once kept the land safe from Nightbeasts. From a time that only old men remember, when we tilled the land and gathered fruit without looking over our shoulders in fear. A curse on all Kings!"

"There will be a new King!" he had shouted back. "The Nightbeast army runs before the warriors of Elundium!" But the villagers had only laughed at him, pulling their high barricades shut against the world they feared.

Sighing, Kyot sank back against the saddle and closed his eyes. The warm smell of cured oiled leather filled his nose and the soft sable fur of the dogs on either side finally helped him drift off to sleep. Sprint snorted a quiet greeting to Rockspray as the owl stooped silently down onto the high cantle of the saddle to sit out the watches of the night.

Unblinking, he stared into the darkness just before the dawn and watched a shadowy figure move towards them. Slowly he unhooked his talons and spread his wings, his beak half open, to call a warning, but two eyes looked into his; dark eyes that held the secrets of twilight, clear eyes that were strong enough to bid him to be still and give no warning. Sprint snorted and turned his head, letting a neigh of rage turn to a soft whinny of greeting, the dogs looked up and bared their teeth in silent snarls.

"Be still," whispered a gentle voice. Sprint pricked his ears, letting Eventine, the daughter of Fairday of Clatterford, stroke his shoulder as she knelt beside Kyot and took the sixth arrow from its place in the earth beside the saddle. Reaching back into the quiver she replaced it with one of her own arrows.

Smiling down at Kyot she whispered, "My father is more than just a whispered legend; and he has waited overlong for the Archer who carries the Bow of Orm. Keep faith in your heart and you will find us. Follow the sun to Clatterford."

Kyot murmured in his sleep and turned on the hard earth. Eventine stepped back hastily into the shadows away from the fire's glowing embers, then sprang lightly over the ring of kindling sticks and disappeared into the growing dawn light.

Kyot yawned, stretching his arms beneath the cloak and rose stiffly to his feet. The chill dawn had coated the grasslands with a fine layer of hoarfrost and the morning was rich with the smell of autumn. "Beautiful! This is beautiful!" he said, looking at the fine threaded patterns the frost had spread onto the blades of grass, marvelling at the jeweled lace in the spiders' webs that bent before the early breezes.

"We ride with the sun," he laughed, stooping to

pick up the saddle, but instead of taking the saddle he stared foolishly at the small footprint, slender and delicate, imprinted in the crisp grass a hand's span from where he had slept.

Falling to his knees he touched the print. "By Nevian!" he whispered, standing and looking out beyond the kindling wood to where other prints in the frost led in the direction that he was about to travel. Frowning, he collected his arrows and returned them to the quiver. The sixth felt different, the shaft was smoother and the goose feather flight had a different shape to it. Rubbing the dirt from the blade on the edge of his cloak he gazed at a slender glass blade that burned with a white fire, catching all the glory of the morning sun.

"There is magic here!" he whispered, turning the arrow cautiously in his hand. "I did not take this arrow from the armory of Stumble Hill and I did not push it into the ground last night before I slept." Sprint neighed and Rockspray hooted, nodding his head backward and forward. Kyot slipped the arrow into his quiver then quickly saddled and bridled Sprint.

"Something must have come with the arrow in the night," he muttered, putting his foot into the stirrup and mounting. "Run, Sprint, and take us away from this magic place. Run!"

Sprint neighed and took the bridle, cantering fast across the grassland, following the frosty footprints. All day Kyot rode Sprint hard, putting as many leagues as the little horse could run between them and their last resting place. He avoided a small cluster of houses ringed by a deep dyke, keeping well away from their harvest fields, galloping Sprint into a white lather until the houses had disappeared behind them in the noonday haze and they were once more alone. Fear had made him edgy and he jumped at shadows and noises in the long grass, loosing two arrows foolishly at rising skylarks. As the sun began to sink towards evening time Sprint's head hung wearily forward. Kyot dismounted and took the reins over the horse's head. "Let us find a place, somewhere safer than last night, a ridge or a hill, somewhere that I can defend."

Rockspray lifted off his shoulder and searched far ahead, rising up on warm draughts of evening air. Hovering, he saw below black shapes moving through the long grasses, encircling a small hamlet of stone houses. He shrieked a warning, flying low across the weatherslated roofs. His cry spread panic through the crowded streets as animals and children were herded into safety, doors were slammed shut, bolts were shot and windows shuttered.

The Nightbeasts broke cover. Roaring and screaming they stormed the wattle-woven walls of defense, smashing them down. Soon they were swarming through the streets.

Kyot had heard Rockspray's cry and remounted Sprint. "Run!" he cried, "the Nightbeasts are here before us."

Riding hard through a gap in the broken wall

Kyot nocked arrow after arrow onto the string and the great Bow of Orm sang with a clear voice in the evening light, destroying the Nightbeasts. Again and again the Border Runners leapt at the monsters' throats. Twice Kyot thought he heard the voice of another bow but he had no time to look behind or to the left or right. Before him the last three beasts towered; reaching into the quiver his fingers closed on the strange arrow. Aiming at the center beast he loosed the arrow and it sang through the air, exploding with a flash of blinding light against the Nightbeast's chest. Kyot reached for another arrow but before he could take aim, or the dogs tear them down, the two other Nightbeasts had fallen with arrows in their throats. Kyot pirouetted Sprint, searching each street; he galloped out into the grasslands and circled the hamlet, but he was alone. Slowly the doors opened and the villagers came forward.

"Who has a bow?" he shouted. "Where is the Archer who fought at my side?"

"Lord," answered a white-haired elder, "if the arrowheads be made of glass then it was the Lady of Clatterford."

"Lady of Clatterford?" Kyot whispered as he knelt and examined the arrows in the fallen Nightbeasts. The blades were smooth as ice and reflected the evening sunlight. Paling, he slowly stood up. "Tell me of this Lady of Clatterford. Where may I find her?"

The elder spread his hands. "Lord, she is nowhere—and yet she is everywhere. She is the light in the morning and the soft sun in the evening. She is beauty beyond a whisper and she keeps us safe from the roving bands of Nightbeasts."

"Rockspray warned you, and I rode to your defense," Kyot answered, an edge of anger in his voice. "Where is this Lady of Clatterford? Does she have a name?"

"Lord, greatly we thank you. Our lives are in the palm of your hand. Take anything you desire. We are now yours to clean the arrowheads and oil the bow, but we cannot show you the Lady of Clatterford for she is her own mistress and she goes where she pleases."

Kyot laughed, taking both the elder's hands and pulled him to his feet. "I want nothing but the way to Clatterford. I seek nothing but to kneel at the feet of Fairday, the Crystal Maker."

"But Lord, we owe you our lives!"

Kyot looked past the elder at the rough stone houses and the mean, worn streets. "Does the Lady of Clatterford own this village? Are you in her keeping?"

"Lord, she takes nothing but the grains of corn we leave in a dish at the village edge."

"How can you offer me more than you offer the Lady of Clatterford?" Kyot questioned.

"She has never stood before us, as you have, my Lord, but if she did all she desired would be laid at her feet."

"I will take nothing from you, elder, for I have

seen the beauty of Elundium and that is riches enough."

Kyot gathered the reins and remounted Sprint. "I bid you a night free of shadows," he cried as Sprint took the bridle and headed out into the grasslands.

"Stay with us and honor our village!" cried the elder, as Kyot, with the Border Runners on each side, passed through the dyke.

"There is no time!" he shouted back. "I must find Clatterford. But I will return when the Nightmare is no more."

Kyot rode without ceasing until the lights of the village had vanished far behind him. Slowing Sprint to a walk he dismounted and found a place they could rest, a slight mound of bare earth that rose above the grassland, surmounted by a single gnarled hawthorn tree. Setting his remaining four arrows, points deep, into the ground he sat and waited, watching the darkness.

"Stay close," he whispered to Sprint. "Be my eyes lest I should sleep," he asked Rockspray, stroking the smooth brittle horn of his talons.

Rockspray hooted and ruffled his chest feathers as Kyot slipped from wakefulness into sleep. Eventine smiled in the darkness of the grasslands and silently climbed to the top of the mound; there she knelt at Kyot's side and quickly took two arrows from her quiver and exchanged them, pressing the glass points firmly into the ground. Laughing to herself she placed a small wooden bowl at his feet, filling it with a small mound of uncooked grain.

"It is his share of the payment from the village," she whispered to Sprint, kissing the velvet-smooth skin of his muzzle. Reaching out to the Border Runners she playfully pulled their ears. "Guard my Archer well, and bring him safely to Clatterford," she whispered before leaving as quietly as she had arrived.

Kyot stretched out feeling the early warmth of the morning sun touch his face. Opening his eyes he looked down at the arrows he had fixed into the ground and smiled. "You have great magic, Lady of Clatterford."

He took her arrows out of the ground and rubbed the damp earth from their smooth glass blades. "Magic enough to silence even you, Rockspray, a sharp-eyed Lord of Owls, and brave enough to risk your hooves, Sprint, and the teeth of two savage dogs."

Sprint snorted, rubbing his head against Kyot's arm, and Rockspray ruffled his feathers and hooted quietly, his eyes half closed. Kyot sighed, collected the other two arrows and rose to his feet. Looking at the base of the mound he saw small cloven hoofprints that led away into the grasslands.

Kneeling, he examined the prints and measured their stride. "She rides a great beast! Come," he called to Sprint. "Today we will follow the Lady of Clatterford."

Sprint lifted his head, smelled the morning breeze and snorted in alarm. Rockspray lifted from Kyot's shoulder and shrieked a warning. Kyot turned and ran quickly to the top of the mound. He gazed out across the grassland, shading his eyes against the morning sunlight. "Nightbeasts!" he hissed, quickly counting the line of dark shapes running towards him as he saddled Sprint. "Follow the lady's hoofprints!" Kyot whispered, mounting and urging him forward. "We do not have enough arrows to stand and fight."

Sprint cantered down the mound, kicking over the wooden bowl that Eventine had left. In his haste to flee from the Nightbeasts Kyot saw the grains of wheat scatter across the ground and laughed. "This will be our cornfield, Lady, and we will harvest it for the village in better times. Now, run, Sprint, run!"

Sprint bounded forward, galloping hard to catch his shadow as the grasslands swallowed them up. Only at noon did Kyot slow the horse to a trot and stood on the saddle looking back at the distant line of Nightbeasts. He could see that they were blind to him in the noonday glare by the way they beat the tall grass with their spear blades and cruel hooked scythes.

"We must run again," he whispered to the Border Runners, "but I will run beside you for as many leagues as I can, as they are spread wide to catch us and follow close on our scent. There is no way but forward."

Sprint neighed and waited while Kyot tied the reins in a knot. Rockspray took to the air and stooped on the line of Nightbeasts, tearing off two sets of wolfskin eye shields before Kyot called him back. "Stay with us, Lord of Owls, and fight beside us when we can run no farther. Fly ahead now and find us a place where we can face the Nightbeasts with the dying sun on our shoulders. A hill or a mound where Father's bow can sing out against the darkness."

Rockspray lifted silently and flew far ahead. Sprint, Kyot and the dogs followed, running side by side, heads bent in effort, over the rough grassland. Behind them the line of Nightbeasts lengthened their stride and gradually, as the afternoon wore into evening, they closed the gap between them. Kyot could hear them now, roaring and screaming just behind him. Sprint flattened his ears and rolled his eyes in fear, the dogs turned, hackles up, ready to fight. Rockspray stooped out of the late afternoon sky to the cantle of the saddle, hooting about the place that he had found.

"Follow, follow," he shrieked, rising up and hovering just above Kyot's head. Kyot looked up and saw through the long grasses a long low mound of bare-trodden earth. Running to the base of the mound he reached back into his quiver and nocked one of the Lady's arrows onto his bow. Six labored strides took him to the top and there he stopped, the arrow resting lightly against the bow, and stared with wide eyes at the neat rows of arrows, ready-pressed into the earth to form a makeshift arrow stand.

"The Lady of Clatterford is with us!" he cried, taking arrow after arrow from the stand and loosing them into the advancing line of Nightbeasts.

Rockspray stooped at their eyes, ripping and tearing at their wolfskin shields, the dogs leapt at the Nightbeasts' throats, tearing them down and Sprint turned, rearing and plunging through the broken enemy line.

Behind them, beyond the mound, a shadow crossed the low evening sun, making Kyot pause and turn his head. Laughing, he raised his bow hand in salute.

"I thank you, Lady of Clatterford," he cried, watching for a moment as the mighty stag she rode halted and lifted its crown of sweeping antlers up towards the first evening stars. "I thank you, Lady!" he cried again, looking at the slender figure in the flowing cloak that held a bow as large as the great Bow of Orm.

"Follow me to Clatterford!" she called in a voice that cut through the Nightbeasts' screams. "Follow me when the last arrow has found its mark!" She urged her mount forward and vanished amongst the tall grasses.

Rockspray stooped roughly to Kyot's shoulder and dug his sticky blood-soaked talons through his cloak, shrieking a warning that the last swarm of Nightbeasts were crouching at the base of the mound. Kyot shook his head, scattering the mem-

ory of Eventine's beauty, and set about destroying
the remaining Nightbeasts. He could smell their
foul odor and see the scales of their armor rattling
and swaying as they breasted the mound. He loosed
arrow after arrow until only one beast was still
rushing forward. Taking the last glass arrow he
knelt and released it, turning his head from the
blinding flash of light as the blade sheared through
the armored scales, shattering the breastbone.

"Die, Nightbeast!" he shouted as the arrow strike
forced the beast backwards, tumbling it to the bottom of the mound. Kyot rose slowly from his knees
and looked out across the heaps of Nightbeast dead
into the silent empty twilight. "We have won!" he
whispered to Rockspray, ruffling the owl's chest
feathers. Sprint snorted, the dogs barked as they
picked their way through the Nightbeast carcasses
and wearily climbed the mound.

"We will follow the Lady!" he laughed, clipping
the Bow of Orm onto the saddle, and led Sprint
down off the mound in the direction she had taken.

Midnight slipped by unmarked before the Border
Runners led Kyot and Sprint through the edge of
the grasslands and passed unheralded into Clatterford. Kyot yawned and stopped, sniffing at the
night air; kneeling he touched the ground, feeling
the difference in the length and texture of the grass.
"Hush!" he whispered, putting his finger to his lips
and listening to the night.

Rising to his feet he looked across a rolling moonlit landscape that stretched away to a dark horizon of tall trees. "This must be Clatterford. Smell the new-mown grass and listen to the Nightingales."

Turning his head he heard the noise of shallow water rushing over gravel. "There must be a stream close by. Come, we will find it and rest there until the new sun rises."

Sprint nickered and trotted off into the darkness. Kyot wearily followed the noise of the stream, which grew louder with each step he took, until he came to the bank. He slipped down and drank deeply, splashing the crystal-cold water onto his face and hands. It tasted better than the wine of Stumble Hill and slightly sweeter on his tongue. Smiling, he dried his hands and settled back against the bank. Thinking of the Lady's beautiful face silhouetted against the setting sun he fell into a trouble-free sleep.

After sunrise Sprint roughly woke him by snorting fiercely into his face. Rockspray perched at his side, preening his feathers. Sitting up, Kyot stretched, yawned, then quickly dropped his arms to his sides and scrambled to his feet. "We are at Clatterford!" he hissed, brushing his fingers through his hair and trying to straighten his travel-stained jerkin and cloak.

"Welcome to Clatterford!" called out a voice from beyond the stream.

Kyot looked out across the stream towards a hall of glowing crystal set amongst neat lawns and flow-ered walkways. Bright-colored peacocks strutted

on the lawns, and between the flowers that swept
down in neat rows to the water's edge and filled the
morning with a heavy scent. Upon the first step of
the Hall of Clatterford stood a tall, white-haired figure dressed in robes of pale sky-washed blue.

"Welcome," he called again, beckoning to Kyot
to come across the stream to the hall. "There is a
ford," he said, pointing away to Kyot's left.

Kyot followed the stream and turned down an
avenue of tall yew trees; he came to the ford and
heard a roar and thunder of two waterfalls that
guarded the dark entrance to the lawns. Covering
his ears against the noise he crossed, nimbly jumping from stone to stone, and stepped up onto the
close-mown grass. The peacocks shrieked in warning and, shaking out their feathers into brilliant
glowing patterns, they watched his every step as
they flanked him in escort to the doors of Clatterford.

Kyot reached out a hand and touched the wall beside the doors, running his fingertips across the
smooth transparent crystal. He bent down and
stared in wonder at the glass, forgetting the impatient peacocks on either side and Fairday, the Master of Clatterford, waiting a few paces farther on.

A hand on his shoulder made him jump and turn
in confusion to face his journey's end. "Lord," he
cried, falling onto his knees. "My father bid me
bring you grave news. I was to tell you that the
Nightmare, Krulshards, is once more loose in

Elundium and that I need new arrowheads to pierce the darkness."

Fairday smiled down at Kyot and reaching out, he took hold of his hands and turned them over. "You have the hands of an Archer and, I am sure, the heart to match them. But why do you seek these arrow blades?"

Kyot looked up, his eyes clouding with anger. "The Nightmare tortured my father to death and took his hands. I seek the Nightbeast, Krulshards, in revenge."

Fairday laughed with a sound of silver touching crystal and pulled Kyot to his feet. "There are no glass arrows for revenge. Steel is a better blade for that. Steel is hard, cold and unfeeling."

"Steel will not enter the malice the Nightmare wears, only light trapped in the glass can harm him. Nevian taught me that on the night my father died."

Fairday turned and took Kyot's hand and led him into the gardens. "I would load your quiver to over-flowing to fight against the Nightmare but not one spine or blade will I give you to use in revenge." Stopping, he turned sharply and looked deeply into Kyot's eyes. "Archer does not want your revenge. He would curse you for it. He chose to stand against the Nightmare and keep pure his pledge. He sent you to carry his burden, not to add to it."

Kyot frowned. "What was his burden?"

"To guard the daylight, that was his burden, just as it was every Wayhouse Keeper's task. But the

Tower on Stumble Hill stands at the great cross-roads and is the first Wayhouse against the dark-ness, that is why Nevian gave your father the Bow of Orm and one quiver of glass-bladed arrows from my forge. Now all the arrows are spent, that is why your father sent you, full grown, to stand in his place, clear-eyed against the darkness. He would not have wanted this revenge that you carry."

Fairday laughed. "Come, my young warrior. Eat, drink and rest away your troubles. We will talk more on this at supper time and clear your heart for the task ahead."

He clapped his hands and summoned the white-robed servers out onto the lawn. "Tend to your guest," he commanded. "Give him everything he desires for he is Kyotorm, the new Keeper of the Tower at Stumble Hill."

Kyot turned and stared at the Crystal Maker. "How do you know my name and where I come from?"

Fairday smiled. "It was foretold long ago that the Bow of Orm would one daylight come to Clatter-ford and long have I waited. The Nightmare thought he took the hands of the greatest Archer in all Elundium, but malice and hatred blinded his purpose. Kyot, you are the best Archer in all Elundium, full grown beyond your father's power, and I knew you long before you crossed into Clat-terford. With the first rumor of Nightbeasts abroad the watchers have brought me much news."

"So you knew of my journey and still you let me

wander helplessly in the grasslands?" whispered Kyot.

Fairday smiled, looking past Kyot to a slender figure that stood, cloak-wrapped, between the flowered walkways. Raising his arm the Crystal Maker gently turned Kyot around. "Eventine, my daughter. She has watched over your long journey and brought me news of your coming. You wandered no farther than to lay a crooked path should the Nightbeasts follow you."

"Eventine!" Kyot whispered, dazzled by her beauty. Crossing the lawn to her he said, "Twice you saved my life from the Nightbeasts and I thank you for it." Taking her hands into his he kissed them, feeling her cool slender fingers against his lips.

Frowning, she pulled away from him and stood a moment, her eyelashes fluttering against her tanned cheeks. "There is darkness in your heart, Kyot, a hatred that feeds on revenge. It is a shadow that comes between us."

"But Eventine," he cried, looking into her gentle eyes, "I owe you my life, surely I can thank you for that?"

"You owe me nothing, Prince of Archers," she whispered, shaking her head, making her hair shimmer with the color of fire-burned gold. "All I did was to strengthen your resolve to find us."

"I have found more than just Clatterford," he answered, blushing at his own forwardness.

Eventine smiled, holding his gaze for a second before she turned and ran quickly into the Crystal Hall. Fairday smiled silently, watching Kyot follow Eventine with his eyes until she had vanished out of sight. "A daughter is a rare treasure," he said quietly, guiding Kyot into the care of the servers. "Be rested and refreshed, young man, we will meet again at supper time." Gathering his sky-washed robe across his arm Fairday left the lawns to the strutting peacocks and entered the long forging hall, pulling the glass doors shut behind him.

"Glassmakers!" he called above the muted roar of the furnaces. "Come to my molding chair and listen, for I have grave news to tell. News of Krulshards, that Master of Nightmares, who is loose once more in Elundium."

"Then the news of the Nightbeasts is not just gossip!" gasped Tyadall, the vase master, dropping his blowpipes onto the veined marble floor.

"The time has come," Fairday shouted, rising up out of his molding chair. "The time has come to forge new arrowheads against the darkness and rekindle our lost skills to trap a ray of sunlight in each blade. See to the forges and fan them white-hot to mirror the center of the sun."

"What of the crystal bowls, the plates and the window panes?" said Tyadall, waving a goatskin sheet of demands.

"And the fluted flower vases and trinkets?" asked another glass maker.

Fairday scowled, drawing his bushy white eyebrows fiercely together. He reached out and snatched the demands from Tyadall and threw them into the forge. "Elundium will have no use for bowl or crystal glass to keep out the cold if the Nightmare is not destroyed. Clean down the anvils and set them in the waters of the ford; polish the brass hammers and the silver blowpipes. Be ready when the new sun rises!"

The Secret
Road

KING Holbian sighed and sat down, resting his aching back against the black tunnel wall. "How long, Breakmaster?" he asked, feeding a few grains of corn to Beacon Light. "How long have we been in the darkness?"

Breakmaster moved close to the King, following the musical whispers of the steelsilver coat. "I have lost count, my Lord, but we must be many leagues away from the Granite City."

"Has there been any sign of the Chancellors or my treacherous warriors?" the King asked.

"Lord," replied the horseman, "Gray Goose leads the way and he has found us much to eat that the Chancellors have discarded. They were careless in their haste to flee the ruined city and I doubt if they know we have followed them."

"They shall pay for their treachery, mark these words and remember them, Breakmaster. They stole the last few moments of the Granite Kings and I set a high price on the daylight that we lost."

King Holbian fell silent then slowly climbed to

his feet and moved forward again, a hand stretched out against the rough rock wall to guide him. For many leagues the secret road that led out of the Granite City had wound downwards, following a hidden fault through the bones of Elundium, twisting and turning before it turned to the north and passed in a straight line under the roots of the Black Forest. Far ahead of the King Gray Goose could hear the sound of the Chancellors and lifted his hand to halt the column of city folk that followed him.

"Put out the sparks, and snuff the candles," he whispered. "Send for the King and ask him to come forward." Gray Goose settled back to wait for the King, counting the arrows that remained in his quiver.

The sound of the steelsilver coat brought Gray Goose to his feet. "Lord, the Chancellors and the Marchers are before us, I cannot tell how far, perhaps a league or maybe two, but they are shouting and arguing, ignorant that we follow."

"What do they say?" asked Holbian.

Gray Goose hesitated, looking down at the ground.

"Speak plainly, Captain, for I hold you as a true friend."

"They call you a fool, my Lord, and a weak shadow of a King, easily deceived, who walks in fear of the darkness."

"Was that all they said?" asked King Holbian, after a long silence.

"Proudpurse's voice was the loudest and he scorned your fears saying that since they had trapped you in the Granite City they should deliver you up to the Nightbeasts for a dozen barrels of wax."

King Holbian laughed, bitterly, without humor. "Well, my last two Captains, what say you? Am I worth as much here, alone and an easy victim in this darkness? What say you to the Chancellors' twisted tongues?"

Gray Goose laughed, taking the King's hand. "You are here, my Lord, without a spark to light the way, hot on the Chancellors' heels. I can hear your power through the music of your cloak and I know the Chancellors and the warrior traitors will be made to bite their twisted tongues and eat every treacherous word they have uttered."

"But," muttered the King, thinking aloud, "how can we challenge them? We are only three."

"We will walk in their shadows," whispered Breakmaster, "and await an opportunity."

"We will be ready, my Lord," added Gray Goose.

Holbian smiled. "Here I stand, a light, wasted King, with just two friends, and we talk of victory. How many arrows have you, Archer, or fierce Marchers to marshal?"

"It is not the number, my Lord, but the heart and the eye that aims the bow. That is where victory lies."

"Who taught you that, Captain?" asked the King, reaching out and taking Gray Goose's bow hand.

"The greatest Archer in all Elundium, my Lord. Archerorm, the Keeper of Stumble Hill."

"Then lead us forward, brave Captain, with his wisdom in our hearts; but tread with cautious stealth and keep a good distance behind the traitors. Remember we will choose the moment, not them. Now lead on!"

Gray Goose turned, reaching out into the darkness for the rough rock wall and moved forward. Breakmaster held back.

"The horses' hooves will echo on the rock floor, my Lord. I must muffle them before we follow."

Moving amongst the city dwellers huddled against the wall Breakmaster found what he sought and returned to the King triumphantly holding up a dozen coarse hessian sacks and leather binding thongs. Picking up each hoof in turn he tied the heavy sacks over their iron shoes.

"Now we can follow with less than a whisper in Gray Goose's quiet footsteps," he laughed, leading both horses forward, one at either shoulder.

King Holbian took Beacon Light's reins from the horsemaster's hand and followed in his footsteps. Slowly, one by one, the city dwellers overtook the King for he walked lost in the music of his steel-silver coat, re-living summers he had too easily squandered before the Nightbeasts arose.

"Move along," growled a voice, breaking through the music of the coat to the left of the King. A ragged figure was pushed, stumbling forward, tripping over and spilling a meager bundle of possessions at Beacon Light's hooves. Holbian turned his head irritably towards the scuffle and gripped the collar of the figure that had done the pushing.

"Who dares to harass my people?" he hissed.

"We are falling behind, my Lord. The old woman was slowing our pace."

"Quiet, fool," snapped the King, bending to help the old woman to her feet.

"Lord, you are a great King, who cares as the shepherd does for his flock, no matter how weak they are," she sighed.

King Holbian laughed and then frowned. There was something in the voice he recognized, a tone that he had heard somewhere before. "What is your name, old woman?" he asked, staring at her through the darkness.

"Angishand, my Lord, the Candleman's wife."

"Ironhand," whispered the King, gripping her hands tightly, and remembering how the Candleman had, for all his simplemindedness, been his first true friend against the darkness. "You should be carried in honor, Angishand, for if fate had treated us better you would have been the mother of Kings, the handmaiden of greatness."

Smiling sadly, he lifted her, bird-light and frail as she was, and set her side-saddle on Beacon Light's back. "Ride beside me, lady of Elundium, and share my dark hours for this is all we have, all that is left."

Before Angis could answer Holbian had knelt and scooped up her bundle of belongings and thrust them into the hands that had pushed her onto her knees. "Guard these treasures well," he commanded, taking the reins and leading Beacon Light forward.

Looking up into Angishand's face he smiled. "We will talk of things to come; of the daylight at the end of the road and of your son, Thanehand, who took a darker road than this to try and save the daylight. There was a moment when I thought he might have the power to be a King, but now there is nothing left to rule."

"Lord, is he dead?" she whispered, her eyes misting with tears.

"Do you have the second sight?" asked the King, fear filling his voice.

"No, Lord, I was only the weaver, the threadlady of the great Granite Hall, and my life was spent repairing the emblems of Elundium, painting in new colors where they had faded with age or neatening ragged endings, binding them bright with fine gold thread."

King Holbian sighed with relief. "Your son may live yet. Thanehand may still be growing strong at Underfall. We must not give up hope no matter how dark the road becomes."

"He took nothing, Lord, save a summer scarf I had woven from the spare ends of emblem thread. I fear that he was so ill prepared he must have perished in that first winter's snow."

"Emblem thread!" cried the King, turning

sharply and setting the steelsilver coat rattling in the darkness.

"Lord," Angis whispered, shrinking back away from the King. "I did not steal the threads, they were rag ends only fit for burning."

"No, no, I care nothing for what you took, but what pictures did you weave? What was upon that scarf? Tell me, tell me!" cried the King, his heart racing with excitement as he tried to remember Nevian's prophecies. There had been words about a standard, that he was sure.

"It was a picture of the sun, my Lord, a summer sun in a blue sky."

"Did you edge it with blue and silver?" persisted the King. "Was it like the royal standards that hung in the Towers of Granite?"

"Oh no, my Lord, that would have been far too grand for the likes of a Candleman's wife. People would have laughed at me or stolen it to exchange for tallow or other treasure of the light. It was a simple picture of the sun."

"There must have been an owl in blue and gold somewhere in the picture," persisted the King. "What size was the scarf?"

Angis smiled, remembering her last few moments with Thane before he started his dangerous journey into exile. "No, my Lord, it was a summer sun and in my hands it was nothing more than a scarf, but the moment Thane took it, it seemed to change in shape and size and yet it passed easily into his pocket."

"Did it burn or shine with light?" pressed the King.

Angis frowned and then slowly nodded. "The picture did seem to come alive as Thane touched it."

King Holbian laughed, his heart lighter than it had been for many daylights. There was still room for hope, even here in this dark hole beneath the ground, and he forged ahead to come to Breakmaster and Gray Goose in heated argument.

"The road divides here, my Lord," Breakmaster said, as the King drew level.

"Can you tell which way the Chancellors chose?" asked Holbian, searching in his pocket for a spark.

"They took the left-hand road," Gray Goose replied in the fierce light of the spark.

"That is our road then. We must follow them," commanded the King.

"What is that?" asked Angis, pointing up into the roof of the secret road. Taking the King's spark she reached up into the roof, moving her hand backward and forward.

"It is roots," laughed Breakmaster, "the roots of a giant tree. Look, they arch the road in both directions. We must be passing beneath a great forest."

With the extinguished spark safely back inside his pocket King Holbian moved on. He felt warm inside the steelsilver coat but a chill wind now blew against his face and far ahead he could hear a roaring noise and he shivered, fearing what might lie across their path.

Swanwater

*O*GION looked across the darkening landscape, searching for a place to rest. Far behind on a broken ridge the horsemen had
slowed to a walk.

"Rest, rest," he hissed, descending towards a gray
stretch of marshland water. Fanning his wings he
touched the lake and ploughed up a white-crested
wave, sending small ripples through the tall black-
flecked bullrushes. One by one the gray swans followed Ogion down and landed on the lake.

Thane saw the sun reflected in the ripples from
the swans which spread across the lake and he dismounted. Yawning he led Stumble down through
jagged thorn bushes to the water's edge and began
cutting branches for a fire.

"No fire!" Ogion hissed, wading ashore and
knocking the bundle of wood roughly out of
Thane's arms. "The Nightmare has set many
Nightbeast watchers. No fire."

Thane shivered, wrapping the ragged half-cloak
tightly around his shoulders, and sat down on the

cold damp marshy earth. He had lost count of the
daylights and half daylights they had followed the
Nightmare, cantering and galloping whenever they
could to keep pace with the swans, never daring to
rest while the great birds were in the sky. "Elionbel," he whispered, looking into Ogion's eyes.

Ogion turned his long neck and brushed beaks
in greeting with Ousious, his life mate, as she left
the lake. Turning back to Thane he hissed, "She
runs at the Nightmare's heels, cruelly driven by the
one-clawed beast. She is proud and bitter with hatred and suffers each daylight for her pride."

"And Martbel, her mother?" Thane whispered,
his eyes haunted with dread.

"She runs," Ogion hissed, turning away to seek
a safe place on the bank for the night ahead.

Ousious paused before Thane, looking deeply
into his eyes, seeing the power of his love for the
Nightmare's prisoner. "How will you rescue her?"
she asked, rubbing her beak against Thane's arm.

Thane looked up, a smile touching the corners
of his mouth. "I had not thought. I only live to catch
the Nightmare. I must do that first, but when he
stands before me I shall find a way."

"They are tied by the Nightmare's life thread,"
Ogion hissed, returning to the bank and roughly
pushing Thane away from Ousious. "There is no
way you can sever that thread, foolish man. Keep
your distance, stay clear of my swans. I only
pledged to lead you at your peril, not to befriend
you."

Thane moved away and sat down beside Stumble, huddling against him for warmth. In the growing darkness he gripped the hilt of his dagger from inside his cloak. "Give me courage," he whispered, falling asleep.

Near the water's edge the swans settled close to one another, whispering late into the night. Ogion sat alone, his hard eyes watchful and alert, his long neck casting a sharp black shadow across the bank. Slowly his head sank back and his eyelids closed.

Crack! Snap! Faint noises in the undergrowth woke Stumble. Snorting, he nudged Thane awake. Blinking his sleep away Thane drew the dagger and turned his head towards the noise. Two Nightbeasts were silhouetted against the starlight on the top of the bank. Thane guessed they were swan-hunting by the nets and three-pronged spears they carried. Slowly he rose into a crouch, the dagger ready in his right hand. The Nightbeasts had crept down the bank and were almost level with him. Stumble flattened his ears, curled back his lips and sank noiselessly onto his hocks. The Nightbeasts had raised their spears to strike.

"Now!" Thane shouted, leaping forward, plunging the dagger hilt deep up beneath the nearest beast's outstretched arm.

Stumble reared up and smashed both forelegs against the other Nightbeast's iron cap, crushing his skull down into his chest. The gray swans hissed and flapped in alarm, running across the bank, fleeing into the water and surging out into the lake.

Only Ogion turned, head outstretched, and tore at the lifeless Nightbeasts. Thane wiped the dagger on the bank and returned it to his belt. Stumble snorted, arching his neck with pride. Turning, they both returned to their place on the edge of the clearing.

Ogion hissed and spread his wings. "I misjudged you, Thanehand, and doubted why you carried that blade."

Thane drew the dagger and placed it on the ground at Ogion's webbed feet. "This blade was forged to cut through Nightbeast armor. It was hammered out by Durondell, the Armorer. I could not, nor would I wish to, harm one soft downy feather on your chest."

"The Magician said you would protect us. He foresaw this night."

"Nevian is the Master of Magic. He sees everything," Thane replied, returning the dagger to his belt.

Ogion stared steadily at Thane, his dark eyes shining in the starlight, before bending his neck to preen his chest feathers. One by one the gray swans returned to the bank and settled less than a neck's distance from the water's edge to sleep. "Sit with us," Ogion commanded, pointing with his beak to a clear space in the center of the swans. "You have shown great bravery and have earned a place among us."

Thane settled inside the cluster of swans and, sheltered by their warm feathers, fell easily into sleep. Stumble stood close by cropping at the short, bitter lakeside grasses. He could sense the changing weather and turned his quarters against the bitter wind that had begun to blow, before the gray hours brought the next daylight.

Thane woke to see a layer of hoarfrost on the folds of his cloak and rose, shivering, to his feet.

Ogion stood at the water's edge, staring out across the lake towards the broken hills that showed in the distance. "He has run before us in the darkness. The Nightmare has turned beyond the edge of the grasslands into a place of deserts and broken rocks. Hurry or we will lose him."

Thane quickly saddled Stumble and cantered him along the bank towards the far end of the lake. Ogion flew low over his head before he lifted away towards the broken line of hills.

By noontime the sky had darkened and ice-cold rain had begun to fall. Thane dismounted as Stumble floundered on the slippery ground and led him forward, hunching his shoulders against the weather. "We will keep on for that gap in the hills," he shouted, against the dull roar of the rain as it worsened, misting the horizon and filling the gullies they were climbing with racing muddy streams.

The cloak kept out the worst of the rain, but the flooded gullies soon filled Thane's ruined boots with cold muddy water. The downpour matted his straw-colored hair and trickled into his eyes in stinging drops. The cold numbed his fingers and burned into his knuckles as he scrambled forward over the rough, rising ground towards the gap he knew must lie ahead. The higher they climbed the colder it became; driving sleet stung their faces and covered Thane's shoulders and Stumble's quarters with a gray layer of wet ice. Soaked through and shivering they eventually reached the gap in the hills and looked out in despair across a bleak tumble of rocks, gray-white under ice and snow, that stretched away to a black horizon.

"Thanehand! Thanehand!" Ogion called in a musical voice, flying in a wide searching circle over the line of the hills. Thane heard the swans call and climbed as high as he could, waving and shouting at the low snow-filled clouds until Ogion saw him and swooped over his head.

"We are lost!" Thane shouted, rubbing the sleet out of his eyes.

"Follow the hills, Thanehand, and do not stray into the ice fields. Follow the hills until you reach Swanwater."

Moving as fast as they could Thane and Stumble descended from the hills following the gray swans, but darkness overtook them, covering their path and they wandered down, unaware that they had strayed into the edge of an ice field. "Stop!" Thane cried, pulling hard on the reins.

The ground beneath their feet had begun to shift, faintly creaking and groaning. Stumble neighed and moved backwards onto higher ground. Thane followed him, jumping to safety just before the ice field opened, gushing up in a fountain of black water. Climbing farther away from the ice field Thane shouted into the darkness. "We are lost, Ogion, and cannot find Swanwater."

Stumble snorted and began to scrape at the light covering of ice and snow, trying to trample a place to weather out the night. Thane put a hand on the little horse's shoulder and bid him be still. "Listen!" he whispered, straining his ears at the snow-silence. "Listen."

Far ahead a single cry, musical and piercing, cut through the darkness; moments later another cry echoed the first. Then another and another. "The swans are calling us," Thane laughed, blowing on his fingers to warm them up. "Come, Stumble, keep to the high ground and follow the music."

Moving slowly forward from ridge to ridge they heard the swans' voices grow louder and louder until Thane had to cover his ears to mute their calls. Suddenly the singing stopped and Ogion waddled out of the darkness to greet them, filling the silence with his strong voice. "Come, Thanehand, come into the flock gathering and rest, for here on Swanwater you are safe from the Nightbeasts."

"What of Elionbel?" Thane asked, stumbling forward onto the flat pebble-strewn beach, dense with the long-necked shapes of the swans. "Where is the Nightmare?"

Ogion hissed, stretching his neck, "He has gone, Thane, through the ice field beyond my sight. He traveled far while we slept and has taken a path that we cannot follow."

"But we must follow them!" Thane cried, turning towards the ice field.

"No, you cannot! The ice field will swallow you, it is a treacherous place where you cannot travel. One step inside and you would vanish without a trace."

"Then I have lost everything," Thane whispered, sinking onto his knees. Bowing his head he wept, oblivious to the biting cold, deaf to the soft sad music of the swans, blind, wrapped in a black mantle of despair.

Ousious came silently to his side, covered him with her soft downy feathers and heard every despair-filled word of his love for Elionbel; of their first meeting in the ring of hawthorn trees when he had rescued her, through his wintering at her father's house when their love had grown and flourished only to be cruelly trimmed by her father's anger.

"I am not bloodworthy of her," he whispered over and over, screwing the edge of his ragged cloak in his hands.

Ousious left Thane as the first light of morning touched the smooth surface of Swanwater. She slipped quietly into the water and swam out through the fingers of still early mist far beyond the last sleeping swans. "I will find her, Thane," she whispered, stretching her neck and spreading her wings. "I will tell her of your search."

Her wings beat against the surface of the lake and she gathered speed and rose into the air. "I will find your Elionbel, for you are lovematched forever."

The Nightmare
Vanishes

*K*RULSHARDS spat at the ground and pulled the malice up around his shoulders. "They still follow us!" he shouted, pointing with a bone black finger at the line of swans silhouetted by the dying sun. Elionbel stole a glance at the horizon and saw the swans. Secretly her heart beat faster. Perhaps they were marking the Nightmare's path for Thane. Krulshards laughed, roughly pulling on the life thread and breaking into her thoughts. "They are gray swans—bearers of ill omens, carriers of the Buryman's list. They foretell your fate, Elionbel, Marcherspawn!"

Elionbel turned her head and looked steadily into the Nightmare's face, past the loops of hanging rotten flesh and the dead locks of wasted hair that swung as forgotten flags in the cold evening air. "I do not fear you!" she hissed, staring into his eyes. "My hate makes me strong and gives me power. Each morning as the first ray of sunlight shows above World's Edge I eat the hate and drink from its cup, and one daylight I will be stronger than you and then I shall tear this life thread out of your black heart and strangle you with it!"

Krulshards laughed, pushing Elionbel onto her knees. "Strong!" he sneered. "Powerful!" he mocked. Reaching out he put his hands around her wasted arms. "You are barely flesh and bones, Marcherwoman, not even worthy as a decent meal!"

Laughing, he cast her aside and beckoned Kerzolde to come forward. "Send two Nightbeasts to hunt down the swans. I fear they are waymarking our path. Bring us swan meat, kill every one of them. The Marcher women have little appetite for our tastier dishes; perhaps they will enjoy swans."

Elionbel's stomach tightened and turned at the mention of food. She dreaded the foul maggot-strewn flesh they forced on her at the beginning of each daylight, but to eat swan meat was somehow worse. They were such beautiful creatures, strong and yet gentle, and she had always imagined she could hear something in their music, not words but voices, perhaps the voices of the dead seeking a place to rest. She turned angrily on the Nightmare but Martbel stopped her with a firm hand on her arm.

"Quiet, daughter," she whispered, pulling Elionbel down onto the ground beside her. There were tears in Martbel's eyes and her shoulders shook with little uncontrollable movements as she wept.

"What is it, Mother?" Elionbel asked in hushed tones, wrapping her arms around her mother's shoulders.

Between her sobs Martbel whispered into Elionbel's ear, "The Nightmare raped me on the top of the wall when he dragged me inside the malice."

"I know, Mother!" Elionbel hissed, gripping her hand and squeezing it tight. "And one daylight he will pay dearly for it."

"But worse than that," continued Martbel, "his seed is growing inside me; it is tearing and gnawing at me, feeding on me. Oh, what am I to do?"

Elionbel stared at the hood of the malice, her heart pounding with hatred, her eyes glittering with rage. Slowly her hand sought amongst the secret folds of her skirt and found the cold brass handle of a dagger that she had kept well hidden. "I will kill him," she muttered, closing her fingers around the hilt.

"No, no!" cried Martbel, taking Elionbel's hand away from the dagger. "Keep the blade a secret and use it to kill the Nightmare's seed the moment it is born. It must not survive and grow for I fear it will have uncontrollable power and spread a terrible shadow across Elundium. Promise me that you will kill it. Promise me!"

"I will kill it. I promise!" Elionbel replied, taking her mother back into her arms and rocking her gently backward and forward. "I will destroy the Nightmare's bastard before it takes its first breath."

Krulshards pulled the hood of the malice down over his face and laughed, gloating in the darkness. He had heard every word and whisper through the life thread, and now sat wondering at the power he had created through raping the Marcherwoman, searching amongst all the Nightbeasts and Nightshades he had ever spawned for a parallel, but there was none. Nothing he had hatched in the darkness could have carried his seed out into Elundium. Nothing he had made before was both light and dark. Bending his finger he summoned Kerzolde to him and pulled him into the malice, wrapping it tightly around them both.

"The Marcherwoman, Martbel, carries my seed. What does that mean? How will she spawn it?" he asked.

Kerzolde thought for a moment, a cruel leer splitting his hideous face. "She will give birth to a child, Master. It is the way the people of Elundium spawn. It will be a part of both of you, but since you are the Lord of Darkness she will carry the strength and power of your image in her belly."

"My image!" he whispered. "That would think as I do and hold all I hold as beautiful. That would spread my darkness throughout Elundium!"

"Yes, Master. It is already a part of you. It is your seed!"

Krulshards laughed, suddenly realizing a part of the power that he had created. Gripping Kerzolde in tight fingers he hissed, "Guard my seed, and keep sharp eyes on the other woman. She has a blade hidden in the folds of her skirt. Let her keep the blade and give her no warning that we know that she wishes to kill my seed."

"Master, she is a great danger. Let me kill her now!"

"No!" hissed the Nightmare. "She is payment against Thanehand and she must hang in the City of Night. Snatch my seed the moment it is born and kill the Marcherwoman, Martbel. She has pledged to kill my seed and will be a greater danger."

"Master," Kerzolde answered, "the newborn Lord of Night will need its mother's milk for nourishment. It is the custom for the people of Elundium for they are weak born and helpless and need time to grow strong."

Krulshards laughed, "Nightbeasts are hatched and battle-ready before the new sun rises. Even Nightshards are only a few daylights in the making, but take the newborn seed from the Marcherwoman and keep it safe. Let her feed it until it is strong enough to stand alone, bind her if necessary, then you must kill her!"

"It will mean many daylights of careful watching."

"Then watch carefully, Captainbeast!" Krulshards snarled, "and let not the Elionbel near my seed. Its life is your life, its death will be your despair."

Kerzolde bent and licked once at the Nightmare's toes, then slipped out of the malice into the gathering darkness.

Elionbel sat huddled beside her mother, unable to sleep. The cuts on her knees wept and oozed from the daylight's hard climbing through the desolate landscape and yet they were nothing but scratches against what Martbel had told her. How was she to kill the monster when every movement was watched by the broken-clawed Nightbeast? Below where they had stopped, a dark stretch of water reflected the star-bright sky and she stared down at it, searching for an answer. A cry broke the night silence, scattering the gray swans across the lake. Krulshards sprang to his feet, the malice billowing against the night sky. Below, a blade flashed in the darkness and a horse neighed fiercely. Silence once more blanketed the surface of the lake and the swans returned to the shadows of the bank.

"Thanehand!" Krulshards hissed, putting a hand over the women's mouths and pulling them behind the malice. Elion struggled against the Nightmare's grip, biting at his smothering fingers, trying to shout a warning to whoever held the blade.

"Run!" snarled Krulshards, pushing Elionbel and Martbel before him. "Run!" Kerzolde snatched up Elionbel and Kerhunge bundled Martbel beneath his arm, and tirelessly they followed the Nighmare through a broken gap in the line of bare hills that towered before them. Krulshards halted on the lower slopes and put a dribble-wet finger up into the bitter wind.

"The marshes will freeze!" he laughed. "Before the daylight they will have become the winter ice fields, treacherous and impassable. Bring the Marcherwoman into the shadow of the malice and walk in my footsteps. Tread to either side at your peril."

Krulshards drew the hood of the malice up over the top of his head and hurried down the slope into the rock-strewn marshes. "Keep to my footprints!" he shouted into the first drop of freezing rain.

Elionbel kicked against Kerzolde's iron grip but he only sneered and squeezed her tighter. "Keep still, Marcherwoman, or I will disobey the Master and throw you into the black marshwater."

Elionbel stopped struggling and pushed her anger and frustration back deep into her heart. Thane had been close to her, she had felt his presence in the darkness. It must have been him with the swans. Looking backwards over Kerzolde's scaly shoulders she thought she saw the graceful long-necked swans searching the edge of the marshes in the gloomy morning light.

"Thanehand!" she whispered, letting her head sink forward, too tired to care that her long golden hair was snagging on Kerzolde's shoulder scales. "Please find us. Please come quickly and rescue us from the Nightmare."

"Faster! Faster!" shouted Krulshards, springing from rock to rock. The black marshwater was beginning to ice over and push the rocks and boulders that marked the path into treacherous ground. Soon the way would vanish beneath the shifting ice field, covered by the snow that cut into their faces in stinging squalls. Krulshards looked ahead and saw the lowcut river meadows rising above the marsh edge. Sneering with delight he climbed up onto the firm grass-covered bank and pointed back across the frozen marshes. "We are safe, Marcherwomen. Nobody, not even Thanehand, could follow us across the ice field. Watch a while and see the truth in what I say."

Elionbel and Martbel stood dejected and huddled against the cold, watching the ice field spread out across the marshes, picking up huge boulders that lay in its path and hurling them into the black stinking waters. Fountains of sludge boiled up across the ice and froze into petrified slippery ridges. Rank grasses and bullrush flags became brittle ice-filled spears, rattling in the bitter wind. Everywhere they looked the gray-white ice whispered and groaned.

"None can follow us!" sneered the Nightmare. "Not until the new sun melts the ice." Laughing he turned, pulling Elionbel and Martbel along behind him.

"Let us rest!" Elionbel shouted, stumbling onto her knees.

Krulshards halted and spread the malice over them. "There is no rest now, Marcherwoman, not until we reach the City of Night. We are on the edges of Clatterford and must hurry to escape the cursed light the Crystal Maker forges into his arrowheads." Taking Kerhunge's twelve-tailed whip he cracked it at Elionbel's heels. "Run, Marcherwomen, run!" he shouted, chasing them forward across the gray winter grasses.

Elionbel lost track of the passing daylight as they

ran through the bleak, seemingly endless grassland and nightfall brought no easing of the pace, only deeper despair as dark shadowy Nightbeasts sprang up out of the tall grasses around them and formed into two dense columns, one on either side of the exhausted women.

"Carry the ones who will lure Thanehand into the darkness," laughed the Nightmare. "Carry my Marcherwomen and let no harm come to them."

Kerzolde looked up into the early dawn light and pointed with his broken claw at the dark tree line that stretched across the horizon. "Nearly home, Master. That is the eaves of Meremire Forest."

Krulshards looked anxiously at the paling sky and cracked the twelve-tailed whip across Kerzolde's face. "Silence, fool, none must know of our passing."

Kerhunge touched the hem of the malice where it billowed in the dawn breeze and silently pointed first to a line of twinkling lights that were spread out in a crescent shape far to their left and then towards a lone swan, flying low and fast across the grasslands.

"Faster! Faster!" hissed Krulshards, lengthening his stride for the eaves of the forest.

Ousious had found their tracks with the first morning light and followed their burned and trampled path far across the grasslands until she saw Krulshards's black shadow running for the forest edge. "Elionbel!" she sang in piercing notes. "I bring you word from Thanehand!" she cried, seeing Elionbel roughly held between two Nightbeasts.

Elionbel twisted and struggled, crying out as the shadow of the swan passed over her. Ousious circled, calling to Elionbel, gliding dangerously close to the Nightmare. "Thane cannot follow you until the ice field melts, but his heart yearns to be with you."

Krulshards reached inside his malice, unhooked a black-bladed spear and hurled it up into the dark shape of the flying swan. Ousious shrieked and for a moment plunged towards the ground. Krulshards pulled hard on the fine thread attached to the spear but Ousious fought against him and broke the blade, leaving a splinter of steel embedded deep inside her chest. Struggling, she rose up away from the hail of Nightbeast spears and turned back towards Swanwater and the long journey home. "Thanehand, Thanehand will follow," she weakly cried, vanishing into the beginnings of a new morning.

Krulshards ran the Nightbeasts under the eaves of Meremire Forest into the dense undergrowth, then stopped. Gripping both women firmly, his hands gagging their mouths, he watched a new threat to their safety drawing closer as the crescent of Marchers and Gallopers passed slowly along the forest edge.

Silently gloating he let both women watch as Tombel came into sight. He looked older, worry-worn and tired, yet the two great Marcher swords he carried resting across his shoulders were dirtied and black with Nightbeast blood.

"I smell Nightbeasts!" he shouted, coming onto Krulshards's tracks where they had left the grasslands, turning away from the forest. He followed them for a few paces into the grasslands. Elionbel, with one mighty effort, sank her teeth into the Nightmare's hand, shearing through the rotten sinews of his finger and cried out to her father, one piercing cry before Krulshards smothered her in the malice.

Tombel spun around, both swords sweeping in a glittering arc. "Where did that cry come from?" he shouted, searching the dark forest eaves.

"It must have been the gray swan, Father," Rubel called, running to his father's side. "It passed low overhead, swooping and dipping, singing its strange death chant." Shivering he watched the swan before saying, with an edge of fear in his voice, "The aged crones say that the voice of the swan is someone's death call."

"Crones' tales!" Tombel muttered, lowering the swords and turning his back on Meremire Forest. "Nothing but crones' tales in a swan's voice, and I thought for a moment that I heard Elionbel's voice crying out."

Sighing, Tombel walked a few paces into the grasslands. "Come on, Rubel, we shall marshal the crescent and sweep out across these grasslands. Thane and Arbel could be anywhere in this vastness."

Rubel frowned, wrinkling his nose. "Wait, Father," he said quietly, rubbing at the wound on his arm, "there is something here, something that strikes terror into my heart. It's the Nightmare!" he cried, gripping his father's arm, sniffing the dawn air. "The smell is here, the Nightmare's smell, that same smell that filled our Wayhouse after Krulshards had taken mother and Elionbel, and Arbel struck that sword blow. That same smell is all around us!"

Tombel steadied Rubel, holding him until he had stopped shaking. Turning, he knelt and sniffed the ground, catching the rancid smell of rotten flesh, the smell of Krulshards. "There are different tracks mixed up amongst these Nightbeasts' footprints. Look how the ground has been burned and blackened."

"But which way did the Nightmare travel?" Rubel asked, staring into the shadows of the forest.

Tombel frowned, straightened his back and walked towards the forest edge. "There are too many tracks to tell, they cross and muddle. The Nightmare could have traveled either way."

Krulshards stepped backwards, tightening his grip on Elionbel and Martbel, smothering them with the hem of the malice, and motioning silently with his hand, he spread the Nightbeasts on either side of him, their spear blades pointing out towards the Marchers.

"Which way, Father?" Rubel pressed impatiently.

Tombel sighed and turned away from the forest. "There are too many tangle-trees in this forest. We would be risking the entire crescent of Marchers, putting them in great danger, if we try to pass through the trees, and if we stray off the Greenways the Gallopers cannot follow us. I counsel that we search the grasslands. If Thane had pursued the Nightmare on this road he would have left a sign or waymarked the path. I say that the Nightmare has turned towards Clatterford and the wildlands beyond. I council that these tracks beneath the forest eaves belong to a band of Nightbeasts that are traveling with Krulshards."

"Forward, Marchers, and Gallopers!" Rubel cried, pointing the blade of his sword out across the winter-gray grasses. "We may be on the trail of the Nightbeasts who captured my brother, Arbel. Forward!"

Krulshards laughed and lifted the edge of the malice. "Watch, Marcherwomen," he sneered, "and shout until your lungs burst, but they will not hear you above the tramp of their marching feet and the clatter of their horses' hooves. You are lost forever and our road is clear through the ancient forest to the City of Night and your torment in the darkness."

Great Deeds

*T*HANE woke to the clamor of hissing voices all around him. The gray swans were moving in a dense waddling flock along the beach, craning their necks in alarm towards the ice field. Swanwater echoed to the thunder of beating wings as swan after swan left the surface of the lake and flew searching across the ice field.

Ogion stood statue-still at the water's edge, his head tilted to one side, staring into the distance. "My Queen has gone," he hissed at Thane, as he came hurrying down to the water's edge. "The Queen of Swans has followed the Nightmare and I fear for her life."

Thane spread his hands in a helpless gesture and looked out across Swanwater. "If only Mulcade were here," he whispered, "he would find her for you, for he is the sharpest-eyed Lord of Owls that ever flew in Elundium."

Stumble snorted and drank deeply from the lake. Ogion spread his wings and ran into the water. "I can hear her, far, far away, across the ice field."

Beating his wings, he rose up out of a plume of white spray and headed low across the tumble of creaking ridges that marked the edge of the ice field.

Thane paced the empty beach, watching the clouded gray horizon. It was bitterly cold and he rubbed his hands together to warm them. He could hear the swan music, haunting as it cut across the wind, gradually getting closer. Stumble heard a change in the swan voices and pricked his ears. Neighing fiercely he urged Thane to mount and cantered out into the lake, swimming as fast as he could through the ice-cold water.

The sky above the lake darkened as Ogion led his Queen over the last tumbled ridges of the ice field. On either side two swans supported her tired wings, easing her down onto the water. Ousious crashed, ungracefully, in a spray of white foam and lay floating, head down and wings outstretched. Ogion landed beside her and pulled at her head, pecking at the close downy feathers to keep it above the water.

Stumble had reached the place where Ousious lay and Thane reached out and pulled the drowning swan up out of the cold water then laid her across the high pommel of the saddle. Gently he took her head and tucked it inside his shirt, folded her wings and wrapped his cloak around her cold shivering body. Stumble slowly turned and swam back to the bank, flanked on either side by the whispering swans.

Jumping quickly out of the wet saddle Thane

opened his cloak and laid Ousious on the beach. Turning her over he saw the broken spear blade protruding out of her chest. "Krulshards's black metal!" he muttered between clenched teeth, loosing the dagger from his belt and drawing it out.

Standing up he faced Ogion and the close-packed beach of swans that encircled him. "Ogion, your Queen will die if I do not try to pull the Nightmare's blade out of her chest."

Ogion stepped forward hissing and touched the dagger with his beak. Thane smiled and dropped onto his knees, spreading his ragged travel-worn cloak across Ousious' shivering body. "Fetch me kindling sticks and firewood. I must clean the blade of my dagger of any trace of Nightbeast blood with fire before it touches the Queen of Swans. Go quickly for time is our enemy."

Thane searched out his spark and dried it in the palm of his hand while the swans built a pile of kindling sticks on the beach. Kneeling again he held Ousious's head in his hands and whispered to her, "The blade will be white, fire-hot and as pure as the day Durondel hammered it on his anvil."

Ousious opened her eyes.

"We will follow Elionbel together," Thane whispered, "when you are strong and healed from this terrible wound."

Ousious closed her eyes and hissed quietly, her orange beak quivering in his hand. Turning his head, Thane threw the spark, lighting the pile of kindling and waited until the base of the fire had burned into a bed of white-hot ash. Picking up the dagger he thrust it hilt deep into the ashes and watched the almost invisible smears of foul Nightbeast blood bubble and hiss as they burned away.

"Merion, give me your skill!" Thane whispered, trying to remember what he had seen the Healer do to remove the broken spear blades from the injured warriors of Underfall.

Gripping the jagged protruding splinter of black steel he pulled hard. Ousious screamed, arching her back away from the ground. Easing his hand from the broken blade he sat and thought, forming a picture of the dark fortress at Underfall and the small stone cell where Merion mended the Nightmare wounds. Clearly he saw him hurrying and singing as he opened the edges of a wound with a long curved blade and easily removed the slivers of steel or broken arrowheads. Something glittered in his hands—thread, gold and silver. Deftly, the Healer would sew the jagged tears together, sometimes pouring new blood into the wound. "Now I know," he whispered, closing his hand on the hilt of his dagger, but he had forgotten the fire and screamed as the hot metal burned his skin.

"Nevian, give me courage!" he shouted, clenching his burned fingers around the hot metal hilt and cutting two deep incisions into the swan's chest beside the broken splinter. Warm blood gushed up, cooling the blade and flooding across his burning knuckles. With his other hand he grabbed the splinter and wrenched it free. Ousious lay limp and still on the ground, her chest feathers matted and sticky, and the edges of the wound slipped in Thane's fingers as he tried to stop the bleeding. He knew she would die if he could not give her new blood and close the edges of the wound. In despair he turned the dagger and with one stroke gashed his wrist, crying out and biting his tongue as the blade cut through the skin.

"Live, Queen of Swans," he cried, forcing his bleeding wrist against Ousious' chest, plunging it deep into the gaping wound.

Stumble neighed and pushed hard against his arm, rubbing his coarse mane on Thane's cheek. Thane turned his head crossly to send Stumble away, but a shaft of winter sunlight broke through the clouds at that moment and touched the little horse's neck, shining on the mane.

"Silver and gold!" Thane cried, dropping the dagger and reaching out with his free hand he pulled a handful of the coarse hair from Stumble's crest. Faintness was sweeping over Thane in waves, he felt dizzy and light-headed. "I must hurry," he whispered, using the point of the dagger to pierce small holes on either side of the wound. Deftly he threaded strands of hair from hole to hole, looping the ends with his free hand. Bending forward he gripped each hair in turn in his teeth and pulled the knots tight. The last strand tied he sank back onto his heels and smiled weakly at Ogion.

"It is done!" he whispered, closing his eyes and falling forward in a black faint.

Ogion pecked gently at his Queen's wing, nudging her against Thane's side out of the bitter wind. Motioning to the leader of swans he bade them cover Thane and Ousious with the cloak and keep the beach fire ablaze with kindling wood until he returned. Bending his neck he stared at the bloody splinter of black steel that lay where Thane had dropped it and hissed in rage. Picking it up in his beak he walked towards the water's edge to throw it away.

"What treasure do you carry, Lord of Swans?" called an ancient voice from the top of the bank above the pebble-strewn beach. Ogion turned, dropping the broken blade and spread his wings to charge. Nevian laughed and sprang lightly down the bank onto the beach.

"Master of Magic!" Ogion hissed, folding his wings. "It is as you foretold. This search for Krulshards has led us to our doom. Ousious, my Queen, lies near to death and I fear that the spear thrust cut more than just flesh. I fear that it is the beginning of our silence."

Nevian frowned and shook the rainbow cloak, sending brilliant shafts of summer light across the cold winter beach. "Fate is a cruel master but even your Queen has played her part, for the Master Armorer of Elundium would call that broken blade beside your webbed foot a treasure rare and beautiful!"

"It is Nightmare steel, foul and black with shadows, marked with the blood of my Queen."

"Yet," whispered Nevian, pulling aside the cloak that covered Thane and Ousious, "it failed to take her life and could be turned in purpose against the hand that threw it, against the Nightmare's heart. Take it, Lord of Swans, and carry it to Durondell for he has a great need of such strong metal."

"Why should I spoil my beak for the skill of the Armorer? He forges our death in the battle tools he makes in the heat of his furnace."

Nevian reached out and touched Ogion's neck and pointed down at Thane. "He gave his blood to save your Queen. The splinter of steel is his by right. Carry it for him to Durondell and repay the debt."

Ogion bent his neck and held closed the ugly slash on Thane's wrist with his beak, until the sluggish flow of blood stopped altogether.

"You foretold he would protect us and for his deeds this day I will carry the blade." Taking up the black metal in his beak he beat a path out across the lake and rose up over the ice field to vanish from the Magician's sight.

Nevian smiled, rubbing his age-wrinkled hand through Stumble's mane and pulled a colored thread from the hem of his rainbow cloak. "Great deeds are in the making," he whispered, neatly sewing up the ugly gash on Thane's wrist before placing it back beneath the travel-worn cloak. "Great deeds!" he sighed, looking out across Swanwater.

The Sword is Reforged

*D*URONDELL, the Master Armorer, looked across at the dampened forge, rubbed his eyes and peered through the blue haze of wood smoke that drifted out into the winter sunlight. The clatter of hoofbeats filled the air.

"Who comes to the Forge of Durondell?" he shouted, striking his long-handled blemishing hammer on the spike of the anvil. "Come forward, warriors!" he cried, rising from his chair and impatiently wiping his spark-blackened hands on the edge of his leather apron before crossing the ashtrampled floor to where Thoron stood undecided between the wide-flung doors.

"What has brought you in search of me? Hard riding on the Lord of Horses with a proud squadron of Gallopers must warrant a mighty cause. Come forward and speak!"

Thoron drew back out into the sunlight, his hand tight on Equestrius's rein. "Nevian bid me find you."

Durondell laughed, casting his eye over the Gallopers. "You have ridden hard and fast through the great world of Elundium, giving little thought to rest and comfort and yet you hesitate on my threshold stone? Come forward, Thoronhand, be not afraid."

"You know my name!" Thoron whispered, looking into the smoke-filled forge.

"You are as much a legend as I," laughed Durondell, emerging through the smoke to take Thoron's arm. "How could I forget the sword I forged long ago for Nevian to give to you, the last Errant Rider of the Granite Kings, who has come back from the shadows of the City of Night. I knew you by the hilt of the sword at your belt."

Thoron looked down and took the hilt, drawing the sword from its sheath. "Nevin bade me to show you the blade and ask you to reforge it, strong enough to shatter stone."

Durondell frowned, took the sword from Thoron's hand and walked towards the white-hot furnace. "Each blade I have fashioned has served a purpose in the making of Elundium, but to reforge strong enough to shatter stone . . ."

Turning to Thoron he held up the blade. "Only a King could lift the sword if I do as you ask. Only a King would have the power to carry it into battle."

Thoron smiled, ruffling Eagle Owl's chest feathers. "I ride upon the Lord of Horses and Nevian said that Eagle Owl will carry the sword, for he is the King of Battle Owls and pledged to it. The blade is not for my hands, but for my grandson, Thanehand, who runs hard on Krulshards's heels."

"The Master of Nightmares!" Durondell whispered, running his fingers along the worn cutting edges of the blade. "It will need all my skill and more to forge a blade against the Master of Nightmares, much more."

"What will you need?" Thoron cried. "If it is within my power the horsemen will fetch it."

Durondell smiled, pointing to a small pile of seasoned oak splinters stacked beside the forge. "I will need a forest of fuel to fire the forge. Would your horsemen gather wood for me?"

"It will be done!" Thoron cried, motioning to the long column of horsemen to scatter through the nearby forest.

"Gather only fallen boughs," Durondell shouted. "Touch nothing that lives, it will spoil the molten steel."

Turning back Durondell rummaged through the tall stands of steel, ringing his hammer on each length, searching for the perfect note. Darkness was falling and the first horses had returned, pulling long heavy wind-blown boughs behind them, before he found the piece of steel he sought and laid it beside the forge. "The steel must be fire warm for one night. Come, warriors, and rest and talk of battle days before the Nightmare ran loose in our fair Elundium. Tell me of the Granite City and the tall towers that mark the passing daylights with their pencil-thin shadows. Tell me of the Granite King who keeps the sunlight pure and bright."

"The King has gone!" Thoron whispered. "Vanished without a trace, and the Granite City has been laid to ruins by a mighty Nightbeast army. Nothing remains but broken stone. The Nightbeasts are spreading terror and fear far across Elundium."

"Then we must hurry with this blade and forge it with strength against their shadows. You will be my striker when I split and laminate the blade. Be at my side as the new sun rides clear of World's Edge. Be ready!"

Long after the last horseman had fallen asleep Durondell returned to the forge and banked up the furnace in preparation for the forging. Pausing, he picked up the firewarmed sword and examined the blade, smiling in the soft glow of the fire. "Tomorrowlight I will open your heart and temper you with a new strength for the task ahead."

Putting the sword back into the charcoal cinders he frowned; this sword would need more than steel to make it Kingworthy. It would need something with more strength than ordinary steel that he could hammer into the blade. Looking into the heart of the fire he whispered out every metal known to him, in his head, balancing and blending them to make a sword that would shatter stone. Threads of gold and slivers of silver, tumbles of brass, coils of copper. Sighing, he shrugged his shoulders and walked out into the cold night to watch the stars, but no matter where he looked the answer he sought remained hidden. Far away on the edge of the night wind he could hear a single swan's voice, clear and haunting, calling to him through the darkness.

"Durondell—I have what you seek. Come to me, come to me."

Durondell spun around, following the swan's voice in the darkness. "You have what I seek?" he whispered, a frown creasing his forehead. "But where are you? Where will you land on such a dark night?"

Durondell passed the forge trying to remember each lake and waterway that crossed the world of Elundium. Many were too narrow or weed choked for swans to use but there was the mirror lake that legends named as Clearwater, and that would shine as bright as daylight on a star-filled night. That was the only stretch of water the swans could land safely on. "Equestrius, Lord of Horses," he called, softly leaving the forge and hurrying through the horse lines, "will you carry me to Clearwater, for the key to the forging of this sword is in the swan's voice."

Equestrius snorted and knelt for the Master Armorer of Elundium to climb upon his back, and then cantered into the darkness beyond the forge. For what seemed an age the Armorer clung on tightly letting Equestrius have his head and find the shortest route through narrow valleys and tight copses of tangle-trees until they slowed to a trot and crossed the water meadows that stretched along the banks of Clearwater. Blinking his eyes against the water's glare Durondell looked for the swan.

Ogion heard the thunder of Equestrius's hooves and swam into the shadows of the wide sandy bank then waded ashore. Statue-like he waited on the steep sandy beach. Durondell climbed stiffly to the ground and knelt before the Lord of Swans.

Lifting his eyes he saw the broken splinter of steel in the swan's beak. "Black metal!" he whispered, reaching out a trembling hand towards the broken spear blade that the swan carried. "You carry the strength for the new sword!" he cried, closing his fingers on the black splinter. "There is nothing in my forge to match it."

Ogion hissed, drawing his head back from the Armorer's hand, holding Durondell's eyes with a hard stare. Durondell dropped his hand to his side, brushing his knuckles through the dew-wet sand. "Nevian has asked me to reforge a sword strong enough to shatter stone. A sword of Kings, to be used by Thanehand against the Nightmare, Krulshards."

"Thanehand!" Ogion hissed, seeing now how their fates were mixed. He allowed the Armorer to pick up the broken black metal spear blade. "Forge it hard to avenge my Queen!" Ogion hissed before he entered the water and swam out into the center of the lake. Dawn had begun to break and the first blackbirds stirred in the trees. Ogion beat the still water beneath his dark wings and rose up into the first shaft of sunlight, then turned towards Swanwater, flying high across the rolling hills of Elundium.

The broken spear blade weighed heavy in Durondell's hands as he wrapped the black metal in the tail of his cloak and remounted Equestrius. "Tread carefully, for we carry a rare treasure to the forging and we must not lose it on the way!"

Equestrius snorted and arched his neck, keeping to the center of the way, well clear of the shadows, as he retraced their path back to the forge.

"Strike the wedge squarely, and with each blow see the Nightmare's death!" Durondell instructed, giving the heavy forging hammer to Thoron.

"But . . ." Thoron whispered, his eyes straying to the roaring furnace where the black metal splinter bubbled and hissed in the heat of the fire.

"Close your ears, warrior, to everything but the sweet song of the hammer and look to nothing but the wedge as it opens the blade. Are you ready?"

Thoron nodded silently, flexing his fingers around the smooth polished handle of the hammer. Durondell turned to the forge and gripped the hilt of the sword between the long-handled tongs and laid it white-hot across the anvil. Tiny star sparks fizzed along the blade and fell burning on to the floor. Taking the sharp wedge in his free hand he balanced it on the cutting edge of the sword, squeezing the fine tines to hold it steady.

"Now!" he cried. "Strike! Each time I move the wedge, strike!"

Blow by blow the wedge moved along the sword, biting into the blade, cutting through the thin metal. Twice Durondell returned the sword to the fire to reheat it before striking was complete and the sword lay with its two cutting edges hammered into splayed strips of still fire-hot metal upon the anvil.

"It is a wonder," Thoron exclaimed, bending forward to study the strange star-shaped blade.

Durondell laughed and tossed the sword hilt deep back into the fire. "That is nothing but fancy forge work, any smith can do that. Now comes the task to test the Master Armorer of Elundium. Stand back lest the black metal strikes out."

Carefully, with the shortest blunt-nosed tongs, Durondell withdrew the black splinter of steel from the furnace. Sullen and brooding, glowing dark red, it scattered sparks across the anvil. Durondell took a deep breath and swung his hammer. Thoron leapt back as blood-red sparks fountained up, and blocked his ears as the metal screamed out, echoing all his worst nightmares.

Durondell laughed and struck again and again, flattening and drawing the splinter, changing its shape until he had fashioned it into a long thin strip, twice the length of the sword. Taking a cold chisel from the cooling tank he cut the strip in two and placed both parts beside the sword in the forge. Wiping his blackened, burned hand across his forehead he stepped back and motioned to Thoron to feed the fire with the wood they had gathered.

"I have never worked with black metal before," he said to Thoron, taking him out into the noonday sunlight. "It is Nightmare steel fashioned in the darkness of the City of Night, but caution warned me and prudence armed me well. Look!"

Durondell lifted his old spark-scarred leather apron and showed Thoron where two thin slithers of black metal had pierced through the leather. Thoron gasped, looking at the Armorer's chest, expecting to see blood on his shirt. Durondell laughed and opened his coarse woven shirt to reveal a smooth sheet of shining metal that rose and fell with each breath.

"Steelsilver!" Thoron gasped, reaching out to touch it.

Durondell smiled. "In my youth it was my triumph against the darkness. Then this forge rang night and day to the sweet music of my hammer. I had found the secret of steelsilver and forged all the battle coats for the Warhorses."

"A steelsilver cloak would render a warrior unbeatable in battle," Thoron whispered.

"I lost the secret when the horses' battle coats were finished. This fragment is all that remains and I kept it in memory of my true power. Come, the forge will be hot enough now to reforge the sword."

"Would steelsilver have made the sword strong enough?" Thoron asked as they passed through the doors back into the smoke-hazed forge.

Durondell smiled, picking up his long-handled

tongs. He gripped the hilt of the sword and passed it to Thoron.

"I would have used steelsilver but its strength was to defend against the darkness, not to attack. It would have made the sword shine and given it the sound of larksong as it cut through the air. The new power in this reforged blade will be to use the Nightmare's own steel against him, it will shine enough from the honing stone and yet be black enough to penetrate the malice. Now, hold the blade steady across the anvil while I laminate the black steel inside the sword and the new steel on the outside. It will take all my skill to weld them together."

Thoron held the sword with the fire tongs while Durondell placed the thin strips of black steel inside the blade and eased them together with soft, carefully aimed blows from the flat blennishing hammer. The black steel hissed and spat as the blade closed about it. Quickly the Armorer hammered on the new steel and thrust the sword back into the fire, working furiously at the bellows until the blade glowed white-hot. Calling forward two of the horsemen he gave them strong fire tongs. "When I lay the sword on the anvil hold it steady, no matter what happens."

Thoron helped draw the sword out of the forge and held it steady while the horsemen clamped their tongs beside his. Durondell swung his heaviest hammer down over his shoulder and struck the blade, sending it buckling up into the air. "Hold it steady!" he shouted, striking again.

"Why does it fight against us?" Thoron cried, struggling to keep the blade still.

"Light against darkness. Good against evil!" Durondell shouted above the tortured screams of the metal as his hammer struck again and again along the length of the blade. Showers of blood-red sparks flew up to the roof of the forge, driving back the circle of horsemen that had gathered to watch the reforging. Gradually the hammer blows lessened and their crashing changed from harsh screams to notes of sweet music. The steels had welded together, rough hammered but fast stuck. Durondell laughed and pushed the blade back into the fire.

"Now for the tempering," he cried, pulling an old charred wooden anvil out of the far end of the forge and placing it beside the fire. Blinding smoke enveloped the Armorer as he hammered the blade across the wooden anvil, cooling the hot metal in the heavy oak sap.

"The sword is reforged!" he shouted, carrying the still-smoking blade out into the winter sunlight and putting it into Thoron's hands.

Thoron tested the cutting edge against his fingers and unhooked a sharp stone from his belt.

"Hone it well until it shines!" Durondell laughed. "Hone it until the moment the Lord of Owls takes to the air!"

Thoron gripped Durondell's hand and thanked

him for the reforged sword before he climbed slowly up into Equestrius's saddle.

"Do not thank me until the sword has pierced the Nightmare's heart."

"All Elundium will thank you then," answered Thoron grimly.

"Then hurry, horseman, and deliver the sword before time blunts its edge," urged Durondell.

Equestrius snorted and neighed fiercely, turning away from the forge and cantering across the edges of Mantern's Forest and the great road that led to World's End.

Light at Clatterford

*K*YOT walked alone in the gardens of Clatterford, listening to the haunting cries of the peacocks as they strutted, shadows long, across the lawns. He shivered and pulled his cloak tighter against the winter chill and turned towards the house.

"Without revenge!" he muttered for the thousandth time, waiting for the darkness to cover his confusion and hide his misery. He felt unsettled and unsure of his purpose and ill-at-ease in the company of the beautiful Lady of Clatterford. Sighing, he watched the colors deepen as the sun slipped out of sight behind the crystal halls, reflecting in countless soft glowing patterns as darkness crept forward covering everything. "Clatterford, beautiful Clatterford!" he cried, clenching his hands together, "show me my purpose!"

"Kyot?" a voice whispered in the darkness at his side. Kyot jumped and spun around. "Why do you hide out here and walk alone amongst the peacocks?"

Kyot could see the slender figure of Eventine against the darkening sky and smelled the cold night damp on the cloth of her cloak.

"You and your father are both angry with me," he answered, "and I do not wish to displease you further. I walk alone searching for my purpose, and trying to shut out revenge. I am ashamed that it still burns in my heart. It casts a shadow across the beauty of Clatterford. Yet, if I give it up I turn my back on my father's torment and the Nightmare runs free. You see, I have vowed to shoot an arrow strike into his black heart."

Eventine smiled and touched his hand. "If you treasure the light the Nightmare can never escape from you."

Kyot breathed deeply, inhaling Eventine's night-fresh scent and his heart raced. He had laughed when Thane had told him of his love for Elionbel because he had never known love but now he could almost cast aside all thought of the Nightmare for one soft smile . . . Kyot shook his head, scattering the picture, remembering how he had found his father in the courtyard of Stumble Hill.

Eventine smiled in the darkness and took out a spark, lighting it so that she could look into Kyot's eyes. "There is a shadow in your heart. A shadow of anger because my father denied the glass-bladed arrows."

Kyot blushed again, looking down at the lawn. "No, if there is anger in my heart it is aimed inwards at myself because I know I cannot shut out revenge. I *must* avenge my father's death. Nevian cast the rainbow cloak across my shoulders and showed me his torment. I must follow the Nightmare to the end of Elundium to clear my mind of that picture before it burns my eyes into blindness."

Eventine let the spark fall onto the lawn and sadly shook her head. There were moments in the grasslands when she had seen him with a clear heart and a straight eye.

Kyot frowned and drew back. "I was at Thane's side in the battle before the Gates of Night, and I wounded the Nightmare with one of your father's arrows. That is why Krulshards took my father's life. Now I must kill him."

"Was it only revenge and hate that brought you twenty daylights into the grasslands?" Eventine asked, turning to him. "What of all the other reasons for fighting against the darkness? Do they have a place in your heart, or does revenge shut them out?"

"Purpose? What other purpose? As the Wayhouse Keeper's son my task is to fight against the Nightbeasts. Now I seek their master, Krulshards's, death. That is my purpose."

"Was there nothing but the Nightbeasts before your father's death?"

Kyot shook his head. "My father was pledged against the darkness and now I must take his place to rid the world of all Nightbeasts."

Eventine took both of Kyot's hands and held

them tightly. "What of the daylight? Are you blind to the beauty of the land and all things that move within it?"

"No!" cried Kyot. "Here at Clatterford I can see the beauty you talk of, but the picture of my father's torment is more powerful. It drives me to leave this place. It drives me back on to the road to seek revenge."

Eventine sighed, wrapped her cloak tightly around her shoulders and turned towards the house. "Perhaps if you could see and love the daylight it would ease your pain. Perhaps then you could see that there might be other ways to destroy the Nightmare's heart."

Kyot took a step to follow, stopped and sank to his knees. "Nevian, help me!" he whispered, burying his head in his hands. "Take away this revenge. I know not what to do!"

"Be at peace, Kyot," Fairday said quietly.

Kyot looked up, startled by the voice. The Crystal Maker was standing before him, his sky-washed cloak a shade of pale purple in the starlight. In his hands he held a glass-bladed arrow that still showed the beauty of the setting sun in its tip. Bending, Fairday placed the glass blade against Kyot's forehead.

"Nevian, the Master of Magic, only showed you the tragedy of your father's death. Close your eyes; watch with me now and see what he loved in the daylight."

Kyot closed his eyes and felt the warmth of the

setting sun on his forehead and heard birdsong in the hedgerows, then he saw his father on the high platform of the tower looking out over a beautiful evening landscape of rippling grasslands. The sun touched each polished stalk of grass in waves of glittering light. Wild deer sprang quickly through the grasses and owls hovered in the deepening gloom. The picture faded as Kyot opened his eyes, the first smile of Clatterford on his lips.

"Your father was pledged to keep the wayhouse safe, but his love of the daylight far outmeasured his duty, and his victory over the Nightmare was to hear the first blackbird herald the new morning. I did not counsel you to turn away from the Nightmare but to follow him with this clear picture in your mind. See your father now with the new sun rising above World's Edge, filling the courtyard of the tower on Stumble Hill with the pure morning light that he loved."

Kyot smiled, tears running down his face and rose to his feet. Taking Fairday's hand into his he kissed the Crystal Maker's knuckles. "He could not retreat and let the Nightmare steal one moment of the daylight. He stood there for us all that we might see the new sun rise."

"Give me your hand," Fairday asked. "This is the hand that must be steady for it holds the great Bow of Elundium, but this hand," whispered Fairday, catching hold of Kyot's other hand, "will now hold the future of Elundium tight on the bowstring."

"How so?" cried Kyot. "How can I carry such a burden?"

Fairday smiled. "It will be but a moment's choice in the darkness. That is why your heart must be pure and your eyes clear sighted. Your father, if he lived, could have made that choice, but it has fallen to you to stand in his place."

"Yes, now I can see purpose," Kyot cried, kneeling and offering his empty quiver.

Fairday laughed, and pulled the young Archer to his feet. "Go to my daughter. She has two quivers ready loaded with spine-matched arrows. She has waited impatiently since your arrival at Clatterford for this moment."

Kyot blushed but Fairday laughed, for he had seen Kyot's love for his daughter at their first meeting on the lawns of Clatterford and it had saddened him to watch the shadow of revenge stand between them. Putting his arm around Kyot's shoulders he turned him towards the house.

"Long ago, when your father had just carved the great Bow of Orm he came to me for glass arrows to use against the Nightmare. As payment for the arrows he fashioned a bow from the waste wood and left it in my care. It is the sister, the wife, the perfect match to the Bow of Orm. Go to Eventine for she has that bow, and let the bows sing out together against the Nightmare. Go, for Nevian foretold your meeting and the love that would grow out of it. Go quickly."

Laughing, Kyot thanked Fairday, ran across the

lawn and sprang lightly up the wide glass steps to stand before Eventine. "Forgive me," he stammered, "but revenge had clouded my purpose and made me blind."

Eventine closed her fingers around his hand and brought it to her lips. "When I first saw you in the grasslands I knew our lives were to be interwoven. I know now that I loved you even then."

Kyot smiled, looking deeply into her eyes. "Your arrows, pressed silently into the ground while I slept, were a token!"

"To keep you safe from the Nightbeasts!" she replied laughing. "As a child my father often told me the legend of the Archer who would one daylight cross the grasslands in search of this house. It was a beautiful story, yet full of sadness, for the Archer carried the tragedy of his father's cruel death in his heart. He was lost and alone with only the sun to guide him."

"You were beside me in the village?"

Eventine smiled, reached beneath her cloak and took out the Bow of Clatterford. "Your father left this bow, it is a part of the legend. As a child I would stand before it making myself as tall as possible, eager to nock an arrow onto the bowstring and ride out in search of the lonely Archer. I counted the Nightbeasts and shadowed your every step, you did not hear me because our bows sing the same tune."

Kyot took the bow from Eventine and held it against his own listening to the gentle music the bowstrings made together in the chill night draft blowing through the open doorway. Eventine shivered and put her arm through Kyot's. "Come and see the beauty of Clatterford now that the blindness has gone," she whispered, pointing into the darkened halls where Candlemen were lighting the lamps, bringing the house to life.

Carrying the two bows Kyot entered the inner halls and stood spellbound, staring from wall to wall. Eventine followed his gaze. "Clatterford is a mirror, nothing but a mirror held up against an imperfect world. It is the memory of all that is beautiful, all that is good and all that is bad."

Kyot knelt and reached out a hand to touch the smooth glass walls, to touch the flowers and ferns, stalks and stems, that seemed frozen forever fresh, each leaf and vein, in finest detail, etched inside the glass. "Everything has so much beauty!" he murmured.

"Even shadows!" Eventine smiled, and beckoned him to follow her. "We keep the darkness of men's hearts here in a room crowded with thoughts of greed and revenge. For many daylights I feared I would lose you to that place. Come, let me show you."

Eventine led the way through a maze of smooth polished corridors where each wall grew a little more clouded and dull until they stood before a smoke-darkened door. Eventine shivered and drew her cloak tightly around her shoulders before she opened the door. Kyot cried out and jumped backwards, away from crowded half-formed beasts and nightmare shapes.

"Be not afraid," Eventine shouted, catching him by the hand and drawing him into the darkness. She pushed his hand through the nightmares until it touched the cold glass wall. His hand felt icy and brittle and his eyes ached.

"Learn to face the darkness," she urged, tightening her grip on his hand.

"Rockspray was my eyes in the City of Night!" Kyot cried, blinking and not daring to look through the shadows.

"He is a great Bird of War but he may not always be with you. You must overcome your fear of the dark if you are to follow the Nightmare."

Rockspray flew from Kyot's shoulder to perch on Eventine's arm. "Now I am blind!" Kyot cried, scratching wildly at the wall.

"Open your eyes, Kyot," Eventine whispered, brushing her fingertips across his eyelids. "You can see in the dark if you want to. You have the power."

Slowly he opened his eyes, feeling them widen as the lashes parted.

"What do you see?" Eventine asked.

"Shadowy shapes and dark walls, envy, greed, hatred, revenge," he replied, slowly turning his head.

Eventine laughed and threw open the door. "We will come here each evening until you can look without blinking at what hides in the walls of the shadow room."

"What hides there?" he began to ask as they

walked back towards the crystal halls, but Eventine put a finger on his lips.

"Your love of the daylight will overcome the darkness," she answered, frowning with concern as her father came running through the outer halls.

"Eventine! Kyot!" he cried, "my watchers have seen Nightbeasts swarming through the grasslands in their thousands. They will reach the edges of Clatterford. We must warn the villagers!"

Kyot ran to the top of the wide glass steps and called out against the darkness for Sprint to come to him. Twice he shouted his name and twice in echo a stag roared at the cold evening stars, closely followed by Sprint's proud neigh.

"He runs with Tanglecrown," Eventine said, running to Kyot's side. "Listen! I can hear their hoofbeats near the ford."

Kyot laughed softly as he listened to the jingle of harness mingled with the growing thunder of hooves. "We will strike terror into the Nightbeasts' hearts," he cried.

"And scythe them down as thick as summer corn!" Eventine added, springing lightly down onto the lawn.

Fairday hurried through the doorway holding two twisted glass torches aloft that sparkled and fizzed fountains of cold white light, illuminating the wide sweep of lawns.

"The Lord of Stags!" Kyot cried, stepping back out of Tanglecrown's way as he halted before Eventine.

She laughed and taking Kyot's hand she placed it between the razor-sharp tangle of crystal-tipped antlers on his soft velvet forehead. "My father has armed him against the Nightbeasts," she said, plucking a slender stalk of grass and slicing it in two on the crystal-covered antler tips. "He is proud and brave and stands beside me in the struggle against the darkness. He is the Lord of his kind."

Sprint snorted, arching his neck and rearing up above Kyot's head.

"Sprint is the bravest relay horse from the Tower on Stumble Hill, and he has carried me fearlessly against the shadows many times," Kyot cried, reaching up and catching a loop of rein.

"They will run together!" Fairday shouted above the rising clamor of voices from inside the house. "Together on the edge of the grassland wind, and they will buy the time that we need to forge the arrowheads that will strike at Krulshards's heart."

"You have my pledge on it," Kyot cried, pirouetting Sprint on a tight bridle.

"Come back to the House at Clatterford when the frost before morning is little more than a whisper to chill the fingers. Come then, and the arrows you seek will be ready!" Fairday passed the torches to a waiting Candleman and descended the steps. "Take care, my precious daughter," he begged, reaching up and gripping her hand.

Tanglecrown pawed the ground, sweeping his antlers in a glittering arch.

"I have the Lord of Stags, Father, and the greatest

Archer that ever walked Elundium at my side. I have nothing to fear."

"Krulshards is loose and travels where he pleases. He spreads despair and darkness that blind my second sight. Beware, daughter!"

Eventine smiled down at her father, her eyes full of love. "I treasure the daylight, and thus I must defend it."

Fairday frowned, rubbing his long, age-flecked hand across his forehead, catching a glimpse of a daylight yet to come. "Wait!" he cried, holding on to his daughter's cloak as she turned Tanglecrown to follow Sprint towards the ford. Tanglecrown halted and Eventine looked over her shoulder to her father.

"You will find two travelers on the road, wearied and worn to rags. Pass them by and all Elundium will fall into darkness. Find them and bring them here to the Crystal House of Clatterford."

The River in
the Darkness

WITH each step the roaring noise grew louder, filling the dark secret road with a rage of sound, forcing the King and those that followed him to muffle their heads.

"What can it be?" Breakmaster shouted, his hands slipping on the mist-wet reins.

Gray Goose motioned to them to stop and ran ahead, an arrow ready nocked onto the bow. King Holbian sat down on the cold wet floor and, leaning back against the rough rock wall, slipped into sleep. Angis slid down from Beacon Light's saddle and knelt beside the King, wrapping his gnarled knuckles in her shawl.

Holbian murmured and opened his eyes. "To have such friends here, at Road's End, is more than I deserve." His heavy eyelids slowly shut and his head nodded forward.

"He is age worn and brittle," Angis whispered, tugging at Breakmaster's sleeve and pointing to the maze of fine fractures in the King's face and neck.

Breakmaster nodded silently and drew Angis

aside. "Nevian pledged me to keep him warm, but it is impossible in this dark damp place; even the steelsilver coat is not enough to stop the King from shivering."

Gray Goose emerged from the darkness, glistening beneath a layer of clinging water mist. "Breakmaster," he hissed, shaking his arms and rubbing his wet hands vigorously together to make them warm. "Come here quickly."

Drawing Angis and the horseman away from the King he told them what he had seen farther down the tunnel. "We are doomed! Like rats in a trap we are fated to drown in the dark."

"Trapped? How?"

Gray Goose shook his head as if trying to cast away what he had seen. "There is an underground river, fast running and deep and dangerous, less than one hundred paces farther on."

"But the Chancellors?" interrupted Breakmaster. "Surely if we are trapped they must be also."

Gray Goose laughed bitterly. "There was a bridge, a narrow single span, but either it broke beneath their weight or they ruined it once they were across. The way is closed and the broken rubble from the bridge has partly dammed the river. The roaring noise you can hear is the water rising to flood this miserable secret road."

Breakmaster turned and stared back at the huddled city folk spread along the rough rock walls, clenching his fist. He feared water and felt his throat tighten in panic. "I would rather face a thousand Nightbeasts . . ." he began to whisper, when Gray Goose gripped his arm and shook him fiercely.

"You must be strong. There is none but us to lead; the King is aging and growing weaker with each step; we are the only Captains."

Breakmaster laughed, "I have stood before galloping horses and tamed the wildest beasts but . . ."

"Then stand by me now, friend," whispered the Archer, nervously pulling at his bowstring, "and tame the beast that lurks in your heart, it will be your greatest triumph."

"And the hardest battle," Breakmaster added, turning to Angis. "Go gently amongst the people," he instructed her in a hushed whisper, "find Arachatt, the stonemason, and bring him with all haste to me."

Arachatt hurried forward, his stone-chipping tools clinking against each other in a coarse hessian sack thrown across his shoulder.

"The masons that carved this tunnel had skill beyond my understanding," he laughed, swinging the heavy tool sack onto the ground before asking what task they had called him to do.

"Follow," Gray Goose commanded, disappearing into the mist-wet black tunnel. The water had risen almost to Gray Goose's knees before he reached the broken bridge and showed the mason the disaster that blocked the path.

"Wonder of a lost age," Arachatt murmured,

staring at the broken span of the bridge where it rose in a steep arch out of the raging waters.

"Is there a way to cross?" Breakmaster asked, struggling to control his panic and keep his voice level.

Arachatt laughed and waded out onto the bridge. "Light me a spark, horseman! And try to keep it steady in your hand." Kneeling, the mason inspected the smooth stone of the bridge and peered down into the jumble of broken stone blocking the river. Whistling and humming tunelessly he scaled the walls and climbed out over the black boiling water. "Pass me a searcher," he shouted to Gray Goose who was holding the sack of tools above the rising flood.

For what seemed half a daylight Breakmaster shivered, knee deep in the freezing cold water, holding the spark, while Gray Goose passed a steady flow of dull, hammer-blemished tools up to the mason. "Is there a way? Tell us."

Arachatt laughed and climbed down out of the roof, wiping his dirty face on his sleeve. "The stonemen that fashioned this road built two bridges, the one you see ruined and impassable and above that a narrow ledge. I expect the ledge bridge follows a natural fault in the rock and they probably used it to cross the river while they were building the lower one."

"But can we escape using the ledge?" Gray Goose asked above the roar of the water cascading over the fallen rubble. It was deafening and dampened the music of the steelsilver coat as King Holbian came forward to find his Captains in debate.

"Lord," Breakmaster cried, "there was a bridge, but now . . . !"

Arachatt pushed his way forward. "There is a way, my Lord, dangerous and difficult, but there is a way forward."

King Holbian struck his spark and stared out at the broken span of the bridge. "How?" he asked without turning.

"There is a ledge, my Lord, up near the roof of the secret road. It is blocked with rubble and fallen stone choke, but if we clear it we have a path to the daylight."

Holbian looked up at the narrow ledge. "A bird or a quick-footed mason could use that road but what of my people, the old and the infirm, the bent beggars and the small children? They will never be able to scale the walls and reach the ledge."

Arachatt spread his rough calloused hands. "There will be space for all those who can reach the ledge; that is the way forward for the strong, my Lord."

King Holbian looked back along the tunnel to where the first bedraggled city dwellers had halted, knee deep in the cold black water, their few meager possessions held above the flood. He turned back to his mason. "I am the last Granite King of all the people of Elundium, the strong and the weak and you, Mastermason, must fashion a way for us all. None shall be left behind."

"Not even the horses, my Lord?" Breakmaster cried out above the roaring waters.

"Not even the horses!" echoed the King, walking back amongst his people, calling out the strong and the willing to help the mason.

Arachatt frowned and muttered under his breath as he rescaled the wall, measuring with his finger-span and dropping a plumb line from the brink of the ledge down into the black water. "We will build a ramp," he eventually shouted down to the King. "It will be steep and slippery but it will lead us to the daylight."

"You are the Mastermason," King Holbian shouted up, scrambling to the ledge. Angis nimbly followed him and bent to start clearing the stone choke. "No, my Lady of Elundium," he cried, putting his hand on her arm, "this work is not for your gentle hands."

"Lord, I would wear my hands blunt to work beside my King and win a road to the daylight."

Holbian smiled down at her. "You are King-worthy, my Lady, and I am proud to have you by my side."

Arachatt measured and dressed each rough piece of stone choke, before his helpers leveled them into position. Knuckles became scuffed and bled raw before the ramp had risen against the flooding waters.

"Bring the people forward!" Arachatt shouted. "The rubble from the ledge and the newly built ramp has completely dammed the river and the level will rapidly rise. There is not a moment to waste."

"What of the road beyond the river?" Holbian shouted, pushing the last huge blocking boulder to the ledge. "Surely that will flood and drown us before we can escape?"

"No, my Lord," Arachatt replied. "Beyond, the road is above this level and slopes steeply upwards; the water will fill the secret road we have traveled, flooding it all the way back to the Granite City. But hurry the people forward, my Lord, or we will be trapped forever."

King Holbian gripped the mason's arm and quickly thanked him. "It is the greatest wonder in all Elundium," he cried, jumping down into the waist-deep water and urging the long column of city folk forward onto the ramp.

"Bring the children," he shouted, "for they are our tomorrowlights, and then the old, they are the glories of yesterlights. Keep order!"

Gray Goose led the people and Holbian frowned, searching back along the dark tunnel, hurrying past the last stragglers. "Be quick! Hurry!" he ordered, lighting his spark and letting a sigh of relief escape from his lips.

"Hurry, Breakmaster!" he called, running towards the horseman, but Breakmaster was on his knees between the two horses, shaking and crying with fear, the whites of his eyes brighter than the winter's moon.

"Lord, I cannot!" he cried, looking into the

King's face. "I have tried and tried to lead the horses forward but the fear holds me back."

Holbian sank onto his knees beside the horseman and put his arms around his trembling shoulders. "What fear? What fear stops you, my brave champion?"

Breakmaster bent his head. "The water, my Lord, I dread it. I cannot walk for the fear."

King Holbian smiled and held the horseman's head against his chest. "You gave me the strength in the darkness of the siege and showed me the way, now I will lead you through your greatest fear. Come, place your hand on Beacon Light's shoulder for you gave her the courage to stand against the shadows and she will not falter."

King Holbian took a deep breath, unbuckled the steelsilver coat and spread it across Breakmaster's shoulders. The music in the fine shimmering metal held the hint of skylarks rising up in search of the sun and it drowned out the boiling roar of the rising water.

"Walk with me, friend!" the King shouted, as the raging darkness closed about them, and he struggled to lead both horses and the horseman forward towards the ramp without the warmth of the cloak.

The secret road became a cold and dangerous place full of strange noises and hideous shadows and the King shuddered as his courage wavered. The ramp was in sight now but the swirling waters had reached his chest and the rushing current was threatening to sweep him clean off his feet. "Hold on to the reins!" he shouted to the terrified horseman as the horses surged forward onto the first rough stones of the ramp. "Their strength will lift us clear of the water."

Mulberry moved ahead of Beacon Light, scrambling up to safety. Looking back the King saw that Breakmaster's hands were slipping on the reins, the water was closing over his head. He was floundering on the brink of the ramp, dislodging loose stones with his feet. "We will lose him!" he cried, looking desperately for Gray Goose, but the Archer could not help, he was struggling to pull Mulberry out into the tunnel. Drawing a deep breath Holbian let go of Mulberry's tail and ducked beneath the water. Two giant steps backwards and he caught hold of the horseman's arms and looped them through Beacon Light's reins. Rising above the water he urged the horses on.

"Pull us to safety!" he cried, clutching on the high cantle of the saddle. He felt the water swirl over him as the horse struggled up the last part of the steep ramp onto the narrow ledge.

Gray Goose and Arachatt were waiting with strong hands and helped the King pull Breakmaster up into the dry tunnel. Breakmaster rose from his knees, choking and spitting out mouthfuls of water, his fingers fumbling with the catch of the steelsilver coat.

"Lord, you risked your life to save my skin!" he gasped.

Holbian laughed, knelt beside the exhausted

horseman and took his hand. "Who will calm the horses and ready them for battle? Who in all Elundium could do that as well as you, my loyal Captain?"

Shaking the last drops of water out of the beautiful steelsilver coat Breakmaster rose to his feet and gave it back to the King. "To serve you all my days would not repay the debt I now owe you!" he said. "For I know what courage it took to face your fear and put this cloak about my shoulders."

"There is no debt, friend, there never will be one between us, for we are battle-tested in friendship and forged together through our moments of great need."

Looking up into the dark tunnel that stretched before them the King pointed an age-bent finger. "Gray Goose, lead us forward out of this darkness!"

Rising to his feet the Archer nocked an arrow onto his bow and disappeared into the tunnel.

"Come, we must follow," commanded the King, leading Beacon Light forward past the waiting city folk.

"Lord, you have saved us!" the people cried out as the King walked to the head of the column.

Angis fell into step with him, casting her warm shawl across his shoulders. "You have saved us all, my Lord, even the weak and the humble, and they thank you. Listen to the praise in their voices."

Holbian laughed, rubbing his hand through Beacon Light's wet mane. "That is the real task set before Kings, to care for all their people. Power and pomp are nothing but empty moments; rising towers and palaces are empty shells; the greatness of Elundium walks with me here in the dark."

Angis nodded and made to drop back into her place.

"Walk with me," Holbian called, "and listen to the music in the coat, for it tells of where the darkness ends and the new daylight begins."

"Lord, wherever you walk there will be sunlight, for you are a King who loves his people," she answered.

"If only I had discovered all this an age ago there would be no Nightbeasts," King Holbian sighed.

The First Shout
of Silence

*T*HANE murmured in his sleep and curled himself into a tight ball against the cold, snuggling into Ousious's side under the torn cloak. Ogion sat sentry-still nearby, staring out across the blizzard-covered beach, past the sleeping forms of the flock of swans, at the dark lake beyond. The ice had begun to groan and crack yet there was no change in the weather. Rising up, he waddled up the beach and fueled the dying fire, tossing broken beach wreckage onto the glowing embers.

Thane opened his eyes, sat up and smiled at the Lord of Swans. He stretched out his arms and stared at the bright cotton thread sewn neatly across his wrist. Blinking he frowned and remembered slashing his wrist to try to save Ousious's life, but how did the colored thread become sewn across his wrist? Turning he felt under the half-cloak at the stiff blood-encrusted wound on Ousious's chest. She was warm to his touch and her breast rose and fell with each sleeping breath she took. Thane touched the rough stitches he had sewn with strands from Stumble's mane and looked up to the top of the beach where the horse grazed, hunched against the weather.

"The Queen of Swans lives!" he shouted, before falling back exhausted. Thane shivered beneath the cloak and closed his eyes, too tired to worry about the rainbow thread, but the creaking voice of the ice that lay thick across Swanwater made him sit up again. "Why does the ice move?" he asked, staring out across the lake. "Perhaps something unnatural is draining the water," he thought. He watched the buckling ice water shatter under its own weight and collapse into the freezing mud out in the center of the lake.

"A great power is emptying the lake," he said, turning his wrist over and gazing at the colored thread. "Something as great as the hand that sewed up my wrist! Perhaps Nevian, the Master of Magic!" Thane whispered, touching the thread and feeling the warmth of a summer day flow through his numb fingers. "Perhaps he came and found me stranded on this beach, weak from the loss of blood."

Thane rose slowly to his feet, using a twisted water-bleached branch to keep him steady. Dizzily he took one step towards the shattered ice and sank to his knees.

Ogion hissed and flapped his wings, pushing him back towards Ousious. "Rest and become strong, you cannot follow Krulshards until Ousious is strong enough to fly, for only she knows the way."

Thane turned back the corner of the cloak and gently stroked the soft downy feathers on Ousious's neck. "Please tell me, Queen of Swans, which way the Nightmare took Elionbel."

Ousious stirred, moved her wings and straightened her neck. Opening and closing her bright orange beak she brushed it against Thane's cheek.

"Where did the Nightmare run?" Thane asked, pressing his ear against her breast. Far away beyond the edge of the wind he could hear the whisper of her heart and faint murmurs of the dark road through Meremire Forest.

Then Ogion pulled him away. "Leave Ousious to rest, she is weak and burdened with our fate. It was foretold long ago when night first spread across Elundium that the Queen of Swans would lead us into silence. We did not know how this silence would begin, only that it heralds the Nightmare's end, or so the legend tells, for we are the gray swans of his doom. That is why we called his name each time we flew across Elundium, searching without finding, looking without seeing, for we feared the silence."

"But the aged crones say you carry everyone's death in your voices; that is why the people fear you."

"Men are fools who seek themselves in every shadow. If they had listened to our voices they would have heard the Nightmare's name."

"But you resisted chasing the Nightmare when

Nevian asked you to show me his footprints!"
Thane cried.

"Knowing your fate and meeting it are very different things. Knowing that somehow your loved one will be struck mute is not an easy path to follow."

Thane looked across at the sleeping Queen and whispered, "Was it Krulshards's black spear blade that struck her mute or did I damage Ousious as I removed the broken splinter?"

Ogion shook his head. "Fate drew us together, Thane, and your skill and courage saved Ousious's life, for without your blood she would have died. Each daylight as our slender necks intertwine we will echo our love together, for with the rising of the winter sun all our voices shall fall silent with that of our Queen."

"But how shall I find the Nightmare if you do not tell me the way? Stumble cannot keep pace with you, we have followed your voice through all the wildlands."

Ogion searched the night shadows, turning his head from left to right. "Ousious will show you the way when she is strong enough to fly. Fear not what tomorrow may bring, be patient until then."

Thane put his head into his hands and wept, cursing Krulshards for striking Ousious mute, and covered by despair, he was blind to the black night passing through the gray hours into a cold winter's dawn where the first rays of the winter sun shone dully on Swanwater, melting the thick layer of ice that lay across the mud. Thane searched the beach, sifting the pebbles between his fingers.

"Where is the Nightmare's splinter of broken steel? Show me where it fell so that I can destroy it in the fire," he asked Ogion.

Ogion looked up to the winter sun and opened and closed his beak noiselessly then ran out across the ice, flapping his wings.

"Your silence has started, and the cause of it is lost in the mud of the lake. Well, it is as safe there as it is in the fire!" Turning, he knelt beside Ousious and inspected the ugly wound, testing the strength of the horsehair stitches. All around him the flock of swans was moving along the beach searching for food or laying fine down feather nests in shaded dips or clumps of gray reeds that rattled in the chill morning wind.

Ogion brought scraps of half-chewed fish and grass for Thane and Ousious to eat. Stumble trotted down off the thinly-grassed bank and neighed, rubbing his muzzle on Thane's arm.

Stumble whinnied and returned to grazing on the bank, leaving Thane to sit in black brooding silence, feeding the beach wreckage into the roaring fire while he watched the ice slowly thaw. On the twenty-third daylight of silence Ousious paddled out into Swanwater and, beating her wings on the shallow cold muddy water, she slowly rose up into the air and turned to the grasslands. Thane saddled Stumble and quickly mounted him to follow the swans, cantering around the far edge of the shallow lake. Wading through deep, sticky mud they climbed onto the far bank that led to the desolate grasslands. Waiting for Ousious to grow strong on the banks of Swanwater had left Thane weak from the bitter cold and the lack of whole nourishing food and he slipped into a dizzy exhausted half sleep in the saddle as Stumble carried him forward. Driving rain brought him back to his senses long after darkness had fallen. The horse had halted inside a thick clump of brambles where sharp thorns cut through his ragged shirt and breeches. Dismounting carefully he spread his wet cloak across the top of the lowest bramble bush and crept shivering beneath it. Stumble lay down beside him and Thane rested his head on the horse's warm shoulder and quickly fell asleep.

They awoke, stiff and aching, to a cold wet drizzle that misted the horizon and clung to the gray stalks of winter grass in long glistening drops. Stumble lifted his head, sniffed at the morning damp air and flattened his ears against the side of his head.

"What is it?" Thane whispered, peering cautiously through the rain-soaked tangle of brambles. "Nightbeasts!" he hissed, crouching back against the ground. "Nightbeasts are all around us!"

The dull tramp of clawed feet and the harsh rattle of foul armor drew closer and closer. Thane unsheathed his dagger and looked desperately for a gap between the Nightbeasts. "If they discover us we must try and dodge between them. They are almost blind in the daylight and attack by following sounds."

Stumble snorted, arching his neck and accidentally caught his mane in the thorns. By pulling back and violently shaking the thicket he broke free. Thane gripped the sharp thorns in his hands and stilled the bush but it was too late, the nearest Nightbeast had turned at the sound, his spear blade raised to strike. Roaring he took a step closer. Thane shrank back, waiting for the spear blade to cut through the brambles and peered past the advancing Nightbeast into the drifting drizzle mist.

"We must run," he hissed, slipping his leg over the saddle and getting ready to spring forward.

Suddenly two fleeting shapes flanked by huge Border Runners broke through the mist. Arrows sang in the air and the nearest Nightbeast screamed, driving his blade harmlessly into the ground as he collapsed. Roaring and screaming, the mass of Nightbeasts swarmed after the two shadowy figures as they melted back into the mist. Thane laughed and quickly dismounted, putting his ear to the damp earth. Faint hoofbeats made the ground tremble, taking the Nightbeasts away from the bramble thicket in a wide circle. Leaping to his feet, he urged Stumble out of the brambles into the wet grass.

"Run, Stumble, run!" he cried, jumping into the saddle and turning the horse away from the Nightbeast screams into the long grass, and he did not rest or ease the pace until well after noon. The drizzle worsened into heavy rain and Thane hunched his shoulders and turned his soaking cloak collar up against the weather.

"We are lost," he muttered, blinking the water out of his eyes as he searched the low dark sky for the swans. Turning in the saddle, Thane saw dark shapes breast the horizon and start crossing towards them. "The Nightbeasts are everywhere!" he cried, pulling at the reins with numb fingers to turn the horse and find a place to hide.

Stumble stretched his neck and cantered for league after league through the long grass until ahead of them the grasslands broke into low tree-crested ridges of barren earth. Between the first two ridges Thane found a narrow reed-filled gully. Dismounting he led Stumble in amongst the reeds to hide but the ground quickly became marshy and too soft for the horse to go anywhere; he was sinking into the mud. Retreating a few strides Thane commanded him to wait. Unsheathing his dagger he began to cut armfuls of reeds and laid them in a crisscross pattern where the oozing mud was firmest, in the center of the gully. Taking the last bundle of cut reeds he wove them, just as he had seen his mother weave rush mats, threading and pulling each reed until it was bound tightly to the next. Walking back across the mat he took the reins over Stumble's head and led him forward.

The mat swayed with each reluctant footstep and black mud oozed up between the reeds, but it held their weight. "Lie down!" Thane hissed, touching

Stumble's knee with a cold muddy hand. Clearly he could hear the tramp of mailed feet and the rattle of armor above the noise of the pouring rain and the wind moaning through the tall reed stems. Crawling back to the edge of the mat he pushed their path of cut reeds aside, forcing it beneath the treacherous mud.

"Lie down or the Nightbeasts will see you. They are too heavy to follow us into this marsh and will pass us if we are hidden; lie down."

Stumble nickered softly and trembled with fear but he bent his forelegs. Thane pushed firmly on the cantle of the saddle and the horse sank down onto the mat. Cold black mud bubbled up along his side and he snorted, struggling against Thane's hand to stand. The whites of his eyes were wide with panic.

"Steady, Stumble," he whispered, caressing the horse's shoulder. "The mat takes our weight." Stumble shifted his head and rubbed his muzzle on Thane's arm. "The Nightbeasts are near us now," Thane whispered. "We must lie still until they have gone."

Stumble slowly lowered his head until his chin was resting in the cold black mud and Thane spread the dirty cloak across them both. He laid his head wearily on Stumble's shoulder and fought off the waves of sleep that were pulling at his eyelids. Reaching back into his pocket he pulled out the little silver finger bowl that the Nightmare had tarnished and spoiled, and brought it to his lips.

"I will find you, Elionbel, I will never give up," he whispered, tracing her name with a dirty cracked fingernail along the rim of the cup.

The rain had eased with the coming of evening but now as darkness fell it became a roaring torrent that pattered on the cloak and drummed on the mat of reeds. Thane moved as close to Stumble as he could, feeling the layer of sticky mud pull at his rough shirt as he fell asleep.

Sharp Eyes in the Grasslands

*H*UNGER and pain blurred together and the noise of the rain on the reeds drowned out the noise of men and horses crossing the low ridges on the heels of the Nightbeasts. "There is no danger here," Tombel had shouted. "I can smell the Nightbeasts on the evening wind and they have gone before us into the grasslands."

Gathering his Captains he had warned them to cross well clear of the marsh gullies, using only the high ground. "Lord, Lord," a Marcher on the edge of the great crescent of warriors had shouted just before nightfall, "there are two riders approaching. One rides on a mighty stag, before them two Border Runners search the ground."

Tombel had halted the crescent half a league beyond the first earth ridge and set the Marchers and Gallopers into battle order, taking the center of the field as his own while he waited for the riders. Wiping the trickles of rain water out of his eyes he laughed and threw his Marching sword high into the dark night air.

"Kyot, Kyot," he cried, running forward as the Archer rode into the circle of their torchlight, but frowning he turned his eyes on Eventine, quickly took off his metal helm and bowed. "Are you the Lady of Clatterford?" he whispered, offering her the hilt of his Marching sword.

Smiling, Eventine jumped to the ground and lightly touched Tombel's hand. "Great is the legend of the Lord of Marchers," she said, "for he hunts Nightbeasts in all Elundium without rest."

"Greater still is the legend of the fair Lady of Clatterford, who has tamed the Lord of Stags as her mount," he replied, sheathing his sword.

Eventine laughed, putting her hand through Tanglecrown's huge set of crystal-tipped antlers onto his velvet forehead. "He is free, my Lord, and serves no master or mistress; we hunt the Nightbeasts together, side by side."

Tombel smiled, stepping forward. "We run on their heels, Lady, night and day, without rest. They are before us now."

Kyot frowned. "You say they are before you?"

Tombel nodded, pointing past Kyot's shoulder into the darkness.

Eventine stepped back two paces and knelt beside the Border Runners, her hand on the ground. "We have been following the tracks of a single horse for one daylight through the wet grass, but if the Nightbeasts crossed here they must have killed it."

Tombel turned and called his Captains forward,

but each one in turn shook his head when asked if they had seen a horse wandering alone.

Eventine turned and walked to the edge of the torchlight, pulling her cloak tight against the rain. "Where are the two travelers?" she whispered to Rockspray who perched forlornly, soaked through, on her shoulder.

She sighed and returned to Kyot's side and listened eagerly as Tombel told of the wreck of Granite City and the vanished King, but her eyes grew wet with tears as he told of Krulshards's attack on Woodsedge and the loss of his wife and daughter and of Arbel's capture as he tried to follow them.

"I will not rest until every Nightbeast is slaughtered," Tombel concluded, grimly, ordering his Captains back into the crescent to ready the warriors for a night's march.

"Will you not wait and rest until morning?" Eventine asked, but Tombel shook his head.

"These Nightbeast tracks will grow cold. We dare not wait."

Kyot gripped Tombel's hand and asked him quietly if he could take the crescent of warriors towards Clatterford and keep it safe from the Nightbeast attack. "Fairday is forging glass arrowheads for us to use against the Nightmare and he needs as many daylights as we can win."

"Not one Nightbeast claw shall touch the lawns of Clatterford," Tombel cried, leading the warriors forward.

Kyot and Eventine stood hand in hand watching

the slow-moving crescent with its flickering torch-light fade into the grasslands.

"Clatterford will be safe now," Kyot whispered, calling Sprint to his side and gathering the reins into his hand. "Let us ride on and find shelter from this bitter rain."

Eventine hesitated, looking across the dark bulk of the low ridges. "No, Kyot," she whispered, taking his hand again and removing it from the reins. "There is something here, I can feel it. Look, the Border Runners are restless and cast around us in circles; they can scent something. We must wait for the new daylight and then search."

Kyot smiled at her in the darkness and spread his cloak over them both. "If the two travelers passed this way you will find their tracks, I know it."

Sprint and Tanglecrown grazed on the steep slope of the first ridge while Kyot and Eventine sat beneath a makeshift canopy made from their cloaks that they had stretched between the bows of Orm and Clatterford. They sat looking out across the darkened gully, listening to the rattle of the rain on the winter black reeds.

Kyot turned his head and for a moment he gazed at Eventine's still silhouette. "Will you come with me to the Tower of Stumble Hill when the Nightmare is dead?" he asked.

Eventine turned to him in the darkness and rested her head on his shoulder. "Nothing will ever part us. Not even the darkness of the Nightmare, Krulshards," she whispered.

Kyot lifted his hand and gently caressed her tangled wet hair. Long after Eventine had fallen asleep against his shoulder Kyot sat staring out into the rain, knowing a little of how Thane had felt after he had met Elionbel and seeing some of the pain he must be suffering now that the Nightmare had taken her. Eventine moved, snuggling closer without waking. The gray hours had come and Kyot shivered, looking down at the glistening wind-bent reeds that showed in the half light. "I will find the Nightmare, and rid Elundium of his foul shadow forever," he whispered, touching the arrows packed tightly into his quiver.

Eventine awoke with the first light of dawn, stretched stiffly and looked out from beneath the cloak at the pouring rain. Dark shapes crossed the line of the barren ridges, flying close to the ground. "The gray swans of doom!" she whispered, pointing up at the swans as they flew overhead.

"They call out the dead," Kyot answered in fear, covering his ears and turning his head away.

Eventine laughed, and tugged at his arm. "These swans are not gray. At least, the leader has a snow-white breast. Listen, they fly without making a sound."

Kyot lifted his head and watched the swans flying from gully to gully. It was true, their leader was white. "They are searching for something," he whispered, lifting Rockspray up. "Fly with them, search the gullies."

Eventine stood up, took her cloak from the bows

and shook it, scattering raindrops across the steep hillside. Ousious flew low across the reed bed, twisting her head from side to side. Eventine shook Kyot's arm. "The owl sees something in the reed beds. Look!"

Ousious descended into the gully, wheeling and turning slowly across the place where Thane lay, crying out his name with her silent voice. Rockspray stooped beside her shrieking in the dawn light. Eventine shaded her eyes against the stinging rain and stared out at the winter black reeds. "There's something there, in the reed bed," she said, quickly drawing a glass-tipped arrow and nocking it onto her bow.

Sprint had lifted his head as the swans flew over and neighed as if calling to a lost friend. Tanglecrown pawed at the wet grass and cantered down to where Eventine stood. Kyot shook out his cloak, flung it across his shoulders and ran into the shadows of the gully, his hand on the feather flight of an arrow.

The gully had become treacherously swollen from the heavy rainfall and Kyot sank almost to his knees in the black mud on the edge of the reeds. "Nothing could live in there," he called over his shoulder as Eventine ran to join him. "Be careful where you tread."

Eventine suddenly stopped and knelt. "Look, look at this!"

Kyot retreated out of the mud and looked down over her shoulder at a neat hoofprint in the soft earth. Stepping forward he found another, then another, right on the very edge of the reeds.

Sighing sadly he turned to Eventine. "The horse we followed must have wandered into the gully and been swallowed by the marsh."

Eventine shivered and began to turn away, pulling the hood of her cloak up over her wet hair against the weather, but something made her stop.

Something in the reed bed glittered in the gray morning light. "Kyot, what is that?" she cried, pointing.

Kyot followed her hand, balancing on tiptoe to see between the reeds. "There is a dark shape on the surface of the marsh!" he said, uncertainly, stepping back and steadying Eventine on the edge of the reeds while she peered through the tall stems.

"Tanglecrown, stand for me," Eventine asked as she sprang up into the saddle and looked over the top of the reeds. "There is a clearing, the reeds have been cut and woven into a mat. It is floating on the surface of the mud with two figures lying on it. I think one of them is a horse. Wait! Something shines on the mat, something shines with the glint of beaten silver."

Kyot scrambled up onto Sprint's saddle and peered out into the reeds following Eventine's pointing finger. "Search for me, Rockspray!" he urged, calling to the owl who hovered silently into the air above the gully.

Stumble heard Kyot's voice sending the owl to look for them and tried to raise his head but the sticky black mud held him stuck fast onto the mat. Stumble's struggles woke Thane from his dark feverish dreams and he fought to open his mud-heavy eyelids. Far away he could hear a familiar voice above the rattle of the rain. Blinking, he looked up at the owl.

"Rockspray," he cried, weakly, lifting the hand that held the finger bowl. "Find Kyot and tell him . . . tell him that the Nightmare has taken Elionbel."

Thane's hand began to sink back into the mud at his side but as the base of the finger bowl touched the mud Rockspray's talons hooked around the rim and he took it, pulling it free of Thane's weakening grip, taking it up into the rainswept sky, beyond the tall circle of reeds.

Thane smiled, tears running down his dirty face. "Kyot will rescue Elionbel," he whispered, using the last of his strength to lift his hand and stroke his horse's neck. "He will take up the task we cannot finish."

Stumble suddenly freed his head from the mud and lifting it, he neighed as loudly as he could, his flanks shaking from the effort.

Rockspray stooped to Kyot, delivering the finger bowl into his hands. Kyot lifted the little silver bowl and traced the fine letters engraved around the rim, then looking up he shouted at the top of his voice. "THANE! THANE!"

He jumped down from Sprint's back and passed the bowl to Eventine and waded out into the reeds, but with each stride he sank deeper and deeper, clutching and breaking the tough reed stems in an effort to reach his friend.

"Wait!" Eventine called, dropping the cup into her safest pocket. "You will be sucked under the mud if you go any farther. Come back."

Kyot struggled and scrambled back onto the bank. "We must rescue them. We are like brothers, we must . . ."

Eventine gripped his shoulders and tried to calm him. "We cannot cross the marsh; the rain has made it much too treacherous even to lay a reed path. Somehow we must bring them to the bank, there must be a way."

"But Thane may be only moments away from death. The reed mat may be sinking."

Eventine put a finger on Kyot's lips and pressed him into silence. Reaching back into her quiver she withdrew the only steel-bladed arrow she carried, barbed and hooked behind the tip. Unbuckling the pouch on Tanglecrown's saddle she lifted out a fine silken rope of twisted strands of glass no thicker than a needle thread, and carefully tied an end around the barbs.

"Do you trust Thane's life in my hands?" she asked, springing up onto Tanglecrown's saddle and nocking the arrow onto her bowstring. Kyot smiled and reached up to touch her hand.

"Your aim is clear-sighted and true. I would put my own life in your hands, beautiful Lady of Clatterford."

She looked along the spine of the arrow, choosing her moment as the reeds bent in the wind. Easing the arrow she looked down and asked Kyot to tie the loose end of the glass rope onto Sprint's saddle and lead him up onto the slope above the gully. After Kyot had secured the rope she took a deep breath and tried to calm her shaking fingers, hearing her father's words echoing in her head. "Do not pass them by or all Elundium will fall into shadow."

Blinking just once she drew the arrow back and released it into the reeds. Thane laughed as he heard the arrow sing its way through the reeds and cut into the mat at his feet, sinking with a dull splash through the layer of mud that had seeped up between the weaving.

"Kyot has found us!" he cried as the silken rope went taut and the mat began to move towards the bank. Sprint arched his neck and pulled hard, urged on by Kyot as the heavy mud-laden mat broke down the reed stems in its path. Tanglecrown hooked his antlers onto the rope and pulled beside the little horse but the mat twisted and turned, bumping into the tough reed stems, and the barbed arrowhead was tearing through the reed mat. Eventine took the reins from Kyot and sent him back to the edge of the reeds. "Wade out as far as you can and cut them a path. Be quick!" she whispered.

"Thane, Thane!" Kyot shouted, wading out as far as he dared, cutting through the tough reed stems to ease the passage of the mat. Closer and closer it came, pushing a small wave of mud before it. Kyot reached out and caught hold of the edges of the mat, his strong fingers tearing through the reeds as he brought it to the safety of the bank.

"Thane, oh Thane," he cried, seeing the ragged mudblackened figure struggling to crawl towards him. With strong hands he quickly lifted him and laid him on the bank and cast his cloak over him. Turning back he cried out in horror to see Stumble slipping off the sinking mat into the marsh. Running onto the mat he cut the glass rope and tied it around the pommel of Stumble's vanishing saddle.

"Pull, Sprint, pull!" he shouted, grabbing at the reins to keep the horse's head above the mud. "Pull, or Stumble will sink."

Tanglecrown and Sprint dug in their hooves and, shoulder to shoulder, edged forward. Eventine ran back to the gully and took the reins from Kyot while he waded, waist deep in the sticky mud, and helped the floundering horse with both hands. Eventually Stumble scrambled wearily onto firm ground on the edge of the marsh and clambered up on the bank.

"You are safe!" Kyot cried with relief, stripping the filthy saddle and bridle from the exhausted horse. Sprint cantered to Stumble's side, snorting and whinnying in greeting as the muddy horse shook himself and pulled on a mouthful of grass.

Eventine and Kyot knelt at Thane's side and gently pulled back the cloak. "He is bone thin, and near to death," Kyot whispered. "We must get him to shelter out of this rain."

"He needs wholesome food and a good fire to warm him through," Eventine added, calling Tanglecrown to come to her. "We must get him to Clatterford without delay. I will ride ahead of you and warn my father," she said as she sprang onto Tanglecrown's back.

Kyot made to rise as Eventine cantered away but Thane clung weakly to his hand. "The Nightmare has Elionbel. I must find the gray swans and follow them. They will show me the way."

Kyot smiled down at Thane. "The gray swans have been flying over the marsh led by a beautiful swan with a white breast; they have been flying since dawn drove the night away. They led us to where you lay."

"Were they silent?" Thane asked anxiously.

Kyot nodded. "Again and again they swooped silently through the gully, brushing their wing tips on the top of the reeds."

Thane sighed and turned over his wrist to show Kyot the fine rainbow thread. "Ousious is the Queen of the gray swans, she . . ." Thane's head slumped forward as dark dreams overtook him and he slept in the warmth of Kyot's cloak. Kyot hurriedly cut two wind-blown boughs from the trees on the top of the ridge and using the glass rope and Thane's ragged half-cloak he made a rough stretcher which he attached to Sprint's saddle, binding it tight with his stirrup leathers. He tied

Thane onto the stretcher and called Stumble to follow. Mounting Sprint he rode as fast as he could through the tall wet grass, following the clear track Tanglecrown had left.

"Guard Stumble," he called to the Border Runners as they fanned out on either side of the exhausted horse. Sprint arched his neck and, pulling hard on the makeshift harness, he cantered as fast as he dared through the waist-high grass, closing the gap to Clatterford with each measured stride.

Light at
the End of
the Secret Road

"*D*AYLIGHT, Lord! Daylight!" Gray Goose cried, shaking King Holbian's shoulder. "Daylight?" mumbled the King, slowly opening his eyes and looking up at the Archer. For what had seemed an age beyond counting he had bravely led the city folk along the secret road, but little by little the darkness and the cold had crept beneath the steelsilver cloak, weakening his ancient bones.

"Yes, Lord, less than half a league farther the city folk are waiting for you to lead them out."

Holbian carefully took off his battle gloves and stared at the maze of fractures and hairline cracks that had spread across his fingers. Lifting his hands he touched his cheeks and forehead, scratching at the pattern of cracks. "I am old and brittle, Captain," he whispered, "and I am turning back into stone. I cannot go forward."

"Lord, the people will not go into the daylight without you." Gray Goose bit his lip and knelt beside the King. "They have grown to love you, great King. They love you so much they would turn their backs on the sunlight."

Holbian made to rise, then sank back against the tunnel wall. "I have led them this far but I can go no farther. Take the people out and shout our victory to the limits of the sky. I will hear the shout and know I did not fail."

"Lord," Breakmaster cried, bringing the stonemason to the King's side, "let us help you."

"I am turning to stone!" the King hissed. "Each movement makes me weaker. Without the steel-silver cloak I would have fractured long ago into thousands of pieces. Leave me here to rest my last few moments and dream of the daylight I cannot see."

"Lord," ventured Arachatt, the mason, moving closer to the King, "let me try and make you strong enough to see the daylight."

Holbian frowned at Arachatt's outstretched hands, but slowly gave the mason his hand. Arachatt smiled. Opening a heavy leather pouch that hung at his waist, he scooped out a handful of fine stone dust. Taking a pinch of stone the mason mixed it with a few drops of water leaking from a fissure in the tunnel wall and kneaded it to a thick paste. He worked it into the maze of cracks in the King's hand, smoothing and wiping the surface of each finger with a silver trowel. "There, Lord," he whispered, letting the King lift the hand.

Holbian gazed at the hand, bent the fingers and made to clench the fist.

"Easy, Lord, the stone dust needs time to settle and bond. But it should make you strong enough for many daylights."

Holbian smiled, offering his other hand to the mason. "You are a Lord amongst masons to have such magic at your fingertips; twice now you have helped me towards the daylight. Ask and all shall be yours."

"Lord, I carry no magic, only a bag of dust from the ruins of the great granite wall that once surrounded the city. It is fitting that it should now help you back into the sunlight," Arachatt replied, squeezing the stone paste into the cracks of the other hand and smoothing it between the fingers.

Holbian sighed and settled back against the wall to let Arachatt work the stone paste into the fractures of his face and neck. It tingled and itched, drawing the brittle skin tight as it dried. Arachatt wet his fingers with spittle and smoothed over the last few hairline cracks in the King's eyelids and sat back, nervously, on his haunches. Breakmaster held up a polished knuckle of armor and the King laughed in the feeble sparks of light as he looked at his face. Turning his head from left to right, he felt suns younger and ready to face the light.

Taking Arachatt's hand he rose to his feet and thanked the mason. Pausing a moment, his hand on Beacon Light's saddle, he said, "I said ask and all will be yours, but in truth I have nothing to offer you. I carry the Kingdom about my shoulders and my pockets are empty."

Arachatt laughed, helping the King into the saddle. "Lord, to have reached the end of this dark road is enough, but beware, for I have only hidden the fractures, I do not have the power to make you young again."

Holbian reached down and gripped the mason's arm. "It will last to journey's end, I know it will."

"Journey's end, Lord?" asked the mason, hurrying after the King as he trotted the last stretch of darkness, but the King did not reply, he was lost in the cheering as he trotted out into the bright sunlight onto a wild grassy slope.

"Granite King!" shouted a voice from the top of the bank, stopping the King's headlong rush out of the secret road.

The King turned and stared up the bank, blinking his eyes against the light, his hands closing on the hilt of his sword. "Chancellors!" he snarled, spurring Beacon Light forward.

Proudpurse laughed, and with a sweep of his hand he motioned the treacherous warriors out of hiding behind the bank into a tight line before the King. "We heard you creeping along behind us," sneered Proudpurse, "but the broken bridge should have stopped you and drowned you in darkness."

Holbian turned the point of his sword at the Chancellor and tried to force a passage through the warriors, but much as they hesitated to strike the King they would not let him pass.

Proudpurse took a Marcher's long spear and stepped towards the King. "For suns beyond counting I have sat on the steps of your throne and dreamed of this daylight. Now you shall die and I will have all Elundium in my hand."

"Stay, my Lord," Gray Goose cried out, nocking an arrow onto his bow and taking aim at the Chancellor's heart.

Proudpurse laughed cruelly, pointing at his strike of bowmen. "You are defeated, Archer, and dead if you do not drop your bow. The last Granite King has reached the end of his road and stands all alone."

"He is not alone!" cried Breakmaster, lowering his spear and urging Mulberry forward.

Proudpurse sneered and called his Gallopers out to face the single horseman. "Abandon your King. Look how many stand against you, but if you kneel at my feet there is a place for you amongst my horsemen. Come forward, Breakmaster, and join the new rulers of Elundium."

Breakmaster spat on the ground and dug his spurs into Mulberry's sides, driving him forward.

"No! No!" shouted the King, raising his hand to stop Breakmaster's reckless charge. "I will parley and strike a bargain for the people of the Granite City before blood is spilt."

"Parley?" laughed Chancellor Overlord.

"Bargain!" sneered Proudpurse. "You have nothing to bargain with. Your life is worth less than the sharp stone that honed my spear blade."

King Holbian sat easily in the saddle letting the sunshine warm his face. Laughing, he held the Chancellor's eyes. "There is more to Kingship than just taking a crown, surely my wise Chancellors know that. I do not deal with you for my life, but for the future of the people of Elundium."

Turning in the saddle he swept his arm across the city dwellers that knelt in neat lines in front of the entrance to the secret road, the weapons they had taken from the armory held steady in their hands. "They will be your inheritance if you kill me. They are the future of Elundium."

Chancellor Proudpurse hesitated. He had expected rage or anger, even fear, in the aged King, but not this strength of purpose in the city folk that stood behind him. Their grim and angry faces mocked at his treachery and made him stand back a pace.

"We will kill your city folk. All of them," he cried. "Elundium will belong to the Chancellors and those they choose to share it with."

"Then you will have nothing," answered the King quietly, "nothing at all, for the warriors you whispered into treachery are beyond trust and will in turn betray you at the first twist of fate. It is you who stands alone through your own black thoughts and deeds. It is you who totters on the edge of defeat."

"You lie!" screamed Proudpurse. "It is you who stands alone to die! Those so-called warriors will not fight, they are servers, Candlemen, the scum of the lower circles of the city."

King Holbian laughed and lifted his hand for silence. "It matters not which circle they came from, the Nightbeasts leveled the city and made us one. But we are not alone, listen to the changing wind, brave Chancellors, for it whispers out your fate in sweet music. Listen."

Proudpurse frowned and lowered his spear. Listening, he turned his head from left to right. Faint on the wind it came as horse bells on a summer breeze.

"Look about you, traitors," shouted Gray Goose, bending his bow, "and see the warriors who are true to the King."

Proudpurse spun around and dropped the spear, falling onto his knees in terror as he saw the bright glitter of Dawnrise's steelsilver coat and the shadow of a forest of spears ascending the bank. Errant let his hand fall to his side and the Nighthorses of Underfall swept forward in a fast-moving crescent, galloping beside the Warhorses. The thunder of their hooves drowned out the Chancellor's screams and the cries of the treacherous warriors who, as the King foretold, turned their weapons on the Chancellors, felling them before the Nighthorses could check their pace.

Silverpurse, Proudpurse's son, had been collecting kindling wood in a nearby copse, heard the thunder of hooves and saw his father fall, speared and arrow-struck by their own band of warriors. Ducking out of sight he dropped the wood and crawled deep into the undergrowth and watched the terrible slaughter as the Nighthorses trampled his father's warriors underfoot. Again and again they charged until the riders' spear shafts were blood wet.

"You will pay dearly for this daylight," Silverpurse hissed between clenched teeth as he watched Errant dismount before the King and offer up the hilt of his bloody sword.

Holbian dismounted and embraced Errant, laughing and laughing until the tears ran down his cheeks. "Captain of Captains, our lives were on such slender threads!"

Errant smiled and pointed a gloved fist at the wide crescent of spearmen spread across the bank. "We were hunting Nightbeasts, Lord, throughout these wild lands and were drawn by the smoke from the Chancellors' cooking fires. We were about to attack when you emerged from that dark hole in the ground."

"And not a moment too soon!" laughed Breakmaster, jumping to the ground and gripping Errant's arm.

Holbian frowned, looking from the slaughtered warriors to the Chancellors' twisted bodies. "Hate, I fear, will feed on this," he said quietly, summoning the Loremaster forward and cutting the bonds on his wrists.

"This is the price of their treachery," he said, pointing down at the Chancellors. "Look on it, Loremaster, and learn well, for what you see is the work of a moment's awful judgment. You would lie with them if they had not abandoned you before they fled, but I will not add your death to this day of grief. Thus I shall spare your life that you may teach others the dangers of treachery and falsehood."

Pinchface looked nervously from face to face. "Thank you my Lord," he whispered, retreating a step.

Errant laughed and drew his sword. Gray Goose nocked an arrow onto his bow.

"No!" commanded the King, putting his hand on Errant's arm. "We have blooded this daylight enough, there is much knowledge in the Loremaster's head, knowledge that we would be fools to waste."

"To spare him is a dangerous move, my Lord," muttered Breakmaster, the tip of his long spear a handspan from the Loremaster's throat. "He has betrayed you once and could easily do so again."

"Then let him prove his new loyalty to us, let him win our respect through his true teachings of the world before the destruction of the Granite City," answered the King.

Breakmaster shrugged his shoulders and turned away, unbuckling Mulberry's girths. "Black days," he muttered, moving to the entrance of the secret road to marshal the city folk out into the sunshine.

King Holbian ordered the Loremaster to be given a shovel. "Dig graves for the Chancellors. Bury them deep without a post or a stone to mark the place where they lie for they are nothing but a black memory."

Turning, the King strode up the bank to the top and breathed in the clean sun-sparkling air. "Elundium!" he whispered. Beckoning Errant up onto the bank he said, "Tell me, Captain, how do things stand in the beautiful sunshine of Elundium?"

Errant frowned and pointed down to the dust-weary Nighthorses with their torn battle coats, and ragged warriors snatching a moment out of the saddle. "We hunt the Nightmare, Krulshards, my Lord; without rest we chase his foul shadow across this land."

"Krulshards!" cried the King, his face fading to ash gray, his aged hand clutching at the hilt of his sword.

"Yes, Lord," whispered Errant, drawing closer. "The army I gathered along the Greenway's edge fought and won a great battle on the high plateau before the Gates of Night. They defeated the Nightmare and Thanehand chased him into the darkness."

"Thanehand!" the King cried, "the Candleman's son, the boy I sent to Underfall? He entered the darkness?"

"Lord, he ran on the Nightmare's heels, but in the darkness he lost Krulshards. In a high chamber he found Thoronhand, his grandfather, and brought him back into the light."

"Thoron! Thoronhand, my last Errant rider!" Holbian cried, sweeping his sword aloft.

Turning towards the city folk who were resting at the bottom of the bank he called for Angishand and summoned her up into the sunshine. "Thane is alive!" he laughed, embracing Angis and lifting her off her feet, "and he found Thoronhand, my last Errant rider, and freed him from the darkness."

Angis fell weeping onto her knees, the sunlight sparkling in the tears that ran down her cheeks. "Lord, are they safe?" she whispered, clutching at the hems of her shawl.

"Tell me more," urged Holbian, turning back to Errant. "Tell me how Krulshards escaped into Elundium."

Errant took the King's hand and knelt before him. "Lord, he broke out into Elundium through the vaults that lie beneath the fortress of Underfall. It is whispered that he has the love token that Thane carried into battle and seeks Elionbel, Tombel's daughter, in revenge, for her name was engraved on the token."

"Revenge?" whispered the King, frowning, "why does he seek revenge? When all Elundium is on the brink of darkness he should be leading the Nightbeast army spreading destruction, not seeking revenge."

"Lord," Errant answered, "Thane entered the City of Night after he had led the warriors to victory before the gates. He is not afraid of Krulshards or the darkness."

"Only Kings can walk in the dark," Holbian whispered, turning his head to look at Angishand twisting the hem of her cloak between her fingers. "He walks in the dark and carries a summer scarf woven from emblem thread—old legends are coming to life." King Holbian sat down heavily on the grassy bank, and rested his chin in his hands. "Tell me of Thanehand and all that has come to pass at Underfall. Start with the moment you broke free from the siege-locked Granite City and raised the army along the Greenway's edge. Tell me every twist and turn that I may see which path to tread for we may yet have a new King in Elundium. I must know all there is to know so that I can play my fading part as the last Granite King."

"Lord, you have many daylights yet!" cried Errant.

Holbian smiled and stripped off his battle gloves to show where the fine cracks had appeared again. "I age, brave Captain, it is only the mason's skill that keeps me from turning into brittle stone. I am beyond my time, so tell me quickly of all that has happened."

The Chancellors' rekindled cooking fires blazed in the darkness below the bank before Errant had told the King all he knew, and left him staring out across the wild landscape.

"I must travel to Underfall," King Holbian said quietly, getting to his feet. "For that is where Nevian, the Master of Magic, foretold the new King would set his standard. I must be at the doors of the Palace of Kings to pass on my crown before I turn to stone."

Errant stood beside the King, wrapping his cloak tightly against the cold night air. "Lord, it is a dangerous road to World's End! The Greenways are blocked and overgrown with wildness."

Holbian laughed. "That is the road, Errant. I see now the road Krulshards will run, he will re-enter the City of Night and draw Thane into darkness. None will follow him, for none but a King can walk there. Krulshards has used his revenge well but I will follow and help Thane to end the Nightmare's grip of terror on this beautiful land. It is my task as the last Granite King to walk in the darkness and stand at Thane's side now that I have mastered my fear. Revenge or not, I know it in my heart."

Errant reached out and took the King's hand, feeling the maze of cracks that the chill air had opened. "The Nighthorses of Underfall will lead you, Lord, and the Warhorses and the packs of Border Runners will protect you on the road. But what of the city folk?"

"They will follow you, great King," Angis whispered, kissing his hand. "I will lead them for you," she offered, before she vanished down the bank to marshal them in readiness for their night's march.

Pinchface the Loremaster had barely laid the last

rough-cut turf on the Chancellors' graves before
the last of the city folk had hurried out into the
darkness. Muttering he slung the heavy shovel
aside and turned to follow them.

"Loremaster!" a voice hissed just behind him in
the darkness, and a hand gripped his wrist.

"Silverpurse!" Pinchface cried, seeing the Chancellor's son.

Silverpurse clamped his hand across the Loremaster's mouth and pulled him back into the undergrowth. "You saw what those foul warriors did to
my father and all my friends. You will help me to
destroy the King and take all Elundium as mine,
in my father's name. You will do it or die here in
the darkness."

Pinchface struggled against the strong hands that
held him to the ground, trying to open his mouth
to cry out to the King but he felt the sharp point
of Silverpurse's dagger against his throat and
shrank back silently against the cold earth.

"There will be others who will help us take
Elundium, many others," Silverpurse snarled, easing the dagger away from the Loremaster's throat.

"Yes, Lord, yes, Lord," Pinchface whispered in
fear, wringing his hands in despair as the clatter of
hooves and the tramp of marching feet faded into
the black night air.

The New City

WILLOW Leaf climbed the last two steep steps onto the top of the inner wall that encircled Candlebane Hall and shaded his eyes against the setting sun. Sighing with satisfaction he stared out over the new-built Granite City. "It is in your memory, Elder," he whispered, looking up into the darkening sky for the first evening star.

Running footsteps sounded in the shadows of the inner wall. Willow turned and searched the shadows. Laughing, he bent forward and offered his hand to a slim dark-haired girl who turned the last twist in the stone stairs and ran lightly to the top of the wall. "Mother says you would have missed the noonday food," she said, catching her breath after the steep climb.

Willow smiled, feeling his cheeks blush a deep red as he took the rough woven basket and set it down on the top of the wall. "You Apples are like a family to me," he laughed, lifting the edge of the clean cheesecloth that covered the basket to see an array of forest fruits and finger treats that made his mouth water. "Your mother is a real treasure," he said, taking out a bright yellow fruit and biting into its tough shiny skin.

Oakapple smiled shyly and looked away. "Mother says you never eat properly. Ever since Elder's death, she says."

Willow frowned, his face darkening with anger as he remembered Elder's death beneath that cruel-clawed Nightbeast's foot in the City of Night. "None of us is safe and never will be until the Nightmare is destroyed," he said, angrily stabbing his finger towards the newly-built great wall that had thrown evening shadows across the lower circles of the city. "I dared not rest while the city lay open for the Nightmare to enter."

Oakapple moved closer to Willow, touching his sleeve with her long pale fingers. "Do you watch for the Nightmare? Is that why you sit up here all alone, watching in case he returns?"

Willow smiled, "No, Oakapple, I watch for a friend upon the Greenway. Nevian, the Magician, said that Evening Star would come to the city when the rebuilding was finished; that is who I wait for."

"The last roof slates were laid today. The city is finished now, I am sure she will come," Oakapple answered.

Willow shook his head. "There is still the fallen tower in the inner circle, but something has stopped me from rebuilding it or opening the wall.

It is still sealed against Nightbeast attack just as the King left it."

A noise from below made Willow and Oakapple turn and look down into the inner circle of the city. The moon had ridden high in the clear sky, casting deep shadows across the rubble of the fallen tower. "Hush!" whispered Oakapple, holding her finger against her lips.

Willow stared at the fallen tower, his hand upon the hilt of his dagger. "Look!" he cried, stepping back a pace. "Look, there is water shining amongst the jumble of stones."

Fine jets of water suddenly rose up in graceful fountains, sparkling in the moonlight as the night winds drove them against the inner sheer sides of the wall where they ran in glistening droplets down onto the cobbles. "The wells are dry and dust-choked. This is a miracle!" Willow cried, jumping to his feet and turning to Oakapple.

"Go down and gather the best masons, we must cut a channel through the wall and take the water spiraling down into a new well beside the great gates."

Willow ran down the inner stone stairway and splashed his way through the ice-cold water that was flooding across the cobbles until he stood level with the doors to Candlebane Hall. Laughing he held up his stone searcher, judged the height of the first broad step and drove it into the wall. "The inner circle of the city will be a lake, the Candle Hall and the fallen tower will be islands, gardened and set with flowers! A beautiful lake of pure sweet water," he whispered, scooping a handful to his mouth and drinking.

"Cut the channel here!" he called to the tunnelers who were hurrying down the stone steps armed with heavy sacks of tools.

Dawn had grayed the sky before the water channels were finished and the overflow of water was following the newly built spiral down into the shadows of the great gate. Willow sought out Oakapple from amongst the women treading earth between the granite blocks from the fallen tower and took her up to the top of the wall. "Please watch with me," he asked, turning his eyes towards the dark horizon line.

Oakapple smiled and spread her cloak around them both. "The city is finished now," she whispered, sleepily resting her head on his shoulder.

Willow nodded silently, watching the Greenway appear through the ghost tails of the dawn mist. He knew she would come now, deep down in his heart he knew it and he stretched out his hand and touched the cold metal stone searcher that lay beside him. Oakapple snuggled closer, and murmured as she fell asleep.

The first ray of sunlight had begun to burn above World's Edge, warming them and drying out the dew that had settled on the cloak. Willow stiffened and sat up straight, blinking against the low rays of golden light. There were figures on the Greenway, small dots, far away but moving towards the city. "Oakapple, Oakapple, look!" he cried, shaking her awake.

Lifting her head, she blinked and rubbed her eyes and smiled at Willow. "I dreamed of horses just like the Warhorses that fought beside us on the high plateau before the Gates of Night."

"Yes, yes!" Willow interrupted, "but look out there on the Greenway."

Oakapple rubbed her eyes and stared out along the bright morning road. "They are just like the dream," she cried.

"It is Evening Star and her foal, surrounded by a company of Warhorses!" Willow shouted and leaping to his feet ran to the top of the steps, then he stopped and turned and looked into Oakapple's eyes. "Nevian said that I must follow my fate wherever it may lead."

Oakapple reached into the forgotten supper basket and withdrew a crisp orange forest fruit. "Take this gift for comfort on the journey," she whispered, pressing it into his hands.

"When the Nightmare is dead I will return," he cried, gathering up his stone searcher and running down into the morning shadows.

"Star! Star!" he shouted, halting on the crown of the Greenway. The safety of the great gate lay at least a league behind him. Before him the company of Warhorses had grown longer and longer and was filling the road and the pounding of their hooves had churned up a dense cloud of dust. "Star!" he shouted again against the thunder of their hooves.

As one the Warhorses slowed and halted before Willow. The leading horses trotted up to him and stretched their necks and snorted in greeting. Evening Star neighed and trotted forward, brushing her soft muzzle against his cheek.

"Willow," a calm gentle voice whispered in his head, "we have crossed Elundium to your call, without rest. Night and day we have traveled."

Willow stepped back and let his hands fall to his sides. "But I haven't called for you," he cried. "You have been in my thoughts with each waking moment and I have watched the Greenway each night and every daylight ever since Nevian foretold that you would come to the city when it was newly built; but I did not send word."

Star snorted and pawed at the ground, nudging her foal forward.

"Fate draws you together," laughed a voice from the Greenway's edge.

"Nevian!" Willow gasped, spinning around and shading his eyes against the bright colors in the rainbow cloak.

"It was my voice in the wind. It was I who tugged at the threads of your fates, drawing them once more together."

Willow reached out and touched the rainbow cloak, feeling its soft warm colors. "But why?" he asked, turning his head towards Evening Star. "Why did Star and her foal have to travel through great danger to come here? Was it to shelter in the safety of the newly-built city? Is Elundium too wild for her to roam in?"

Nevian smiled and shook his head, and taking Willow's hand he placed it on Evening Star's shoulder. "Because there is a bond of love between you that grew out of the despair and darkness of the City of Night. A love so strong that not even Krulshards, the Master of Nightmares, can tear it apart."

Willow nodded, but his face paled at the Nightmare's name. Star snorted, arching her neck and pushed her foal towards the Warhorses.

Nevian put his hand on Willow's shoulder and turned him towards World's End. "Krulshards has turned towards the City of Night. He has taken Elionbel and her mother in revenge for Thane entering the city. They are helpless lures tied onto the end of his life thread."

"Lures?" interrupted Willow, drawing his eyebrows together. "What are they?"

Nevian lifted the rainbow cloak and carefully drew out a fine silver shimmering thread. "If I tie you to my life thread, Willow, you are a part of me, and suffer each and every one of my hurts. The Nightmare uses Elionbel and her mother to draw Thane into the darkness. There he will take him and peel his skin back to the bones, destroying him slowly, and if he dies I fear Elundium will fall into the shadows."

"But how are we to help?" Willow asked, looking up into Nevian's face.

The magician smiled, his face crinkling into a thousand wrinkles. "I know not, Willow," he whispered. "It is beyond my sight, but I fear that Thane will be powerless against Krulshards while Elionbel suffers hurt and I would ask you to be at Thane's side in the darkness, because you know of the Nightmare's weakness. You know of his shadow."

Willow frowned and looked out across the green rolling countryside and asked quietly, "What if Thane cannot destroy the Nightmare? What if even he fails?"

Nevian lifted his hand and pointed at the sun. "Your time of freedom in the daylight will be nothing but a brief moment to treasure in the darkness that will come."

"And the foal? Must he travel back into the darkness?"

"No, he will stay with the Warhorses, they will protect him."

Willow smiled and as he moved among the Warhorses he reached out to put his hand upon the foal's shoulder. The foal squealed and reared, boxing the air above Willow's head. "Easy! Easy!" he cried, jumping backwards clear of the thrashing hooves.

"He is a Lord of Horses," laughed Nevian, "and is not yet ready to come quietly to the bridle."

Star snorted and pushed her foal deeper among the Warhorses, scolding him for being so savage.

Turning she trotted quickly back to Willow and stood quietly while he mounted her.

Nevian picked up the heavy metal stone searcher that Willow had dropped onto the Greenway when he first greeted Star and placed it in his hands. "Far sight tells me that you must carry the stone searcher to the City of Night. Beyond that I can see nothing but darkness."

"Lord, what of my people now that the Granite City is rebuilt?"

Nevian smiled, casting back the rainbow cloak. "The city is theirs until a new King comes to claim it, but you must turn your mind to the road to World's End or there will be no more Kings. Ride hard and fast to reach the City of Night before Thane enters the darkness."

"Where shall we meet? Mantern's Mountain is a rambling wilderness that almost touches the stars," cried Willow. Star pawed at the Greenway, neighed fiercely and sprang forward.

"I know not," Nevian shouted against the thunder of her hooves. "But Evening Star was once a great relay horse and knows all the secret ways to World's End. Give her her head, she will find the way!"

Willow waved his hand in salute to Nevian and then wound it tightly into Star's mane and clung on for all he was worth as they left the Greenway and cantered into a long avenue of young sapling trees. The sun flashed and flickered behind the trees

and he laughed, remembering a dream from long
ago when he lay, a prisoner in the City of Night,
and he had watched the sunlight behind a forest of
shafts. And he galloped forward to this dream.

Glass Arrow Blades

*T*HANE awoke to the bumping clatter of the rough-made stretcher and looked out at the gray grasses bent beneath the pouring rain. He shivered, trying to remember what had happened as he twisted his head to see who was pulling him along. "Kyot!" he shouted, looking past Sprint's rain-soaked flank up at his friend's shoulder where a quiver of feather-flighted arrows swung from side to side.

Kyot heard Thane's weak cry and eased Sprint to a halt. He dismounted and knelt beside the stretcher; a frown of worry creased his forehead as he tucked his cloak more firmly around Thane's shivering body.

"Where is Stumble?" Thane asked in a broken whisper, trying to shake the raindrops from his eyes. "Where are you taking me trussed up like a prisoner?"

Kyot laughed softly, "I'd let you walk if you could stand but you are fevered, bird thin and near to starvation. Lie easy on the stretcher until we get to Clatterford. Eventine has gone before us to warn them, and then you will be hot-fed and a warm fire will dry out your rain-soaked bones."

"But Stumble . . ." Thane worried.

Kyot pointed back into the trampled grasses along the two broad lines the stretcher had left. "He is following our tracks at his own pace. He is as weak as you after the ordeal in the marsh gully but the Border Runners are guarding him and they will keep him safe."

Thane struggled against the bindings that held him to the stretcher. "Krulshards has Elionbel. I must follow him, I must."

Kyot sadly shook his head and stood up. "You cannot follow anybody until you have rested and found new strength at Clatterford, but when you are strong I promise I will come with you to hunt down the Nightmare."

Thane cursed and muttered helplessly as Kyot remounted, but there was nothing he could do. Closing his eyes he sank into dark dreams lulled by the rattle of the rain as they passed through the tall grasses. The low gray rain clouds darkened with the coming night. Kyot turned in the saddle and searched the trampled grass; he was worried that Stumble would be lost once darkness fell but he laughed with relief to see the little horse had almost caught up with them. He looked gaunt and tired but there was a flicker of pride in his eyes as he whinnied a greeting to Sprint.

A stag roared out in the half light and Kyot saw

Tanglecrown and Eventine galloping towards them. "There are Nightbeasts on the borders of Clatterford. Tombel has cleared a wide path through them but we must hurry!"

"How long will it take us to reach Clatterford?" he called out as Eventine moved in beside him.

"If we ride hard, without rest, dawn will be breaking as we cross the ford before my father's house," she answered, looking down at Thane's fever-lined face, worrying that he might die from the rough journey long before they were threatened by a Nightbeast attack.

Thane opened his eyes and for a moment he caught sight of Eventine, but all he saw was a blurred face framed in a halo of fire-gold hair and edged by the dark gray rain clouds. "Elionbel," he whispered as the face slipped away from him and he sank back into darkness.

Kyot called Stumble to him and caught his reins, drawing him in close to Sprint's flank. The two huge Border Runners dropped back one on either side of the stretcher as the company forged ahead and the only sounds above the pouring rain were the jingle of their harness and the thunder of their hooves as they passed through league after league of the night-dark grasslands.

The gray hours came, cold, wet and forbidding to show them Nightbeast carcasses strewn in rough battle order across the trampled grasses.

Eventine turned anxious eyes from left to right searching for signs of life amongst the Nightbeasts.

"It looks as though the path is still ours," she whispered, nocking an arrow onto her bow, but the Border Runners smelled danger and their hackles rose.

Rockspray lifted quickly from Kyot's shoulder and flew in a wide circle. "Nightbeasts!" he shrieked, stooping at a black shadow and plunging towards its hideous upturned face as the monster rose to hurl its spear at Kyot.

All about them Nightbeasts leapt to their feet. Eventine and Kyot loosed their arrows, the Border Runners leapt snarling at the Nightbeasts' throats while Tanglecrown lowered his antlers and swinging his head from side to side he scythed a path through the swarming beasts, cutting and tearing with the glittering crystal tips that Fairday had woven into his antlers.

"Follow me," Eventine shouted as Tanglecrown surged ahead.

Kyot dug his spurs in Sprint's sides to keep pace with the Lord of Stags for now he could see the ford of Clatterford less than sixty strides ahead. All around him Nightbeasts were screaming and shouting, rising up to block out the breaking dawn and fighting to block the gap Tanglecrown had made.

Tanglecrown reached the ford and halted. He lifted his head to the gray morning light, roared, turned and charged again.

"Follow me, faster!" Eventine called out as Sprint broke free from the mass of Nightbeasts and followed Tanglecrown into the ford. "My father's

Archers will not let the Nightbeasts onto the lawns of Clatterford."

Bright water sprayed up from Sprint's fleeing hooves, bubbling and swirling over the stretcher, soaking Thane to the skin. Roughly woken and terrified of the seething mass of Nightbeasts less than a dozen strides behind him he began to shout, struggling frantically against the binding cord that held him onto the stretcher. With a mighty bump they left the water and climbed the steep slopes onto the lawns of Clatterford. Brilliant peacocks surrounded the stretcher, fanning out their plumage and turning a thousand eyes against the Nightbeasts, and the last Thane saw of the battle was the two huge Border Runners crouching side by side defending the ford.

The stretcher had stopped. Kyot was at his side, cutting the cords and helping him slowly to his feet. Before him, in all its dazzling beauty, rose the House of Clatterford. Thane looked up and gasped, catching his breath at the sheer beauty of the sunlight trapped in a thousand interwoven patterns, from bright white on the gables and roof tops to indigo and deep purples where the walls rested their feet in the neat shadow-covered lawns. Each brick and beam seemed to be fashioned out of smooth crystal, transparent and yet solid, and they all glowed in countless soft hues.

"It is beautiful, truly beautiful," he whispered, stepping dizzily forward.

Fairday stood on the glass steps, his sky-washed

cloak shining out in the first rays of sunlight to break through the rain clouds. "Welcome! Welcome!" he cried, descending and taking both of Thane's hands in his. "You did not fail me, daughter," he said quietly, sweeping his gentle eyes over Thane's ragged clothes and fever-wasted face. "You found the ones that all Elundium waits for."

Stumble snorted and lowered his head as Fairday ran his hand through his mane. "You ran a hard road, hard enough to wear this great-hearted horse into a shadow."

Thane blinked and then held Fairday's eyes. "We chase the Nightmare, Krulshards. I gave Stumble his freedom, but he chose to stay with me."

Fairday nodded, a smile touching the corners of his eyes as he led the company into the house of Clatterford. "You will stay with us long enough to take meat and build up your strength or I fear that road will be the death of you for that is indeed a hard and desperate road to travel alone."

"He is not alone, Father," Eventine cried, interrupting. "We, Kyot and I, will travel into the darkness with Thane."

Fairday frowned. "No, child, hunting Nightbeasts on the edge of the morning is one thing, dangerous enough. But to chase the Nightmare, Krulshards!"

"The Nightmare has Elionbel and her mother, Martbel, as prisoners. I shall ride with Thane, we are as brothers," Kyot said fiercely, taking Thane's hand.

"And we are love-matched, our bowstrings are intertwined," whispered Eventine, looking into Kyot's eyes.

"Enough! Enough!" cried Fairday, raising his hands for silence. "What would you do with the Nightmare, Thane, if you caught him?"

Thane shook his head. "I know not, Lord. Nevian said that Elionbel and Martbel were tied to the Nightmare by his life thread and if I was to hurt him they would be strangled to death."

Fairday placed a hand on Thane's shoulders and looked deeply into his eyes. "He will destroy you, Thane, through that moment of weakness if you hesitate because of your love for Elionbel. Remember, whatever the price, if you come face to face with Krulshards you must drive the blade hard and quick through the shadowy malice into his rotten heart. More than Elionbel's life is in the balance. You must strive to win the daylight for all Elundium!"

Thane paled; the marsh fever was making him feel dizzy with despair.

Fairday smiled and summoned two of his furnace men to come forward. "Did Nevian counsel you to let fate find a way to destroy the Nightmare?"

"Yes!" cried Thane, looking up at the two glass-makers carrying slender arrow-filled quivers in their hands. "But I am no Archer, my Lord, I am a swordsman!"

Fairday laughed, drawing two polished arrows, one from each quiver. "They are spine-matched,

Thane, for the two greatest bows in Elundium. Spine-matched to sing with one voice as they cut through the air."

Eventine took one of the arrows from her father and wet the blade with her tongue. Spinning the arrow between her fingers she filled the grand crystal hall with pure shafts of scattered light.

Fairday smiled, taking the arrow from his daughter and gently replaced both in the quivers. "Legend foretold of a time when the great bows would sing together against the darkness. I feared that moment, knowing it would take my daughter into great danger but I cannot fight against fate. Thus each morning since Kyot first entered my house I have stolen a little drop of sunlight and hot-forged it into the arrow blades."

"Stolen the sunlight?" Thane whispered, looking in fear at the gray goose arrow flights that stood just proud of the rims of the quivers.

Fairday laughed, taking Thane's hand. "As the sun rose, fiery and powerful above the grasslands and cast its first ray across my polished anvil I hammered out the molten glass, smoothing it and folding it over the sunlight, trapping a tiny point of light within the blade. They are rare indeed; forged a moment too soon and the sun is too weak, a moment too late and the light has faded."

Turning to Kyot and Eventine he warned them to use the glass arrows only against the Nightmare. Turning back to Thane he held him for a moment, searching with his second sight in the dark daylights yet to come. "Fate has armed your companions with the Bows of Orm and Clatterford. Fate will arm you with bright metal," he said quietly. "It will arm you with a sword fit for a King to use against the Nightmare. Cry out and the sword shall be yours."

"Sword?" questioned Thane, leaning forward.

But Fairday laughed, clapping his hands for the servers to lead them to breakfast and dismissing Thane's question. "Let fate pull the threads that draw us all together, let fate keep you safe on the way into the blackest night. Come, or breakfast will turn into noonday food."

Long after breakfast had been cleared away and the house of Clatterford stood wrapped in silence Thane took Kyot out onto the rain-wet grass and walked beside him, asking with fear in his voice, "Did Esteron reach Underfall?"

Kyot stopped and turned towards Thane. "He is with the Healer, Merion, at World's End. He is sorely wounded but safe from the Nightbeasts. He limped slowly onto the Causeway Field, with Mulcade battle-perched on his withers, putting our council to rout."

Thane smiled, seeing again the proud arched neck and hearing the thunder of his hooves. "Esteron," he whispered, "oh, how I need you now."

Rockspray dug his talons into Kyot's shoulder and hooted. Thane looked at the owl. "Would you find them for me?" he asked in a whisper, stroking the owl's chest feathers. "Would you fly to World's

End and tell them that the Nightmare has Elion-bel?"

Rockspray spread his wings and hooted just once more before lifting silently into the sun-bright sky and turning towards the line of shadowy mountains that hid World's End from their sight.

Thane and Kyot passed into the shadows of the tall yew hedge that bordered the waters of Clatterford and looked towards World's End. "We will travel as soon as Stumble is strong enough to carry me," Thane murmured as he turned towards the river bank. Laughing, he knelt and reached out his hands to the dark shapes that sat silently paddling against the current. "The gray swans will find the fastest road," he whispered.

Sliding down the bank into the water he gently stroked Ousious's downy chest, feeling for the wound Krulshards had made but all that he could find were the knot ends of Stumble's mane that he had used to sew the edges of the wound together. Easily he cut them with his dagger and let them drift with the current away beyond the lawns of Clatterford.

"You must sleep," Kyot insisted, kneeling on the edge of the bank, beside Ousious. "Sleep and rest and grow strong before we journey to the City of Night."

A New Nightmare

"*M*OTHER!*"* Elionbel cried, reaching out a steadying hand as Martbel stumbled on the steep mountain slope.

Martbel sank onto her knees, both hands pressed against her stomach. "I cannot go on," she wept, bending double with the pain.

Krulshards felt the tug of the life thread and stopped and turned, a snarl of impatience on his skinless face. "Hurry, hurry!" he spat, with one eye watching the empty sky for danger. "Get to your feet, Marcherwoman."

"She is too weak to walk," Elionbel shouted, her fists clenched in anger, her lips trembling with hatred.

The Nightmare's seed had grown too quickly inside her mother's belly, it had drained her strength as if sucking her life away, withering her with each daylight that passed.

"Carry the Marcherwoman!" Krulshards ordered pulling the hood of the malice over the top of his head against the sunlight.

Kerzolde roughly slung Martbel across his shoulder and savagely pinched Elionbel's arm with his one good claw. "Move!" he screamed, prodding her forward after his master.

A shadow slowly crossed the mountainside towards them. Krulshards saw it and scrambled for shelter in a rough outcrop of rocks, pulling Elionbel after him. Kerzolde and Kerhunge followed, pushing Martbel into the shadows of an overhang of boulders.

"Quiet," hissed the Nightmare, clamping his fingers across Elionbel's mouth. "Quiet!"

Above them, high in the cloudless sky, an owl flew towards World's End. Elionbel struggled against the Nightmare's grip, kicking her feet wildly, sending the loose shale cascading in a steady stream into the depths below.

Rockspray saw the rocks slide and circled and stooped low over the outcrop of rocks. "Nightmare!" he shrieked, seeing the edges of the malice where it overshadowed Elionbel's cloak.

Beating the thin mountain air beneath his wings he flew away from the rocks into the bleached weather-ruined branches of a mountain pine and sat frozen still, watching and waiting.

"Owls!" sneered Krulshards, pushing Elionbel back out into the sunlight. "Meddling blinkless birds!" he muttered, dismissing the owl from his dark thoughts as he searched for the secret ways back into the City of Night, cursing Thanehand and his warriors for blocking the Gates of Night and sealing them against him. "Follow!" he snarled, tugging on the life thread.

Rockspray sat unmoving throughout the long afternoon, watching the Nightmare scale the steep slopes. He heard the curses and brutal screams as each new path they found led to a false ending.

"Blind fools!" the Nightmare shrieked, raising the lash again and again to beat his Captain.

"Master, the entrance is near. I can smell the pure dark air," Kerzolde cried, cowering backwards.

Krulshards looked eagerly from left to right, his nose almost touching the barren shale. He could also smell the sulphurous fumes and knew that the journey's end was but a pace away. "There, it is there!" he shouted, pulling on the life thread, drawing Elionbel to him.

Gurgling with victory he pointed a bone black finger at a narrow crack high up above their heads. "There is the doorway. There is the doom-slit of your torment, Marcherwoman!"

Elionbel looked up at the sulfur-stained yellow rocks that rose in sheer columns on either side of a narrow crack and shrank back. "No!" she whispered, crouching beside her mother.

Krulshards hooked his fingers into the weave of Elionbel's cloak and lifted her roughly to her feet. "You are lost, Marcherwoman, these are the last moments of your daylight. Nobody shall see you vanish into the darkness. Thanehand has not overtaken us on the road!"

Elionbel turned her head desperately searching the barren shale slopes without hope. She cried out in desperation, "Thane! Thane!"

The Nightmare laughed, sneering with victory as he wound the life thread between his fingers and dragged her up through the narrow crack. Kerzolde and Kerhunge lifted and pushed Martbel after their master but, in the last glimpse of daylight before the darkness swallowed them, Elionbel thought she saw an owl rise silently from the weather-bleached branches of a single pine tree that grew in the shadow of the foul entrance.

"Tell Thane!" she called. "Tell Thane!" but the darkness muffled her voice, deadening all hope, as Krulshards hurried them forward.

"Nightshards!" he called, summoning the guardians of the City of Night. "Come to your master. Come to me!"

Far away in the depths Elionbel heard dry rattling footsteps and screams of delight. Foul fumes blew all around them, choking bitter scents that made Krulshards dance with delight.

"Blind beasts," he crowed licking at the cold black walls, "your master has the Elionbel as a lure to trap Thanehand. Soon he will come, and with his death we will reopen the Gates of Night and destroy the daylight of all Elundium."

Martbel screamed, arching backwards in pain. "Elion!" she cried, falling heavily onto her knees, "it is beginning. Help me!"

Kerzolde bent, sniffing at Martbel's skirts and

tugged at the folds of Krulshards's malice. "Master, Master, the seed is flowering!"

"Show me the seed!" Krulshards shouted, pushing aside the first of the Nightshards that had gathered around him.

Kerhunge gripped Elionbel's wrists and pulled her away from Martbel as far as the life thread would allow.

"Mother!" she cried, struggling helplessly against the Nightbeast's strong claws.

Krulshards took one giant stride and tore Martbel's skirts into shreds. "Where is the seed?" he hissed, crouching on his haunches, staring without pity or shame at her stretched pulsating belly. Eagerly he dug his fingernails into the highest point of the dome. "Where is the seed?"

"Soon, Master, soon," soothed Kerzolde, easing the Nightmare's hand away and motioning four Nightshards to hold the woman down.

"What shape will it be?" Krulshards whispered, watching Martbel's belly contort as she fought against the claws that held her.

"The shape of a man, Master," Kerzolde began to say, but he stopped, pointing excitedly with his broken claw at a small blood-soaked split that had begun to open in the angle between Martbel's legs. "It has begun, Master!"

Martbel lifted her head, her eyes glazed with pain and pushed. With all her strength she pushed, trying to force the foul burden out. "Help me, help me, Elion!" she screamed, grinding her teeth as the

Nightmare's seed clawed at her insides. Far away she heard Elionbel call out in the darkness.

"Remember your promise!" Martbel shouted through the blinding pain. "For all Elundium's sake, kill it!"

Grunting with the effort, she pushed again and again until suddenly her stomach split, and through the blinding pain she saw a face, leering and blood-wet, through the broken birth sack. "No!" she screamed, thrashing her head from side to side, fighting helplessly against the claws that held her, but the Nightmare seed was almost born. Freeing first one longfingered hand then the other, tearing savagely at the edges of the birth sack, it emerged. Lifting its head it cried out, shrill and piercing in the darkness. Krulshards leapt backwards and the Nightshards gathered in a tight circle and trembled. Stepping forward Krulshards carefully lifted the baby free, holding it up as far as the birth cord would allow. He stared at it, turning it this way and that.

Looking down he frowned. "How can this seed be as powerful as me? The life thread traps it to the Marcherwoman!"

"No, Master, it is the way of the people of Elundium; once the seed is born the thread must be severed before it withers away."

Bending, Kerzolde took the birth cord in his teeth and quickly bit through it. Standing up and wiping a trickle of blood from his chin, he smiled at the baby. "You must name him, Master. He is your heir to the darkness."

Krulshards leered as the Nightshards crowded around him in the darkness and lifted the baby above his head. "Kruel! I name you Kruel, Master of Nightmares, Lord of the Night!"

Kruel turned his head and stared at his father and made soft gurgling noises. Kerhunge, in awe of the birth, eased his grip on Elionbel and, forgetting her, stepped closer to see his Master's seed. Elionbel saw her chance, and silently slipping a hand underneath her skirts drew out the narrow-bladed dagger she had long kept hidden. Without a moment's hesitation she lunged forward, the dagger held firmly in both hands. Krulshards saw the flickering metal and snatched the baby into the folds of the malice. Kruel turned his wrinkled infant head and screamed, high-pitched and piercing, as the folds of the malice closed about him.

The mountain trembled, the floor buckled, rippling beneath their feet. Krulshards, holding the baby tightly against his chest, reached out with his other hand and snapped Elionbel's dagger, melting the bright metal between his fingertips. "There is a new power in the darkness," he cried, forcing Elionbel down onto her knees. "A new power that shall have all Elundium as his own."

Lifting the baby out of the malice he held him above his head and shouted out his name, "Kruel! Kruel! You shall be the Lord of Darkness!"

Kruel waved his tiny arms, flexed his long fingers

and gurgled with delight, turning his head slowly towards Elionbel. He fell silent and stared at her through ice-cold pale eyes, then opening his mouth he screamed, sending a tremor deep through the City of Night, making the tall columns of sulphurous rock that marked the secret entrance sway backward and forward. Kruel screamed again, louder and more piercing, pointing at Elionbel with his long fingernails and the columns of rocks shattered, cascading down over the loose yellow shale into the dark valleys below.

"A new power in the darkness!" laughed Krulshards, turning towards the long dark road that led up into the City of Night.

"Bring the Marcherwomen to the high chamber," he ordered, cuddling the baby, touching the bright pink wrinkled skin on its face.

"Gently, Master, babies are very fragile and break easily."

Krulshards turned his head, dead locks of lank hair fanning out across the malice. "The power! Did you feel the power when he screamed!"

"Yes, Master," answered Kerzolde touching the baby's arm, "enough power to move this mountain."

Krulshards frowned, looking down at the tiny baby. "How do we feed so small a mouth?"

"Master," Kerzolde whispered, pointing back at Martbel where she lay unconscious and bloody across Kerhunge's shoulders, "the baby must feed from his mother, drinking her life force, until he is big enough to eat."

"Then guard him closely when he is with the Marcherwoman, and keep him well clear of Elionbel," Krulshards ordered.

"Yes, Master," whispered Kerzolde, running to keep pace with the Nightmare as he hurried towards his high chambers.

The Palace
of Kings

*T*HUNDERSTONE felt the first earth tremor
as it tore at the walls of Underfall and he
ran as quickly as he could up the winding
stairs to the lamp gallery. Behind him the stairway
crumbled, collapsing in a crash of blinding stone
dust. Breathlessly he steadied the lamp, holding it
with both hands as the wooden mounting rocked
backward and forward. Twice he tried to reach inside and catch hold of the last jewel from the cloak
of jewels that he had laid so carefully beside the
wick to reflect light into the darkness, but the jewel
skidded on the smooth polished surface of the glass,
cutting a small deep groove as it evaded his grasp.
The fortress of Underfall settled and grew still.
Thunderstone stretched out his hand inside the
lamp but just as his fingers were closing on the
jewel another tremor fiercely shook the fortress and
tipped the lamp violently towards him. The jewel
scratched across the glass and caught in the groove
it had cut beside the wick, fusing in a blinding flash
of white light into the glass.

Thunderstone gingerly touched the edge of the jewel and cried out with pain as he licked at his burned fingertips. "Magic! Pure magic!" he muttered, shielding his eyes against the shaft of brilliant white light that had begun flooding through the jewel and out across the shadowy Causeway Field.

Following the shaft of light to the wild edge of Mantern's Forest Thunderstone cried out, reaching for his horsetail sword. "Lord of Lords!" he shouted, stumbling and sliding down the ruined stairway. "Greatest of Kings!" he laughed, running through the maze of inner courtyards, throwing door after door open wide. "The greatest Granite King, King Holbian, has returned to Underfall!"

Thunderstone called out to the servants and undergrooms, crying with joy. He threw the bolts on the outer doors and rolled them wide open across the cobbles.

Rockspray flew low, close to the Causeway, shrieking a warning to the Keeper of World's End as he entered the fortress but Thunderstone merely laughed, pointing down at the weary column of city folk flanked by the Nighthorses of Underfall, the wild Warhorses and the packs of Border Runners. At the head of the column rode King Holbian, aglitter in the steelsilver coat. Errant was at his side riding Dawnrise and beside him another warrior sat on a dark rough-coated pony.

"Lord, greatest of Kings," Thunderstone cried,

falling onto his knees in the center of the Causeway and offering up the hilt of the horsetail sword.

King Holbian reined Beacon Light to a halt before the Keeper of World's End and stiffly dismounted. Smiling he reached down and took Thunderstone's hands into his own and pulled him to his feet. "Rise, true friend," he laughed. "Rise and be easy at my side."

Thunderstone looked up into the maze of fine cracks that covered the King's face and frowned with concern. "Lord," he whispered, stepping forward.

King Holbian laughed, slowly ungloving his hands. "I have grown brittle, Thunderstone, old and brittle from the rub of time." The King looked past the Keeper's shoulder, sweeping his gaze across the sheer granite-gray walls of Underfall. "I have come home, dear friend," he whispered. "Home to the Palace of Kings."

Beyond the great doors hoofbeats echoed in the inner courtyards thundering across the cobbles. "Who in all Elundium?" Thunderstone cried, spinning around just in time to see Esteron gallop out into the sunlight, a broken halter chain dangling from his head collar, his mane streaming in the wind.

Mulcade and Rockspray stooped onto Thunderstone's shoulders and together, with quick beaks and talons, they took Thane's summer scarf from beneath the Keeper's cloak and rising up, the scarf spread out between them, they flew towards Mantern's Mountain. "The banner of light!" shouted the King, pointing with his sword after the vanishing owls. "That is the standard; the summer scarf that Angis told me about."

Angis saw the owls carrying her scarf, broke away from the column of city folk and knelt upon the short grass of the Causeway Field. "Thane! Take care," she called, twisting her shawl between her fingers.

King Holbian turned, shading his eyes against the sunlight and followed the flight of the owls. "It is indeed a royal standard, for it is made from the rag ends of the great banners in the Towers of Granite. See how it sparkles in the daylight."

Turning back the King faced Esteron who had halted a pace away. Smiling, he reached out a hand towards the horse he had given to Thane to carry him to World's End. "Who would have thought that we would be standing here in the shadow of the Palace of Kings on the threshold of a new Elundium? There are great deeds in the making, I can feel it in my ancient bones. Were I young again I would vault upon your back, Esteron, and follow the owls, but I am burdened with old age and I will have to follow as best as I can. Tell Thanehand, tell him that the King will follow with all haste. Tell him that I am here at the Palace of Kings."

Esteron neighed, pawed at the Causeway road and reared up, thrashing the air with his hooves, before jumping the shadow-filled dyke and galloping after the owls.

King Holbian stood for a moment watching Esteron gallop away before he turned to Thunderstone. "The Granite City is no more. The Chancellors are dead, and these," here the King paused, pointing at the dusty column of travelers, "are all that are left of the people of the city."

Thunderstone clapped his hands, calling every server and underling out of the fortress onto the Causeway, ordering them to find a bed and food for each of the people of the city. Kneeling before the King he offered him the suite of rooms just below the lamp gallery, saying, "They look over World's End, my Lord, and they glorify each sunset."

But Holbian shook his head. "No," he answered quietly, pointing into the darkened courtyards. "When I enter the Palace of Kings it will be to take my place among the other Granite Kings who sleep within the bones of the mountain and I cannot do that while the Nightmare lives. No, I shall set my pavilion on the Causeway Field and prepare to enter the City of Night and stand against Krulshards."

Turning towards the long column of city folk he called Breakmaster to come to him, placing Beacon Light's reins into his hand. "Let her rest with a full belly of corn, but in the gray hours before morning ready her for battle, ready her for my ride into the City of Night."

The steep mountain stank of death as it towered over them. Thoron reined Equestrius to a halt as the first earth tremor shook the ground. He had carried the heavy sword that Durondell had forged far across Elundium while Eagle Owl had waited patiently on his shoulder, waiting for the call to carry the sword to a new King. He looked up the steep side of the shale-strewn valley they were about to enter. "This is a dangerous place," he called out to the long column of Gallopers that waited behind him.

Far above the sunlight touched the mountainside burning fiercely on two tall columns of sulfur-yellow rocks. Eagle Owl tensed, spreading his wings. Equestrius backed a pace, snorting fiercely. Thoron loosed the hilt of the sword and edged it out of the sheath. "Now may be the moment!" he said, resting his hand briefly on the owl's talons.

Somewhere above them a piercing cry broke the silence, tearing through the columns of yellow rock, shattering them into a thousand pieces. "Back! Retreat!" Thoron shouted against the thunder of the rockslide as shale stones rained down into the narrow valley, creating a cloud of stinging dust. Equestrius turned and galloped clear of the rock slide. Thoron felt a tug at his belt and when he looked down he saw that his sword had gone. Shading his eyes he looked up across the mountain's barren slopes and saw the flash of sunlight on bright metal as Eagle Owl labored to lift the blade high up into the thin mountain air.

"Kingspeed, great bird of war!" he shouted lifting his hand to wave farewell. "Kingspeed!"

A Door Crack into Darkness

*S*TUMBLE and Sprint galloped hard throughout the morning to keep pace with Tanglecrown and together they reached the edges of the grasslands before the sun had dropped towards World's End. Two daylights they had rested and waited for Stumble to recover while Thane impatiently paced the lawns. On the third daylight the swans had taken to the air and they had quickly followed them for fear of losing their path.

"This looks a barren place," Thane shouted as they passed into the shadows of the wild mountains that marched away beyond the edge of sight in a ragged line before them.

"It is desolate and bleak," Eventine called out, "but it is not barren. Wild flowers grow against the shale and pine trees cling to the higher slopes and there are secret lakes and heather meadows where the grassland people graze the mountain deer."

Thane slowed Stumble to a walk and began to pick his way across the first steep shale slope. The horse skidded, sinking in the shale as it moved beneath his feet and twice he almost fell onto his knees. Thane dismounted.

"It will take us forever to cross these mountains," he cried, scrambling over the loose shale, pulling Stumble along by the reins.

Kyot and Eventine dismounted and began slowly crossing the slopes. Ogion swooped low over their heads, his shadow racing across the uneven shale. Opening his beak he sang in silence of the way to Mantern's Mountain and the City of Night. "Follow! Follow!" he sang, turning into a narrow valley a hundred paces beyond where Thane struggled on the slope. Reaching a small bluff of dark rock Thane clambered into the floor of the valley and found firmer moss-covered ground that led up towards a high saddle of rocks. The moss felt damp and in places it covered pools of stagnant water. "There is a hidden stream," he whispered to Stumble before turning to wave to Kyot and Eventine, beckoning them forward. "Follow the gray swans," he shouted, "they will show us the best road."

Darkness had fallen before they reached the saddle of rocks and climbed up over them, using a narrow gully fashioned in the shape of a giant's staircase.

"Legends say that the Granite Kings built these mountains," Eventine whispered, testing each dark shadow before she climbed up through it. "They built it with their bare hands in battle with the Nightmare," she added.

Thane climbed up the last step and stood on the

highest point of the saddle, looking out across a wide lake of still black water.

"Mantern's Mountain!" he whispered fearfully, pointing at the huge dark shape that rose sheer and terrible on the far side of the lake, blotting out the canopy of stars, casting a black shadow across the water. Kyot moved silently to his side and stared up at the black mountain. Somewhere near the summit a rock slide began, turning from a hollow rattle of sharp shale into the thunderous roar of falling rocks that plunged down into the lake, sending ripples far out across its surface.

"The most dangerous place in all Elundium!" Kyot gasped, stepping back a pace and taking Eventine's hand.

Thane turned his head and smiled softly at his two love-matched friends. "Take nothing you treasure or would fear to lose," he whispered, pulling his half-cloak tight against the cold night wind.

Kyot squeezed Eventine's hand and knelt beside Thane. "We treasure each moment we are together, we must walk into the darkness as one."

Thane gripped Kyot's hand, his eyes wet with tears. "No, Kyot, stay here and wait for me. It is enough to lose Elionbel to the Nightmare, but to lose you and for you to risk losing Eventine . . ."

Kyot shook his head gently, resting his hands on Thane's shoulders. "We are as brothers, Thane. I would not leave your side, not if all the Nightbeasts of Elundium were before us."

"To face Krulshards will be far worse," Thane

cried, shaking himself free. "Don't you understand? To destroy the Nightmare I must destroy Elionbel, I can see no other way. Fate has driven me along this path and I must travel it to the bitter end, but it would be a great comfort to me in the darkness to know that you are both here beneath the canopy of stars, walking free in soft summer sunlight. And if I fail you must gather every warrior, Marcher, Galloper and Archer in a last desperate attempt to save the sunlight for I think that if Krulshards kills me he will come to claim Elundium. That will be the moment when the great Bows of Orm and Clatterford should sing together."

Eventine knelt before Thane, holding his gaze with her gentle clear eyes. "Fate has armed us to walk with you," she whispered, "you cannot turn away from the twists of fate."

Thane blinked and looked away. Ousious, the Queen of Swans, had waded ashore and stood silently beside him. Reaching out a hand he caressed her soft, downy neck. "Promise me," he whispered, looking back into Eventine's eyes. "Promise me that Elionbel will not suffer, that if I cannot cut the Nightmare's life thread you will end her pain."

Eventine reached back into her quiver and took out a glass-bladed arrow. "I promise," she whispered, kissing the blade and handing it to Thane.

He lifted it and pressed it against his forehead, feeling the hot sunlight trapped in the blade. Kyot also drew an arrow and pledged his kiss upon the blade that Elionbel would feel no pain as the Nightmare died.

Thane stood up, tears streaming down his face, and lightly touched both the glass arrow blades against his lips before he gave them back. "You have eased my heart and freed me to destroy the Nightmare," he whispered, turning away to hide his grief and walk alone along the dark edge of the lake.

Kyot rose to follow him, but Eventine gripped his hand, stopping him. "He is with her now, walking in happier days. Leave him with his sweet memories."

Thane, unable to rest, had saddled Stumble in the gray hours and waited impatiently until the light grew strong enough for the swans to rise from the lake and find them an entrance to the City of Night. Ogion and Ousious paddled to the water's edge and bent their necks in salute, singing in haunted whispers of the dark mountainside that loomed before them and of the love that Thane had for Elionbel. Thane knelt on the bank, putting his head between them and thanked them for all they had done to lead him this far through the wildness of Elundium.

"All Elundium shall be yours to fly freely in, and any lake that you choose shall be called Swanwater. I know the King will pledge it to you if I can destroy the Nightmare."

Ousious rubbed her beak against his cheek and sang Elionbel's name just once before she turned away and beat a path across the still water, rising up into the new morning's light. Ogion stayed a moment, his glittering eyes looking deeply into Thane's. Blinking, he touched the hilt of the dagger with his beak, turned and followed Ousious out across the lake.

Kyot tested the string of his bow and mounted Sprint. Eventine smiled and sprang lightly onto Tanglecrown's back, but Thane stood awhile, watching the swans dip and swoop across the bleak mountainside, searching out the road.

"There, there is the path," Eventine cried, urging Tanglecrown forward to where the swans were circling above a tall ridge of shale that had its beginnings in the shallow waters of the lake. Tanglecrown was a Lord of Stags and sure-footed in the mountain crags. He roared a warning and led the way, picking a route through the treacherous shifting shale.

Kyot followed a little way behind, a glass-tipped arrow ready on the string. Stumble found the pace too fast on the steep ridge, slipping and sliding with every footfall. Thane dismounted, leading the horse, and followed as quickly as he could. Twice during the long ascent he turned back, thinking he saw a movement far below in the dark shadowy valleys. Breathlessly he caught up with Kyot and showed him, pointing downwards. Kyot followed Thane's arm, shading his eyes against the noonday glare reflected on the slate-gray shale.

"They are horsemen, I think!" he said. "Marchers and Gallopers spread out in a great crescent around the base of this black mountain. It must be Tombel or Thoron. Nevian pledged them to hunt the Nightbeasts clear across Elundium."

Eventine had halted just above them, where the ridge curved away from the mountainside. She laughed softly, sweeping the end of her bow in a wide semicircle. "All Elundium has gathered to watch our battle with the Nightmare. I can see the roofs of Underfall far away to the right and the glass spires of Clatterford far away to the left. The emblem of the owl in blue and gold is everywhere between them spread in a great line that moves towards us."

"But how many of them have the courage to follow us into the darkness?" Thane asked. Turning back to face the mountain he began to climb again.

Ousious swooped past him, flying straight at the mountainside. At the last moment she turned away, her bright orange beak opening and closing noiselessly. Again and again, in great danger from Nightbeasts' spear thrusts, the swans flew close to a narrow crack in the mountain wall, showing where day turned into night.

"I see it, that dark split just above us. That is the beginnings of night," Thane shouted to the circling swans, waving his hand in thanks as they glided down towards the still black water of the lake at the foot of the mountain.

"I can see the beginnings of the darkness," he whispered to himself, touching the silver finger bowl that Eventine had given back to him before he left Clatterford. Carefully he placed it in the pocket closest to his heart before he loosed the dagger from his belt and moved forward.

Burnt footprints spoiled the opening but the dark crack in the mountain stood empty and beckoning. Any Nightbeast watchers guarding the entrance had retreated, hurrying, Thane guessed, to the high chambers to tell Krulshards that he had found the secret way into the City of Night. Taking deep breaths he turned and searched the blue-domed sky. Fate was to arm him. But how?

Daylight and Darkness

*E*VENING Star passed through the last tangle of ancient trees in the eaves of Mantern's Forest and trotted onto the Causeway Field. Away in the distance the fortress of Underfall rose sheer and powerful in the sunlight.

The Causeway road before the giant doors was thronged with a long column of travelers; lines of horsemen and beautiful Warhorses were passing through the dykes to fill the Causeway Field. Willow shaded his eyes and saw Thunderstone kneel before a tall age-bent figure wearing a glittering coat.

"Nevian?" he whispered, turning Evening Star towards the fortress. Star hesitated, pricked her ears and snorted fiercely. Willow leaned forward and picked up the faint sound of galloping hoof-beats.

"Esteron!" he cried, seeing the Warhorse burst through the darkened entrance and pause before the figure in the glittering coat before galloping out across the Causeway Field. "Look, Star, the owls are carrying the standard belonging to Thane. They will lead us to him—quickly, follow, follow Esteron."

Evening Star arched her neck, neighed and turned away from Underfall, following Esteron up into the thick pine forest that covered the lower slopes of Mantern's Mountain. High above the dark trees the standard carried in the owls' talons glittered and sparkled in the sunlight, flashing as a beacon to the weary crescent of Marchers and Gallopers, hard on the heels of the remnants of the Nightbeast army.

"Thane is before us!" Thoron shouted, reining Equestrius to a halt and pointing up at the owls as they turned and flew over the steep pine forest that grew on the shoulders of the mountain.

"The standard of the sun!" Tombel cried, pointing with the blade of his Marching sword. "Follow the standard!"

Turning to his son, Rubel, he lowered his voice and whispered, "We stand on the skirts of Mantern's Mountain; above us is the City of Night. Elionbel and Martbel are now beyond our power to save them."

"Curse Thanehand!" Rubel spat, clenching his gloved fists.

"No, no!" Tombel shouted. "Follow the standard and let no foul Nightbeast enter the City of Night. If Thane is on the Nightmare's heels then we must do all we can to help him. Nevian foretold it."

Rubel hesitated, his face white with anger. "First

he takes my sister's heart, then Mother falls beneath the Nightmare's shadow and my brother, Arbel, is at best a prisoner of the Nightbeasts. Base Candlebrat!" he shouted, "I curse him and all candlecurs that meddle in magic and cling to the magician's skirts. Thanehand is the root of this Nightmare's hate; without his meddling none of this would have happened."

Rubel stuttered in rage against Thane, making himself dizzy and lightheaded. Tombel stared at his son, the blood draining from his face, the tips of his fingers tingling with anger. "Fool!" he hissed, snatching Rubel's Marching sword out of his hands. "You shout base Chancellor's words; ignorant words built on false pride."

Turning the sword and holding it with both hands he brought it firmly down across his knee, snapping the blade in two. "You are no son of mine to judge another man by his station, be he base or high born. Thane did not choose to bring these tragedies upon our house; fate runs him on a harder road than ours. Now go from my sight and seek true wisdom. Seek out the Master of Magic and beg him to show you the measure of Thanehand. Go!"

Rubel stepped back a pace and, bending, he gathered up the two pieces of the sword. "I cursed Thanehand for bringing the Nightmare to our house and the curse shall stay until Mother and Elionbel are safe home. I will not help him, save with another curse."

Without another word Rubel left the crescent of

Marchers, turning his back on Mantern's Mountain and the shadowy line of Nightbeasts that ran before them towards the Gates of Night. Tombel watched him walk away and took a step to follow, then stopped.

"Nevian," he whispered, blinking back his tears, "forgive Rubel his anger, forgive my son his hatred, show him as you showed me how to judge."

Sighing, Tombel moved into his place in the crescent and, heavy-hearted, he led the Marchers up out of the heather meadows into the cool pine forest that covered Mantern's towering shoulders. Far away to the right where the pine trees thinned and the steep shale slopes began he saw Thoron marshalling the Gallopers and swept his sword in a glittering arc in the sunlight. Seeing Tombel, Thoron halted and waved his hand, pointing up towards the summit.

"Run, Marchers, run," he shouted, urging Equestrius forward. Tombel shaded his eyes and thought for a moment that he saw a flash of sunlight on bright metal somewhere near the summit, somewhere near the high plateau. "Run, Marchers," he shouted.

Willow and Evening Star had cantered clear of the pine trees and slowed to a trot as they passed through the heather meadows. Soon they would breast the edge of the high plateau and the ruined Gates of Night. Before them, clear to see, were Esteron's hoofprints, pressed deep into the heather.

Willow shifted the stone searcher, resting the butt end on his foot, holding it upright as he would a spear. There was no sign of the owls but to the left and right Warhorses and Border Runners broke free of the pine trees and entered the heather meadows, forming into fast-moving lines behind them. Star whinnied and neighed, lengthening her stride as the steep slope leveled. Cantering easily she reached the high plateau and halted. Before them rose the three grassy mounds of battle dead from the battle before the Gates of Night, and each mound was covered with a mighty stoop of owls; still they sat, unblinking, waiting and watching the ruined gates. Rockspray and Mulcade were perched on the small grassy mound of Amarch and Silverwing, the summer scarf still hooked into their talons.

"Can you lead me to Thane?" Willow called out as Star trotted towards the burial mounds. "Nevian forewarned me to meet Thane here before he entered the City of Night."

Rockspray turned his head and hooted in shrill notes, telling how the Nightmare had taken Elionbel and Martbel into the darkness. "Thane is on his heels," he shrieked, ducking his head backward and forward.

Evening Star quickly passed on all the owl's news to Willow, snorting and neighing, striking her hoof upon the ground.

"The Gates of Night are closed and ruined, beyond my skill to open! If Thane has followed the

Nightmare by another path how shall we find it, where shall we find it on all this dark mountain?"

Mulcade hooted softly, tilting his head and looking upwards at a shadow that slowly passed over the high plateau.

"Is that Eagle Owl?" Willow whispered, crinkling his eyelids against the sun's glare as a shaft of light reflected from a blade held in the owl's talons. "He is searching the mountainside, he is looking for a way into the City of Night!" Willow cried, urging Evening Star forward, sending the stoops of owls up noiselessly to darken the sun. "Look in every crack and hole, turn over every boulder and loose stone. We must find a way into the City of Night!"

Behind him, with the noise of thunder, the dense crescent of Warhorses moved across the plateau, the Border Runners fanned out, noses to the ground, sniffing for any trace of the Nightmare's prints. Higher and higher Evening Star scrambled amongst the rough boulders and slippery shale. Willow dismounted, spun the stone searcher in his hand and began the long task of searching under every stone and rock. Behind his shoulder the sun slowly sank out of sight, casting a blood red shadow over the roofs of Underfall far below.

"We must search on," he cried. "By silver moonlight or the glow of a million stars we must find a way."

*   *   *

King Holbian shivered, drawing the steelsilver coat tightly against the chill night air and looked up at the black mountain that filled the sky. "Breakmaster," he called softly, turning his head.

"Lord, I am here."

Holbian smiled, gripping Breakmaster's arm. "The new sun will see the last of the Granite Kings. I am at the end of my road."

"No, no, my Lord!" Breakmaster cried, falling onto his knees. "I will be first into battle. I will protect you."

King Holbian smiled softly and took the horseman's hand. "There will be no more battles for me, dear friend, nor work for Arachatt to hide the cracks or plaster over the truth. I am turning into stone; cold brittle granite. Here, feel it in my fingertips."

Sighing the King turned away from the black mountain. "I had hoped to ride with the morning sunlight into the darkness of the City of Night but it is beyond me, gone forever."

"Lord . . ." Breakmaster began to interrupt, but the King bid him be silent.

"It is my place as the King to stand at Thane's side just as, in the darkest hours of the siege lock on the Granite City you stood faithful and firm beside me, a true friend against despair. My heart is strong and does not falter; it is the body that cannot scale the mountain. Judge me not as a coward."

Breakmaster blinked back his tears and bent his head to kiss the King's hand, and he felt the cold touch of stone against his lips. "Lord, you have the courage of the wild Warhorses and stand head and shoulders above us all against the Nightbeasts."

"With the first light of the new sun saddle Beacon Light," the King continued in a hushed whisper. "Spread the steelsilver coat across her back and help me up into the saddle. Be near me as the day wears on and see that I sit as a King, tall and proud, upon the Causeway Field. Let none know that my body weakens; I must be a King to the last breath. Errant shall draw the Nighthorses into a wide battle crescent behind us and Thunderstone shall stand at my right hand, his horsetail sword driven point-deep into the turf. The city folk will form the second sweep of the crescent with Angis before them, for they must witness the Nightmare's end and the new beginnings of Elundium."

King Holbian sighed, leaning wearily on the horseman's arm. "What of Gray Goose and the mason, my Lord; where shall they wait out the new daylight?"

Holbian laughed, a flicker of warmth flooding through his fingertips. "Where else, Breakmaster, but in their rightful place, beside their King at the center of the battle crescent?"

"It shall be done, Lord," the horseman whispered, rising to search out Errant, Gray Goose and Thunderstone, the Keeper of World's End, and marshal them for the new daylight.

"Wait!" Holbian cried, clinging onto Breakmaster's hand. "If fate turns against us and Krulshards brings his darkest Nightmares down onto the Causeway Field the battle crescent must stand against him and we as its center must lead the way into battle, and be the first to face Krulshards!"

"Here you have led us, Lord, to win the daylight and here we shall stand, glad to be at your side, singing aloud the name of the greatest Granite King."

Holbian sighed and eased his grip on Breakmaster's hand. "Stand with me awhile, dear friend, and remember how we helped him start, a mere boy, thrust forward by fate."

"Who, Lord?" asked the horseman, drawing his eyebrows into a frown.

King Holbian laughed quietly. "Once your life hung in the balance, waiting for the noonday bell to strike while he lay at the feet of the untamable horse. Have you forgotten?"

"Thanehand!" Breakmaster cried, turning to look at the King. "Thoron's grandson, Thane?"

Holbian nodded and turned back towards the dark shape of Mantern's Mountain.

"Now we wait once more, only this time all of Elundium waits with us. His name is on every warrior's lips and the sparkling standard that the owls took from Thunderstone is the scarf that he took from his mother's pocket before he left the Granite City. The boy we helped along the road has grown in strength and purpose, Breakmaster, and holds all our fates in his sword arm. I knew it, or half guessed it a long time ago. I am sure that he is the one that will make old legends come to life."

"Legends, Lord? What legends do we wait for upon the Causeway?"

King Holbian smiled and in little more than a whisper repeated what he could remember of Nevian's words from long ago. "And he shall set his standard and it shall light the shadowy Causeway Field and it will be the sign of the new Elundium, the sign of our new King!"

"Lord! You are my King, young in heart, strong and brave enough. You have led the people through their blackest despair."

"No! I cannot climb to the high plateau. I am too old to face the Nightmare but any man who can walk in the darkness and destroy Krulshards, he shall be the new King, and you must treat him so, with full honor, for he will have stepped where no other would or could and saved the daylight for all to share."

Breakmaster sadly shook his head. "But I will lose you, Lord, and I could never serve another."

"It may be hard, dear friend, and in memory of me you will give all of that love to whoever walks free of the darkness. Pledge yourself now, for he will need someone to trust in the daylights to come. Someone strong who will watch the shadows without flinching and someone honest who takes nothing for himself. Pledge it and ease my troubled heart, for it is no easy matter to hand over a kingdom. Pledge it and lighten my last daylight."

Breakmaster reluctantly knelt and, kissing the hilt of his sword, offered it to the King. Teardrops glistened, reflecting the starlight on the smooth fluted handle of the sword.

"It is done!" said the King, passing the sword back into Breakmaster's hand and helping him to his feet. "The new kingdom of Elundium is lucky to have such a friend. Go now and ready the battle crescent for the greatest daylight of the Granite Kings. Go, before the gray hours touch the sky!"

A Sword in
the Sunlight

"WHERE is Thaneland?" Krulshards
hissed, cracking the twelve-tailed
whip impatiently at Kerhunge's head.
"Master," Kerhunge cried, ducking under the
flailing whip tails, "the foul Galloperspawn waits
at the doorcrack; he watches the sky and looks out
across the wildness of Elundium towards the wide
crescent of Marchers and Gallopers that have
ringed our beautiful city."

Krulshards sneered, pulling at the life thread,
and rattling the chains that bound Elionbel from
the domed roof of the chamber. "Marchers are gathering, Marcherwomen, but they cannot help you.
Gallopers are riding on the lower slopes, but they
are all afraid of the dark. Even the brave Galloperspawn, Thanehand, hesitates; perhaps he is also
afraid!"

Laughing, the Nightmare lifted Kruel above his
head, holding him easily in his bone black fingers,
taunting Elionbel with the baby, just beyond her
reach. "When the Galloperspawn is dead all

Elundium shall be yours!" Chuckling he tossed the baby high into the darkness.

"Master!" Kerhunge whispered, touching the edge of the malice, "the foul Galloperspawn is not alone; the Archer with the Great Bow of Orm and the lady who rides the crystal-tipped stag are with him."

Krulshards caught the baby and quickly hid it in the folds of his malice. "Do they fear the dark, Captainbeast?" he hissed, picking at the loose strips of gray flesh that hung below his cheekbone. "Will they enter the darkness?"

"Master, they wait, statue still, watching the sky."

"Wait!" shrieked the Nightmare, raising the twelve-tailed whip. "I will teach them to wait!"

With both hands on the twisted black handle he brought the whip down across Elionbel's back, cutting through the fabric of her cloak and bodice. Twelve iron whip tails tore into her skin, making her scream out, sending an echo of her pain rippling through the City of Night.

Krulshards raised the whip again, hesitated and tossed it aside. "One cry is enough from my lure, that will draw Thanehand to us!"

Turning to Kerzolde he grasped him by his iron collar and pulled him into the malice. Secretly he drew the baby out of the folds of his cloak and kissed him, dribbling black bubbling spittle across the top of his head.

"I cannot risk Kruel, he is not strong enough to

defend the darkness or enjoy my revenge, you shall be the guardian of my seed," he said, pushing the baby, Kruel, through the narrow opening in Kerzolde's armored jerkin.

"If Thanehand comes too close to me or the Archer threatens my life, kill both the Marcherwomen and escape with it. Take it far away into a darker place and make it strong; feed it on dark meats and carrion flesh for it is the new Power of Darkness that will blacken all Elundium."

"Master, I hear footsteps," Kerhunge cried, tugging at the hems of the malice. "Thanehand and the two followers have entered the City of Night."

Elionbel heard Thane's distant footsteps and shook her mother's shoulder urgently, desperately trying to wake her from the dark dreams she had sunk into. But the Nightmare birth and the greedy feeding of the infant as he sat astride Martbel's belly had almost drained her life away. Wearily she mumbled, half opening her eyes.

"Mother! Mother! Thane has come to rescue us!" Elionbel shouted fiercely, slapping Martbel's sunken cheeks. "Mother wake up!"

Krulshards laughed, pulling Elionbel away behind the folds of his malice.

Beyond the door crack, muffled by the darkness, Thane heard the single tortured scream and took a giant stride towards the mountain wall.

"Elionbel!" he cried, clenching his empty hands.

Turning, he once again searched the dawn-bright sky. "Fate has abandoned me," he whispered, his face drawn into tight lines of despair. "I cannot wait any longer for a sword to use against Krulshards. I will go with nothing in my hands other than the dagger blade that Duclos gave me on the lawns of Gildersleeves."

"You have the great Bows of Orm and Clatterford and the crystal-tipped arrows forged with the light of the sun," Eventine said, quietly nocking her pledge arrow onto the string.

"No! You are both pledged to end Elionbel's torment; do not weaken my purpose. There is no room for doubt or a second arrow strike if I am to charge straight at the Nightmare. In my moment of despair let me hear the sweet music of your bows and know that you have ended Elion's pain."

Silently Eventine and Kyot locked hands with Thane, the two pledged arrow shafts and the blade of the dagger touching. "It will be done," Kyot whispered as they walked towards the black door crack.

Eventine paused beside Tanglecrown, putting her hand into the center of his antlers, touching the velvet-soft crown. "Guard the entrance, watch over the daylight until we return."

Stumble and Sprint reared, neighing, while Tanglecrown lifted his glittering antlers towards the rising sun and roared out a challenge at the dark shadows in the valley below. Kyot trembled and cried out as the darkness swallowed him up but Eventine reached out her hand and comforted him in the dark.

"Remember the dark chamber at Clatterford; reach out and touch the darkness and put your fear behind you."

Thane walked two paces ahead, his left hand outstretched against the rough rock wall. Before them the stench of Krulshards grew stronger and stronger, filling the dark road.

"Thanehand!" taunted a cruel voice, whispering them forward. "Come to me, Thanehand, and see how the Elionbel dangles on my life thread, chained in my high chamber!"

Thane swallowed his fear, shutting his ears to the Nightmare's taunts and forged ahead. Twice during the long morning climb up through the darkness Eventine called out, begging Thane to ease the pace. "Kyot has no sight in the dark; he stumbles and trips with each footstep."

Thane halted and waited, taking Kyot's hand into his own to help him forward. "I am a burden without Rockspray's sharp eyes at my shoulder," Kyot muttered, gritting his teeth against the darkness. "A useless blundering blind man who slows you up."

Thane squeezed Kyot's hand. "Only a true friend would have the courage to step into the darkness and I love you for it."

Kyot stumbled on in silence, his bow arm locked through Eventine's, his arrow hand gripping Thane's sleeve.

The walls on either side of them suddenly fell away, the dark road had reached a vast low-domed chamber. Thane stopped, choking on the rotten stench.

"Thanehand!" shrieked a voice.

"Nightstealer!" sneered another.

"Welcome, welcome, Thanehand," whispered Krulshards, raising his bone black fingers for silence, and shaking the chains that bound Elionbel's wrists.

Thane took a step forward and saw that the chamber walls were lined with Nightshards; huge shadowy figures that dry-rattled as they turned their blind faces towards him. In the center of the chamber Krulshards waited beside two long loops of chain. The folds of his malice and the outer edges of the hems had been spread in the shape of a black fan, each tuck and twist cleverly piled on top of the next. Beside the Nightmare on either side crouched his Captainbeasts, Kerzolde and Kerhunge. Kerzolde spat Thane's name onto the dusty floor, leaving a trickle of bubbling spittle dribbling down his scaly chin.

Krulshards laughed, his skinless face bloated with victory. "Thanehand," he hissed, slowly drawing aside the hem of his malice to reveal Elionbel. "Here is your Elionbel, the lure that brought you into the darkness," he shrieked with delight, grasping her wrist and pulling her forward, tripping her on the black folds of the malice.

"Thane! Thane!" she began to shout, stumbling onto her knees, fighting with both hands to stop the glistening life thread from choking her.

Krulshards snarled, sweeping the other hem of the malice aside and kicking Martbel out onto the dusty floor. Thane reached for the dagger but froze as Elionbel screamed, her face blackened and distorted by the choking thread. The Nightmare laughed.

"Touch me, Thanehand, or even move one little finger and the thread tightens!"

Looking past Thane the Nightmare froze Eventine and Kyot with a hateful stare. "I will take your arrows, foul Archers, pluck them from the bows, before you ease your fingers on the strings."

Thrusting both women aside Krulshards strode across the chamber towards Thane. "You are mine, Galloperspawn!" he shouted, throwing his head back and cackling with delight, but he stopped, rooted with doubt, his mouth hanging silently open, his bone black fingers pointing up into the domed roof. "What is that?" he hissed, releasing the Archers from his hateful stare, and they both bent their bows, the gray goose flight feathers touching their cheeks.

"Wait!" cried Eventine. "Look at the glass arrow blades; they are beginning to glow. There must be daylight here in the City of Night."

Thane made a grab for the dagger but stopped, looking up into the dome above his head to see what had made Krulshards hesitate in his moment of victory. A fine trickle of stone dust was falling, he could hear a grating sound in the roof. A sharp metal point, twisting and turning, suddenly broke through the black rock; a pinpoint of light flooded through the darkness, burning a bright white light on to the glass-tipped arrow blades.

"Thane," a faint voice shouted from somewhere above the dome. The trickle of dust and pebbles became a torrent as the chamber roof collapsed in a thunderous shower of rocks. Sunlight flooded the high chamber, casting long shadows across the dusty floor.

Krulshards screamed, shrinking back into the malice away from the light, grabbing with his fingers for the shadowy hood. Twisting his head he saw his own shadow spread out across the floor and jumped backwards away from it. The life thread glittered in the sunlight as it closed around Elionbel's throat.

"Aim at the life thread," Eventine cried and in that instance Kyot knew the wisdom of Fairday's words and, clear-eyed he aimed at the spider-thin and glittering thread. Both bows sang together, loosing their blazing glass-tipped spines across the chamber.

Thane looked up past the shadowy malice up through the collapsing roof and saw the sky edged with stoops of owls, proud Warhouses and fierce Border Runners. Wave after wave of them leapt down into the chamber, neighing and growling, as they fell upon the Nightshards. Mulcade and Rockspray stooped through the ragged hole, the summer scarf stretched taut in their talons, its sparkling light driving back the shadows. Thane laughed and pointed out into the sunlight where high above the mountainside a mighty owl hovered, shadowing the sun as he searched, following the Warhorses towards a black dust-filled hole.

"Eagle Owl!" Thane shouted, seeing the flash of bright metal in the owl's talons. "Fairday foretold that you would come to me but I doubted his wisdom. Come to me quickly for I have great need of the blade you carry!"

"Tread on the Nightmare's shadow!" Willow cried out as he struggled to free himself from the pile of roof rubble that had collapsed and brought him down into the chamber.

Thane hesitated, turning to search for Willow's voice as Eagle Owl plunged to earth.

"Step on his shadow and freeze him before he vanishes amongst the Nightshards! Quickly, quickly!" Willow urged, rising to his feet, his stone searcher ready to plunge into the nearest Nightshard.

Eagle Owl burst into the chamber, delivering the sword into Thane's outstretched hand.

Elionbel choked as the life thread burned a black mark around her throat, she heard the arrows sing and shut her eyes as the glass blades cut into the life thread, exploding in one flash of white light. Briefly the thread tightened, the severed ends thrashing and wriggling as it withered away. Reaching up Elionbel tore at it, digging her broken fingernails into the slippery skinless sinews.

"Mother!" she screamed, kicking out at the

Nightbeast, Kerzolde, as he bent over Martbel, stabbing at her with his cruel curved dagger.

Kerzolde jumped away beyond the full stretch of her chains and fled. Clutching the baby, Kruel, secretly inside his armored jerkin he dodged away amongst the Nightshards and vanished into a dark hole at the far end of the chamber. Elionbel rose, shouting a curse, to follow but Kerhunge rushed past her, knocking her down next to Martbel.

"Mother!" Elionbel cried, gathering her up into her arms, "oh Mother, Mother!" she wept, rocking her backward and forward.

Martbel slowly opened her eyes, searching blindly in the shafts of sunlight. "Daughter," she whispered, her lips hardly moving.

"I am here," Elionbel answered, weaving their fingers together.

"Hide my shame, child, bury all knowledge of the bastard beast. Promise me that you will take it from the folds of the malice. Promise me."

Elionbel bent low, tears of despair and love coursing down her cheeks. "None will ever know of it, Mother."

"Not even Thane. Promise me, child."

Elionbel nodded, biting her lips.

Martbel sighed, a trickle of blood escaping from the corner of her mouth.

"Kill it, Elionbel, I beg you. Kill it before all Elundium is cursed with its eternal darkness."

Elionbel blinked away her tears and dabbed away

at the blood on her mother's lips. "I swear that I will kill it," she whispered.

Martbel smiled, her eyes growing pale and distant. "Tell your father that I love him. Tell him..."

Martbel slumped forward, her head sinking into the crook of Elionbel's arm. For long moments she knelt holding her mother, whispering her promise, deaf and blind to the battle that raged all about her as the Warhorses and the savage Border Runners fought amongst the Nightshards and the Nightbeasts that flooded into the chamber. Kyot and Eventine moved as one through the chamber following Krulshards, felling every blind beast he tried to reach. The center of the chamber was littered with dead Nightshards. Krulshards ran amongst them, trying to lose his shadow, but always Thane was a pace behind him and whichever way he turned the Archers were destroying his Nightshards, crumpling their shadows to nothing. There was nowhere left to hide.

Turning, he lunged with two black blades he had drawn from beneath the malice. Slashing with hatred he cursed at Thanehand.

"Here, Nightmare, here," cried Thane, ducking under Krulshards's thrust. Gradually he had been moving into the main shaft of sunlight away from where Elionbel was chained, drawing the Nightmare towards a tall column of stone that rose towards the broken roof. Movement on the edge of his sight made him look quickly back.

"Elionbel!" he cried with joy to see her safe and

alive, huddled on the chamber floor with Martbel in her arms. Laughing, he looked back into Krulshards's eyes. Now there was no lure, nothing to trap him and divide his purpose. Now he could destroy the Nightmare.

Krulshards stepped backwards, into the bright ray of sunlight, stumbling with fear, and turned to flee but the severing of his life thread had weakened him and Thane quickly overtook him, treading firmly on his shadow, freezing him to the floor.

"I know your weakness, Nightmare!" he cried, raising his sword.

"NO! NO!" Krulshards screamed, dropping both black blades and throwing his hands across his face to shut out the light. The Nightshards and the Nightbeasts in the chamber hesitated at their master's scream, turning helplessly towards him.

Thane lunged forward, both hands gripping the hilt of the sword Eagle Owl had delivered and drove it against the folds of the malice. Bright sparks danced along the blade, spraying up in stinging fountains of hot metal as the shadowy fabric shredded into ribbons. Deeper and deeper the blade sank, melting the armorer's new-forged steel, buckling and splitting it away from the long splinter of black Nightmare steel forged into its center.

Krulshards felt the point of the sword cut into his flesh and lashed out, tearing desperately at Thane's face, hooking his bone black fingers around his neck.

"Thanehand!" he screamed, tightening his grip.

Thane choked, stumbling onto his knees, gasping for breath.

"Nightmare!" he gurgled, throwing his weight against the sword, feeling it slice through the Nightmare's layers of rotten flesh until it pierced into his black heart. Krulshards's fingers twitched and trembled, his head jerked backwards and the ruined blade tore through the back of the malice and struck the tall column, shearing into the black marble, fusing with the rock.

Thane took his hands off the hilt of the sword and reached for the dagger in one hand, and with the other he snatched a handful of the Nightmare's dead locks and slashed with the dagger at Krulshards's throat, cutting through layer after layer of the rotten flesh. Sparks burned his hands and black blood splashed onto his face but he was blind to the terror that fought at him and deaf to the screams of defeat as Krulshards writhed against the sword. One last mighty slash and he tore the Nightmare's head away from his shoulders, threw it high up into the shaft of sunlight and watched it tumble slowly back onto the chamber floor.

"Die, foul Nightmare and rid Elundium of your darkness," Thane cried, rising from his knees and tearing Krulshards's lifeless bone black fingers from his throat.

An eerie silence filled the chamber. Everywhere Nightbeasts and Nightshards lay dead or dying in the shafts of the morning sunlight. It was over. The shadows were lifting. Krulshards was no more.

Elionbel's chains snapped as the Nightmare died and she ran to Thane's side and began searching frantically between the folds of the malice, crying with despair. She sank onto her knees, clutching at the last shadowy threads and tore them apart.

Thane knelt beside her, pushing the ruined malice aside. "Elion!" he whispered, gathering her into his arms and gently lifting her chin with his hand. "The Nightmare is dead, we are forever free of his darkness!"

Elionbel looked away towards the dark hole where Kerzolde had escaped and a shadow crossed her face, haunting her eyes. "No, Thane," she whispered, slowly shaking her head. "This is only the beginning of the real Nightmare darkness that will cover all Elundium."

MIKE JEFFERIES was born in Kent but spent his early years in Australia. He attended the Goldsmiths School of Arts and then taught art in schools and in prisons. He now lives in Norfolk where he works, among other things, as an illustrator, with his wife and three stepchildren. *The Palace of Kings* is the second volume of the trilogy, *Loremasters of Elundium*.

You have just finished reading
one of the first books published
by Harper Paperbacks!

Please continue to look for
the sign of the 'H', below.

It will appear on many fiction
and non-fiction books, from
literary classics to dazzling
international bestsellers.

And it will always stand for a
great reading experience and a
well-made book.

Harper Paperbacks
10 East 53rd St.
New York, NY 10022

VOLUME THREE OF
THE ACCLAIMED
*LOREMASTERS OF
ELUNDIUM* TRILOGY

SHADOWLIGHT

by Mike Jefferies

Krulshards, Master of Darkness, lies dead,
his nightbeast armies destroyed. But
Elundium's joy is mingled with sorrow as
King Holbian goes to his rest at last.
Thane returns as king with Elionbel as his
bride to the newly built Granite City, bidding the people to return to their homes.
But many murmur that this is an uneasy
peace. Where are the unhappy warriors
who rejected Thane as king? And what is
the deadly secret that Elionbel refuses to
divulge, even as a terrible shadowlight
swirls like mist across Elundium?

**Coming Soon From
Harper Paperbacks**